MW01608434

SHERRYL WOODS

Whether she's living in Florida or Virginia, Sherryl Woods always makes her home by the sea. A walk on the beach, the sound of waves and the smell of the salt air all provide inspiration for this author of over seventy-five romance and mystery novels. You can write to Sherryl January through March at P.O. Box 490326, Key Biscayne, FL 33149 or check out her Web site at www.sherrylwoods.com. From April through December, stop by and meet her at her bookstore: Potomac Sunrise, 114 Washington Avenue, Colonial Beach, VA 22443.

BEVERLY BARTON

An avid reader since childhood, Beverly Barton wrote her first book at the age of nine. After marriage to her own "hero" and the births of her daughter and son, Beverly chose to be a full-time homemaker, aka wife, mother, friend and volunteer. The author of over thirty-five books, Beverly is a member of Romance Writers of America and helped found the Heart of Dixie chapter in Alabama. She has won numerous awards and has made the Waldenbooks and USA TODAY bestseller lists.

MARGOT EARLY

says she's written romance fiction since she was twelve. (Her first hero and heroine were kids as well, solving a mystery together.) She's been writing ever since— humour, features, scripts, as well as fiction. In fact, Margot met her husband at a "murder mystery" for which she wrote the script. He played an undertaker, she played a nun. In a matter of hours, he told her he was falling in love. Margot lives in Colorado with her husband and son.

Sherryl Woods
Beverly Barton
MARGOT EARLY

So This Is
Christmas

Harlequin
Mills & Boon

First Published 2002
First Australian Paperback Edition 2005
ISBN 0 733 56516 6

THE PERFECT HOLIDAY © 2002 by Sherryl Woods
FAITH, HOPE AND LOVE © 2002 by Beverly Beaver
THE THIRD CHRISTMAS © 1994 by Margot Early
Philippine Copyright 2002
Australian Copyright 2002
New Zealand Copyright 2002

Published by
Harlequin Mills & Boon
3 Gibbes Street
CHATSWOOD NSW 2067
AUSTRALIA

HARLEQUIN MILLS & BOON and the Rose Device are trademarks used
under license and registered in Australia, New Zealand, Philippines, United
States Patent & Trademark Office and in other countries.

Printed and bound in Australia by
McPherson's Printing Group

CONTENTS

THE PERFECT HOLIDAY
Sherryl Woods

Dear Friends,

The holiday season has always seemed to me to be a time for gathering those we love close to share old memories and create new ones. I've always found it especially sad when families are separated or when holiday memories hold only disappointment.

In "The Perfect Holiday," I've written about two people who've been disillusioned by most of the people in their lives. Yet both hold fond memories of one incredible woman who touched them in the past and whose death brings them back together. In the special atmosphere of Holiday Retreat, they're able to open their hearts to the possibility of love.

This story of hope and renewal is my holiday gift to you. May the joy of the season touch your life now and forever.

Sherryl Woods

Chapter 1

"**M**om, it's snowing," Hannah shouted from the living room.

Savannah heard the pounding of her daughter's footsteps on the wood floors, then the eight-year-old skidded to a stop in front of her, eyes shining.

"Can I go outside? *Please?*" Hannah begged. "This is so cool. I've never seen snow before."

"I know," Savannah told her, amused despite herself. "We don't get a lot of snow in Florida."

"Wait till my friends back home hear we're going to have a white Christmas. It is *so* awesome. I am *sooo* glad we moved to Vermont."

Though she could understand her daughter's excited reaction to her first snowfall, from Savannah's perspective the snow was anything but a blessing. Since her arrival a couple of days ago, she'd discovered that the furnace at Holiday Retreat wasn't reliable. The wind had a nasty way of sneaking in through all sorts of unexpected cracks in the insulation, and the roof—well, the best she could say about that was that it hadn't fallen in on their heads…yet. With the weight of a foot of damp snow on it, who knew what could happen?

It had been three weeks since the call had come from the attorney informing her that she was a beneficiary of her aunt Mae's estate. The bittersweet news had come the day before Thanksgiving, and for the first time since her divorce the year before, Savannah had thought she finally had something for which to be thankful besides her feisty, incredible daughter. Now that she'd seen the inn, she was beginning to wonder if this wasn't just another of Fate's cruel jokes.

Holiday Retreat had been in the family for generations. Built in the early 1800s as a home for a wealthy ancestor, the huge, gracious house in the heart of Vermont ski country had become an inn when the family had fallen on hard times. Savannah could still remember coming here as a child and thinking it was like a Christmas fantasy, with the lights on the eaves and in the branches of the evergreens outside, a fire blazing in the living room and the aroma of banana-nut bread and cookies drifting from the kitchen. The tree, which they cut down themselves and decorated on Christmas Eve, always scraped the twelve-foot ceiling.

Aunt Mae—Savannah's great-aunt actually—had

been in her prime then. A hearty fifty-something, she came from sturdy New England stock. She had bustled through the house making everyone in the family feel welcome, fixing elaborate meals effortlessly and singing carols boisterously, if a bit tunelessly. It was the one time of the year when there were no paying guests at the inn—just aunts and uncles and cousins all gathered for holiday festivities. To an only child like Savannah, the atmosphere had seemed magical.

If the house had been in a state of disrepair then and if the furniture had been shabby, she hadn't noticed it. Now it promised to be one of the world's worst money pits.

"Mom, did you hear me?" Hannah said again. "I said it's snowing."

"I heard," Savannah said glumly.

Hannah's blue eyes were alight with excitement. "Isn't it great?"

Savannah tried to work up some enthusiasm to match her daughter's, but all she could think about was the probability that too much snow would make the sagging roof plummet down on top of their heads as they slept. Still, she forced a smile.

"There's nothing like a white Christmas," she agreed.

"Can we get a tree and make hot chocolate and sing carols like you used to do when you were a kid?" Hannah pleaded. "Then it won't matter if we don't have any presents."

Savannah cringed at the realistic assessment of their financial plight. The divorce had left her with

next to nothing. Her ex-husband hadn't yet been persuaded to send even the paltry child support payments
required by the court. As for alimony, she had a
hunch hell would freeze over before she saw a penny
of that. Since their divorce had hinged on her objections to his workaholic tendencies, Rob clearly saw
no reason she should benefit from the income derived
from those tendencies.

Last night, after Hannah had gone to bed, Savannah
had sat for hours with her checkbook, a pile of final
bills from Florida, and a list of the repairs needed
before the inn could be opened to paying guests in
the new year. Her conclusion had left her feeling
more despondent than ever. It was going to take more
than a glistening snowfall and a few carols to brighten
her spirits.

No matter how hard she tried telling herself that
they were better off than they had been, she still
wasn't totally convinced. Maybe if they'd stayed in
Florida, she would have found a better-paying job,
something that wouldn't have left them scraping by
after making house payments and buying groceries.
At least they wouldn't have had to worry about the
kind of exorbitant heating bill from last winter that
she'd found in a kitchen drawer here. Maybe selling
the heavily mortgaged house that had been her home
with Rob had been another error in judgment. It had
given her barely enough cash to make the trip and to
make a start on the repairs the inn needed.

"Mom, what's wrong?" Hannah asked. "Are you
afraid we made a mistake?"

Seeing the concern that filled her daughter's eyes and the worried crease in her forehead, Savannah shook off her fears. Hannah deserved better than the hand she'd been dealt up to now. For the first time since the divorce, she was acting like a kid again. Savannah refused to let her own worries steal that from her daughter.

"Absolutely not!" she said emphatically. "I think coming here was exactly the right thing to do. We're going to make it work. How many people get to live in a place that looks like a picture on a Christmas card?"

She gave her daughter a fierce hug. "How about some hot chocolate?"

"Then can we go out in the snow?" Hannah pleaded.

"Tell you what—why don't you bundle up in your new winter jacket and go outside for a few minutes so you can see what it feels like? I'll call you when the hot chocolate's ready."

Hannah shook her head. "No, Mom, I want you to come, too. Please."

Savannah thought of all she had to do, then dismissed it. It was only a few days till Christmas. Most of the contractors she'd spoken to said they couldn't come by till after the first of the year. Until she and Hannah made a trip into the small town at the foot of the mountain, she couldn't strip the old wallpaper or paint. Why not think of this as an unexpected gift of time?

"Okay, kiddo, let's do it," she said, grabbing her

coat off a hook by the door. ''Only for a few minutes, though. We're going to need some heavy boots, wool scarves and thick gloves before we spend much time outside. We don't want to start the new year with frostbite.''

''Whatever,'' Hannah said, tugging her out the door, seemingly oblivious to the blast of icy air that greeted them and froze their breath.

There was an inch of damp, heavy snow on the ground and clinging to the towering evergreens already, and it was still falling steadily. With no chains or snow tires on the car, they'd be lucky if they got out of the driveway for a couple of days, Savannah concluded, sinking back into gloominess.

Then she caught the awed expression on Hannah's face as she tilted her head up and caught snowflakes on her tongue. She remembered doing the exact same thing the first time she'd visited Aunt Mae and seen snow. She'd been even younger than Hannah, and for several years the Christmas trips to Vermont had been the highlight of her life. She couldn't recall why they'd stopped coming as a family.

She'd come on her own several times after she was grown, but those visits had dwindled off when she'd met, then married, Rob. He was a Florida boy through and through and flatly refused to visit anyplace where the temperature dropped below the midfifties.

Now that Aunt Mae was gone, Savannah deeply regretted not having done more than write an occasional letter enclosing pictures of Hannah. Her aunt had never once judged her, though, and she'd been totally supportive when Savannah had told her about the breakup of her marriage. She'd sent one check explained away as a birthday gift and offered more, but Savannah had turned her down. She'd lied and said they were getting along okay, but she knew now that her aunt had seen through her. She had done in death what Savannah hadn't permitted her to do while she was living.

If other members of her family resented the gesture, Savannah didn't know about it. She'd lost touch with most of them years ago. She'd been estranged from her parents ever since she'd divorced a man of whom they enthusiastically approved. Aunt Mae had tried to broker a peace agreement between Savannah and her father, but he'd remained stubbornly silent and un-yielding. He'd been convinced Savannah was a fool for divorcing a man who brought home a steady paycheck.

"Mom, I love it here!" Hannah announced, throwing her arms around Savannah. She was shivering even in her heavy coat. "I want to build a snowman. Can we?"

"I think we'll need a little more snow than this," Savannah told her. "Besides, I'm freezing. How about that hot chocolate?"

"I want to stay out here. I'm not cold," Hannah insisted.

"Then why are your teeth chattering?" Savannah teased. "Come on, baby. Even if you won't admit to freezing, I will. There will be more snow once we've warmed up. I'll teach you how to make snow angels."

"What are snow angels?" Hannah asked, her interest immediately piqued.

"You'll see. Aunt Mae taught me when I was a little girl. Now come inside and get warm."

Far more agreeable lately than she had been for months, Hannah finally acquiesced, following Savannah into the kitchen. Savannah studied her daughter's sparkling eyes, pink cheeks and tousled hair and knew she'd done the right thing, no matter what struggles might lay ahead.

Despite the sad state of the inn, they were going to have the fresh beginning they both deserved, she decided with a surge of determination. And it was going to start with the very best Christmas Hannah had ever had, even if she was going to have to do it on a shoestring. Some of her very best holiday memories had cost nothing.

As for the practicalities—the repairs, the marketing plan she needed to devise—they would just have to wait for the new year.

Mae Holiday had been one of the most eccentric people Trace Franklin had ever known. He had met her when he'd been dragged to Vermont for an idyllic summer getaway by one of the women he'd dated. That had been eight or nine years ago. Twice that number of women had passed through his life since then. Of them all, the one he hadn't dated—Mae—had been the most memorable.

She'd been the grandmother he'd never had, the mentor who tried her best to bring some balance into his life. Until the day she'd died at seventy-eight, it had frustrated her no end that she hadn't managed to convince him that romance was just as important as money.

Trace knew better. His parents had been madly in love, but it hadn't brought either one of them a blasted thing except heartache. Love had kept his mother with a man who never had two nickels to rub together, a man whose big killing was always ''just around the corner.''

While John Franklin had spun his dreams, his wife had cleaned houses, worked in fast-food chains and, finally, when it was almost too late to matter, gotten a steady job selling toys to families that could afford to give their kids elaborate backyard swing sets and fancy computer games.

When Trace was fifteen, his mom had brought one of those games home to him, but by then he'd been way past playing childish games. He'd been working with single-minded focus on graduating from high school with honors and getting a scholarship to the best college in the state. He didn't want to play with toys. He wanted to own a whole blasted toy company.

And now he did. The irony, which Mae had seen right away, was that he still didn't have time to play. He wasn't even sure he knew how.

He was driving along the snow-covered roads of Vermont right now, because of Mae. On his last visit to see her at the end of October, she had made a final request. She had known she was dying, had known it for fully a year before the cancer had finally taken

her, but she hadn't said a word to Trace until that last
visit when she had detailed her losing battle, reciting
the facts with a stoicism and acceptance that had
awed him.

"I want you to promise me something," she had
said as they'd sat in front of the fire on his last night
there. Despite the heat of the blaze, she'd been
wrapped in blankets, and still she had shivered.

"Anything," Trace had responded, and meant it.
Not only was Mae one of the earliest investors and
biggest stockholders in Franklin Toys, she was his
friend.

"I want you to spend Christmas here at Holiday
Retreat."

It was only a couple of months away and it would
require some juggling of his schedule, but there was
no question that he would do it. "Of course, I will,"
he said at once. "We'll have a wonderful time."

She had squeezed his hand. "I won't be here,
Trace. You know that."

Even now, the memory of that moment brought the
sharp sting of tears to his eyes. Her gaze had been
unrelenting. From the beginning of her illness, she
had refused to sugarcoat the truth to herself. Now that
she was revealing it to others, she expected them to
face it, as well. The cancer had spread too far and too
fast before the doctors had had the first inkling there
was anything wrong. She was dying and there was
going to be no reprieve.

Trace had returned her unflinching gaze, heartbroken yet unable to face her death with less bravery

than she was showing. "Why, Mae? Why would you want me here after you're gone?"

"Just do it for me," she whispered, her voice fading. "Promise."

"I promise," he'd said just as her eyes drifted close. He'd been willing to do anything that would give her comfort. He owed her that much, and more.

Two weeks later Mae Holiday had died peacefully, a lifelong friend—a man she had loved deeply but never married—by her side. Now Trace was on his way to Vermont to pay his respects…and to keep his promise.

Chapter 2

There was smoke curling from the chimney at Holiday Retreat. Lights were blazing from the downstairs windows. Trace sat in his car and stared, trying to make sense of it. He'd expected to spend the Christmas holiday alone here, mourning Mae in private, reliving the happy times they'd spent together over the years they'd known each other.

And, he conceded with a rueful grimace, catching up on the mounds of paperwork he'd brought with him, along with his cell phone, laptop computer and fax machine.

What the dickens was going on? he wondered, thoroughly disgruntled by this turn of events. Mae had said nothing about anyone else being here. Nor had the attorney in the note that had accompanied a key to the inn. The note had merely advised that Mae had seen to having plenty of food and firewood on hand and that she hoped his visit would be a memorable one. If he had any problems, he was to contact Nate Daniels, the man Trace had heard of, but never met, the man who was the shadowy love of Mae's life.

Trace fingered the old-fashioned key in his pocket as he walked through the foot or so of recently accumulated snow. He was halfway to the door when he spotted indentations, a hectic swirl of footsteps and something else. He looked more closely and saw...not one but two snow angels, the sort made by flopping down in new-fallen snow and moving outstretched arms to create wings.

At first the sight brought a smile, reminding him of innocent, long-ago days as a kid before the unpredictability of the family's day-to-day existence had registered with him. Winters back home had been relatively mild, so that rare snowfalls had been regarded with sheer delight. He hadn't owned a sled, but he'd had his share of snowball fights and made more than a few snow angels.

Then the full implication of the snow angels sank in, and pleasant memories gave way to edginess. Judging from the smaller size of one snow angel, there was a kid on the premises and that generally meant noisy chaos, the last thing he'd anticipated when he'd made the commitment to Mae to spend the Christmas holidays here. For a man who made his living by providing expensive hobbies and toys to children, Trace was amazingly uneasy when confronted with an individual child. For him, toys were a multimillion-dollar business, not entertainment. Unless he could persuade himself to use whatever child was around to conduct market research, this whole situation had just gone from bad to worse.

He was about to turn tail and run, but then he heard Mae's voice in his head as she'd extracted that promise from him. He'd never gone back on his word to her, ever. He wasn't about to start now.

Filled with a sense of dread, he made his way to the front door. He stood on the slick porch debating whether to ring the bell, rather than walking in on whoever was here. Then, again, he had just as much right to be here as the unknown occupant did. More, perhaps. That remained to be seen.

He stuck the key in the lock, turned it and pushed open the heavy door, noting as he did that it was in serious need of paint. It had once been bright red, as had all the shutters on the house. Now it was faded to a shade only slightly deeper than pink. Maybe he'd take care of that while he was here. It would be a fitting homage to Mae to see the doors and shutters restored to their scarlet holiday brilliance.

He was about to close the door when a girl—just about the size of the snow angel outside, he noted—skidded to a stop in front of him on one of the scooters his company made. It had been the hottest gift of the holiday season two years ago. It was not meant to be used indoors, though he could understand the temptation given the wide expanse of hardwood floors. And it wasn't as if those floors were in partic-

ularly great shape. They could do with sanding and a
fresh coat of wax. Something else he could do while
he was here…in Mae's memory.

First, though, he had to figure out who was this
imp of a child regarding him with blatant curiosity,
her golden hair scooped through the opening of a
baseball cap, her T-shirt half in and half out of her
jeans.

"Who are you and what are you doing here?" he
demanded in the no-nonsense tone he used on exec-
utives who'd failed to deliver on their division's
projections.

The kid didn't even flinch. "I'm Hannah and I live
here. Who are you? And how come you have a key
to my house?"

Trace's head began to throb. What the devil was
Mae up to? "Are your parents here?"

"Just my mom. My dad divorced us. He lives in
Florida. My mom's baking Christmas cookies." She
cast an appealing smile at him. "Don't they smell
great?"

Trace automatically sniffed the air. They did smell
fantastic, just the way Mae's always had. He'd eaten
fancier food than what was served at Holiday Retreat,
but he'd never had any that tasted better or was prepared with more love. He wondered if Hannah's mom
shared Mae's talents in the kitchen, then sighed. That
was hardly the point.

"Want me to get my mom?" Hannah inquired.

"I'll find her," Trace said, heading determinedly
toward the kitchen. He'd taken only a step before he

turned back. "By the way, that scooter is not an indoor toy."

The kid's smile never faltered. "Maybe not, but it works great in here." And off she went, completely unimpressed by his admonishment.

Trace sighed and went in search of her mother.

He wasn't sure what he expected, but it certainly wasn't the frail wisp of a woman who was bent over in an incredibly provocative pose, her head stuck halfway into the huge, professional quality stainless steel oven that had been Mae's pride and joy.

This room was where Mae had splurged, spending her money to design a kitchen that was both welcoming and efficient. Everything in it, from the refrigerator to the granite countertops, was top of the line. When she had shown it to Trace a few years ago, she'd been as excited as a kid on Christmas morning. She told him it was how she'd spent her first dividends from her stock in Franklin Toys.

And now there was an interloper in here, he thought, feeling oddly possessive on Mae's behalf. Unless this woman could prove her right to be on the premises, Trace would have her packed up and out of here before nightfall, even if he had to call on local law enforcement to toss her out on her attractive backside.

Despite his impatience to accomplish that task, and rather than risk scaring her half to death while she was that close to incinerating herself, he waited, barely resisting the desire to haul her out of there immediately and demand an explanation for her presence.

Of course, he was also having some difficulty resisting the urge to smooth his hand over that narrow curve of her denim-clad bottom. That, he concluded, was a very dangerous temptation. He admonished himself to forget it the same way he'd scolded Hannah only moments earlier. He hoped he paid more attention to the warning than she had, since there was likely a lot more at stake than scarred floorboards.

The woman finally retreated, holding a tray almost as big as she was. As she turned to set it on the granite countertop, she spotted him and let go of the tray with a yelp of surprise. Trace caught it in midair, then let out a curse of his own as the hot metal seared his fingers. He dropped the tray with a clatter. Cookies went flying. And the woman regarded him as if he were a living, breathing embodiment of Scrooge and he'd deliberately set out to ruin her Christmas.

"Look what you've done," she said, scowling at him as she bent to pick up the broken remains of sugar cookies decorated with pretty red and green designs. She waved a hatless Santa with half a beard under Trace's nose. "Just look at this."

She didn't seem one bit concerned with the fact that he'd burned himself trying to save her blasted cookies. He stepped past her and stuck his hands under cold running water. That finally got her attention.

"Oh, fudge, you burned yourself, didn't you?" she said. "What was I thinking? I'm sorry. Here, let me see."

She nudged up against him and grabbed his hand. Her touch was anything but soothing. In fact, now Trace was suddenly burning on the inside, too.

"Sit," she ordered before he could unscramble his thoughts. "There's a first-aid kit around here somewhere."

"Cabinet next to the stove," Trace told her, blowing on his fingers.

She stopped and stared. "How do you know that?"

"Mae was always getting distracted and having little accidents in the kitchen. She said it paid to keep the bandages close at hand."

Rather than fetching the first-aid supplies, the woman sank down onto a chair, her eyes promptly filling with unshed tears. "She did say that, didn't she?" she whispered. "I must have heard her say it a hundred times. And even before she remodeled in here, she kept aloe and antiseptic spray and bandages right by the stove."

Trace was startled by the depth of emotion in this stranger's voice. Her love for Mae was written all over her face. That much raw pain was more than he knew how to deal with...his own emotions were shaky enough. He stepped carefully around her and got his own ointment and bandages, using the time to collect himself and try to fill with renewed resolve the tiny chink she'd created in his desire to be rid of her.

When he was finished repairing the damage to his hand, he finally risked another look at her. The color had returned to her cheeks, but there was no mistaking the signs of a woman on the edge. He'd seen that same stressed expression often enough on his mother's face, the same tightness around the mouth, the wariness in her eyes.

"You okay?" he asked at last.

She nodded, still blinking back tears. "Sometimes it just catches me off guard, the fact that she's gone. I hadn't seen her in several years, but I always had such wonderful memories of being here, especially around the holidays."

That must have been a long time ago, Trace thought with a surprising surge of anger on Mae's behalf. He'd been here with Mae every year since that trip when they'd first met. He'd never been entirely sure how she'd cajoled him into coming, but year after year he'd found himself driving north from New York City, looking forward to spending time with the closest thing he had to family now that his folks were both dead.

Oddly, on none of those trips had he ever caught a glimpse of the man in Mae's life. Only at the end had she explained why, that Nate had his own family responsibilities, duties that he had never once shirked through all the years they had loved each other. It had been an unconventional love—an impossible love— she had explained to Trace. The man's wife had suffered a nervous breakdown years before, when his children were little more than toddlers. Nate could never bring himself to divorce her during all the long lonely years when he'd struggled as a single dad, watching his wife's mind deteriorate degree by de-

gree. He had been the rock that held his family together...and the other half of Mae's soul. If she regretted anything about their long, secret affair, she
never once complained of it to Trace. And it had certainly never soured her on the possibilities of
romance.

It was little wonder, though, that Mae had sought
out Trace's company around the holidays, he had realized as she told him the story. The loneliness at a
season meant for sharing with family and friends must
have been unbearable. Trace wondered if this woman
even knew about that part of Mae's life.

"If you hadn't been here for years, why are you
here now?" Trace asked, unable to hide the note of
bitterness in his voice. "Did you come to pick over
her belongings?"

She seemed startled by the hostility in the question—or maybe by the fact that he thought he had the
right to ask it.

"I'm here because my aunt left Holiday Retreat to
me," she said eventually. "Not that it's any of your
business, but I'm Savannah Holiday. Mae was my
grandfather's sister. And you are? How did you get
in here, anyway?" She sighed. "Hannah, I suppose.
I've told her and told her about not opening the door
to strangers."

It didn't seem to occur to Savannah Holiday that it
had taken her a long time to get around to asking
about his identity. In New York, the police would
probably have been called the second he appeared in

the kitchen doorway and the answers to all those questions could have been sorted out later.

"I'm Trace Franklin," he said. "A friend of Mae's." He retrieved the key from his pocket and plunked it on the table where it glinted in the sunlight. "And I got in with this, though I did see your daughter as I came in."

She stared at the key. "Where did you get that?"

"From your aunt."

"Why would she give you a key to Holiday Retreat?"

"Because she'd invited me here for the holidays." He was only now beginning to grasp just how diabolical that invitation had been. His finding the alluring Savannah Holiday and her daughter underfoot was clearly no accident, but Mae's last-ditch effort at matchmaking. He wondered if Savannah Holiday had figured out what her aunt was up to.

He regarded his unexpected housemate with a wry expression. "Merry Christmas!"

Chapter 3

Compared to the man sitting across from her with his cool, flinty gaze and designer wardrobe, Savannah felt like a dowdy waif. She was pretty sure there was flour in her hair and, more than likely, red and green sprinkles on her nose. When it came to baking, she did it with more enthusiasm than tidiness or expertise. The results were equally unpredictable, though she'd been particularly proud of the batch of golden cookies that were currently lying in crumbles around her feet.

She regarded this interloper with caution, in part at least because his presence rattled her. She'd felt a little flicker of awareness the instant he'd entered the kitchen. At first she'd attributed it to surprise, but then she'd realized it was a whole lot more like the sensation she'd experienced the first time she'd met Rob. It was the caught-off-guard, heart-stopping reaction of a woman to a virile, attractive male…or a doe when confronted by a rifle-toting hunter. She was stunned to discover that she was even remotely susceptible to a man after the bitterness of her divorce, especially to a man wearing the clothes of a business executive to a country inn. It was something her uptight ex-husband would have done.

Because her reaction made her uneasy, she focused on the one topic guaranteed to take her mind off of it. "You said Mae invited you here. You do know that my aunt died, right?" she asked.

"Yes."

His expression was almost as bleak as the one Savannah saw in the mirror every morning. "But you came anyway," she said, impressed despite the instinct that told her this man was anything but sentimental.

"It's what she wanted," he said simply. "I promised I would."

"And you always keep your promises?"

"I try," he said. "I don't make that many, and the ones I do make mean something."

"What about your family? Won't they miss you over the holidays?"

"In recent years Mae was the closest thing I had to family. What about *your* family?"

"Hannah's here. For all intents and purposes, she's all I have. My husband and I divorced a year ago." She hesitated, then added, "My parents and I aren't on speaking terms at the moment."

"I see."

She was grateful that he didn't bombard her with a lot of questions about that. "How did you know Mae? Forgive me, but you don't look as if you spend a lot of time in the country."

He laughed at that, and it transformed his face. The tight lines around his mouth eased. His dark eyes sparkled. "What gave me away?"

"The clothes, for starters. I'm amazed you stayed upright walking from the car to the house in those shoes. I don't think snow is kind to Italian leather. And I can't imagine that you'd be able to spend more than a few minutes outdoors before freezing in that shirt. Men around here tend toward flannel."

"But I think the real secret is what they wear under it," he said, barely containing what promised to be a wicked grin.

Savannah's thoughts automatically veered off in a very dangerous direction. She had the oddest desire to strip off his clothes to see if there were practical long johns underneath. She'd never thought that sort of men's underwear to be particularly sexy, but she imagined Trace Franklin could do amazing things for the look.

"You're blushing," he said, regarding her with amusement.

"Well, of course I am! I hardly know you, and here we are discussing underwear."

"It can be a fascinating topic, especially if we move from cotton to satin and lace."

She frowned at him. "You're deliberately trying to rattle me, aren't you?"

"Why would I do that?" he asked, trying for a serious expression. The twinkle in his gray eyes betrayed him.

"I can't imagine, especially when all I was trying to find out was what drew a city man like you to spend time in a country retreat." She studied him thoughtfully, then said, "There must have been a woman involved."

"Bingo. The woman who brought me here years ago was envisioning a quiet, romantic getaway with long hikes through the woods." He shrugged and gave her a beguilingly sheepish look. "Instead I spent the weekend holed up in Mae's study with my computer and fax machine taking care of a business crisis."

Savannah immediately felt a surprising empathy for the woman. "Now, *that* I can imagine. Your friend must have been disappointed."

"Dreadfully."

"What sort of business?"

"I own a company in New York," he said in such a dismissive way that it sparked her curiosity.

"Franklin," Savannah recalled thoughtfully. "Not Franklin Toys, by any chance?"

He seemed startled that she'd grasped it so quickly. "That's the one. How on earth did you figure that out?"

"There were some articles about that company on Mae's desk. Obviously she kept up with it."

"I imagine so," he said, his expression noncommittal.

"Because she knew you from your visits here?" Savannah persisted, sensing there was more.

He shrugged. "That was the start of her interest, I suppose."

She frowned at his evasiveness. "What aren't you saying?"

"What makes you think I'm leaving something out?"

"Instinct."

"Okay, then, here's the whole story in a nutshell. I suppose I owe you that, since I've shown up on your doorstep out of the blue," he said. "Your aunt was the one who encouraged me to start the company. I'd been with another toy manufacturer for a few years. I'd learned all I could, and I had a lot of ideas for ways to do it better. Mae was an early investor in Franklin Toys. Over the years she and I made a lot of money together, but I owe every bit of that success to her initial encouragement."

"I see," Savannah said slowly. "So that first trip here wasn't a waste of your time after all. Did your relationship with the woman last?"

"Only for as long as it took me to get her back to her apartment in New York that Sunday night," he said with no hint of regret. "My friendship with Mae lasted much longer."

"Then you came back here often?" she asked, feeling a vague sense of regret and guilt that he'd spent these last years with her aunt, when she should have been the one spending time here.

"As frequently as I could," he said. "Your aunt

was a remarkable woman. I enjoyed my visits with her.''

. ''Even if she did live essentially in the middle of nowhere,'' Savannah said, needing to remind herself that this man bore way too many resemblances to her ex-husband.

''Funny thing about that,'' he said, picking up one of the few sugar cookies they'd managed to salvage and breaking off a bite. ''I got used to the peace and quiet. And the phone lines, fax and Internet connections work just fine.''

''So even though you're here for the holidays, I suppose you brought all of your equipment along,'' she guessed.

''Of course.''

Savannah shook her head. ''I hope you watch your cholesterol. Anybody's who's as much of a workaholic as you appear to be is clearly a heart attack waiting to happen.''

''I'll try not to have one while I'm here,'' he promised solemnly.

''Thank you for that. I'm afraid I don't have the kind of insurance it would take to cover your medical expenses if you collapse and fall down the stairs.''

He grinned. ''I do.''

''Well, then, I suppose you can stay,'' she said grudgingly, thinking of the extra work involved in having a guest in a house that was all but falling down around them.

He regarded her with a wry expression. ''I had no intention of doing anything else.''

''You'll have to pitch in and help,'' she said, deliberately ignoring his remark. ''I'm afraid the inn isn't officially ready for guests again.''

''I'm not a guest—not the way you mean, anyway. And I came expecting to take care of myself. The attorney said the refrigerator would be stocked, and I brought along plenty of food from the city.''

''Caviar, I imagine,'' she said, feeling strangely testy at the thought of sharing the house with a man whose tastes, like Rob's, probably ran to the expensive and exotic. ''Maybe some imported Stilton cheese? Smoked salmon? The finer things you absolutely couldn't live without?''

His grin spread. ''Junk food, if you must know.''

Once again, Savannah felt the full effects of that devastating smile. She hoped he wouldn't do it too often. It might make her forget that he was completely unsuitable for a woman who'd already been burned by a man who put his work before his family.

''What exactly do you consider junk food?'' she asked.

''Potato chips. Popcorn.'' He leaned closer and lowered his voice to confide, ''I also have a cooler filled with chocolate mocha almond ice cream. I'm addicted to the stuff.''

Her eyes widened. Chocolate mocha almond was an indulgence she rarely allowed herself. Aside from the calories, the brand she loved was outrageously expensive. She'd developed a taste for it during her marriage, but had had to forego it since the divorce. The store brands simply didn't live up to the gourmet ice cream. She had a hunch that cooler of Trace's was stocked with the best.

"Exactly how much ice cream did you bring?" she asked, hoping it sounded like a purely casual inquiry.

"Enough for you and Hannah...if you're good," he teased.

"When it comes to chocolate mocha almond, I can eat a lot," she warned him.

He surveyed her slowly, appreciatively, then shook his head. "Not as much as I can," he said. "And I brought enough for a week. I'll make you a deal. If you let me share in whatever you're fixing for Christmas dinner, I'll provide dessert."

"But that's three days away," Savannah protested.

He winked. "I know. Patience is a virtue."

"Another of Mae's favorite sayings," Savannah recalled as again a wave of nostalgia hit. "Are you sure I can't talk you into sharing sooner?"

He glanced at the piles of cookies on the table and the obvious remnants of hot chocolate in two mugs. "Are you absolutely certain you won't go into some sort of sugar overload crisis?"

"Absolutely."

"Then I'll bring it in," he said.

"I'll help," Savannah said eagerly, grabbing a jacket off a hook by the door and following him outside.

The instant she spotted his fancy new four-wheel-drive sports utility vehicle out front, she was momentarily distracted from thoughts of ice cream. It could turn out that Trace Franklin was the answer to her prayers.

"I don't suppose you'd be willing to let me borrow your car?" she asked.

"First you want my ice cream, and now you're after my car," he said, shaking his head. "You ask a lot for someone I've barely met."

"I need to get to town to pick up paint and things to start on the work that's needed around here." She glanced toward her own car, a faded six-year-old sedan with questionable tires. "I doubt my car will make it down the mountain, much less back up on these icy roads."

His expression grew thoughtful. "Okay, here's my best offer. I'll trade you breakfast tomorrow for a trip into town."

Apparently the man's obsession with business never quit. "You really do like to negotiate, don't you?"

He shrugged. "Force of habit. I like creating win-win situations. Is it a deal?"

Savannah held out her hand. "Deal." She hesitated. "You could have dinner with Hannah and me this evening, if you like. It won't be fancy. I'm fixing spaghetti."

He seemed startled by the invitation. "It just so happens that I love spaghetti." His gaze narrowed suspiciously. "What do you want in return for that?"

"Ice cream for dessert?" she asked hopefully.

Rather than answering, he reached in the car, then turned back with something in hand and tossed it to her. Savannah caught it instinctively. It was a pint of ice cream. And she'd been right—it was the best.

"It's all yours," he said. "Consider it a gesture of good faith."

He retrieved a huge cooler, which obviously contained the rest. Savannah eyed it enviously. "Is that thing really filled with more of this?"

"Packed solid," he told her. He studied her warily. "Am I going to have to put a lock on the freezer?"

"I would never steal your ice cream," she said with a hint of indignation, then grinned. "That doesn't mean I won't try to talk you out of it."

His gaze locked with hers and anticipation slid over her once again, making her senses come alive.

"This is really, really good ice cream," he said quietly. "It could take more than talk."

Savannah barely resisted the urge to fan herself. She was surprised steam wasn't rising around her. Oh, this man was dangerous, all right. She was obviously going to have to watch her step the whole time he was underfoot. Any man who prided himself on being a shark when it came to business was likely to be equally determined when it came to anything else he wanted.

Well, she'd just have to make sure he didn't decide he wanted her. One glance comparing her flour-streaked jeans to his tailored wool slacks put that notion to rest. They weren't in the same league at all.

She lifted her gaze to his, caught the desire darkening those gray eyes. Uh-oh, she thought. Apparently clothes didn't matter to Trace, because the look in his eyes was anything but neutral.

More worrisome, though, than that discovery was the realization that she wasn't nearly as upset by it as she probably ought to be. In fact, a little *zing* of anticipation had her blood heating up quite nicely. She could probably strip off her sheepskin-lined jacket and be quite comfortable in the twenty-degree temperature out here.

"You'll want to get all your stuff inside," she said, her tone suddenly brisk. "Who knows how many deals you might have missed while we've been talking?"

"The ones worth making can always wait," he said.

"Still, I'd hate to feel responsible for you missing out on something important. Besides, I promised Hannah that she and I would go cut down a Christmas tree this afternoon."

He regarded her as if she'd just mentioned a plan to cut down the entire forest.

"There's a perfectly good tree lot in town. I passed it on my way out here," he said. "Those trees are already cut. Less work. Less waste."

"Is that an expression of environmental concern?" she inquired. "Because the trees I'm talking about are grown specifically for the holidays. It's how some people make their living."

He looked skeptical. "Still seems like a lot of work."

"But this is a tradition," she countered.

He looked as if she'd used a foreign term.

"Didn't you have any holiday traditions when you were growing up?" she asked.

"Sure," he said at once. "Staying out from underfoot while Mom and Dad argued over how much money was being wasted on presents."

Savannah couldn't imagine a home in which the

holidays had meant anything other than a joyful cel-
ebration. For all of the problems she and her parents
were having now, they had given her years of memories of idyllic Christmases. Very little of that had
had anything at all to do with the materialistic things.
It had been about family togetherness, laughter…traditions. For some reason, she suddenly
wanted to share just a little of that with this man to
whom tradition meant so little. She'd never been able
to get through to Rob, but maybe Trace Franklin
wasn't a lost cause.

"Would you like to help us?" she asked
impulsively.

He looked even more disconcerted by that invitation than he had been by her request that he join them
for dinner. "I had planned to get some work done
this afternoon," he said predictably.

"Surely the company founder can take a break for
a couple of hours," she coaxed. "Most people do
relax around the holidays. I doubt anyone will be too
upset if they don't get a fax today or even tomorrow.
Some people might actually be hoping to leave work
early to finish their holiday shopping."

A vaguely guilty expression passed across his face,
as if he'd already forgotten that Christmas was only
a few days away.

"You're right," he said eventually. "The work can
wait. In fact, maybe I'll call my secretary and tell her
to let everyone leave early."

Savannah grinned at the unexpected evidence that
Scrooge had a heart. "That's the spirit," she said.
"I'll get my coat and hurry Hannah along. You'd
better change into something warmer, too. My hunch

is that this could take a long time. Hannah rushes through most things, but she's never made a quick decision about a Christmas tree in her life.''

As Savannah left Trace to finish putting his groceries away, she was all too aware that his gaze followed her as she exited from the kitchen. And that she unconsciously put a little extra sway in her hips because of it.

Oh, so what? she thought as a guilty blush crept into her cheeks. If she could grant Hannah's not-so-secret Christmas fantasy of a pair of skis, then surely Fate wouldn't mind granting her the chance to flirt with a handsome man for a couple of days. After the holidays, what were the chances she'd ever see Trace again? Slim to none, more than likely. He was the perfect guy on which to practice a little harmless flirting. She had to get back into the dating game one of these days. Here was her chance relearn the rules with a man who absolutely, positively was not her type, and better yet, a man who wouldn't be around long enough to break her heart.

Then she recalled that desire she'd read in Trace's eyes only moments before. Harmless was not the first word that came to mind. Okay, she concluded, wicked would be nice, too.

Chapter 4

Trace hauled all of his business equipment into Mae's den, but before he could plug any of it in he was so overcome with emotion that he sank into the chair behind her antique desk and drew in a deep breath. As he did, he was almost certain he could still smell the soft, old-fashioned floral scent she had worn.

The room looked as if she'd just left it moments earlier. A jar of her favorite gourmet jelly beans sat on the desk. He noted with amusement that most of the grape-flavored ones were gone. They had been her favorites, though she had claimed that she continued to buy assorted flavors precisely so she wouldn't get in a rut. She'd never realized that Trace had added a half-pound or so of the grape-flavored jelly beans each and every time he came to visit, secretly stirring them into the mix.

The inn's guest book was still beside the phone with reservations carefully noted. He turned to to-day's date and saw his own name written in her grace-ful, flowing script. He saw that Savannah's arrival had been noted for a date only a few days earlier in a script that seemed less steady.

Had she made those final arrangements for her niece's inheritance when she'd known the end was near? Had she cleverly schemed to bring him together with Savannah even as her health was failing? It would have been just like her to plot something for those she loved, something to make them less lonely once she was gone.

Ironically he didn't think Savannah had picked up on the scheme yet. He'd been the subject of so much matchmaking in recent years that he'd seen what Mae was up to the instant he'd realized he wasn't going to be alone at Holiday Retreat over the holidays. It was no accident that he and Savannah were here at the same time. Mae had wanted some of the seasonal magic to rub off on her heart-weary niece and a man she thought was missing out on romance.

So, why hadn't he run? He could have apologized for the intrusion and headed back to New York and the safety of his workaholic routine. It wasn't entirely duty to Mae that had kept him here but—mostly, he had to admit—the sweetly vulnerable Savannah her-self. Though she wasn't complaining, it was obvious that her life hadn't been easy lately. Still, she'd maintained an air of determination and her sense of humor. She was too unsophisticated to be his type, but there was something about her—a fragility encased in steel—that drew him just the same. It reminded him of a young man who'd fled Tennessee years ago with little more than a dream and the determination to make it come true. And in many ways it reminded him of his mother, who'd had the strength to endure poverty and hardship. Only in recent years—after spending most of his youth condemning her for the choices she had made—had he come to realize just how strong she had been.

"Trace, are you ready yet?" Savannah asked quietly, startling him. "My goodness, you're not even changed. Is everything okay?"

He met her concerned gaze. "Sorry. I got distracted."

Savannah came closer and perched on the edge of the desk. She regarded him with sympathy. "You feel her presence in here, don't you? I feel it most in the kitchen. It's like she's watching over my shoulder." A grin tugged at the corners of her mouth. "Making sure I don't burn the place down, more than likely."

"She wouldn't have left the inn to you if she didn't trust you to take care of it," he told her, knowing with everything in him that it was true. Mae had been sentimental, but she had also had a practical streak. Her New England heritage, no doubt. "This place meant everything to her. When Franklin Toys started doing really well, I suggested she retire. She had plenty of money to live comfortably for the rest of her life. Know what she told me?''

"That retirement was for people waiting to die," Savannah said. "She told me the same thing. She loved having her company, as she referred to the guests who came here year after year. She said they kept her young. What she missed was having family underfoot for the holidays."

"You and Hannah and I are here this year," Trace said, unable to keep a note of sorrow from his voice.

"Too late," Savannah said, a tear sliding down her cheek.

Trace thought of his suspicions about Mae's reason for bringing them together. Not that he intended to get too carried away trying to see that *all* of her wish came true, but celebrating this Christmas with her niece was the least he could do for the woman who'd believed in him.

"You said yourself that you think she's watching over you," he reminded Savannah. "What makes you think she's not here right this second, gloating over having gotten us up here to celebrate the holiday and her memory at the same time?"

Savannah's expression brightened. "You're absolutely right! Let's not disappoint her. We'll make this the most memorable holiday ever. We'll do everything just the way she used to do it, from the greens in the front hall to the candles on the mantel and in the windows."

"Perfect," he said enthusiastically. "Give me a minute to call my office and change, and I'll meet you and Hannah out front. We'll find the best tree on the tree farm.''

''It has to be huge,'' Savannah warned.

He hesitated, phone receiver in hand. ''How huge?''

''Really, really big.'' She held her arms wide. ''And very, very tall.''

''How were you and Hannah going to get such a huge tree back here by yourselves?''

''I was counting on help.''

''Are you sure you didn't know I was coming?''

''Nope. Mr. Johnson has a truck. He also has a fondness for Mae's sugar cookies.''

Trace winced. ''The ones on the kitchen floor?''

''Those are the ones.''

''Think he'll accept any other sort of bribe?'' he asked, knowing that he was going to hate the alternative if Mr. Johnson declined to haul that tree.

''Nope. I think this tree is riding in your pristine, shiny SUV, shedding needles all the way,'' she said happily.

Trace groaned. ''I was afraid of that.''

She patted his hand, sending a jolt of awareness through him.

''I'll go get a blanket to lay in the back,'' she said soothingly. ''Now, hurry, or you'll have Hannah to deal with. Trust me, she's worse than a nagging splinter when she's anxious to get someplace. Right now she's making a family of snow angels on the front lawn, but her enthusiasm for that will wear off shortly.''

"I'll hurry," Trace promised, unable to tear his gaze away as she left the room. He sighed, then dialed his office.

Two minutes later, he'd told his stunned secretary to shut the company down until after the new year, changed into warmer clothes and was heading out the front door, only to be greeted by squeals of delight as Hannah upended her mother into a snowbank. Savannah was sputtering and scraping snow out of her mouth. There was a dangerous glint in her eyes as she regarded her traitorous daughter.

Oblivious to her mother's reaction, Hannah spotted Trace. Emboldened by her success with her mother, she raced in his direction. Trace braced for the hit. "Oh, no, you don't," he said, scooping her up when she would have tried to knock him on his backside. He held out a hand and helped Savannah up, even as Hannah tried to squirm free of his grip.

He looked into Savannah's dancing eyes. "What do you think? Should I drop her in that snowdrift over there?"

"No!" Hannah squealed. "Put me down. I'll be good. I promise."

Trace kept his gaze on Savannah's. "Your call."

"Hannah does keep her promises," she began thoughtfully. "Then again, that snow was really, really cold. She needs to know that."

"I know it. I know it," Hannah said. "Really, Mom. I swear."

Before he realized what she intended, Savannah scooped up a handful of snow and rubbed her daughter's face with it, dribbling a fair amount inside the collar of his coat while she was at it. Accident? he wondered. Probably not.

"Mom!" Hannah squealed, laughing.

Savannah clapped her gloved hands together to get rid of the excess snow and regarded Trace with a pleased expression. "I think it's okay to put her down now."

He lowered Hannah to her feet and caught her grin. "I hope you learned a lesson," he said, fighting to keep his own expression somber.

"Oh, yes," she retorted just as seriously. "I learned that my mom is very, very sneaky."

Trace nodded, shivering as the snow melted against his suddenly overheated skin. "I caught that, too. What do you think we should do about it?"

"Hey," Savannah protested, backing up a step. "Don't you two even *think* about ganging up on me."

"Never dream of it," Trace said, winking at Hannah.

She winked back, then giggled. "Never," she agreed.

Savannah looked from one to the other. "I'm going to regret this eventually, aren't I?"

"Could be," Trace said. He took a step closer, reached out and tucked a flyaway strand of hair back behind her ear. "But you'll never see it coming."

Her gaze locked with his, and suddenly the tables were turned. The desire to kiss her, to taste her, slammed through him with enough force to rock him on his heels. He hadn't seen that coming, either.

* * *

"We are never in a million years going to get this tree into the house," Trace said, eyeing the giant-size pine that Hannah had picked out. "What about that one over there?" He pointed to a nice, round, five-foot-tall tree. It was cute. It was manageable. Hannah was already shaking her head.

"No," daughter and mother replied in an emphatic chorus.

"I suppose it's also a tradition that the tree has to be too big to fit inside," he grumbled as he began to saw through the trunk. He'd worked for a lawn service one summer and had some skill at sawing down trees and branches, but nothing this size. He should have brought along a chain saw.

"Exactly," Savannah said, grinning and apparently thoroughly enjoying his struggle with the tree.

"I think my mother had the right idea after all," he said. "A ceramic tree that lit up when she plugged it in."

"Oh, yuck," Hannah said. "That's so sad."

As he breathed in the scent of pine and fresh, crisp air, Trace was forced to agree with her. Despite his grumbling about the endless search for the perfect tree and his protests over the size of their choice, he hadn't felt this alive in years. Something that might have been the faint stirrings of holiday spirit spread through him. He couldn't remember the last time he'd felt like this.

"Stand back, you two. When this thing falls, you don't want to be in the way," he warned as he heard the crack of the wood and felt the tree begin to wobble. One hard shove and it would hit the ground. Before he could touch it, the tree began to topple…straight at him. It knocked him on his back in the deep snow. He found himself staring straight toward the sky through a tangle of fragrant branches.

''Uh-oh,'' he heard Hannah whisper.

Her mother choked back a giggle and peered through the branches. ''Are you okay?''

''What the devil happened?'' he asked, frowning up at her.

''I gave the tree a teeny little push to help it along. I guess I pushed the wrong way. You aren't hurt, are you?'' The twinkle in her eyes suggested she wasn't all that worried.

Trace bit back his own laughter and scrambled out from beneath the tree. ''You are in such trouble,'' he warned even as she began backing away, her nervous scramble hampered by the deep snow.

''You wouldn't,'' she said, regarding him warily.

''Oh, but I would,'' he responded quietly. ''Nobody pulls off a sneak attack on me twice in one afternoon and gets away with it.''

She tried to escape, but she was no match for his long legs. He caught up with her in a few steps, scooped her up and dropped her into the cushion of snow.

Hannah's laughter mingled with theirs. He whirled on her. ''Okay, young lady, you're next. Don't you know better than to injure a man's pride?''

Hannah was quicker to scamper away, but Trace

still caught up with her, grabbed a handful of snow and rubbed her face with it. Just then he felt himself being pelted with snowballs from behind. In seconds all three of them were engaged in a full-fledged snowball fight.

"Oh, my," Savannah said a few minutes later, collapsing into the snow. "I haven't laughed that hard in ages."

"Me, either," Trace said, his gaze clashing with hers. In fact, he could barely recall ever laughing that hard.

Or wanting a woman as much as he wanted the virtual stranger lying beside him in the icy snow right this minute. With all the heat crackling between them, he was surprised they hadn't melted the snow right out from under them.

He started to reach out to touch her cheek, but recalling Hannah's presence, he drew back. "Do you know what I'd like to do right now?" he asked, his gaze locked with Savannah's.

She swallowed hard at the question and shook her head.

Trace realized that her thoughts had drifted down the same dangerous path as his own. "Not *that*," he protested, deliberately teasing her.

Her cheeks, already pink from the chill in the air, turned an even brighter shade. Another woman might have called his bluff, but she merely kept her gaze on him, apparently waiting to see just how deep a hole he intended to dig for himself.

"What *I'd* like to do," he said, "is go back to the

house, build a nice warm fire in the fireplace, and…''
He deliberately let the suspense build. He saw the
pulse beating a little more rapidly in her neck. He
permitted himself a hint of a smile, then said softly,
''Take a nap.''

She was still blinking in confusion when Hannah
plopped down between them and said, ''Grown-ups
don't take naps.''

''Sure we do,'' Trace told her. His gaze went back
to Savannah. ''In fact, sometimes when adults take
naps, we have the very best dreams ever.''

Savannah shot him a knowing look, then rose
gracefully to her feet. ''Well, by all means, let's get
home so you can get some sleep,'' she said testily.

She muttered something more, something obviously meant for Trace's ears, not Hannah's. He
caught her hand and held her back until they were
well out of Hannah's hearing.

''What was that?'' he inquired.

She leveled a look straight at him. ''I said, I hope
you have nightmares.''

''No dream with you in it could ever be a nightmare,'' he said, locking gazes with her once more.
''Then, again, you could take a nap with me.''

''In your dreams,'' she retorted.

He winked at her. ''Exactly.''

She stopped in her tracks and scowled up at him.
''Is this some sort of game with you?''

There was a hint of anger behind the question that
threw Trace completely. ''Game? I'm not sure what
you mean.''

"When you found me at the inn, did you decide I was Aunt Mae's gift to you or something? Because I am here to tell you that hell will freeze over before I fall into bed with you just because it's convenient."

With that, she whirled away and stalked off as gracefully as the deep snow permitted, leaving him to deal with the tree. He considered running after her, trying to explain, but maybe it was better to give her time to cool down.

So he struggled with the monster tree, finally getting a firm grip on the trunk, then dragging it through the snow. The trek took forever. By the time he reached the car, Savannah and Hannah were nowhere to be seen. Since the inn was less than a mile down the road, they'd probably decided to walk.

Trace wrestled with the tree and finally got it half in and half out of the SUV, cursing at the mess it was making of the car's interior. He tied it securely, then climbed into the vehicle and turned the heater up full blast.

He was still stinging from Savannah's tongue-lashing as he drove back to the inn. Granted, he'd only been teasing her, but she didn't know him well enough to understand that. He'd deserved every bit of scorn she'd heaped on him.

As he pulled up in front of the house, he noted that the lights were blazing and that smoke was curling from the chimney. Dusk was falling rapidly, and along with it, the temperature was dropping.

He lugged the tree onto the porch, then left it there to be dealt with after he warmed up with a cup of

coffee or maybe some of that hot chocolate Savannah
and her daughter were so fond of.

Inside, he stomped the snow off his boots and
tossed his jacket over a chair, then headed for the
kitchen where he could hear the low murmur of
voices. He found Savannah at the stove stirring a pot
of spaghetti sauce. The weathered older man to whom
she was talking caught sight of Trace and gave him
a wink.

"You must be Trace. Savannah here's been giving
me an earful about you," he said. "'Course, it's not
exactly the same high praise I was used to hearing
from Mae."

Trace saw Savannah's back stiffen, but she didn't
turn around. Obviously, the walk had done nothing to
cool her temper. She was still royally ticked at him.
The apology he owed her would have to wait, though.
The man regarding him with such amusement had to
be Mae's longtime lover.

"You must be Nate Daniels," Trace guessed at
once. "I heard a lot about you over the years, as well,
all of it good."

"Only because Mae never had a sharp word to say
about anyone," Nate said. "Maybe that's because she
brought out the best in people."

"I know she did in me," Trace said solemnly, his
gaze on Savannah.

Nate looked from him to Savannah, then stood up
and began pulling on his jacket. "Think I'll be going
along now."

Savannah whirled around at that. "I thought you might like to stay for dinner."

"Not tonight," Nate said, shooting a commiserating look toward Trace. "I'll be around next time you're interested in having company. Meantime, you two need anything, you give me a call. I'll be happy to do what I can. You both meant a lot to Mae. I know she'd be happy that you're here together for the holidays."

Savannah regarded him with a disappointed expression. "Come by anytime," she said, her voice husky, her eyes shimmering with unshed tears. "I want to hear everything you can tell me about my aunt."

Nate clasped her hand in his. "Come on, now, girl. Don't you be crying for your aunt. She's at peace."

"I know. I just wish I'd been here for her."

"She understood why you couldn't be here," Nate assured her. "And I was here. She wasn't alone."

"Thank you for that," Savannah said.

"No need to thank me. My place was by her side," he said simply. "I only wish I'd been able to give her more. Now let me get out from underfoot, so you folks can have your dinner." He regarded Trace with a stern expression. "And a nice long talk."

Trace accepted the admonishment without comment. "I'll walk you out," he offered.

Nate shook his head. "No need. I know the way. Seems to me like you have better things to do," he said, casting a pointed look at Savannah, who'd deliberately turned her back again.

"Yes," Trace agreed.

He waited until he heard the front door close before attempting his apology. "Savannah?"

"What?"

"I'm sorry if I offended you earlier."

"*If?*" she asked with a hint of disdain. She faced him, eyes flashing heatedly. "You all but propositioned me in front of my daughter!"

"I made sure that Hannah was out of earshot before I said a word," he reminded her, but she didn't seem the least bit pacified. She turned away and began stirring the spaghetti sauce with a vengeance. "Okay, I'm just plain sorry. I never meant to give the impression that I seriously thought you and I ought to be back here tumbling around in bed together."

"Oh, really?" she asked skeptically. "Then exactly what *did* you mean?"

"I was just teasing. Your cheeks get all flushed and your eyes sparkle when you get indignant. That was the only reaction I was going for. I was out of line."

She turned slowly and studied him. "Apology accepted. I probably overreacted anyway. It's been a long time since I've flirted with a man."

"You'll get the hang of it again." He reached for her hand and tugged lightly until she was standing directly in front of him. "I only think it's fair to warn you, though."

"Warn me? About what?"

"Next time I might not be teasing."

She gulped visibly, then nodded. "I'll keep that in mind."

"Is it all right if I stay here, or would you rather I go?"

She seemed startled—perhaps even dismayed—by his offer to leave. "Aunt Mae invited you here. I'm certainly not going to kick you out."

"I know what Mae wanted," Trace said. "What do you want?"

She drew in a deep, shuddering breath, then stiffened her shoulders as she looked straight into his eyes. "I want you to stay."

The satisfaction that swept through Trace felt a lot like the exhilaration he felt when a difficult business negotiation ended well. "Then that's what I'll do," he told her solemnly.

She muttered something that he couldn't quite make out.

"What was that?" he asked.

A flush crept up the back of her neck. "I said, like I really had a choice."

"Of course you have a choice."

"Not if I want that tree to get put up tonight," she said, facing him with a renewed sparkle in her eyes.

Trace laughed despite himself. "I do love a woman who's always working an angle."

"Of course you do," Savannah said. "Makes you feel more at home, doesn't it? I'll bet you spend most of your time with female boardroom piranha types."

Trace chuckled at the all-too-accurate assessment. "True enough," he admitted. "But something tells me that's about to change."

Chapter 5

Savannah sent Trace in search of Hannah, while she got dinner on the table. She also needed the time to compose herself. She knew precisely why she had overreacted to Trace's teasing. It was because she had actually been tempted to take him up on his offer to slip away for a so-called *nap*. Even if they'd actually done no more than crawl into bed together and snuggle, it would have satisfied the yearning that had been building in her ever since he'd arrived earlier in the day.

Of course, she doubted a man like Trace would have settled for simply holding her in his arms. He would have wanted much more, and while she was tempted by that, she didn't want to wind up with her heart broken when he left in a few days. It was better that she'd made her position perfectly clear. If she was lucky, there would be no more temptations.

Next time I might not be teasing.

Trace's words suddenly came back to haunt her. How convenient that she had forgotten the warning.

At the sound of his laughter as he and Hannah came toward the kitchen, Savannah's pulse raced a little faster. The same wicked yearning that had gripped her earlier teased her senses now. She sighed. Resisting him was going to be a whole lot harder than she'd ever imagined. She'd just have to keep reminding herself that he was cut from the same cloth as her workaholic ex-husband.

"Mom, can we put the Christmas tree up tonight?" Hannah pleaded as they finished up bowls of ice cream after the best spaghetti Trace had eaten in years.

"According to tradition, we never put it up till Christmas Eve," Savannah told her, but she sounded regretful, as if this were one tradition she could be persuaded to change.

"Maybe it's time to start your own tradition," Trace suggested, earning a high-five from Hannah. "Besides, the sooner the tree is in its stand and has some water, the better it will be, right? It'll last much longer, and it will fill the house with the scent of pine. Why not start enjoying it now?"

Hannah studied her mother, clearly trying to gauge her mood. "Please," she begged finally. "I'll go up in the attic and bring down all the decorations you said are up there. Trace will put it up and string up the lights. You won't have to do anything."

"Except keep the carols going on the CD player and the hot chocolate flowing," Trace corrected. "What do you say, Savannah?"

"I say that you two are a formidable team," she said, feigning an air of resignation that was belied by the spark of excitement in her eyes. "Go on. Bring in the tree."

"Do you know where you want it?" Trace asked. "Once it's up, I don't want to be hauling it all over the house."

She frowned at him. "It goes in front of the window in the living room. That's where it's always been."

"And you're happy with that?" he persisted.

"Why wouldn't I be?"

"Since you're starting new traditions and all, I just thought you might want to go for broke and pick a new location."

"I think the old one is just fine," she said. "That way, anyone driving up to the house will be able to see the lights on the tree."

Trace resigned himself to moving the sofa that normally sat in front of that window. "Where should I move the sofa?"

Savannah regarded him blankly. "The sofa?"

"The one in front of that window."

Her eyes suddenly lit with understanding. "So that's why you were so eager to have me put the tree somewhere else. You're going to be stuck moving furniture."

"Hey, I'm not complaining." He glanced at Hannah. "Did you hear me complain?"

"No," she said at once.

"I'll put that sofa just about anywhere you want it except the attic," he insisted.

Savannah regarded him with a wry expression. "I think on the wall facing the fireplace will do."

"Got it. Tree in front of the window. Sofa in front of the fireplace. And the easy chairs currently on that wall? Where should they go?"

A chuckle erupted from deep inside her, lighting up her face. "Maybe Hannah and I can rearrange the furniture while you get the tree in its stand."

"No way," Trace protested. "I'm providing the brawn here. Just give me instructions."

By the time Savannah finished with the instructions, he was pretty sure that not one single piece of furniture in the living room would be where it had started out. He figured he could live with that, as long as she didn't change her mind a million times.

"That's it?" he questioned. "You're sure?"

"As sure as I can be before I see what it looks like," she said.

Trace sighed. "I'll get started. You might want to hunt for some painkillers and a heating pad in the meantime."

"Very funny."

He leveled a look at her. "Who's joking?" he

asked as he headed for the living room to rearrange the furniture.

By the time everything was in its newly designated place, including the tree, the room did have a cozier, more festive air about it. A fire crackled in the fireplace, and the fresh scent of pine filled the air.

Hannah had brought down stacks of boxes of decorations from the attic. They were now scattered over every surface, as she took each one from its tissue and examined it with wide-eyed delight.

"These must be really, really old, huh?" she asked him.

"They certainly look as if they're antiques," Trace said, noting the loving care with which she handled them. It must be nice to have family heirlooms to be brought out year after year, each with its own story. But now with Mae gone, who would share those stores with Hannah?

Savannah came in just then carrying a tray of steaming mugs filled with hot chocolate. Her eyes widened as she saw the decorations.

"Oh, my," she whispered. "I remember these. Mae used to tell us kids about them when she'd take them out of the boxes. We were never allowed to touch them because they were so old and fragile, but we each had our favorites."

She immediately picked up a blown-glass rocking horse, its paint beginning to wear away. "This was mine. This and the angel that goes on the top of the tree. Is that still here?"

"Over here," Hannah said excitedly, picking it up gingerly. "She's beautiful."

Dressed in white satin with red velvet trim, the angel had flaxen hair and golden wings. The delicate porcelain face had been rendered with a serene look totally appropriate for gazing down on the holiday festivities year after year. Even Trace, with his jaded, unsentimental view of the season, could see the beauty of it.

"We always drew straws to see who would get to put it on the top after all the other decorations were on the tree," Savannah said as she held the angel. "My dad or one of my uncles would lift up whoever won so we could reach the very top."

"Can I put it on this year?" Hannah asked. "Trace could lift me high enough."

"Maybe this year your mom ought to do it," Trace suggested, seeing the nostalgia in Savannah's eyes.

"No," Savannah said at once. "It was always one of the kids. Of course Hannah should do it—that's the tradition."

"Well, it'll be morning before we get to it unless we get started," Trace said. "There are a lot of lights here, and there must be hundreds of decorations. You two sit back and relax while I get the lights on. You can tell me when they're in the right place."

"Ah, my favorite job," Savannah teased, settling onto the sofa with Hannah beside her. "Supervisor."

Trace had a devil of a time untangling all the lights, making sure they worked and then getting them on the tree. It was the first time such a task had fallen to him, and he was beginning to see why his father had always grumbled about it. Trace would have settled for three or four strands strategically placed, but Savannah was having none of that.

"At least four more strands," she insisted. "I like a lot of lights."

"I'm not hearing any carols while I work," Trace chided. "What happened to the music? Isn't that your job?"

"Oops. I forgot. What will it be?" She shuffled through a stack of CDs. "Bing Crosby? Nat King Cole? Kenny G? The Mormon Tabernacle Choir? Vince Gill? The Vienna Boys Choir?"

"Your aunt certainly had eclectic taste," Trace commented.

"She loved Christmas music. She used to buy at least one new album every year. Obviously she kept up that tradition. So, what's your pleasure?"

"Surprise me," Trace said.

Despite the suggestion, Savannah didn't surprise him at all when she chose the old standards of Nat King Cole. As the singer's voice filled the room, Trace recalled the way his father had scoffed at the sentimentality of the holiday music. Trace had inadvertently carried that same disdain with him into adulthood. Now, though, with Savannah and Hannah singing along with the music, he began to enjoy the songs.

"Come on," Savannah encouraged. "Sing with us."

"No, thanks, I'd rather listen to you," he said as he wrapped the final strand of lights around the tree.

"But singing helps to get you into the holiday spirit. It doesn't matter if you're off-key," she told him.

"Sorry," he said, his voice a little tight. "I don't know the words."

She stared at him with obvious astonishment. "You never learned the words to all the old standard Christmas carols?"

"They weren't played much at our house. My father objected. He said it was just more crass commercialism. We were lucky he let us put up a tree. After a few years, he carried on so about that, that my mother settled for the little ceramic tree I told you about earlier."

"But you must have heard the carols when you were at your friends' houses," she persisted. "Or on the radio."

"I didn't pay much attention," he said defensively.

"How awful," she said, studying him with sympathy.

"Savannah, I got along okay without knowing the words to a bunch of songs that get played once a year."

She studied him seriously. "Can I ask you something?"

"Sure," he said, despite the wariness creeping over him.

"As a man who doesn't seem to have many happy

memories of the holidays, how did you end up running a toy company?"

"Long story," he said.

"It's still early. We have time."

"I don't want to bore Hannah with all this. Besides, we've got a tree to decorate." He deliberately turned to Hannah. "Sweetie, are you ready to start hanging those decorations?" he asked, shutting down the topic of his career.

"Sure," Hannah said eagerly. "Mom, you've got to help."

Savannah cast one last curious look at him, before smiling and picking up several decorations.

By the time they were finally finished and all the boxes were empty, there wasn't a bare spot on the tree's branches.

"Ready for the lights?" Trace asked.

"Wait. Let me turn off the overhead lights," Savannah said. "It's better in the dark."

As soon as the main lights were off, Trace plugged in the tree's. The hundreds of lights shimmered, reflecting off the ornaments and filling the room with dazzling color. Even he was a bit in awe as he stared at it.

"It's beautiful," Hannah whispered.

"The very best tree ever," Savannah agreed.

Suddenly she was slipping her hand into Trace's. "Thank you," she said.

"Just following directions," he said.

"No. It's more than that. I think we all need a

touch of magic in our lives this year, and you've made sure we have it.''

"All I did—"

She cut off his protest. *"Thank you,"* she repeated emphatically, gazing up at him.

Trace thought he'd never seen anything so lovely in his life as he gazed into her sparkling eyes, which put the lights on the tree to shame. "You're welcome," he said softly, resisting the need to kiss her only because Hannah was in the room.

"I think I'll go to bed," Hannah announced with rare impeccable timing.

"Night, baby," Savannah said, sounding just a little breathless.

"Good night, Trace. Thanks for helping with the tree." Hannah stood on tiptoe to give him a peck on the cheek.

"Good night, angel."

"I'm glad you're here," she murmured sleepily as she headed for the stairs.

Trace looked into Savannah's eyes, aware suddenly that he was caught up in something he couldn't explain with his usual rational practicality. "I'm glad I'm here, too."

The most amazing sense of contentment stole through Savannah as she settled onto the sofa with Trace beside her. He was careful not to sit too close, but she could still feel the heat radiating from him, and she was drawn to it more than ever.

It had been an incredible evening. Even listening

to Trace and Hannah bickering over where to place the ornaments on the tree had been wonderful. Hannah wouldn't have risked such a debate with her father. Things were always done Rob's way. It was a lesson Hannah had learned early, to keep peace in the family.

It was more than that, though. Maybe it was the cozy fire. Maybe it was the hot chocolate and salvaged chunks of sugar cookies.

Or maybe it was simply that for the first time in years, there was no real dissension as the holidays got under way. It had always been a battle to get her husband home from the office in time to help with the preparations. And unlike the bantering between Hannah and Trace, there had been a superior edge to her ex's tone that had always sent Hannah to her room in tears.

"Can I ask you something?" Savannah said, studying Trace intently.

He kept his guarded gaze directed toward the fire, but he nodded.

"Christmas is still a couple of days away. Why did you come up here early?"

"I told you."

"I know. You promised my aunt. But she's been gone for several weeks now. You could have waited till the last second and still fulfilled your promise."

He glanced at her, then looked back at the fire. "You'll think I'm crazy."

Savannah laughed. "I doubt that. Even in the brief

time I've known you, I can tell you definitely have all your wits about you.''

"Okay, then, here it is. I was planning to wait till Christmas Eve, rush up here, spend the night and rush right back to the city on Christmas Day.''

"But you changed your mind. Why?''

"I woke up this morning with this weird feeling that I needed to be up here today.'' He met her gaze. "Normally I would have dismissed it and kept to my original plan...." His voice trailed off.

"But?'' Savannah prodded, intrigued by the distinctly uncomfortable expression on his face. For a man who exuded confidence, it was a rare display of vulnerability.

"You know that cooler of chocolate mocha almond ice cream?''

"Very well. What does that have to do with anything?''

"It was delivered to my apartment this morning with a note that said I should get it up here before it melted.''

Savannah stared at him. "Someone sent you that ice cream as a gift?''

His gaze held hers. "Not just *someone*. It was your aunt's handwriting.''

"Oh, my,'' Savannah whispered. "How could that be?''

"I called the store and the delivery service. The arrangements had been made weeks ago.'' He shrugged ruefully. "I guess Mae was afraid I might not keep my promise without a little nudge from beyond the grave. Needless to say, I packed my bags and hit the road.''

She studied him closely. ''Are you teasing me?''

''Absolutely not,'' he said. ''I have no sense of humor. Ask the people who work for me. Heck, it's even in most of the articles about Franklin Toys.''

''That's absurd,'' Savannah said, dismissing the suggestion out of hand. ''You've been joking and laughing with Hannah and me since you got here.''

''I know,'' he said, his expression serious. ''What do you make of that?''

''We're good for you,'' she said, her voice suddenly a little breathless. Could it really be that she had something to offer this man who had everything money could buy?

''Which, I suspect, is exactly what your aunt had in mind when she plotted this meeting.''

Suddenly it all made sense to Savannah. The inheritance of Holiday Retreat at a time when she desperately needed a change in her life. The unexpected arrival of a handsome stranger on the inn's doorstep. Yes, indeed, Aunt Mae had been scheming, all right. The realization horrified her.

''I am so sorry,'' she told Trace with total sincerity. ''She shouldn't have dragged you up here with an ulterior motive. If you want to get back to the city and your friends for Christmas, I will certainly understand.''

Her declaration seemed to amuse Trace for some reason. His eyes were glinting humorously, when he reached out to caress her cheek. "Are you kicking me out, Savannah?"

"No, of course not. I just wanted you to understand that you're free to go if there's someplace you'd rather be, people you'd rather be spending the holiday with."

As an answer he leaned forward and touched his lips to hers in the lightest, tenderest of kisses. There was a whisper of heat, the promise of fire…and then he was on his feet.

"I'll see you in the morning," he said as he headed for the stairs.

"You're staying?" she asked.

"Of course I'm staying."

"Because it was what Mae wanted?" she asked, determined to clarify the reason.

"No, darlin'. Because it's what *I* want." He winked at her. "Besides, I promised to take you into town tomorrow."

With that he was gone, leaving Savannah staring after him. She touched a finger to her lips, where she could still feel his mouth against hers. "And you always keep your promises," she whispered to herself. It was such a little thing, but it meant more than Trace could possibly imagine.

She lifted her gaze to seek out a picture of Aunt Mae that sat on the mantel. "Thank you."

Just knowing that there was one man left who kept his promises restored her faith that the future would turn out all right.

Chapter 6

The scent of fresh-brewed coffee drifted upstairs, pulling Trace out of a perfectly fascinating dream. For once it had nothing to do with mergers and acquisitions, but with a woman—Savannah, to be precise.

How could a woman with so little guile, so little sophistication, get under his skin the way she had? That kiss the night before—little more than a friendly peck by most standards—had packed more punch than any kiss he'd experienced in years. He'd left the room, not because he believed in hasty, uncomplicated exits, but because he wanted so much more. If he'd gone after what he'd wanted, more than likely he would have scared her to death. Then she would have kicked him out and he would have spent another lonely holiday season back in New York.

"I hope to hell you knew what you were doing, Mae," he muttered.

When the scent of sizzling bacon joined that of the coffee, Trace quickly showered and dressed in a pair of old jeans, a dress shirt and a heavy pullover sweater. That was about as casual as his attire ever got these days. He reminded himself if he was going to paint the front door and trim and sand the floors, he needed to buy something else to wear.

When he walked into the kitchen, Savannah regarded him with flushed cheeks and wisps of curls teasing her face. "Is that your idea of work clothes?" she asked. "Or do you intend to supervise today, the way I did last night?"

Trace noted that she, too, was wearing jeans, but her University of Florida sweatshirt had seen better days, as had her sneakers. She still looked fabulous. He still wanted her. A part of him had been hoping that last night's desire had been an aberration.

"Did I say I was working?" he inquired as he poured himself a cup of coffee, breathed in its rich scent, then took his first sip. "Good coffee, by the way."

She grinned. "Glad you like it, since it's yours. I figured you wouldn't approve of the instant I had on hand."

Trace shuddered. "Good guess." He met her gaze. "Exactly what sort of work are you planning to do today?"

"I want to pick up paint for the guest rooms, a tarp for the roof and…"

"Whoa! Why a tarp for the roof?"

"Because it's leaking."

"Why not get it fixed?"

"I would if I could get the contractor over here," she explained with exaggerated patience. "He said he can't come till after the first of the year."

"Then call another contractor."

She frowned at him. "Don't you think I thought of that?"

"I'll handle it," he said at once.

"What do you mean, you'll 'handle it'?"

"I'll get someone over here to repair the roof."

"Even if you are a business mogul, I doubt you'll be any more successful than I've been," she said. "Besides, there's at least a foot of snow up there. They won't even be able to look at it, much less start the repairs."

"Okay, you have a point," he conceded. "Though that would also seem to make the tarp a waste of time, too, unless you're planning to put it over the snow."

She frowned at him. "Okay, then, no tarp."

"What else do you want from the hardware store?"

"The paint and tools to scrape the wallpaper will do it. I don't want to spend any more till I know what the rest of the repairs are going to cost. And I have to set some money aside for new brochures and advertising. I need to start getting paying guests back in here as soon as possible. I've already missed the start of the ski season."

Trace thought he heard a hint of desperation in her voice that she was trying hard to hide. "Savannah,

do you have the money to get this place up and running again?''

''I have enough,'' she said tightly.

''What about a loan? I could—''

''Absolutely not. I won't take money from you.''

''Then let me talk to the bank.''

''No, I am not going to start off my new life with
a pile of debts. Things will get done when I can afford
to do them.''

Trace admired her pride and her independent
streak, but as a practical matter he knew it was better
for a business to present its best face from the outset
so that word-of-mouth would spread. She might not
take money from him, but she wasn't in a position to
turn down a little practical assistance in the form of
labor. She could hardly tell him not to pick up his
own supplies. He'd just have to be a little sneaky
about it. That meant getting in and out of the hardware store without her catching sight of his purchases.

''Fine,'' he said. ''Holiday Retreat is yours.''

There was one more thing he could do, too. It
would require a few phone calls, routing his attorney
away from his new girlfriend for a couple of hours,
but he could pull it off by Christmas.

''Is Hannah coming into town with us?'' he asked
as he ate the scrambled eggs Savannah put in front
of him.

''Of course. She's dying to take a look around. We
stopped at the grocery store on our way up here, but
that's all she's seen. I'll go get her. We can be ready
to leave whenever you're finished with breakfast.''

"Did you eat?"

"I had a piece of toast," she said.

Trace frowned at her. "I have enough eggs here for three people." He stood up, grabbed a plate from the cupboard, then divided up his eggs, added two slices of bacon and set it on the table. "Sit. You need the protein."

Savannah opened her mouth to protest, but his scowl achieved what his directive had not. She sat down and picked up her fork.

"You know, I have to get used to serving the guests around here without sitting down to eat with each and every one of them," she told him.

"I'm not a guest."

She nibbled thoughtfully on a piece of bacon. "Which means I probably shouldn't have cooked this for you," she said.

"Right. I told you I'd look out for myself."

"I'll remember that tomorrow morning."

He regarded her slyly. "Of course, it wouldn't hurt to get in a little practice in the kitchen. You wouldn't want the first real guests to starve, would you?"

She laughed. "I don't think there's any chance of that. I may not have had a lot of practice at cooking for a crowd, but Aunt Mae has a whole box filled with recipes she perfected over the years. I can read directions with the best of them."

"I seem to recall some sort of baked French toast Mae used to make," Trace said, his gaze on Savannah. "I don't suppose…"

To his surprise, Savannah's eyes lit up. "I remember that. She always made it Christmas morning."

"Then it's a tradition?" Trace asked hopefully.

"Yes, it's a tradition. And, yes, I'll make it. And, yes, you can have breakfast with Hannah and me on Christmas morning."

"Before or after we open presents?" Trace asked, only to see her shoulders stiffen slightly.

Hannah arrived in the kitchen just in time to hear the question. "We're not having presents this year, 'cause we're poor," she said with absolutely no hint of self-pity.

"We are *not* poor," Savannah said, obviously embarrassed by her daughter's comment. "It's just that the divorce and the renovations needed on this place have left us temporarily strapped for cash, so we're keeping Christmas simple."

"I see," Trace said slowly.

Simple might be good enough for Savannah, maybe even for Hannah, who seemed resigned to it, but not for him. For the first time in years, he had the desire to splurge on the holidays.

Oh, he always sent truckloads of toys to various homeless shelters in the city, but his personal gift list was small and mostly confined to business associates. He couldn't recall the last time he'd had anyone in his life to whom he'd wanted to offer even a small token of affection.

He made a mental note to make a few more calls the second he had some privacy.

"Why don't you guys grab your coats, while I

clean up in here?'' he suggested. ''I'll meet you at the car in a few minutes.''

Savannah regarded him curiously, almost as if she suspected something was up because he'd let her description of their financial plight pass without comment.

''Go on. Warm up the car,'' he encouraged, tossing her the keys. ''You cooked. I'll clean up. That's *my* tradition.''

''I thought you didn't have any traditions,'' she replied.

''I'm starting a new one.''

To his relief, she seemed to accept that.

''We'll be outside,'' she said. ''Try not to break any dishes.''

''Hey,'' he protested, ''I know what I'm doing.''

He loaded the dishwasher, turned it on, then grabbed his cell phone. It took less than ten minutes to set things in motion. That was one of the benefits of being rich. Trace rarely threw his weight or his money around. When he did, people were eager enough to do as he asked. He'd always been satisfied in a distant sort of way when he thought of the delight his toys would bring to kids on Christmas morning, but he'd never actually experienced that sense of awe and wonder that was pictured in his commercials. Maybe this year things would be different.

Satisfied that Christmas was under control, he grabbed his coat and joined Savannah and Hannah, who'd already retreated to the slowly warming interior of the car. Hannah shivered dramatically when he opened the door.

"I hate cold weather," she declared.

Trace regarded her in the rearview mirror. "You're living in the wrong place, then, kiddo. Weren't you the one who was out here half-buried in snowdrifts yesterday?"

"It's colder today," she insisted. "And now I've seen snow. Yesterday I hadn't."

"Does that mean you want to move back to Florida?" Savannah asked.

There was no mistaking the note of trepidation in her voice, Trace thought. He glanced over and saw the tight lines around her mouth.

"No," Hannah said at once. "Even if it is cold, I want to stay here."

Savannah's relief was almost palpable. "Why?" she asked.

"Because since we got here, you've started laughing again," Hannah said quietly. "You never laughed in Florida."

Savannah turned her head away, but not before Trace saw a tear sliding down her cheek. He wanted to reach for her, to hold her...to make her laugh.

Instead he glanced toward Hannah. "How about you and me making a pact?" he said. "The one who makes your mom laugh the most today wins."

Hannah's eyes lit up. "Okay. What's the prize?"

"Hmm," Trace began thoughtfully. "If you win, I make us all hot fudge sundaes for dessert tonight."

"Good prize," Hannah said enthusiastically. "What if *you* win?"

"Then you make me the biggest, mushiest Christmas card ever, something I can hang on my office wall."

"Deal," Hannah said, slapping his hand in a high five.

He glanced toward Savannah and saw that her lips were twitching. It wasn't a real laugh, but it was at least the beginning of a smile. He pointed it out to Hannah.

"I get the first point," he said.

"That's not a real laugh," Hannah scoffed. She leaned over, slipped her hand down her mother's back and tickled Savannah until she giggled aloud. "*That's* a real laugh," Hannah said triumphantly.

Savannah wriggled away, then scowled at both of them. "What do *I* get, if I maintain a totally stoic facade all day long?"

"Never happen," Trace said.

"No way," Hannah agreed.

"Bet I can," Savannah retorted, her eyes twinkling.

"Okay, that does make it more interesting," Trace agreed. "If you win—and that's a really big *if*—you get Hannah's mushy card."

"What about you? What will you give me?"

Trace met her gaze evenly and felt his heart take a leap into overdrive. "Same as last night," he said softly.

He noted the flush that crept into her cheeks as she remembered that fleeting kiss they'd shared.

"You'll have to do better than that," she challenged.

His gazed remained steady. "Oh, I promise you, darlin', it will take your breath away."

The blasted heater in the car must have shot the temperature into the nineties, Savannah thought, barely resisting the urge to fan herself as Trace's words hung in the air.

Unlike the day before, when his seductive teasing had merely irritated her, today she was immediately all hot and bothered and wishing for more...maybe because she knew for a fact exactly what Trace's kiss could do to her. Worse, she wanted another of those kisses so badly, she was going to have to try really, really hard not to laugh for the remainder of the day. Given Hannah's determination to win that bet she'd made with Trace, Savannah was going to have a real struggle on her hands.

She could do it, though. She just had to remember her resolve...and keep a whole lot of distance between herself and those two co-conspirators.

The second they reached the hardware store, Hannah begged to take a walk through town.

"Back here in thirty minutes," Savannah instructed, relieved to be rid of one of them. She looked at Trace. "I'll meet you back here in a half hour, too."

"You sure you don't need my help?" he asked, regarding her with a knowing grin.

"Nope. I'm sure someone will help me carry whatever I buy."

"Here's the spare key, then, in case you finish before I get back. You don't mind if I come in and pick up a few things myself, do you?" he asked.

"What sort of things?" she asked suspiciously. Trace didn't strike her as the type who had a lot of fix-it projects back home. Then again, didn't most men get a little giddy around wrenches and screwdrivers and power tools? Maybe he just wanted to soak up the atmosphere.

"This and that," he said vaguely. "I'll know when I see it."

"Fine. It's a big store. I'm sure you won't be in my way," she said.

They parted at the front door. Savannah headed straight for the paint supplies. She'd already thought about the colors she wanted for each of the guest rooms—rich, deep tones, accented by white trim. In no time at all, she'd picked out the appropriate paint chips and had the colors being mixed, while she chose brushes, rollers, an edger for trimming, and a paint pan.

Just as she headed through the store toward wallpaper-removal materials, she thought she spotted Trace coming around the end of the paint aisle, but then he vanished from sight. She didn't see him again until she was unloading her purchases into the back of his SUV.

"Find everything you were looking for?" he asked, tucking his own mysterious packages beside hers.

"Yes. What about you?" she asked as he lifted something heavy into the car. "What on earth is that? It looks as if it weighs a ton."

"Just a tool," he said, immediately turning his attention to the street. "Any sign of Hannah yet? Maybe we should go meet her. We could grab some lunch while we're in town. There's a little restaurant on Main Street that Mae used to like."

"The Burger Shack," Savannah said at once. "Is it still in business?"

"It was last time I was here. I took Mae a burger, fries and a chocolate shake from there."

"I can almost taste their shakes," Savannah said. "They made 'em the old-fashioned way with milk and ice cream. They were so thick, a straw would stand straight up in them."

When she looked at Trace, his lips were curving into a grin.

"Sounds like that's a yes," he said.

"Absolutely," she said eagerly. "And here comes Hannah."

She noticed that her daughter was carrying a shopping bag and that her eyes were sparkling with excitement. "What did you buy?" Savannah asked.

"Mom, I can't tell. It's almost Christmas, remember?"

Savannah started to question where Hannah had gotten the money to buy a gift, then stopped herself. Rob had probably slipped her a little money before they'd left Florida. Knowing him, that had been his gift to her, and she was turning right around and spending it on Savannah. On Trace, too, more than likely. Her daughter had the most generous heart of anyone Savannah knew, something she clearly hadn't inherited from her father.

"And that's all you need to tell us," Trace said, making room in the back of the car for Hannah's purchases. "Your mom and I were just talking about lunch. You interested?"

"Only if you're talking about that burger place on Main Street. The smell coming out of there is awesome. And I saw lots of kids my age going in. It must be the cool place to go."

Trace grinned. "Then it sounds like it's unanimous."

"Guess what?" Hannah asked excitedly. She went on without waiting for a response. "I met this girl at the store. Her name's Jolie. Isn't that a great name? And she's my age. We'll be in the same class at school. She says the teacher is really great. Her name's Mrs. Peterson. She's been here like forever, but everyone loves her, because she's so nice."

"Really?" Savannah said, since Hannah didn't seem to expect much of a response. She was already rushing on.

"And guess what else?" she said. "Jolie says there's going to be caroling in town tonight and that everyone will be there, so we should come, too." She regarded Savannah hopefully. "Can we, please?"

Savannah instinctively thought of how uncomfortable Trace had been when she'd asked him to sing carols at the house the night before. She glanced at him.

"I think it sounds like a wonderful idea," he said with apparent sincerity.

Hannah grinned at him. "Jolie says they give out song sheets, so you'll know all the words."

"Then I definitely say we do it," Trace said. "Savannah?"

Being out on a cold, snowy evening two days before Christmas singing carols with her daughter and Trace? Savannah couldn't imagine anything more romantic. That probably meant she ought to say no, but of course she wouldn't. Not if it meant disappointing Hannah.

Sure, as if that were the real reason, she mentally scolded herself. She was going to do it because there was no place on earth she'd rather be tomorrow night.

"Yes," she said, noting the smile that spread across Hannah's face. It was almost as bright as the warmth stealing through her.

Chapter 7

Savannah had the radio blasting as she got into a rhythm of applying paint to the walls of the first guest room. The beautiful deep shade of green brought the color of the evergreens in the surrounding forest inside. When the white trim was added, it would be reminiscent of the way the scenery looked right now with snow clinging to the trees' branches. She envisioned a thick, warm comforter in shades of green and burgundy on the queen-size bed, with aromatic candles to match on the dresser.

Glancing out the window, she caught a glimpse of Hannah building her first snowman and chattering happily, no doubt to Trace, though Savannah couldn't figure out exactly where he was. He'd been up to something, though for the life of her she couldn't figure out what it was. The instant they'd arrived home after lunch, he'd disappeared into Mae's den. She hadn't seen him since.

Despite her declaration that she intended to handle the painting task on her own, a part of her had been counting on his defiance of that. She'd expected him to show up by now, if only to critique her work, maybe try to coax a laugh out of her in his ongoing attempt to win that bet with Hannah. Instead, much as her ex-husband would have done, Trace had retreated to whatever work he considered more important.

Oh, well, this was her job, not his, she thought with a sigh. And a man she barely knew was hardly in a position to disappoint her.

Besides, the painting was going very well, she decided, as she stood back and surveyed the room. There was an elegance and warmth to the result. Once the finishing touches were in place—probably after she could hit the January white sales at the Boston department stores—it would be perfect.

Satisfied, she snapped the lid back on the can of paint and prepared to move on to another room, the one she thought of as the blue room, though at the moment it had faded wallpaper that needed to be stripped. It was already late afternoon, so she probably wouldn't get much of the stripping completed before they left for the caroling in town, but any progress on the messy task was better than none.

She was about to peel off her first chunk of paper when something that sounded a lot like a big-time power tool kicked on downstairs, followed by a muttered curse, then giggles and deep, booming laughter. Savannah went to the top of the stairs and looked down just in time to see Hannah and Trace cast a furtive look in her direction.

"Uh-oh, we're busted," Trace said.

"If she heard you cussing, she'll probably send us to our rooms," Hannah said, looking downcast.

Hands on hips, Savannah scowled at them. "What are you two doing?"

"Nothing bad, Mom. Honest." Hannah's expression was filled with sincerity.

"Trace?"

"She's right. It's just a little surprise," he said.

Savannah remained skeptical. "A surprise, or a shock?"

Hannah giggled. "Mom's not real good with surprises."

"Maybe because I've had so many bad ones," Savannah said. "By the way, I'm not hearing any reassuring explanations. Do I need to come down there?"

"No," they both said at once.

The quick chorus only roused her suspicions further. She started down the steps, only to have Trace take the bottom steps two at a time and meet her when she was less than halfway down. Putting both hands on her shoulders, he gazed into her eyes.

"Do you trust me?" he asked.

Now there was a sixty-four-thousand-dollar question. "I suppose," she said, hedging. Only Mae's faith in him was giving him her current benefit of the doubt.

"Well, you can," he said, clearly disappointed by the less than wholehearted response. "You need to go back to whatever you were doing and let Hannah and me finish up what we're doing."

She returned his gaze without blinking. "I was thinking of quitting for the day, maybe coming downstairs for a snack."

"I'll bring you a snack," he said at once. "Anything you want."

"An entire pint of your ice cream?"

"If that's what you want," he said at once.

"Okay, that's it. Something bad is going on down there, isn't it?" she said, trying to brush past him.

"Mom, please," Hannah wailed. "You'll spoil everything. It's not bad. I promise."

Savannah told herself that it was her daughter's plea, not the pleading expression in Trace's eyes that won her over. "You can't keep me up here forever, you know."

"Just another couple of hours," he said, looking relieved. "Still want that ice cream?"

"No, that was just a test."

He grinned. "I figured as much."

Savannah sighed. "I'm going back to strip wallpaper."

"Maybe you ought to take a break," he suggested. "Maybe take a long, leisurely bubble bath or something."

"Who has time for that?" Savannah grumbled. "This place isn't going to get fixed up by itself."

He tucked a finger under her chin. "When you start saying things like that, it's exactly the time when you need a break the most."

"This from a workaholic like you?" she scoffed.

"Actually that's something your aunt used to say to me every time I protested that I couldn't get away from the office to come visit. It got me up here every time," he said, an unmistakable hint of nostalgia in his voice. "And she was always right. I always felt better after a few days with her. I even got so I barely cracked open my briefcase the whole time I was here."

"Did she talk you into taking a bubble bath, too?" Savannah teased.

"Nope, but you probably could," he retorted, then added in an undertone, "especially if you were joining me."

Heat and desire shot through Savannah like a bolt of lightning. "Any bubble bath I take, I'll be taking alone," she told him, keeping her own voice muted.

"Too bad."

Before she made the fatal mistake of agreeing with him, she whirled around and went back upstairs. She started toward the room where she'd been about to work, then changed her mind and headed another floor up to her bathroom, where she poured some lavender-scented bubble bath into the tub and turned on the water, knowing that the sound would be enough to keep Trace's imagination stirred up. He wasn't the only one under this roof who had a wicked streak, she thought with satisfaction as she sank into the warm water. Hers had just been on hold for a while.

Unfortunately the memory of his suggestion that he join her and the sensual feel of the water against her skin combined to make the bath far less relaxing than she'd envisioned. In fact, she concluded as she stepped from the tub and wrapped herself in a thick terry cloth towel, it really was too bad that she wouldn't find Trace waiting for her in her bed. Thank goodness they were going caroling in a couple of hours. It was definitely going to take a blast of icy air to cool off her wayward thoughts.

"Quiet," Trace admonished Hannah when they heard Savannah moving around upstairs. Since they were due to leave for the caroling in less than a half hour, he figured they had five minutes, maybe less, before she started down from the private quarters on the third floor. He squeezed Hannah's hand. "Not a word till she gets all the way down and sees what we've done."

They'd only made a dent in the work that was needed to put Holiday Retreat back into shape for guests, but the outside of the front door and the exterior trim were now a bright red, the brass fixtures glistened and the foyer and living room floors were polished to a mellow sheen. Hannah had even fashioned some greens and ribbon into a decoration that had been hung from the brass knocker. In his opinion, with just a little effort, they had made a vast difference in the appearance of the inn. It looked as it had on his first few visits, before Mae had let some of the maintenance slip.

Beside him, Hannah was practically bursting with excitement as they waited for her mother.

"I should open the door," she whispered. "Otherwise, how will she know about the paint and the decoration?"

Trace grinned at her. "Good point. Why don't you sneak out the back door, run around to the front and open it when I give the word that she's almost down the steps? I'll make sure it's unlocked."

Hannah took off, thundering across the floor in her eagerness.

"Don't forget your coat," Trace called after her just as he heard Savannah's footsteps descending from the third floor to the second.

Since he didn't want Savannah to miss Hannah's grand entrance, he stepped into view as she started down the last flight and blocked her way. She paused halfway down, regarding him warily.

"I am not going back up," she told him.

"Never said you should."

"Then why are you standing in my way?"

"Am I in your way?" he asked, still not budging.

Savannah sighed heavily, just as Trace heard Hannah hit the porch running.

"You look lovely," he said in a voice meant to carry outside.

Her gazed narrowed. ''Announcing it to the world?''

''Why not?'' he said. ''It's worth announcing.''

At that instant he heard Hannah turn the doorknob. He stepped aside as the door burst open.

Clearly startled, Savannah looked straight at her daughter, then caught sight of the freshly painted door. Her eyes lit up.

''Oh, my,'' she said softly. ''It's beautiful.'' She looked from Hannah to Trace. ''Is that what you two were up to?''

''Only part of it, Mom,'' Hannah said. ''Come down the rest of the way and look around some more.''

As soon as Savannah stepped off the bottom stair, she glanced around, her expression puzzled.

''Down,'' Hannah said impatiently.

Savannah's gaze shifted to the floor with its brand-new shine. ''What on earth?'' There were tears in her eyes when she turned to Trace. ''You did this? That's what I heard down here? I couldn't imagine the wood ever looking like this again. It's beautiful.''

Hannah beamed at her. ''I helped, Mom. Trace and I did it together.''

''It's just a start,'' Trace said. ''We only had time to do the foyer and the living room. We'll do the dining room tomorrow.''

The tears in Savannah's eyes spilled down her cheeks. ''I don't know how to thank you.''

''You could start by not crying,'' Trace said mildly, stepping closer to brush the dampness from her cheeks. "We wanted to do something to help. Hannah made the decoration for the door. She's got a real knack for that sort of thing."

Savannah's gaze shifted to the greens. "Trace is right, sweetie. It's absolutely beautiful. Aunt Mae would be so pleased with all of this."

She turned to Trace. "I know you did it for her, but thank you."

It had started as something he wanted to do for Mae, but that wasn't how it had ended up. Trace realized he had done it to put that sparkle into Savannah's eyes, the sparkle that shimmered even through her tears.

"It was the least I could do," he said. "Now, do you want to admire our work some more, or shall we head into town for the caroling?"

"Let's go," Hannah said at once. "Mom can look at this forever when we come home."

Savannah laughed. "So much for savoring the moment."

"I made you laugh," Hannah gloated. "That's a whole bunch of points for me and hardly any for Trace. Those sundaes are mine!"

"Ah, well," Trace said with an exaggerated air of resignation. "I suppose the art already on my office wall will have to do."

Savannah was quiet on the ride into town. Too quiet, in Trace's opinion. When they'd finally found a parking place a few blocks from the town square and Savannah was exiting the car, he pulled her aside. "Everything okay?"

"Of course," she said brightly, though her smile was as phony as that too-chipper tone.

"Tell me," he persisted.

She sighed. "I was just thinking about all the Christmases I missed with Aunt Mae, years when I could have had this, instead of…well, instead of what we had."

"You can't go back and change things," Trace reminded her. "You can only learn from your mistakes and look ahead."

She regarded him intently. "Are there things about your life that you'd change, mistakes you regret?"

He hesitated over the answer. "I wish things had been easier for my mother," he said slowly. "But I was a boy. I had no control over that. She made her own choice to stay married to a dreamer who was very good at criticizing everything *she* did, but did nothing himself."

A half smile touched Savannah's lips. "You say that, but you sound as if you still believe that you should have fixed it somehow."

"I suppose I do believe that," he admitted. "But by the time I had the money to make a difference in her life, it was too late. She'd already died of pneumonia. She'd let a flu go untreated too long, because my father thought she was making too much out of a little cold. Once she got to the hospital, there was nothing they could do. That was the beginning of the end for my dad. He was devastated. I finally saw that in his own way, he had felt my mother was everything to him. He died less than six months later."

"Oh, Trace, I'm so sorry," Savannah said.

He forced aside the guilt that the memory always brought. "Time to take my own advice. I can't change the past. I have to let it go. We all do." He managed a smile. "I think I hear a band warming up. It must be about time for the caroling to begin."

As if on cue, Hannah, who'd been hurrying ahead of them, bolted back. "Hurry up, you guys. The carols are starting. And I see Jolie. Can I go say hi to her?"

"Of course," Savannah said. "But then you come back to join us. Got it?"

"Got it," Hannah said, racing away from them.

Left alone with Savannah, Trace reached for her hand and tucked it through his arm. "This is nice," he said, looking into her shining eyes. "The stars are out. The air is crisp. I can smell the bonfire up ahead. It definitely feels as if Christmas is in the air. And there's a beautiful woman on my arm."

In the glow of the gas lamps on the street, Trace could see Savannah blush. If a simple compliment rattled her so, it must have been years since she'd heard any. Which made her ex-husband even more of a fool than Trace had imagined.

"You know, as much as I loved growing up in Florida," Savannah said, "this is the only place it's ever really felt like Christmas to me. Just look around. All the stores are decorated along Main Street. There's a tree in the center of the green that's all lit up, and snow underfoot. It's like a Currier and Ives Christmas card. What could be more perfect?"

She looked up into Trace's eyes, and he felt his heart slam to a stop.

"You," he said softly.

"What?"

"You're the only thing I can think of that's more perfect than all of this."

For the second time that evening, she was blinking back tears.

"Hey," he protested. "I didn't mean to make you cry again."

She gave him a watery smile. "It's just that no one's ever said anything so sweet to me before."

"Then you've been spending time with the wrong people," he said emphatically.

Suddenly she stood on tiptoe, and before he realized what she intended, she was pressing a kiss to his cheek. "Thank you. I'm really glad you're spending Christmas with us."

Trace could have let it go at that. It was a tender gesture, not an invitation, but the night was cold and that kiss promised heat. He captured her chin and gazed into her eyes, then slowly lowered his head until his mouth covered hers.

She tasted of mint and felt like satin. Then the anticipated heat began to work its way through his system, hinting of a simmering passion just waiting to be unleashed. He unzipped her jacket and slid his arms inside, pulling her close until their body heat mingled. She melted against him. They were a perfect fit, her curves soft and yielding, his body hard and demanding.

Trace could have been content to stay right here, doing nothing more than learning the shape and texture and taste of Savannah's mouth for hours on end, but sanity finally prevailed. This was a small town. Savannah was a newcomer. The last thing she needed was him stirring up gossip. Whatever happened between them—and there was little doubt that something would—he didn't want there to be regrets. Not of any kind.

With a sigh, he slowly released her. His gaze clung to hers as he slid the zipper of her jacket up, then tucked her scarf more securely around her neck.

"Trace, what…?" She swallowed hard. "What was that about?"

"New beginnings," he suggested. He drew in a deep breath of the cold air, then added, "And speaking of that, I had an idea I thought I'd run by you."

"If it's anything like that last one, the answer's yes," she replied, amusement threading through her voice.

"Don't agree until you've heard it," he said. "What about holding an open house at the inn tomorrow before midnight church services? The downstairs rooms can be ready by then, and it would get people talking about the place."

She was staring at him, her expression dazed. "Are you crazy? I can't be ready for an open house tomorrow night! Even if we could finish up with the downstairs rooms, what about food? We'd need wine and eggnog. All of the good dishes would have to be washed, the table decorated. I can think of a million reasons why it would never work.''

He waited through the tirade, then asked, ''Is that it? Any other objections?''

''I think those are quite enough.''

''Okay, your turn to listen to me. I can have a caterer here first thing in the morning. He's already on standby. He'll bring all the food, the drinks, the table decorations, linens, crystal and china. All you need to do is say yes and stay out of his way.'' He pulled his cell phone out of his pocket. ''What's it going to be?''

She regarded him with obvious astonishment. ''You've already done all that?''

''I put it into motion, checked to make sure the caterer I use for our big marketing events was available. I haven't given the go-ahead. That's up to you. I thought it might be the perfect way for you and Hannah to get to know your neighbors, a way to let them know that the inn is back in business.''

She looked torn. ''It's a wonderful idea, but I can't let you do it.''

''Why?''

''Because…'' Her voice faltered. She frowned at him. ''I don't know why exactly. It's just too much. Besides, how would we let people know?''

He sensed that she was weakening and pressed his advantage. ''I think we can count on Hannah and her friend to take care of that. Say the word, and we can send the two of them through this crowd. It'll be faster than an instant-message e-mail.''

"What if no one comes?" she asked worriedly. "It is Christmas Eve, after all. People have plans. Then you would've gone to all that expense for nothing."

"I'm not worried about that. I'm sure people are curious. Some are probably anxious to know if you intend to reopen the inn. It's been an historic landmark in the town for years. I think they'll be more than eager to take a little side trip on their way to church." He waited while the wheels turned in her head. He could practically see the pros and cons warring in her brain, as her expression shifted from dismay to hope and back again.

"You're absolutely certain we can pull this off?" she said at last. "It won't be the biggest mistake either of us has ever made?"

"Darlin', when it comes to business, I try really hard never to make mistakes."

"Okay, then," she said decisively. "Make that call. Then let's find Hannah and Jolie and put them to work."

Trace confirmed the plans with the caterer, who was eager to do anything for the bonus Trace had promised him. After that, finding the girls wasn't all that difficult. They were right in front, singing at the top of their lungs. Trace pulled Hannah aside and told her the plan.

"That is so awesome!" she said. "Jolie will help."

She pulled her friend over, introduced her to Trace and Savannah, then told her the plan.

"Sure," Jolie said at once. "I'll tell my mom and dad to spread the word, too. They know everybody.

And this will be way better than sitting around at home while my relatives say the same old things they say every year.''

''Tell them I'll appreciate whatever they can do to let people know,'' Savannah told her.

The two girls were about to race off when Jolie turned back. ''I was supposed to ask you if it would be okay for Hannah to spend the night at my house tonight. A couple of my other friends are coming over, and my mom said it would be okay. She's right over there, if you want to meet her.''

Trace saw the indecision on Savannah's face, but he also saw the anticipation on Hannah's. ''Let's go over and say hello,'' he suggested. ''You can discuss it with Jolie's mother.''

Five minutes later, Savannah had given her approval for Hannah to spend the night at Jolie's. Donna Jones had been reassuring about the slumber party and enthusiastic about the open house at Holiday Retreat.

''I can't wait to see it,'' she said. ''And I know all my friends are dying to meet you. Mae Holiday was loved and respected, and everyone wants to let you know that. You'll have a huge crowd. An open house on Christmas Eve is a lovely thing to do for the community.''

Savannah looked relieved by her genuine excitement. ''I'll see you then. What time should I pick Hannah up tomorrow morning?''

''Oh, don't worry about that,'' Donna said.

"You'll have enough to do. I'll bring her by around noon, unless you'd like her there earlier to help out."

"Noon will be perfect," Savannah said, just as the band began to play "Silent Night." She slipped her hand into Trace's and began to sing.

A sensation that felt a whole lot like contentment stole through Trace. Not that he was familiar with the concept. For all of his success, for all of the people who filled his life day in and day out, he'd never experienced a moment quite like this. Maybe there was something magical about the holidays after all.

Or maybe Mae had been even wiser than he'd realized. Maybe she'd known exactly how to grant wishes before they'd even been made.

Chapter 8

The bright-red front door closed softly behind Savannah, and she suddenly realized that she was all alone in the house with Trace. Her heart thundered in her chest as she met his gaze and saw the familiar heat slowly begin to stir.

As he had earlier, he reached for the toggle on her jacket zipper and slowly slid it down, his intense gaze never once straying from her face. His knuckles skimmed along the front of her sweater, barely touching it, yet provocative enough to have her breasts swelling, the peaks instantly sensitive.

"Tell me to stop now, if that's what you want," he said quietly.

"I..." Her voice quavered. She swallowed hard and kept her gaze level. "I don't want you to stop."

"Thank God," he murmured, his mouth covering hers.

Savannah hadn't expected the whirlwind of sensations that tore through her at his touch. Trace had kissed her before, each time more amazing than the last, but this was different somehow. Probably because of where it was destined to lead.

It had been so long since any man had wanted her, since she'd been open to feeling this reckless surge of desire. From the moment of her divorce, she had resolved never to let another man take away even one tiny bit of her control over her life or her body. In little more than a couple of days, Trace had made that resolve crumble. She'd wanted him almost from the moment he'd stepped into the kitchen on that first day.

The reaction then had been purely physical. Now it was so much more. She knew the kind of man he was, had seen for herself that the workaholic traits she despised covered a vulnerability spawned years ago. She knew he was kind and generous. Best of all, he'd had Aunt Mae's apparently unwavering faith. That stamp of approval alone would have been enough to convince Savannah that Trace was someone to be respected and admired...maybe even loved.

In one corner of her brain, she wanted to apply reason to all of the feelings he stirred in her, wanted to dissect them with logic, but the rest of her mind was clamoring for something else entirely. Majority wins, she thought, barely containing a giddy desire to laugh with sheer exhilaration.

And then Trace's tongue was teasing her lips, tasting her, and the last rational thought in her head fled. From that instant on, it was all about sensation, about dark, swirling heat and a racing heartbeat, about the brush of his hand over flesh, about the clean male scent of him and the way his eyes seemed to devour her as he gauged the effect of each lingering, provocative caress.

She felt a connection with this near-stranger that she hadn't felt in years with her ex-husband. It was as if Trace could read her mind, as if he knew exactly which part of her was screaming for his touch. Savannah knew he believed that Mae had brought them together with something exactly like this in mind. And maybe that was how it had happened. It hardly mattered, because it felt right. It felt as if she was exactly where she belonged with exactly the right man. Fate or Aunt Mae—it hardly mattered which— had brought them to this moment.

She was breathing hard and barely able to stand when he finally paused to take a breath. ''Come upstairs with me,'' she said, then hesitated, suddenly uncertain. ''That is what you want, isn't it?''

''Darlin', I've never wanted any woman more than I want you right this second,'' he said with flattering sincerity. ''Are *you* sure, though? I don't ever want you to regret this.''

''I've made mistakes and I have my share of regrets, but this won't be one of them,'' she said with total conviction.

She held out her hand and Trace took it. Together

they walked up the stairs, past the floor of guest rooms and on to the private quarters on the third floor. In recent years Mae had kept a small room for herself on the ground floor, but Savannah had opted for the privacy upstairs for herself and Hannah. She led Trace to her room, which had a panoramic view of the mountains lit by moonlight glistening on the snow.

She walked to the window and stood looking out. "Every time I look at this view, I feel this amazing sense of peace come over me. It's so incredibly beautiful."

She felt Trace come up behind her, his arms circling her waist.

"I think you're more beautiful," he said softly, his breath whispering against her cheek.

His hands slid up to her breasts, cupping them. As if the exquisite sensation weren't enough, the reflection in the window of his hands exploring her so intimately doubled the sweet tug deep inside her.

She was already shivering when his fingers slid beneath her sweater to caress bare skin. Eyes closed, she leaned back against his chest as he made her body come alive. Her breasts were heavy and aching before he undid the zipper on her jeans and repeated the delicious torment between her legs. She shuddered at the deliberate touches, each more intimate than the last, each coming closer to sending her over the edge.

She could feel the press of his arousal against her backside, could feel the heat radiating from him in waves. When she risked another look into the glass, she saw the tension in his shoulders, the hooded look in his eyes as he pleasured her. She'd never known a man could give so much without demanding anything in return.

The complete lack of selfishness inflamed her even beyond the effect of Trace's touch. Savannah turned in his arms, then slipped from his embrace. Her gaze locked with his, she stripped her sweater over her head, then let her already-unhooked bra fall to the floor. She knew the precise instant when he saw the reflection of her actions in the window, when that image merged with the one before him and deepened his desire.

She shimmied out of her jeans and panties, then reached for the hem of his sweater. She slid her hands over his chest, which felt like a furnace in the chilly room.

"One of us has way too many clothes on," he said in a husky growl as he tried to push her hands aside to relieve her of the task of ridding him of his sweater.

"Oh, no, you don't. I get to do this my way," she challenged.

A smile curved his lips. "By all means," he said. "Just hurry it up, will you?"

"Some things should never be rushed."

"And some things can't be stopped," he said, drawing her to him, bending down to circle each throbbing nipple with his tongue in a way that had her gasping.

The gesture pretty much destroyed her intent to torment him. Instead, she began to rush the task that only moments before she'd planned to draw out until he felt the same urgency she felt. Within seconds, they were both naked and moving toward the bed, knees weakened by exploring hands, desire ratcheted up to a height Savannah had never before experienced.

When Trace finally entered her, she was already crying out with the first explosive climax. He stilled while the pulsing sensations slowly died away. Then he began to move deep inside her, stirring her all over again, turning restless need into a demanding urgency that stretched every muscle taut with anticipation, until at last, with one sure, deep stroke, he took them both tumbling into a whirlpool of shuddering sensation.

Finally, still cradled in his arms, she fell into the first dreamless sleep she'd had in months.

Trace's heartbeat was easing, his pulse slowly quieting as he gazed down at Savannah. Such a sweet, innocent face to pack so much heat. If he hadn't been enthralled before, the last few hours would have been a revelation. She had a wicked, wanton streak that could lure a man into the fires of hell. Who would have thought it?

The strength and resilience he'd seen in her from the beginning took on new meaning when it came to making love. She'd all but exhausted him, yet he couldn't seem to stop looking at her—touching her— long enough to fall into desperately needed sleep.

Her porcelain-fine skin was still flushed, her hair tousled. Her chest rose and fell with each breath she took, drawing attention to breasts so perfect they took his breath away. Amazingly he wanted her again. In fact, he suspected that after tonight there would never come a day when he didn't want her.

Forever? The word he'd always avoided like the plague popped into his head and wouldn't go away. Forever meant commitment. It meant compromising, joining his life with someone else's, putting her needs above his own. Was he capable of such a thing? Or was he his father's son in that regard? His father had certainly never considered for a second what his irresponsible choices meant for the rest of the family. Trace had always made sure that there would be no one in his life to be affected by the choices he made.

Oh, really? This time when he heard the voice in his head, it was Mae's. More than once she'd scolded him for such self-deprecating comments. She'd pointed out that he had hundreds of employees who counted on him for their livelihoods, that he'd never once let them down, that he'd never let *her* down.

He let his gaze linger on Savannah. Was it possible that he could give her everything she needed? Everything she deserved?

And what about Hannah? Being a stepparent wasn't easy. Oh, they got along well enough now, but what if the rules changed? What if he were here all the time? Would she balk at any attempt by him to take the place of her father...in her life or in her mother's?

He chided himself for getting way ahead of himself. Just because he and Savannah were compatible in bed, just because they'd spent a couple of incredible days that felt magical, didn't mean there was a future for the two of them. She might not even want that. Hell, *he* might not want it. If ever there was a time for clear, rational thought, for not looking beyond the moment, this was it.

Just then, Savannah sighed deeply and snuggled more tightly against him. Heat shot through him. Heat and need. The need went beyond sex, he realized. He needed what she represented—steadiness, love, family—things he'd never imagined himself wanting.

It was his turn to sigh then, his turn to tuck his arms more tightly around her. Maybe morning was soon enough for answers. Maybe tonight was simply meant for feeling fresh, new, enticing emotions.

He breathed in her scent—flowers with a hint of musk—then pressed a kiss to her shoulder. In minutes, he was asleep.

Savannah lay perfectly still, her eyes closed against the brilliance of the sun and against whatever she might discover in Trace's expression. It had been so many years since she'd experienced a "morning after" that she had no idea what to expect. Awkwardness topped the list of possibilities, though.

"You're playing possum," Trace teased, his voice low and husky and warm as it whispered against her cheek.

"Am not," she denied, feeling a smile tug the corners of her mouth.

"Come on, Sleeping Beauty, wake up. We have a million things to do today."

"I don't suppose any of them include staying right here in bed?" she asked wistfully.

"Afraid not."

To her relief, he sounded as disappointed about that as she felt. "And once Hannah's back under this roof, I suppose any more nights like this are out of the question, too."

"Your call, but I'd say that's the sensible way to go."

She opened her eyes then and met his gaze. Fighting against the uncertainty spilling over her, she asked, "Then this was a one-night thing?"

His gaze never wavered. "Not if I can help it," he said emphatically. "I think that's something we need to discuss in detail, don't you?"

Actions seemed vastly preferable to words in Savannah's current frame of mind, but he was right. Talking was definitely indicated, someplace and at a time when temptation wasn't inches away.

"I suppose there's enough time for me to do this," he murmured after a quick glance at the clock on the bedside table. "And this."

Kiss followed kiss until Savannah was writhing and crying out for him to slide inside her. The sweet urgency, the rush for one more taste, one more touch, made their joining even better than any they'd shared during the night before.

"Now we really do have to get up," Trace said with obvious regret. "The caterer will be here in an hour, and I've got to polish the dining room floor and be out from underfoot when he gets here."

"I'll fix breakfast," Savannah said. "And clean up the kitchen."

Trace's heated gaze roamed over her. "Or we could take a leisurely shower together, and to heck with breakfast and polishing the floor."

She grinned. "I think breakfast is highly overrated anyway."

"Not a sentiment you should be sharing with prospective guests," Trace advised as he scooped her up and carried her to the shower.

They were still damp and barely dressed when the doorbell rang.

"Nick of time," he said with a wink. "I'll get it. You might want to see if you can tone down that blush before you meet Henri. He's French and considers himself an expert on the nuances of romance. One glimpse of you, and he'll be offering more unsolicited advice than you ever dreamed of."

"Heaven help me," Savannah said wholeheartedly. "I'll be down in a minute...or an hour. However long it takes."

When Trace had gone, she sat down at her dressing table and studied her face in the mirror. He was right. She was flushed in a way that was entirely too revealing. Even so, she couldn't seem to stop the grin that spread across her face.

"Get a grip," she told herself firmly. "Tonight's too important for you to be frittering away time up here."

But no matter how important tonight was, she had

a very strong hunch it wouldn't hold a candle to last night, especially if Trace refused to share her bed again.

By eight-thirty, Savannah knew that the open house was going to be a roaring success. Neighbors were crowded into every room, sharing holiday toasts, commenting on the delicious food as Henri basked in their compliments. Again and again, they had paused to welcome her and Hannah and tell them how delighted they were that Holiday Retreat would be reopened.

"My parents honeymooned here," Donna Jones confided when she caught up with Savannah during a quiet moment in the dining room. "My mother claims I was conceived here, since I was born almost nine months to the day after their wedding night."

Savannah grinned. "I'll bet I know which room," she said. "Aunt Mae always referred to it as her honeymoon suite, because it's the largest room here. Want to take a peek? The decorating isn't finished, but I painted it yesterday."

"Oh, I'd love to," Donna said, following her upstairs.

At the door of the freshly painted green room with its white antique iron bed, she turned to Savannah with a gleam in her eyes. "It's going to be beautiful." She moved to the window that faced the mountains. "And the view is fabulous. I wonder if I could convince my husband to sneak off here for a weekend sometime."

Savannah heard the wistfulness in her voice and

considered it thoughtfully. "You know, it might not be a bad idea to offer an introductory weekend getaway special for locals. People get so used to living in a place like this, they forget that the tourists who come here see it entirely differently."

"And it seems silly to spend money to stay just a few miles from home," Donna said enthusiastically. "But if it were a special promotion, I'll bet you'd be jammed with reservations. There's no better way to build word-of-mouth. People would start sending all their out-of-town guests here. It could fill in the slack once ski season dies down."

"I'm going to do it," Savannah said, delighted by the whole idea. "And for giving me the idea, your stay will be free."

"Absolutely not," Donna protested. "That's no way to start a business."

"Sure it is. You'll tell everyone you know how fabulous it is, so when I offer the promotion, it will be sold out in minutes."

As they walked back downstairs, Donna regarded Savannah with open curiosity. "So, what's the story with you and Trace Franklin? I'm sorry if I'm being nosy, but everybody in town remembers his coming to visit Mae. A handsome, single man who owns his own company is bound to stir up comment. Have you known him long?"

Savannah felt a now-familiar flush creep into her cheeks. "Only a few days," she admitted.

"My, my," Donna teased, "you work fast! I know a lot of women who tried to get to know him on his prior visits, and he never gave any of them a second glance. Last night he couldn't take his eyes off of you, and, if anything, he's watching you even more intently tonight."

"We're just—"

"If you say you're just friends, I'll lose all respect for you," Donna teased. "Any woman who doesn't grab a man like that ought to have her head examined."

"Talking about me, by any chance?" Trace inquired, stepping up beside Savannah and slipping an arm around her waist.

Savannah felt her face heat another ten degrees. "We were talking about—" she frantically searched her brain for a suitably attractive, sexy bachelor "—Kevin Costner."

Trace regarded her with amusement. "Oh? Is he in town?"

"No, but we do like to dream," she said, as Donna coughed to cover her laughter.

Trace leaned down to whisper in her ear. "Liar," he said softly.

"I think I'll go chat with my husband and tell him about your offer," Donna said. She grinned at Trace. "Nice to see you again. Merry Christmas."

"You, too," he said.

When Donna had gone in search of her husband, Savannah lifted her gaze to meet Trace's. "I think the party's a success. Thank you for talking me into it."

"It's been fun," he said, as if that surprised him just a little. "Mae's introduced me around before, but this is the first chance I've had to really talk to some of the locals. They're good people, and they really are delighted that you're reopening the inn. Not only has this place been a boon to the economy, its history and charm provide something that the chain hotels can't. I didn't realize that in its heyday, Holiday Retreat employed several full-time people on staff and that the dining room was open to the public for dinner. Is that part of your plan, as well?''

''Eventually,'' Savannah said. ''I'm going to have to take things slowly, so that I don't get overextended financially. Once all the rooms are ready for paying guests, then I can start thinking about whether to offer more than breakfast. I can cope with making eggs or French toast—I'm not so sure I could handle gourmet dinners. And I know I can't afford any help yet.''

''Your spaghetti was pretty good,'' he said.

She frowned at him. ''Somehow I doubt that's up to the standard the guests would expect. Remind me and I'll show you some of the old menus. Mae stopped doing the dinners about ten years ago, when it got to be too much for her, but she saved all the records. Since she left the file right where she knew I'd find it first thing, I'm sure she was hoping that I'd open the dining room again in the evenings.''

The rest of the party passed in a blur. Soon guests were putting on coats, thanking Savannah for having them over and leaving for the Christmas Eve services planned by the local churches. When the last guest had departed, Hannah found Savannah and Trace standing on the front porch.

"Mom, this was the best. I must have met everybody in my class at school. I can't wait to start after New Year's. And there's going to be an ice skating party in a couple of days and I'm invited. Isn't that totally awesome?"

"Totally," Savannah agreed.

Trace grinned. "Then you're back to being happy about living in Vermont?"

"Absolutely," Hannah said. "Can we go to church now?"

Trace glanced at Savannah. "What about it? Are you too tired?"

"I'm tired, but exhilarated. Besides, going to Christmas Eve services was always part of the tradition. I'll grab my coat."

Trace drove into town, which was teeming with many of the same families who had just left Holiday Retreat. They were all walking toward the various churches within blocks of the town square. Bells were ringing in the clear, crisp air.

As they entered the same little white chapel Savannah had attended with her family so many years ago, the scent of burning candles, the banks of red poinsettias by the altar, the swell of organ music, all combined to carry her back to another time. A wave of nostalgia washed over her.

How had she let moments like this slip away? As a child, she'd had no choice, but she could have insisted on coming back as an adult, even if she'd had to leave Rob behind to sulk in Florida. His mood had always been sullen around the holidays anyway. What would it have mattered if it got a little worse because she was sharing an experience like this with their daughter?

Ah, well, those days were behind her. She glanced at Hannah and saw the wonder in her eyes as the choir began to sing "O, Holy Night." Trace slipped his hand around hers as the familiar notes soared through the tiny, crowded church.

Savannah's eyes filled with tears at the beauty of the moment. Trace regarded her with such a concerned expression that she forced a watery smile. "Merry Christmas," she murmured.

"Merry Christmas, angel."

Hannah heard the murmured exchange and beamed at both of them. "Merry Christmas, Mom. Merry Christmas, Trace. I don't care if we don't have presents, this is the best holiday ever."

Gazing into Trace's eyes, Savannah couldn't help but agree with her daughter. It was definitely the best one ever.

Chapter 9

Savannah was hearing bells. Convinced it was a dream, she rolled over and burrowed farther under the covers.

"Mom! Mom! You've got to see this! Hurry!" Hannah shouted, shaking Savannah.

Groaning, Savannah cracked one eye to stare at her daughter. "This had better be good." She and Trace had sat up talking until well past midnight, and if she wasn't mistaken, the clock on her bedside table said it was barely seven. Even if it was Christmas morning, she had counted on at least another hour's sleep, especially since Hannah wasn't expecting Santa's arrival.

"It's not just good," Hannah said, clearly undaunted by her testy tone, "it's fantastic. Come on, Mom. Hurry. I'm going to wake up Trace."

''Wait!'' Savannah shouted, but it was too late. Hannah was already racing down the stairs screaming for Trace. Savannah heard his groggy reply, which amazingly was far less irritated than her own had been. In fact, he sounded downright cheerful.

Even with all that commotion right downstairs, Savannah could still hear those bells, louder and more distinct now. She tugged on her robe and went to the window, then stood there, mouth gaping at the sight that greeted her.

There was a huge, horse-drawn sleigh coming through the snow toward the house, the bells on its reins jingling merrily. The back was piled high with sacks and wrapped packages. And the driver was... She blinked in disbelief and looked again. Nope, no mistake. The driver was Santa himself.

Savannah whirled around and headed for the stairs, pausing only long enough to run a brush through her hair and take a swipe at scrubbing her face and teeth. She met Trace at the second-floor landing. Hannah was already downstairs with the front door thrown open to allow in a blast of icy air.

Savannah studied Trace's expression, looking for evidence of guilt. ''What do you know about this?''

''Me? I have no idea what you mean.''

''Santa? The sleigh piled with gifts? It has your name written all over it.''

''Actually I don't think you'll find that's true,'' he said, giving her a quick kiss. ''Stop fussing and go down there. Santa's a busy fellow. I doubt he has all day to hang around here.''

"Trace!"

"Go," he said, waiting until she led the way before following along behind.

They arrived downstairs just as Santa trudged up the steps toting two huge sacks. Still filled with suspicion, Savannah stopped him in his tracks. "Are you sure you have the right place?"

"Holiday Retreat?" he said, edging past her. "You're Savannah Holiday, right? And that young lady out there by the sleigh is Hannah?"

"Yes."

"Then this is definitely the place. Even after such a long and busy night, I try not to make mistakes. Sorry about not squeezing down the chimney the traditional way, but if I go home with this suit all covered with cinders, Mrs. Claus will have my hide."

Savannah barely managed to suppress a chuckle. "I had no idea Mrs. Claus was so tough on you."

The jolly old man with a weathered face and white beard, who looked suspiciously like Nate Daniels, rolled his eyes. "You have no idea. Now, where would you like these gifts?"

"Under the tree, I suppose."

"And that would be?"

"Inside, in the living room on the right."

Santa carried two loads of packages inside, declined Savannah's offer of hot chocolate, then left with a cheery wave and a hearty "ho-ho-ho" that echoed across the still air. Hannah stared after him, still wide-eyed.

"Mom, do you think that was really Santa?" she asked.

Savannah exchanged a look with Trace, trying to gauge from his reaction whether her guess about Nate Daniels was correct. Before she could respond, Trace spoke up.

"Looked exactly like Santa to me," he said. "And you said you weren't going to have presents this Christmas, so who else but Santa would bring them?"

"Oh, I have some theories about that," Savannah muttered under her breath, but she kept her opinion to herself. She might have a few words for Trace later in private, but she was not going to strip that excitement from her daughter's eyes. "How about breakfast before we open gifts?"

"No way!" Hannah protested. "I want to see what's in the boxes, especially that great big one. Santa could hardly get it up the steps."

"You know that Christmas is about more than presents," Savannah felt duty-bound to remind her.

"I know, Mom, but these are here and some of them are for me. I checked the tags."

"Only some? Who are the others for?"

"You, silly. And Trace."

"Me?" Trace said, looking more shocked than he had at any time since this incredible morning had begun.

Savannah studied him intently. His surprise seemed genuine. Was it possible he wasn't behind this? Or at least not all of it? Curious to find out for sure, she acquiesced to Hannah's pleas and followed her into the living room.

"Big box first," Hannah said, rushing over to it. "Okay?"

"Your call," Savannah agreed.

The big box turned out to contain skis and ski boots. Hannah immediately had to try them on. "These are so totally awesome," she said, then wailed, "but I don't know how to ski."

"Maybe Santa thought of that," Trace suggested, his expression innocent.

Hannah's expression brightened at once. She began ripping open her remaining presents in a frenzy, *oohing* and *aahing* over each toy, over a new ski jacket and finally over the certificate for ski lessons that came in a deceptively large box.

Though a part of Savannah wanted to protest the degree of excess, she couldn't bring herself to spoil the moment.

"Your turn now, Mom," Hannah said, bringing her a comparatively small box that seemed to weigh a ton.

"What on earth?" Savannah said, when she tried to lift it. She began carefully removing the wrapping paper until Hannah impatiently ripped the rest away, then tugged at the tape on the box. Inside, nestled in packing chips and tissue paper, was a tool kit, painted a ladylike pink but filled with every conceivable practical tool she could ever possibly need.

Her gaze shot to Trace. How had he guessed that she would prefer a gift like this to something totally impractical?

"It's perfect," she said, her gaze locked with his.

"Santa must know you pretty well," he agreed.

"Mom, there's a huge box here for you, too," Hannah said, shoving it across the floor.

This time she discovered a floor polisher, precisely the kind she would need if she was to keep the inn's floors gleaming. For most women, an appliance on Christmas morning would have been cause for weeping, but Savannah's heart swelled with gratitude.

"Wait, Mom. There's something little tucked inside with a note," Hannah said, her expression puzzled as she handed it to Savannah.

At the sight of the jewelry-size package, Savannah's breath caught in her throat. Her gaze shot to Trace, but he looked as puzzled as Hannah had. Then she caught sight of the handwriting on the envelope. It was Aunt Mae's.

Tears stung Savannah's eyes as she opened the note.

My darling girl,
I hope you are happily settled in by now and that you will love your new home as much as I have over the years. I've done what I could to be sure you find joy here.

Here's something else I hope will bring you happiness. It belonged to your great-great-grandmother.

With all my love to you and Hannah. I wish I could be there with you this morning, but please know that wherever I am, I will always be looking out for you.

Mae

Savannah sighed and blinked back tears. Finding Mae's present tucked amid all the others made her question everything. She'd been so sure that Trace had sent them, but now? Recalling Santa's resemblance to Nate made her wonder if Mae hadn't been behind this whole magical morning.

"Aren't you going to open it?" Hannah asked, leaning against her and regarding the box with evident fascination.

Savannah slipped off the wrapping paper, then lifted the lid of the velvet box. Inside, on a delicate gold chain, was an antique gold cross. The workmanship was exquisite. The gold seemed to glow with a soft light of its own. She could remember Mae wearing this cross every day of her life. She had always said it symbolized faith itself—so fragile yet enduring.

She opened the delicate clasp, slipped on the necklace, then fastened it. The gold felt warm against her skin, as if it still held some of Aunt's Mae's body heat. Once more, her eyes turned misty. She felt Trace take her hand and give it a squeeze.

"Merry Christmas," he said quietly.

"Wait!" Hannah said. "There's another box. It's for you, Trace."

Once more, he looked completely disconcerted. Hannah gave him the present. He handled it gingerly, studying the large, flat box with suspicion.

"What does it say on the tag?" Savannah asked, curious herself.

"Just Trace," he said. "No other name."

"Must be from Santa, then," she teased.

He slipped open the paper, then pulled out the box and lifted the lid. The grin that broke over his face was like that of a boy who'd just unexpectedly received his heart's desire.

"What is it?" Savannah asked, trying to peer over his shoulder.

"It's the biggest, mushiest card I could make," Hannah said, grinning. "And Mrs. Jones took me to get it framed so Trace could hang it on his office wall."

Trace stared at her, looking completely mystified. "But I lost the bet."

"I know," Hannah said delightedly. "But I could tell you really, really wanted the card, so I made it anyway." She threw her arms around his neck. "Merry Christmas!"

To Savannah's shock, there was a distinct sheen of tears in Trace's eyes as he hugged her daughter.

"It's the very best present I ever received," he told her with such sincerity that Hannah's whole face lit up.

If this didn't stop, Savannah was going to spend Christmas morning bawling like a baby. She was about to head for the kitchen to start on breakfast, when Trace grabbed her hand and halted her.

"Wait. I think there's one more present for you, Savannah," he said, pointing Hannah toward a flat box beside the chair where he'd been sitting earlier. "Bring that one to your mom."

The box weighed next to nothing, but when Savannah tore off the paper and looked inside, her mouth dropped open. "Stock certificates?" she asked, turning to Trace. "In Franklin Toys? I can't possibly accept such a gift from you."

"It's not from me," he said firmly. "Not directly, anyway. These were Mae's shares of the company. She gave me power of attorney to vote them for her during the last weeks of her illness, but she told me I'd know what to do with the shares after her death." He looked straight into Savannah's eyes. "I think she would want you to have them."

"But she left me the inn," Savannah protested. "And Franklin Toys is your company."

He grinned. "I hope you'll remember that when you vote, but in many ways the company was as much Mae's as it was mine. She'd want you to have the financial independence those shares can give you."

"But I don't know anything about running a corporation."

"You can learn," he said. "Or you can sell the shares back to me, if you'd prefer to have the cash. The choice is yours."

Savannah sat back, still filled with a sense of overwhelming shock and gratitude. And yet... She studied Trace carefully. "Is this really what you want to do? She gave you her power of attorney, not me. I think she wanted you to control these shares."

"She wanted me to do the right thing with them," he corrected. "And I think that's turning them over to you. They're yours, Savannah. My attorney took care of the transfer yesterday."

Once again, Savannah looked at the certificates. She had no idea what each share was worth in today's market, but it had to be a considerable amount. The thought that she would never again have to worry about money was staggering.

This truly was a season of miracles.

Christmas morning had been incredible. It was everything Trace had imagined, from the awe and wonder on Hannah's face to the amazement on Savannah's when she'd realized that her financial future was secure. Trace had given the two of them everything he knew how to give. He'd been deeply touched by their gratitude.

Somehow, though, it wasn't enough. He wanted more, but he had no idea how to ask for it, or even if he had the right to, especially after knowing the two of them for such a short time.

Struggling with too many questions and too few answers, he wandered into the kitchen where Savannah was just putting the turkey into the oven.

She turned at his approach, studied him for a minute, then gave him a hesitant smile. "Everything okay?"

"Sure. Why wouldn't it be?" he asked, feeling defensive.

"I'm not sure. You seem as if you're suddenly a million miles away."

"I've got a lot on my mind. In fact, if you don't need my help right now, I was thinking of taking a walk to try to clear my head."

"Sure," she said at once. "It'll be hours before the turkey's done, and everything else is set to go in the oven once the turkey comes out." She continued to regard him worriedly. "Want some company?"

Trace shook his head. "Not this time. I won't be gone long," he said, turning away before the quick flash of hurt in her eyes made him change his mind. How could he possibly think about what to do about Savannah if she was right by his side tempting him?

He heard her soft sigh as he strode off, but he refused to look back.

Outside the snow was a glistening blanket of white. The temperature was warmer than it had been, though still below freezing if the bite of wind on his face was anything to go by. He almost regretted the decision to take a lonely walk, when he could have been inside in front of a warm fire with Savannah beside him.

He headed for the road, then turned toward town. He'd only gone a hundred yards or so when Nate Daniels appeared at the end of his driveway. He was bundled up warmly, an unlit pipe clamped between his teeth. He paused to light the tobacco, then regarded Trace with a steady, thoughtful look.

"Mind some company?" he asked, already falling into step beside him.

"Did Savannah call you?" Trace asked.

"Nope. Why would she do that?"

"I think she was worried when I took off."

"She called earlier to wish me a merry Christmas, but that was hours ago," Nate said. He regarded Traced curiously. "Funny thing, she seemed to have the idea that I was over there this morning playing Santa. Where would she get a notion like that?"

"Santa did bear a striking resemblance to you," Trace said.

"You didn't tell her, though, did you? You let her go on thinking that Mae was behind all the gifts and that she was the one who conspired with me to bring them."

"Oh, she suspects I had something to do with it, but there were enough surprises to throw her off." He glanced at Nate. "So, if Savannah didn't call, what brings you out into the bitter cold?"

"The truth is, I was all settled down with a new book my son gave me for Christmas when I felt this sudden urge to go for a stroll."

"Really? A sudden urge?" Trace said skeptically.

Nate nodded. "Finding you out here, I'm guessing Mae put the thought in my mind."

Trace kept his opinion about that to himself. Maybe Mae did have her ways even from beyond the grave.

"Something on your mind?" Nate inquired after they'd walked awhile in companionable silence.

Okay, Trace thought, here was his chance to ask someone older and wiser whether there was such a thing as love at first sight, whether a marriage based on such a thing could possibly last.

"Do you think there's such a thing as destiny?" Trace asked.

Nate's lips didn't even twitch at the question. "'Course I do. Only a fool doesn't believe there's a reason we're all put on this earth."

"And that applies to love, too?"

"I imagine you're asking about you and Savannah," Nate said. "Now, granted I've only seen the two of you together once or twice, but looked to me as if there was something special between you. It's not important what I think, though. What do *you* think?"

"I don't know if I even believe in love," Trace said dejectedly.

"Well now, there's a topic with which I'm familiar," Nate said. "You know about Mae and me, I imagine."

Trace nodded.

"You probably don't know so much about me and Janie, my wife. Janie and I met when we were kids barely out of diapers," he said, a nostalgic expression on his face. "By first grade I'd already declared that I wanted to marry her, though at that age I didn't really understand exactly what that meant. Not once in all our years of growing up did I change my mind. Janie was the girl for me. We married as soon as I graduated from college, settled down right here and began raising a family."

He glanced at Trace. "Now that should have been a storybook ending, two people in love their whole lives, married and blessed with kids. But Janie's nerves started giving her problems. The kids upset her. Anytime I was away from the house for more than a few hours, she'd get so distraught, I'd find her in tears when I came home. The doctors checked for a chemical imbalance. They tried her on medicine after medicine, but slowly but surely she slipped away from me.''

Tears glistened in his eyes. ''The day I had to take her to Country Haven was the worst day of my life. I told her she'd be home again, but I think we both knew that day wouldn't come. She's happy at Country Haven. She feels safe there. But there's not a day that goes by that I don't miss the carefree girl I fell in love with.''

''It sounds as though you still love her deeply,'' Trace said.

''I do,'' Nate said simply.

''Then what about Mae?''

''After Janie went into the treatment facility, Mae helped out with the kids from time to time. They adored her. They stopped by the inn every day after school, and she always had cookies and milk waiting for them. Soon enough, I took to stopping by, too. Mae was a godsend for all of us during that first year.''

He met Trace's gaze. ''It's important that you know that nothing improper went on between us. I considered myself a married man and I loved my wife. But I loved Mae, too. Since you're not even sure if love exists, I don't know if you can understand that it's possible for a man to love two women, but I did. If I had thought for a single second that my friendship with Mae would hurt Janie, I would have ended it. But the truth was, there were times when Janie didn't even seem to know who I was, didn't seem to care that I was there to visit. That never kept me from going, but it did make me see that I didn't need to lock my heart away in that place with her. I gave Mae every bit of love I felt free to give her. I also gave her the freedom to choose whether to love me. I admired her too much to do anything less.''

He sighed. ''Given the way of the world now, a lot of men would have divorced a wife like Janie and moved on. That wasn't my way. I'd made a commitment, and I honored it in the only way I knew how. And whether you believe it or not, I honored my commitment to Mae the same way.''

''I'm sorry you were in such a difficult position,'' Trace said. ''It must have been heartbreaking.''

''Having Mae in my life was one of the best things that ever happened to me. I can't possibly regret that it couldn't have been more, except for her sake. She deserved better.''

''I think you made her very happy,'' Trace told him.

''I hope so,'' Nate said, then paused and looked directly into Trace's eyes. ''There's a reason I'm telling you this. I always believed that one day Mae and I would be able to be together openly, that we'd marry and spend our remaining years together. Maybe even do a little traveling. We never had that chance.''

Trace understood what he was saying. ''This is

your way or reminding me that life is short and unpredictable.''

"Exactly. If you love Savannah, don't waste time counting the days until it seems appropriate to tell her. Don't fritter away precious hours planning for the future. Start living every moment. I've lived a good long life, but I'm here to tell you that it's still a whole lot shorter than I'd like.''

They'd circled around and were back at Nate's driveway. "Think about what I said," he told Trace.

"I will," Trace promised. "Would you like to join us for Christmas dinner?"

"I would, but I'll be going out to see Janie in a while. She seems to like it when I come by to read to her.''

"Thank you for sharing your story with me," Trace said, genuinely touched that Nate had told him.

"Don't thank me. Take my advice." He grinned. "Otherwise, I have a feeling Mae will find some way to give me grief for failing her. That woman always did know how to nag.''

Nate was still chuckling as he walked slowly toward his house. Trace watched to make sure he didn't slip on the icy patches, then walked back to Holiday Retreat, his heart somehow lighter and more certain.

Chapter 10

For the life of her, Savannah couldn't read Trace's expression when he got back from his walk. She thought he looked more at peace with himself, but had no idea what that meant.

She was also still puzzling over his magnanimous decision to give her Aunt Mae's stock. Had that been his way of making her financially independent to ease his own conscience and rid himself of some crazy sense of obligation to look after her? Was that going to make it easier for him to pack his bags in a day or two and walk away? When he left, would he go with no intention of ever looking back on her or Holiday Retreat as anything more than a pleasant memory? If that happened, it would break Hannah's heart.

It would break Savannah's heart, too.

''How's the turkey coming?'' Trace inquired, peering over her shoulder to look into the oven. "It certainly smells fantastic."

"Another hour or so," she told him, wishing he would stay right behind her, his body close to hers.

She stood up and turned slowly to face him, relieved that he didn't back away. She reached up and cupped his cheeks. "You're cold. How about some hot chocolate? Or some tea?"

"I'm fine," he said, slipping his arms around her waist. "I'd rather have a kiss. I'm sure it would do a much better job of warming me up."

Savannah tilted her face up for his kiss. His mouth covered hers and brought her blood to a slow simmer. She couldn't be sure if it was working on Trace, but her body temperature had certainly shot up by several degrees. She sighed when he released her.

"Warmer now?" she inquired with forced cheer.

"Definitely," he said, his eyes blazing with desire. "Too bad we can't send Hannah for a ski lesson right this second."

"Are you sure we can't?" Savannah inquired hopefully.

"Nope. They're all booked up at the lodge."

She stared at him, biting back a chuckle. "You actually checked?"

"Of course. I always like to know my options."

"Do we have any?"

"Afraid not."

"Oh, well, once we've eaten, I have it on good authority that the turkey will put us straight to sleep.

Maybe when we wake up, we'll have forgotten all about sneaking upstairs to be alone.''

''I doubt it,'' Trace said, his expression wry. ''Besides, I promised Hannah we'd all go for a walk after dinner.''

''Why on earth would you do that? You just got back from a walk.''

''Which taught me the distracting power of exercise,'' he said. ''Besides, maybe we can have another snowball fight, and I can tackle you in the snow.''

Savannah laughed. ''Now there's something to look forward to.''

''Sweetheart, a frustrated man is willing to take any contact he can get.''

''Interesting. I would think the chill of the snow would be counterproductive.''

''I think I'd have to spend a month outdoors in the Arctic before it would cool the effect you have on me,'' he said with flattering sincerity. He tipped her chin up to look directly into her eyes. ''By the way, let's make a date.''

''A date?''

He grinned. ''You know, a man and a woman, getting together. A date.''

''Out on the town?''

''Or alone in front of a cozy fire.''

''Okay,'' she said with a surge of anticipation. ''When do you want to have this date?''

''Tomorrow night?'' he suggested.

The level of relief Savannah felt when she realized he intended to stay another day was scary. She had a feeling she wanted way too much from this man. Asking for a date—even making love—was hardly a declaration of undying devotion. She really needed to keep things in perspective and not get ahead of herself.

"Tomorrow would be fine. Maybe I'll see if Hannah can spend the night with Jolie again."

Trace grinned. "Best idea I've heard all day."

Savannah's heart beat a little faster at the promise beneath his words. The memory of the last night they had spent alone in this house brought a flush to her cheeks.

"Then I will definitely make it happen," she vowed. Because she was desperate for another one of those sweet kisses despite the risk of Hannah walking in on them, she backed away from Trace and moved to the stove, opening lids and checking on things that were simmering just fine only moments ago.

"Trace," she said without turning around, "if I ask you something, will you tell me the truth?"

"If I can," he said at once.

"You did make all the arrangements for Santa and the presents, didn't you?"

"Do you really want to know?" he asked, sounding vaguely frustrated. "Wouldn't you prefer to think it was part of the Christmas magic?"

She turned to face him. "Sure," she said honestly. "But I also believe in giving credit where credit's due. I'm not an eight-year-old who still believes in Santa, at least when it suits her. I know the kind of effort and money it takes to make a morning like the one we had happen. The person responsible should be thanked."

He shrugged, looking as if her persistence made him uncomfortable. "Look, it was nothing, okay?"

"It was more than that and you know it. You made Hannah's Christmas, and mine."

"I'm glad," he said. "Can we drop it now?"

"Why do you hate admitting that you did something nice?"

"Because I didn't do that much. I just made a few calls, ordered a few little things. Nate was more than willing to play Santa, especially since he had that gift from Mae for you."

"Which was wonderful of him to do, but you bought me a floor polisher and a professional quality tool kit, for heaven's sakes."

"A lot of people would say that gift explains why I'm still single," he said.

"And I say it explains why I find you so completely and utterly irresistible," she said.

"Irresistible, huh?" A grin tugged at the corners of his mouth. "Come over here."

"Oh, no, you don't. We agreed that any more fooling around with Hannah underfoot would be a bad idea."

"Did we agree to that?"

"We did," she said emphatically.

"Does one kiss qualify as fooling around?"

"Probably not with a lot of people, but in my experience with you, it has a tendency to make me want a whole lot more."

His grin spread. "Good to know. I'll have to remember that tomorrow night."

Savannah met his gaze, her own expression deliberately solemn. "I certainly hope you do."

Trace woke up in a dark mood on the morning after Christmas. Rather than inflict his foul temper on Savannah or Hannah, he made a cup of coffee, then shut himself away in Mae's den and turned on his computer.

Even though he'd given his staff the week between Christmas and New Year's off, he checked his e-mails, hoping for some lingering piece of business to distract him. Aside from some unsolicited junk mail, there was nothing. Apparently other people were still in holiday mode. He sighed and shut the thing off, then sat back, brooding.

He'd spent the whole night wondering if he hadn't made the biggest blunder of his life the day before by giving Savannah that stock. It wasn't that he thought it was the wrong thing to do or that Mae would have disapproved. In fact, he was certain she'd known all along what he would do with her shares. No, his concern was over whether he'd given Savannah the kind of financial independence that would make her flat-out reject the proposal he planned to make tonight.

He was still brooding over that when the door to the den cracked open and Savannah peeked in.

"Okay to interrupt?" she asked.

"Sure," he said, forcing the surly tone out of his voice. "Come on in."

To his shock, when she walked through the door, she was wearing some sort of feminine, slinky nightgown that promptly shot his heartbeat into overdrive.

"On second thought," he muttered, his throat suddenly dry, "maybe you should change first."

"Why would I do that?" She glanced down. "Don't you like it?"

"Oh, yeah," he said huskily. "I like it. Maybe just a little too much."

Apparently she didn't get the hint, because she kept right on toward him. The next thing he knew, she was in his lap and his body was so hard and aching, it was all he could do to squeeze out a few words.

"What are you up to?" he inquired, staying very still, hoping that his too-obvious response to that wicked gown of hers would magically vanish. "Where's Hannah?"

"Gone," she said, brushing her mouth across his.

"Gone?"

"For the day," she added, peppering kisses down his neck.

"The entire day?" he asked, suddenly feeling more hopeful and a whole lot less restrained.

"She won't be home till five at the very earliest," Savannah confirmed. "I have Donna's firm commitment on that. She couldn't keep her tonight, so we compromised."

"I see," he murmured, sliding his hand over the

slick fabric barely covering her breast. The nipple peaked at his touch.

"Sorry my present's a day late," she said as she proceeded to unbutton his shirt and slide it away.

Trace gasped as her mouth touched his chest. "Oh, darlin', something tells me it will be worth the wait."

Savannah had never felt so thoroughly cherished as she did lying on the sofa in Trace's arms, a blanket covering them, as a fire blazed across the room. In a few short days, she had discovered what it meant to be truly loved, even if Trace himself hadn't yet put a label on his feelings. She wondered if he ever would.

She turned slightly and found him studying her with a steady gaze.

"You're amazing, you know that, don't you?"

She shook her head. "I'm just a single mom doing the best I can."

"Maybe that's what I find so amazing," he said. "You remind me of my mother."

"Just what every woman wants to hear when she's naked in a man's arms," Savannah said lightly.

He gave her a chiding look. "Just hear me out. You're strong and resilient. You've had some tough times, but you haven't let them turn you bitter. You've just gotten on with the business of living and making a home for Hannah. When I was a kid, I don't think I gave my mother half enough credit for that. I spent too much time being angry because she didn't tell my dad to take a hike. I realize now that she didn't see him the same way I did. She loved him, flaws and all. It was as simple as that, so she did what she could to make the best of his irresponsible ways.''

Trace caressed Savannah's cheek, brushing an errant curl away from her face. "So, here's the bottom line. I meant to do this with a bit more fanfare, but since our date has turned out to be a little unorthodox, this part might as well be, too."

He sounded so serious that Savannah went still. "What's the bottom line?" she asked worriedly.

"Will you marry me? I know we've just met and that you're still recovering from a divorce, but I've fallen in love with you. I talked it over with Nate—" Savannah stared, sorting through the rush of words and seizing on those that made the least sense. "You what?"

"Now don't go ballistic on me," Trace said, then rushed on. "I ran into him yesterday. He saw that I had a lot on my mind, because I had all these feelings and I thought they were probably crazy, but he put it all in perspective for me. He said life is way too short to waste time looking for rational explanations for everything. I'm not all that experienced with falling in love, but apparently it doesn't follow some sort of precise timetable."

Savannah's lips twitched at his vaguely disgruntled tone. "No," she agreed. "It certainly doesn't."

"Then, again, I'm used to making quick decisions. And I do think it's exactly what Mae had in mind when she insisted I come here for Christmas." He met her gaze. "And just so you know, with these quick decisions of mine, I rarely make mistakes."

"Is that so?" Savannah said quietly. "Well, it's certainly true that Aunt Mae was an incredibly wise woman. She hasn't steered me wrong so far."

"Me, either," Trace said, regarding her warily. "So?"

"So what?"

"Bottom line? I've fallen in love with you. Something tells me that if I don't reach out for what I want with you now, it will be the biggest mistake of my life."

"Then reach," she said softly, her gaze locked with his.

Trace held out his hand. Savannah put hers in it, and for the first time in her life, Savannah felt as if she were truly part of a whole, something real and solid, with a future that was destined to last forever.

"There's something about this place," she said with a sense of wonder. "It must be Aunt Mae." She lowered her mouth to Trace's. "She always did get me the best gifts of all."

* * * * *

FAITH, HOPE AND LOVE

Beverly Barton

For my grandson, Mason Bryce Waldrep,
Grammy's precious little angel No. 2.

Prologue

"I think that rain is going to change over to snow," Jody Crenson said as she gazed out the double windows in the living room of Faith Sheridan's duplex apartment. "You'd better not only take an umbrella, but wear a hat and gloves, too."

"I'm way ahead of you. I have my hat and gloves ready." Faith emerged from her bedroom carrying a brown knit hat and matching brown gloves. She laid both on top of her ankle-length camel tan wool coat hanging over the back of the sofa beside the closed umbrella. "I'll have to leave soon." She checked her watch again—for the tenth time in ten minutes. "We're supposed to meet at eight o'clock and it's nearly seven-thirty."

"The town square is only a ten-minute walk from here. You wouldn't be just a little overeager would you?'' As she turned from the windows, Jody grinned. ''Are you sure you don't want me to go with you? I'll disappear the minute he shows up.''

''I'll bring Worth back here and call you to come over and meet him. I promise. But once you meet him, I want you to make yourself scarce and go back to your apartment next door. Worth and I will have a lot of plans to make for our future.''

Jody forced a smile as she sauntered over to Faith and grasped her hands. ''Sweetie, nobody wants this to work out for you more than I do. But don't get your hopes up. I know what I'm talking about. I've had guys sweet-talk me into the sack, then forget my telephone number.''

''Worth didn't sweet-talk me. He's not like that.'' A sudden blush burned Faith's cheeks. ''I actually asked him to…well, you know.''

Jody shook her head. ''Ah, Faithie, I really hope the guy shows, but if he doesn't—''

''He'll be there,'' Faith said, with utter conviction. ''I know he loves me. And I'm sure by now he's figured out for himself just how much he loves me. We were meant to be together.''

''You're terribly in love with him, aren't you?'' Jody sighed. ''When you first told me about him— about the way you two met when he rescued you from those terrorist kidnappers over there in Subria—I thought you just had a major hero-worship crush on him. But it's more than that for you.''

''For him, too.'' Faith swung Jody's hands back

and forth, then released her and twirled around several times. "How do I look?"

"Lovely. I've never seen you looking prettier. You're absolutely glowing."

"That's because I'm in love and I'm happy and I'm—" Faith smiled broadly as she hugged herself. "Just think, less than two months ago I was a kidnap victim who could have been killed and now I'm home and safe and have a wonderful life ahead of me."

"If you and Worth decide not to come back here, you call me. Otherwise, I'll worry about you."

Faith picked up her hat and pulled it down over her long brown hair, the two almost identical in color, then she eased on her gloves and put on her coat. "If for any reason we don't come back here to my apartment, I'll let you know. But don't worry about me if I don't call until late. Worth may have made his own plans for us."

"If you aren't back by midnight and haven't called me, I'll send out the Highway Patrol."

Faith grabbed the umbrella and headed for the door. She glanced over her shoulder. "You're going to be my maid of honor, so you'd better start thinking about a fancy dress. Maybe something in velvet."

"Velvet will be kind of warm for a June wedding."

"We won't be waiting until June." Faith opened the door. "I'm sure when I tell Worth my news, he'll want us to get married right away."

"Your news?" Jody's eyes widened in a speculative stare. "What haven't you told me? And why haven't you told me?"

"Because I just took the test today."

"The test?"

"I've got to go. I want to be early, just in case Worth is."

Jody followed Faith out the door and onto the front porch that ran the length of the old house, which had been built in the thirties and later divided into two apartments.

"You're pregnant, aren't you?" Jody grabbed Faith's shoulder just as Faith opened the big tan umbrella.

Faith jerked away, went down the steps and out onto the sidewalk, then began skipping and humming "Singing In the Rain."

"Don't you dare leave here without telling me," Jody called after her.

"Yes, yes, yes," Faith sang out loud and clear. "I'm going to have Worth's baby and we're going to get married and live happily ever after."

Faith skipped away, the cold evening rain drizzling down all around her as she made her way up Somerset Avenue. She'd never been this happy in her entire life. Very soon she would have what she wanted most—a family of her own. She and Worth and their baby would be that family.

If anyone understood the way she felt, Jody did. They'd met when they were kids, both residents of the Whitewood Girls' Ranch for orphans outside of town. Faith had very little memory of her mother, who'd died in a car crash when Faith was three, but she had lots of wonderful memories of her father.

Alfred Sheridan had been a college professor. A shy, quiet man who'd been a gentle, loving parent. But her dad had been nearly fifty when she was born and suffered with heart problems that took his life when Faith was twelve. Without any close relatives, Faith had become an unwanted orphan. She wasn't particularly pretty and she'd always been shy. And not many people wanted to adopt a twelve-year-old.

Decked in holiday finery, with festive lights twined around roof lines, shrubbery and fences, the homes near downtown Whitewood proclaimed the season. When she passed the Dawsons' house, Horace barked at her from his dry perch on a footstool in front of the white wooden rockers on the front porch. Horace was a spoiled rotten, fourteen-year-old beagle. Lindsey Dawson opened the front door, lifted Horace off the stool, then threw up her hand to wave at Faith.

"Horace won't go out in the yard to do his business when it's raining like this." Lindsey shrugged. "What on earth are you doing out on a night like this? Don't you know it's suppose to start snowing any time now?"

Faith was in the church choir with Lindsey and they had become very friendly acquaintances since Faith's return to Whitewood a month ago. The Dawsons, Lindsey and George, were in their midfifties with three adult children who were spread out across the country; and none of them had given the couple grandchildren, much to Lindsey's consternation.

"I'm meeting Worth in the town square tonight," Faith said.

"Oh, dear me, I'd forgotten that your young man was coming to Whitewood on Christmas Eve. Such a romantic rendevous for the two of you."

Faith beamed with her happiness, feeling it through and through, as if this joyous feeling had taken over her body from the inside out. She wanted to shout from the rooftops that she was in love.

Within five minutes, she had made her way to Main Street. Last minute shoppers were scurrying about, rushing in and out of stores as they purchased Christmas presents. Whitewood, South Carolina—population 6,587—had seen its downtown area almost die out when a lot of businesses moved out near the four-lane highway back in the seventies. But in the late eighties, the townspeople had banded together to revitalize the buildings and the square between Main and Cherry Streets.

"Hey there, Faith." Margaret Tompkins stood in the doorway of her coffee and gift shop. "Off to meet Worth in the square?"

Faith stopped under the green awning over the doorway of Margaret's Goodies. "I thought you were closing up at seven tonight so you and Mr. Tippins could make it over to the Godfreys for their party."

"I had so many last-minute customers that I had to call Mr. Tippins to tell him I'd meet him there." Margaret frowned. "That Moselle Hutton had better not try to make time with my Mr. Tippins. The woman is nothing but a hussy."

"Well, if that's the case, you'd better hurry and lock up and get over to the Godfreys."

"You're absolutely right about that." Margaret's remarkably smooth face wrinkled slightly when she smiled. "Do bring Worth by to see me just as soon as you can."

"Yes, ma'am, I'll do just that."

Faith adored Margaret Tompkins, who'd given Faith her first after-school job when she'd been sixteen. And thanks to Margaret's kindness of keeping her employed at Margaret's Goodies, not only after school but in the summers, she'd been able to save enough money to buy an older model car when she was eighteen.

Margaret was what people had once referred to as an old maid; and sometimes Faith thought the sweet old woman—who was now seventy-four—saw a kindred spirit in Faith. But unlike Margaret, who had lost her fiancé during the Korean War, Faith was going to marry and have a family. And nobody was happier for her than Margaret.

The town square had been a part of Whitewood since the town's conception in the early 1800s. At Christmas the merchants decorated downtown Whitewood so perfectly that it looked like a winter wonderland, and the square was the pièce de résistance, the town's true showcase. The two gazebos were strung with white lights, green garland and huge frosty white bows. Inside one gazebo was a life-size Santa with a pack of presents on his back and Rudolph at his side. A group of five life-size carolers, song books in their hands, stood inside the second gazebo, and a taped selection of Christmas carols

played twenty-four hours a day during the twelve
days of Christmas. But the twenty-foot Christmas
tree, decorated with thousands of sparkling white
lights held the place of honor in the center of the
square.

Faith scanned the square for any sign of Worth,
thinking perhaps he'd been as eager as she for this
night and had shown up early. But maybe Worth
wasn't the type to be early or even on time for that
matter. She knew so little about him, had so many
things to learn. She didn't even know if he liked his
coffee black or with cream and sugar. But they had
the rest of their lives to become acquainted, to get to
know each others' preferences.

Some people—like Jody—might think falling in
love at first sight was a ridiculous notion, but Faith
knew better. Well, maybe it hadn't been exactly at
first sight, but within the first twenty-four hours. And
once they had made love, she'd had no doubts that
they were meant to be together forever.

Faith wandered around through the square, following the concrete sidewalk onto the brick walkway that
led from one gazebo to the other. The recorded music
blasted a cheery rendition of "Let It Snow." Peeking
out beneath the umbrella, Faith saw no sign of snow.
She held out her hand and several icy cold raindrops
hit her knit glove. Suddenly a teenage couple came
racing through the square, called out "Merry Christmas" to Faith, then ran across the street to the boy's
parked Jeep. The kids jumped in, revved the motor
and zoomed away.

Only two months ago she had been living on a Mediterranean island working as the nanny to billionaire tycoon Theo Constantine's seven-year-old daughter, Phila. She had loved her job and adored the Constantines and little Phila. Life had been pleasant and fulfilling. Faith truly believed that no job was as important as the care and nurturing of children. That's why she'd chosen a career as an au pair. But her idyllic life had ended abruptly when Phila and she had been kidnapped by a rebel terrorist group called the Al'alim, taken to the mountains in Subria and held for ransom.

In the end everything had turned out well, but Phila and she had endured a terrifying ordeal. Theo Constantine had hired his own small army to free them from their abductors and Worth Cordell had been Faith's personal rescuer. She would never forget his kindness the moment they first met. He had taken off his jacket and wrapped it around her because she'd been wearing nothing but a thin cotton gown. And when she'd cut her foot during their attempt to flee, Worth had swept her into his arms and carried her, keeping her safe.

Faith checked her watch. Five till eight. He'd be here soon. Then she'd take him back to her apartment, fix them cups of steaming hot cocoa and they'd cuddle on the sofa. The north wind picked up, whooshing fine pellets of sleet right into her face. Oh, dear, the rain had changed over to sleet.

But when Worth arrived, he'd take her into his arms and warm her immediately. Her mind recalled the night they'd spent together in the cave in Subria, the two of them, wet and cold. They'd stripped off naked, laid their clothes out to dry and cuddled together under a thin blanket in order to absorb each other's body heat. She'd been afraid that night might be her last night on earth, that by morning the Subrian rebels would find them and kill them. And one thing she'd known for sure was that she didn't want to die a virgin.

Suddenly the Methodist church bells rang out the hour. Eight o'clock. Faith listened, then smiled as memories washed over her. She'd never know where the courage had come from that night or how she'd been able to ask Worth to make love to her. Maybe it had been a courage born of fear. And Worth had been so sweet, so reluctant at first to take her. But in the end he had made sweet, passionate love to her and her life had changed forever.

Faith decided that she would stay warmer if she kept moving, so she walked around the square twice, then came back through it again. She checked her watch. Eight-twenty. Worth was late. Perhaps he'd run into bad weather on his trip from Atlanta. Or he could have gotten a late start, or taken a wrong turn.

Faith glanced across the street to see if Margaret had closed up shop. She had. All the stores on Main and on Cherry were closed. And there was no one on the streets. Occasionally a car passed, but there was no other sign of life. People were either home with their families, at holiday parties, or congregated in local churches for Christmas Eve services.

Her feet were cold, despite the thick socks she wore. And her hands were like ice under the knit gloves. *Where are you, Worth… Where are you?*

They had said goodbye in Subria six weeks ago, but they had agreed to meet here in the Whitewood town square at eight o'clock on Christmas Eve. If Worth loved her, he would be here. He'd promised. And she believed with all her heart and soul that Worth loved her as she did him. *He's just running a little late, that's all. He'll be here soon.*

For over a week she had suspected she might be pregnant. They hadn't used any protection when they'd made love. And Faith's monthly period was usually as regular as clockwork. This morning she had driven over to Greenville to a drugstore and bought a home pregnancy kit. She thought it best not to let the entire town of Whitewood find out about her condition—not until after she and Worth were married. She'd been excited at the thought of carrying Worth's child, but then she'd wondered how he'd feel about having a baby so soon. After all, even she had planned for them to actually date a few months before they got married. Originally she'd thought a June wedding was ideal, but now they'd have to push up the date. Maybe a New Year's wedding. Something simple at the church with only Jody and Margaret and perhaps the Dawsons.

The Methodist church bells chimed the hour. Nine o'clock. How was it possible that she'd been here for a whole hour? Of course, she was so cold that her hands and feet felt numb. What had happened to

Worth? Why was he an hour late? She knew that if he'd been detained, he would have contacted her. After all, it wouldn't be that much trouble to get her home phone number. She was the only Faith Sheridan living in Whitewood. Oh, God, what if he'd had a wreck? No, she refused to consider the possibility. Worth was on his way here and would show up any minute now.

Suddenly Faith looked through her moist eyes and noticed it was snowing. She sighed deeply and hugged herself, settling down on a bench to wait. When Worth arrived, their reunion would take place with snowflakes falling all around them. It would be like a scene from an old movie. Lovers reuniting in the town square on a snowy Christmas Eve.

Time passed, but Faith wasn't sure how much time. And when she heard Jody's voice calling her, she tried to open her eyes, but couldn't. Was she asleep? No, she couldn't be asleep. She was in the square waiting for Worth. He would be here any minute now.

Jody began shaking Faith as she repeated her name and said, ''Wake up, Faithie, wake up. My God, how long have you been lying here on this bench, out in the snow? Come on, honey, let's get you up on your feet. I'm taking you to the hospital right now.''

''The hospital?'' Faith managed to speak, but even to her own ears her voice sounded weak. ''Why do I need to go to the hospital?''

''Oh, honey, you've been sitting out here in the snow, waiting for that damn man for over four hours.''

She felt Jody lifting her to her feet, then putting an arm around her and urging her to walk.

"What—what time is it?" Faith asked.

Before Jody could reply, the church bells rang out twelve times. Midnight. And Worth hadn't shown up yet.

"I can't leave," Faith said. "Worth might—"

"Damn it, Faithie, he's not coming. The guy's a no-show."

As Jody led Faith to her car, she heard her friend grumbling, "Men! They love you until they've had you, then it's on to the next woman. But don't you worry, honey, we'll be all right. You don't need him. You'll get by just fine without him."

"Worth," Faith whispered. "Worth, where are you?"

Worth Cordell woke from a drug-induced sleep in the ICU of an Atlanta hospital…or he assumed he was in Atlanta. He glanced around the meticulously sterile room. Pale-green walls. No windows. An array of tubes and wires hooking him to various machines. The quiet hum of nurses as they went about their duties within the intensive care facility.

What the hell am I doing here? he asked himself.

His brain was fuzzy. His body ached, but it was a medicated ache that told him his true pain was being masked by some high-powered medicine. Worth felt as if his right leg had been run over by an army tank.

His right leg! Now he remembered. He'd been shot. He tried to raise himself up enough to look at his leg, to make sure it was still there. During his time in the Rangers he'd seen guys get their legs blown off and later in the hospital say they could feel their missing limb.

A strong, feminine hand came down over Worth's chest and gently eased his head down on the pillow. "Lie still, Mr. Cordell. Don't try to move around. Not yet."

"Tell me something." Worth looked squarely at the brown-eyed, middle-aged nurse.

She glanced down at him and smiled. "What would you like to know?"

"Is my leg still there?" he asked.

"Your leg?" Her smiled widened. "Your leg is very much there and it's healing nicely. We should be able to transfer you to a private room by this time tomorrow."

"Thanks."

"You're welcome. Is there anything else I can do for you?"

"I'm not sure. I'm a bit crazy-headed right now."

"Your mind will clear up once we reduce your medication. Now take it easy and—" she pointed to a series of buttons attached to the railing on his hospital bed "—if you need anything, just punch right here and one of us will check on you."

Worth nodded.

The nurse paused at the doorway, glanced over her shoulder and said, "Merry Christmas, Mr. Cordell."

Merry Christmas?

"Is today Christmas Day?" he asked.

"Yes, it is."

"How long have I been in here?"

"You were brought into the E.R. three days ago, on the twenty-second, and Dr. Winthrop did emergency surgery. He saved your life and your leg."

"I am in Atlanta, aren't I?"

"You're in Piedmont Hospital and you've had visitors every day, but you probably don't remember."

"Visitors?"

"Your co-workers from the Dundee agency. A Mr. Sawyer, a Mr. Shea and a Ms. Evans."

"Oh, yeah, my co-workers."

Worth tried to remember exactly what had happened to him, but his memory was messed up. He'd been on an assignment, here in Atlanta, providing private security for some rock star in town for a Christmas concert. He could recall that much, but nothing about the particulars. When one of the guys from Dundee's came back to the hospital, he'd find out the details.

Lying there, his leg aching and his stomach rumbling—when had he eaten last?—he suddenly remembered that he'd had a very important date on Christmas Eve. Faith! He was supposed to have met her in Whitewood, South Carolina, at eight o'clock in the town square.

Well, by now, she realized he wasn't going to show up. She must have been really disappointed. Hell, he'd had every intention of meeting her. He'd owed her that much. After he had rescued her from kidnappers and gotten them back to safety, she'd developed a major crush on him. And he had developed a major case of the hots for her.

Maybe it was better for her—for both of them—that he hadn't been able to meet her. Being laid up in the hospital this way, he had saved them both from an unpleasant scene. He had planned to tell Faith that he wasn't the right man for her, that he wasn't the settling-down, one-woman-man she needed. He was a man with too many emotional battle scars for a sweet woman like Faith. Plain and simple—he was no damn good for her.

She might be crying today, but by this time next year, she'd probably barely remember what he looked like. Yeah, maybe fate had done them both a big favor. He could continue his life as it was and she could move on to that fairy tale happily-ever-after she wanted with some other guy.

Chapter 1

Faith Sheridan locked the door to Toddle Town Day Care, the business she had opened in February, only a few short weeks after her recovery from hypothermia and pneumonia nearly ten months ago. With a bank loan, cosigned by Margaret Tompkins, and seventy-five percent of her savings, Faith had purchased a downtown building that had once housed a dry goods store that had gone out of business a couple of years ago. Located on Hickory Avenue, a back street in Whitewood, the two-story building was ideal. Her office and nursery were upstairs, where the infants were kept away from the toddlers on the ground level. Out back Faith had cleared off the empty half lot and put in playground equipment.

Opening a day-care center had seemed the perfect choice for Faith since her background was in child care; plus she had the added bonus of being able to keep Hope with her all the time. But today, her baby daughter was running a fever and she couldn't risk exposing the other children to what the doctor had said was a twenty-four-hour virus. Luckily Lindsey Dawson had become like a grandmother to Hope, as had Margaret, and today Lindsey was looking after Hope.

Life wasn't perfect, but Faith was content. She had a new business that was thriving, good friends all around her in Whitewood and best of all, four-month-old Hope. Her baby was the absolute joy of her life. But despite everything being well with her, she hadn't forgotten Worth Cordell. How could she, when Hope was a living, breathing reminder of the man Faith still loved? She never talked about Worth anymore, not to Lindsey or Margaret—and certainly not to Jody, who was convinced Worth Cordell was a low-life scum.

As Faith headed toward her car, the November wind whipping chillingly all about her, she paused on the sidewalk and glanced around at both sides of the back street already decked out in holiday gear; not quite as elaborately decorated as Main Street, but shimmering with white lights. And each shop door on Hickory Avenue held a festive wreath. Every year, the decorations went up earlier and earlier. Here it was a few days before Thanksgiving and already the town was in Christmas mode.

The turn-of-the-century reproduction streetlights cast a mellow golden glow over the entire scene. Since she kept the day-care center open until six-thirty and all the other shops on Hickory closed at five-thirty, she was quite alone. But she never felt afraid, not here in Whitewood. Their crime rate was one of the lowest in the state.

Hitching her shoulder bag higher, she reached inside her coat pocket for her car keys, then headed straight for the used SUV she'd bought from one of Lindsey's sons who lived in Columbia. The back seat held Hope's infant seat and an array of toys scattered about, even in the floorboard. She couldn't wait to pick up Hope and head straight home. She was unaccustomed to being away from her child all day and she longed to hold her baby in her arms.

Faith unlocked the driver's door of the Chevy Blazer. Just as she stepped up to get inside, someone grabbed her from behind. She gasped, startled by the unexpected hand on her shoulder. When she tried to turn to face the person, she felt something hit her on the head. For a couple of seconds her vision blurred. What was happening? Was she being attacked? She opened her mouth to scream, but no sound came out. *Oh, God, help me!* Whoever had hit her was dragging her away from the car. She tried to struggle, tried to put up a fight, but she felt so weak. When she managed to squeak out a protest, something struck her head again.

Suddenly everything went black!

Worth Cordell finished the paperwork on his most recent assignment for Dundee's, pushed the print button on the computer and leaned back in his plush office chair as he waited for the information to print out. This job had lasted nearly a month and ended with the apprehension of a stalker who'd been obsessed with her college professor. The twenty-year-old coed had finally moved beyond threatening behavior to actually trying to kill the professor's wife. Worth had come damn close to taking the bullet meant for Marcia Hallmark.

After snatching the pages from the printer, he slipped them into a manilla file folder and laid it on his desk, then started to get up; but a sharp pain splintered through his bad leg. Hell! Leaning slightly to the left, he rubbed his thigh. The bullets he'd taken in that leg nearly a year ago had left him with a slight limp. For months after he'd been released from the hospital, he'd used a cane just to get around, but now, after endless therapy, he was about eight-five percent back to normal. He relied on the cane only when he'd been on his feet for too many hours and his limp grew decidedly worse. His life had pretty much returned to normal, but he'd have both the scars and the limp to always remind him of what had happened. He'd taken three bullets—two in the leg and one in the side—when a crazed fan had decided to become famous attempting to kill a rock star who had been in Atlanta for a concert.

"Worth Cordell," Dundee office manager, Daisy Holbrook, called as she knocked on the door, then stuck her head into Worth's office. "Mr. McNamara wants to see you right this minute. It's urgent."

Worth rose to his full six-four height, nodded to Daisy and said, ''Tell him I'll be right there.''

''Will do.'' Daisy beamed that thousand-watt smile of hers and scurried away.

The young woman ran the Dundee office in downtown Atlanta with unequaled efficiency and had for the past year, since she'd been hired to replace the retiring former office manager. Daisy had been the first employee that new Dundee CEO, Sawyer Mc-Namara, had hired when Sam Dundee had asked Sawyer to take over the top job when Ellen Denby married and left the business. Sawyer was the right kind of guy to run Dundee's. He was smart, shrewd, and hard-nosed, as well as fair-minded. He was a no-nonsense type of man who instilled confidence and loyalty in his employees. Well, everyone except Lucie Evans. Worth had thought one of two things would happen when Sawyer took over the reins: either Lucie would resign or Sawyer would request her resignation. The two had been former FBI agents and the animosity between them apparently had deep roots. No one in the business knew the particulars; they only knew Lucie and Sawyer didn't like each other. But to everyone's surprise Lucie remained a Dundee agent and despite an occasional flare-up between the two, Sawyer and she somehow managed to coexist whenever they were both at the downtown office.

When Worth walked through Sawyer's open office door, he heard the voice of a newscaster coming from the television housed in a compact entertainment center in Sawyer's office suite.

"Come in. I thought you'd want to see this." Sawyer motioned for Worth to come over to his desk. "Wasn't Faith Sheridan the name of the Constantines' nanny?"

A shiver of apprehension raced up Worth's spine. He hadn't heard that name spoken in nearly a year, but he had thought about Faith more often than he liked to admit, even to himself.

"Yeah, that was her name. Why?" Worth made his way over to the side of Sawyer's desk.

"When the noon news first came on, they said something about a report coming up on a missing person named Faith Sheridan. I thought since you rescued Ms. Sheridan and took care of her after she and the Constantine child were kidnapped, you might be interested in finding out what's happened to her."

"It might not be the same Faith Sheridan," Worth said.

"Might not be. The report is coming from someplace in South Carolina."

Worth's heart skipped a beat. "Whitewood, South Carolina?"

"Yes, I think that's—"

"Faith told me she was going home to Whitewood when she handed in her resignation to the Constantines last year."

"Well, this news story must be about her. Take a seat." Sawyer indicated a leather wing chair to the left of his desk. "We'll check out the report together."

Just as Worth eased down in the chair, the local

noon anchorman said, "Now to Connie Beck in Whitewood, South Carolina, where a young mother has been missing for the past thirty-six hours and feared to be the latest victim of the Greenville Slayer, who has murdered two women and left two others close to death in the Greenville, South Carolina area."

Every muscle in Worth's body tensed. Faith dead? No, it wasn't possible. Not sweet little Faith. An overwhelming sense of grief sucker punched Worth, then he recalled something that the newsman had said. He'd said Faith was a young mother. Did Faith have a child? Was it possible that when he hadn't shown up on Christmas Eve last year, she'd turned to another man? But if her name was still Sheridan, she wasn't married. Faith was the old-fashioned sort of woman who would take her husband's name when she married.

The face of the attractive brunette reporter, Connie Beck, appeared on screen. Beside the reporter stood a somber young blonde holding a baby in her arms.

"This is Connie Beck, coming to you from Whitewood, North Carolina, where Faith Sheridan, the owner of a local day-care center and mother of a four-month-old child, has been missing for the past thirty-six hours and is feared dead."

Four-month-old child? Mentally Worth counted back. God in heaven! That meant Faith had given birth in late July or early August, which would mean she had conceived sometime in November.

Was it possible the child was his? No! He wouldn't

believe it. Couldn't believe it. Faith knew how to contact him through the Dundee Agency; if she'd been pregnant, she could have gotten in touch with him.

Worth tried to focus on what the reporter was saying. "Police aren't revealing much about Ms. Sheridan's disappearance, but our sources tell us the police fear she was abducted when she left the day-care center night before last, and with a serial killer—the Greenville Slayer—having recently hit in the town of Sparkman, only twenty miles south of Whitewood, there's a good chance Ms. Sheridan is his latest victim.

"With me today is Ms. Sheridan's best friend since the two were childhood playmates—Ms. Jody Crenson." Connie Beck held the microphone toward Jody. "Jody, you have something you'd like to show us and something you'd like to say."

Jody held up a photograph in one hand as she kept the baby, bundled in a pink blanket, poised on her hip. "This is Faith Sheridan. If anyone has seen her or has information about her, please contact the Whitewood police department. Faith's friends are collecting reward money for anyone with information." Jody removed the blanket from the baby's head and the camera zoomed in on the child.

Worth's heart stopped beating for a split second. Fat, pink cheeks, button nose, rosebud lips. A thick fluff of dark-red hair curled atop the child's head and a set of dark-brown eyes stared into the camera.

She was his! He knew it the moment he looked at her. Faith's baby was his daughter.

"This is Faith's little girl. Hope needs her mother, so please, if you know anything, anything at all, about Faith's disappearance, we need your help." Tears spilled from Jody's eyes.

"Thank you, Ms. Crenson." The reporter caressed the baby's rosy cheek, then turned back to the camera, which focused on her. "It is feared that Faith Sheridan is the fifth victim of the Greenville Slayer. This man murdered one woman and left two for dead in the Greenville area, all within the past two months. Only three weeks ago, his fourth victim was found dead in an abandoned warehouse in Sparkman, twenty miles south of here."

Worth shot up from his chair and bounded out of Sawyer McNamara's office. He had to get to Whitewood as quickly as possible. Every instinct he possessed urged him to find out what had happened to Faith and to see the child he knew had to be his.

Sawyer came out in the hallway and called to Worth, "What's wrong with you? Where are you going in such a hurry?"

Worth slowed for a moment, glanced over his shoulder and replied, "I'm going to Whitewood to find out what happened to Faith."

"I knew she had a major crush on you after you rescued her last year, but I didn't think you reciprocated her feelings."

Worth didn't explain himself to anyone, didn't justify his actions to anyone, not even his boss—not unless those actions directly related to a current case.

But he did owe Sawyer some sort of explanation. "I'll need some time off. I don't know how long."

Sawyer eyed Worth suspiciously. "Sure. Take however long you need. And call me if there's anything I or the agency can do to help you."

"Thanks."

Worth hurried into his office, tossed his overcoat across his arm, then went by Daisy's desk on his way out.

"Call the airlines and get me the first available flight to Whitewood, South Carolina. And arrange for a rental car."

"Yes, sir."

"Call me on my cell phone to let me know about my reservations."

"I'll take care of the arrangements for you, Mr. Cordell."

Ten minutes later, Worth found himself stuck in downtown traffic. Twenty minutes later just as he entered his one-bedroom apartment, his cell phone rang. Daisy rattled off details of his flight and he registered the information mentally, then set about packing. His plane left Atlanta in less than three hours.

Margaret Tompkins and Lindsey and George Dawson sat around the table in Jody Crenson's kitchen. Half-eaten sandwiches and empty coffee cups littered the table, along with piles of money.

Margaret punched the final numbers into her adding machine, then announced, "We have collected two thousand, six hundred and forty-two dollars and twenty cents.''

''George and I want to add a thousand dollars to that,'' Lindsey said as she bounced a wide-eyed Hope on her knee.

''With my thousand, that will bring our total to nearly five thousand.'' Margaret wiped away a tear. ''I feel as if we should be doing something more. I want to go out and search this town, house by house.''

''The police have pretty much already done that,'' Jody said. ''Everyone in Whitewood knows Faith and if anyone has seen anything, this reward money—'' Jody eyed the stack of bills and rolled coins in the middle of her kitchen table ''—should entice even the most reluctant to come forward.''

''I simply can't believe that anyone would harm a sweet child like Faith.'' A portly, fifty-something George Dawson had been little Hope's substitute grandfather since the day she was born and both Lindsey and Margaret shared the grandmother role, while Jody was simply Aunt Jody.

''If—and I'm only saying if—the Greenville Slayer—'' Jody's voice cracked with emotion.

She could not—would not—allow herself to believe Faith was dead. Her dearest friend had been through so much in the past year. Surely God wouldn't be so cruel as to take her away from little Hope when the child didn't have a father. Well, she did have a father, but the heartless bastard had taken advantage of Faith and hadn't even bothered to call to say he was sorry. Jody would never forgive the

man for standing up Faith a year ago on Christmas
Eve. The poor kid had sat on a bench in the town
square and waited for four hours—in the snow. When
Jody had found Faith at midnight, she'd been suffering from hypothermia and had been practically delir-
ious. A week's stay in the hospital battling pneumonia
and nearly a month's recuperation at home had come
at the same time evil bouts of morning sickness had
hit Faith.

Jody had wanted to call Worth Cordell and demand
he take responsibility for his child, but Faith had told
her she wouldn't ask Worth for anything.

"Obviously he doesn't love me," Faith had said.
"If he did, he would have shown up at the square on
Christmas Eve as we'd planned. I don't want him to
feel obligated to me just because I'm pregnant. If he
doesn't love me, my baby and I are better off without
him in our lives."

"Don't you worry, Faithie, you've got people who
care about you. We'll help you," Jody had told Faith,
and the people gathered here tonight in her kitchen
had made Jody's prediction come true. Jody, Margaret and the Dawsons had stood by Faith through
her pregnancy and rallied around her and little Hope
like the family they had become.

Margaret stood and placed her arm around Jody's
shoulders. "It's all right, dear, we know exactly how
you feel. Faith is like a daughter to me. I refuse to
believe that she's dead."

"So do I," Lindsey added. "We can't give in to

our fears. We have to believe in a miracle. For Hope's sake, if for no other reason.''

"I'll take the money to the bank in the morning,'' George said. "And open an account for the Faith Sheridan Reward Fund. And Lindsey will contact the newspapers and the local radio and television stations first thing tomorrow.''

"Thanks.'' Jody offered George a fragile smile. "I don't know what else we can do. We've circulated flyers in Whitewood and all the neighboring towns and the local police have been more than cooperative.''

Hope began whimpering. Lindsey lifted the baby and laid her on her shoulder. "Margaret, warm her bottle for me, will you?''

Margaret got up immediately, retrieved a bottle from the refrigerator and put it in the microwave. "She doesn't seem to like that formula. Sweet little thing is used to mother's milk.''

"Faith is such a good mother. She puts Hope's needs first. Always.'' Fresh tears trickled down Lindsey's cheeks.

The unexpected sound of the doorbell froze everyone for an instant. "I'll get it,'' Jody said. "It might be Reverend and Mrs. Simmons. They mentioned arranging a prayer vigil for tomorrow evening.''

Jody rushed out of the kitchen, through the living room and to the front door. She turned on the porch light, then peered through the window in the door. She didn't recognize her guest. He was tall—very tall—with dark auburn hair, broad shoulders and wore a tan trench coat. She eased open the door.

"Yes, may I help you?"

"Are you Jody Crenson?" he asked, his voice a deep, husky baritone.

"Yes, I am. Who are you?"

"I'm Worth Cordell," he replied. "I believe I'm the father of Faith Sheridan's child."

Jody glared at the big man as shock radiated through her body.

"You're about a year late, you son of a bitch!"

Then she slammed the door in his face.

Chapter 2

Worth rang the doorbell repeatedly. He hadn't come this far just to be turned away by one of Faith's friends. If as he suspected, Faith's child was his daughter, then he had certain responsibilities, as well as certain rights. More than anything he wanted Faith found alive and well, but either way, the child was going to need him.

The front door swung open and a stout, balding, middle-aged man stood there glaring at Worth. Three women hovered behind the man, all of them glowering.

"I'm Worth Cordell. May I come in and talk to y'all. Please."

"Let him come in," an elderly, white-haired lady said as she moved forward and planted her hand on her hip.

"Thank you." Worth entered the living room, then closed the door behind him. "I stopped by the police station and a Detective Rollins told me Faith had friends who were caring for her child and were collecting reward money for information concerning Faith's whereabouts."

"Won't you sit down, Mr. Cordell?" The elderly woman nodded toward the sofa.

The man, the older woman and Jody Crenson flanked Worth as he moved toward the sofa. He felt like a condemned man on his way to the gallows. The third woman, a plump, motherly brunette, held back, staying halfway across the room, but her dark eyes bored into him. Worth's gaze zeroed in on the baby she held on her hip. His heartbeat accelerated as he stared at the little girl. She looked a great deal like his little sister Norma had looked as a baby. Curly red hair and chocolate-brown eyes. Oh, God! No doubt about it—this child was his!

"Sit," the man ordered.

When Worth sat, the threesome formed a semicircle around him.

"I'm George Dawson," the man said, then indicated with a hand gesture first to the older woman, then to the younger. "This is Margaret Tompkins and Jody Crenson." He glanced across the room. "That's my wife Lindsey and…" George cleared his throat. "The baby is Faith's little girl, Hope. We're Faith's friends."

"We're Faith's family." Jody frowned at Worth.

"You said you went by the police station," Margaret said. "Did you learn anything new about Faith's whereabouts?"

"No, ma'am, I'm sorry, there's nothing new to report."

"What are you doing here?" Jody asked.

"I saw your interview on the news at noon today," Worth replied. "I felt I had to come, to see if I could—" All eyes focused hostilely on him. "Faith was…is… I had no idea she had a child."

"If you had bothered to show up last Christmas Eve, she would have told you she was pregnant," Margaret said.

"Why didn't you show up, Mr. Cordell?" Lindsey asked.

"Because he's a low-life scum who didn't care anything about Faith." Jody jumped up out of her chair. "He used Faithie and dumped her. I don't think we should even be talking to him."

"Is Jody right, Mr. Cordell?" Margaret asked.

Worth suddenly understood how a man felt when surrounded by a lynch mob who had already tried and convicted him without a hearing.

"I cared about… I care about Faith. I honestly believed that she was better off without me. If she's told you anything about me, y'all know how we met and—"

"You rescued her from rebels in Subria who had kidnapped her and the Constantine child," George said. "Yes, we know about that. And we know how you make your living. But Faith told us what a good man you were. She's never said one unkind thing about you. Not even when you didn't keep your promise to her.''

''I was in the hospital.'' Worth felt a sudden need to defend himself. ''I'd been critically wounded on a job assignment. They kept me highly sedated, so I didn't come out of it and know where I was until Christmas Day last year.''

''Why didn't you call Faith then?'' Lindsay asked.

''Because he'd never meant to show up at the square on Christmas Eve—'' Jody snapped her head around and pierced Worth with her sharp glare ''—did you?''

''I had planned to meet Faith, to explain why— Look, what does all this matter now? I stayed away because I truly believed Faith was better off without me. I had no idea she was pregnant, that I was a father. If she'd told me, I—''

''You really don't know Faith at all if you think she would have tried to use a baby to trap you into marriage,'' Jody said. ''She loved you. She thought you loved her.''

Worth didn't know how to respond, didn't have any idea how to defend himself against their accusations. He was guilty as charged. After being released from the hospital last year, he should have contacted Faith; instead he'd taken the easy way out.

''I'm sorry I wasn't here when Faith needed me. If I could change things, I would, but I can't. But I'm here now and I intend to stay until we find out what happened to Faith.'' Worth glanced at the baby who had laid her head against Lindsey Dawson's shoulder and fallen asleep. "May I see my daughter?"

"What makes you think she's yours?" Jody asked.

Margaret shook her head. "Jody, dear, you mustn't—"

"He can't waltz in here now and claim Hope. He has no right to assume he can play daddy when it's convenient for him." Jody looked from Margaret to George to Lindsey. "Are y'all forgetting what this man put Faith through?" Jody turned to Worth, her eyes narrowed, her nostrils flared. "Faith went to meet you in the square that night. It was raining and the rain turned to snow. She waited for you for four hours, sitting out in the snow. When I found her she had hyperthermia and wound up in the hospital with pneumonia. And she was pregnant!"

A guilt-ridden pain tightened in Worth's gut. He should have known she'd wait for him hour after hour. Damn it—he should have known!

"Our little Faith is such a romantic," Margaret said. "She convinced herself that you were her white knight, her rescuer and protector. She never considered the possibility that you were just an ordinary man or that you weren't as much in love with her as she was with you."

Lindsey Dawson came forward, but when she started to hand Hope to Worth, Jody grabbed the child away from Lindsey.

"Maybe you aren't Hope's father," Jody said. "You have no proof that you are. We aren't about to turn Hope over to you."

"If I'm not Hope's father, then who is?" Worth asked.

"Now isn't the time to play games with this man," George said. "Jody, let him hold Hope."

Reluctantly Jody handed the sleeping child over to Worth. As his muscles tightened, his body went rigid. He hadn't held a baby since he'd been a kid and held his little sister. Norma had been eight years younger than he—his half sister—and he'd taken care of her when his stepmother had been too drunk to look after her own baby. And that had been just about all the time.

Worth held little Hope as if she were made of spun glass. He didn't think he'd ever seen anything as beautiful. She looked like an angel. Tiny, helpless and sweet beyond belief. His child. He didn't need anyone to tell him she was his. Didn't need any blood or DNA tests. Faith had been a virgin when they'd made love, and there was no way she would have turned to another man so quickly after they'd been together. Jody was right—he didn't know Faith all that well. They'd shared a very brief relationship, having been together for only a few days. But he did know how good and kind and sweet Faith Sheridan had been. Had been? God, she couldn't be dead!

Worth closed his eyes as he held Hope against his heart. The clean, delicate fragrance unique to babies assailed his senses. And an overwhelming feeling of possessiveness claimed him. This tiny bundle lying so trustingly in his arms had been born from the passion he and Faith had shared.

''I...uh...I've checked into the Whitewood Motel out on the strip,'' Worth said as his big hand cradled Hope's small, round head. ''I'm planning on staying in Whitewood until we find out about Faith. I'd appreciate it if y'all would let me know when you hear something from the police.'' Reluctantly Worth handed Hope back to Lindsey.

''We'll let you know as soon as we hear anything,'' George said.

Worth stood. ''I'd like to come by and see my daughter tomorrow.''

''Hope will be at Toddle Town Day Care,'' Margaret told him. ''Lindsey is helping out there temporarily...until Faith comes back.'' Margaret choked with emotion.

''Toddle Town?'' Worth asked.

''Faith's business,'' Jody replied. ''She owns Toddle Town Day Care and keeps Hope there with her. Hope is used to everyone who works there and they're all giving her lots of special attention.''

''May I come by tomorrow to see Hope?'' Worth looked to Lindsey.

She offered him a tentative smile. ''I suppose that would be all right.''

''Thanks.''

George walked Worth to the door, then stepped out

onto the porch behind him. When he reached up and put his hand on Worth's shoulder, Worth tensed.

"Son, you've got to understand how the ladies feel. Our little Faith was counting on you and you let her down. My wife and Margaret and Jody aren't going to make things easy for you. You'll have to prove yourself to them."

"I understand. And thank you, Mr. Dawson."

"Call me George."

"Thanks, George."

Barney Jeffries crept down the alley between Clanton and Mooresville Streets in Sparkman. In the morning the sanitation department would empty all the Dumpsters in town, so he had only tonight to sort through the trash and find any usable items discarded by others. In his experience, this particular Dumpster usually yielded the most bounty. Once he'd even found a gold wristwatch that he'd been able to hock for nearly fifty bucks. Some idiot's loss had been his gain.

As he neared the Dumpster, Barney looked around for something he could use as a step stool. A stack of empty crates piled up in the corner by the back door of Dottie's Diner caught his eye. After dragging one of the crates across the alleyway and to the Dumpster, Barney climbed up, tossed back the lid and crawled over inside of the huge garbage bin. The stench would bother most people, but not Barney. He'd grown used to the odor and even the worst smells didn't turn his stomach. A man had to possess a strong constitution in order to go rummaging around in other people's trash.

Barney removed his flashlight from his back pocket and shined the light left to right, back to front, searching for any tidbits that might rest on top. He did a double take when he saw the white arm lying limply atop a black garbage bag. Holy-moley! He aimed the light at the arm. Human. And by the size, either a child or a small female. Oh, this wasn't good. This wasn't good at all. He moved the light up the arm to the shoulder. A sinking feeling hit him in the belly. The light moved over the shoulder, up the neck and onto the face. A woman. A young woman with her eyes closed. She was dead. Had to be dead. Otherwise why would somebody have dumped her in the trash? His hand shook so badly he dropped his flashlight. Better get it, he told himself. If the police found it, they'd check for fingerprints and he'd be in deep trouble.

When Barney reached down to retrieve his flashlight, which had fallen by the woman's hip, he noticed her chest rise and fall. She was breathing. She wasn't dead!

"Hey, lady." He nudged her hip with the flashlight. She didn't respond. "I can't help you. If I do, they'll run me in for sure and put me in jail. I'm sorry. Really, I am. But I tell you what I'll do, I'll call for help. I swear I will."

Barney crawled out of the Dumpster, hopped down

on the crate and then onto the concrete pavement. Leaving the Dumpster lid open, he hurried out of the alley. He glanced all around, then ran across the street to a pay phone. Taking a dirty rag from his coat pocket, he lifted the receiver, inserted a quarter in the slot and dialed 911. When the emergency operator responded, the machine coughed up his quarter, which he quickly rammed into his pocket.

"Yeah, there's a half-dead woman in a Dumpster over on Clanton and Mooresville." Before the operator could say a word, Barney hung up the phone, dashed out of the booth and scurried up the street as fast as he could go.

Worth slept fitfully, tossing and turning, dreaming about Faith. His subconscious played half a dozen different horrific scenarios inside his brain. Each time he was within arms reach of Faith, a moment away from saving her, she disappeared. Vanished. And each time, Worth awoke in a cold sweat.

Tossing back the covers, he rose from the double bed in Room 214 of the Whitewood Motel, a two-story U-shaped structure on the strip outside of town. Sitting on the side of the bed, Worth rubbed his hands up and down his thighs, then dropped his hands between his knees. Although common sense told him that even if he'd shown up at the town square last Christmas Eve and even if he'd married Faith, he couldn't have prevented what happened to her. If some crazed serial killer had gotten his hands on her, it would have happened regardless of what Worth had or hadn't done. But the illogical, emotional part of his nature ached with guilt and told him that if Faith had been with him instead of trying to make it on her own, all alone, she wouldn't be missing right now.

Worth stood and walked across the room to the window overlooking the parking lot. He opened the blinds and glanced outside at the first light of dawn spreading across the eastern sky. Memories of another dawn over a year ago flashed through his mind. The morning after he and Faith had made love for the first time. Her first time shouldn't have been in some dark, dank cave in a barbaric country half a world away from her home. And it shouldn't have been with a emotionally battle-scarred former Ranger who wasn't capable of genuine love. Faith had deserved so much better.

He closed the blinds and shut his eyes. He could almost hear her voice, almost feel her soft, smooth skin. How sweet she'd been, how incredibly sweet. And how shy. That morning before they'd headed out for the rendezvous point to meet the rescue chopper, she'd been worried that because she was dirty, her gown tattered, and her hair a mess, he'd think she was ugly. She had told him that she'd always been skinny and unattractive. How wrong she'd been. And he'd made his feelings perfectly clear.

You have no idea how appealing you are to me. You're not skinny—you're delicate. And you have beautiful eyes and a cute little nose and the most de-

*licious mouth I've ever tasted. If we didn't have a
helicopter to catch out of this hellhole today, I'd take
you back inside that cave and make love to you until
neither of us could stand up for a week.*

He should have known there might be consequences! After all, he didn't have a condom handy
that night. Why hadn't he at least picked up the phone
and called her after he got out of the hospital last
year? He could have at least seen how she was.
Damn! Had Jody Crenson been right? Had Faith been
too proud to tell him about his child?

Faith had wanted love and commitment. Moon,
June and happily-ever-after. He'd tried to be honest
with her, tried to tell her that he was the wrong man
for her. Yeah, he'd tried all right—just not hard
enough. He had made love to a woman who, because
of her romantic nature, had waited her whole life for
the man of her dreams before giving her innocence.
But because she'd feared dying a virgin if they
couldn't escape from Subria, she'd begged him to
make love to her. He had resisted, at least at first. But
what man could resist such alluring temptation?

The ringing telephone brought Worth from the past
to the present rather quickly. He stomped across the
room, lifted the receiver and said, "Worth Cordell
here."

"Mr. Cordell, this is George Dawson."

Worth's heartbeat went wild.

"They've found Faith," George said. "She's alive,
but just barely."

"Where…when…how?"

"Come to Memorial Hospital. Drive through downtown Whitewood, go half a mile on Main Street until you reach Underwood Lane, turn right and go one block."

"Thanks, George. I'm on my way."

"Mr. Cordell?"

"Yes?"

"You'd better hurry."

Chapter 3

When the elevator doors swung open on the second floor of Memorial, the only hospital within a forty-five mile radius and served Whitewood, Sparkman and South Lake, Worth rushed out and, following the arrows pointing the way, hurried down the corridor to the ICU waiting room. Jody glanced up at him, a somber expression on her face, but not with the hostility he'd seen last night. Margaret offered him a soft smile. George rose from the green vinyl sofa and came to meet him.

Grabbing Worth's arm, George said, "She's alive, but just barely. They told us she came out of surgery about an hour ago. We don't know much, only that they had to stop some internal bleeding."

"Where was she found? What happened to her?" Worth asked.

"Come on outside." George led Worth into the hallway. "The ladies are terribly emotional right now. As a matter of fact, I am, too. Been crying a bit myself. Faith has become like a favorite niece to Lindsey and me. And Hope is like a grandchild."

"What did the police tell y'all about Faith?"

"The Sparkman police received a call from a 911 operator on duty who had gotten an anonymous phone call from a downtown pay phone telling them to look in a certain Dumpster for a woman's body."

"A Dumpster?" Bile rose to Worth's throat. Someone had thrown Faith in a Dumpster? He gritted his teeth as his hands instinctively clutched into tight fists.

"It seems she was beaten. Severely beaten. And thrown in the Dumpster. The police estimate she'd been there, unconscious, for the past forty-eight hours and if she'd stayed there another night, she would have died."

Worth grabbed George by the shoulders. "Do they have any idea who—"

"Detective Rollins of our Whitewood police department told me that the M.O. of the crime fits the M.O. of the Greenville Slayer. All of his victims have been found in similar places—Faith and another woman who died were put in Dumpsters; two were found at landfills; and another was actually discovered in her own garbage can inside an abandoned warehouse."

"My God, this guy is a real psycho." Worth tightened his hold on George's shoulders. "Have y'all spoken to the doctor? What odds are they giving that Faith will live?''

''I spoke to the nurses and they didn't say much, but I got the impression they don't think her chances are very good.''

''Have they let any of you see her?''

''Not yet. But they've told us we can go back, one at a time, during visitation.''

''When?''

George checked his watch. ''In about fifteen minutes.''

''I want to see her.''

George nodded. ''You care about Faith, don't you?''

''Yeah, I care.'' *Admit it,* Worth's inner voice told him, *you care a hell of a lot more than you thought you did.* Ever since he saw that noon news account about Faith missing, he'd been figuratively holding his breath. And when he heard she was still alive, he had released that breath with great relief. *You wanted Faith to be alive because you need a chance to make things right with her.*

Jody came out into the hall. ''I just called Lindsey to check on Hope.'' Jody glanced at Worth. ''They're at Toddle Town and as soon as Hope goes down for her morning nap, Lindsey is coming to the hospital.''

''I should be thanking all of you for taking care of Hope,'' Worth said. ''She's a lucky little girl to have so many people care about her and her mother.''

''You don't need to thank us,'' Jody said. ''We're

Hope's family, the same way we're Faith's family. You, on the other hand, are a stranger to Hope.''

''I'm Hope's father and I don't intend to remain a stranger to her.''

''Well, you'd better wait and see what Faith has to say about it. She might not want—''

George put his arm around Jody's shoulder. ''We all know what Faith wanted. Worth being here when she wakes up is going to be the best medicine possible. Why don't we put aside any misgivings about Worth and give him a chance to prove what kind of man he really is.''

Jody glared at Worth. ''I'll give you a chance, but so help me, if you hurt her again, I'll—I'll make you wish you'd never been born.''

Worth smiled. ''I understand. Faith brings out the protector in everyone, doesn't she? She's so small and delicate, so kind and caring.''

Jody swallowed hard. ''She's too good for her own good most of the time.''

Worth nodded. ''She's too good for me. Don't think I don't already know that. It's one of the reasons I believed she was better off without me.''

Margaret joined the others in the hallway. ''It's about time for visitation. Maybe we should check with the nurse in charge. I won't rest easy until I've seen our girl.''

''I want to see her, but…if she was beaten as badly as they say she was, it'll be hard for us to see her in that condition.'' Jody hugged Margaret and both women brushed away tears from their eyes.

Worth led the others when they entered the intensive care unit en masse and swooped down on the nurses' station.

"May I help you?" A plump, pleasant-faced nurse asked. Her name tag read Wilson.

"We'd like to see Faith Sheridan," Jody said.

"Are you family?"

"Yes, all of us are family."

"Then you may go back, two at a time. But you mustn't stay longer than five minutes." Ms. Wilson rose from her desk and looked directly at Worth. "Are you her husband?"

"No, I'm...I'm her—"

"He's her fiancé," George said.

"Yes, and the father of her baby," Margaret added.

Ms. Wilson blushed and Worth suspected that the middle-aged lady didn't quite approve of unwed parenthood. "I must warn you...all of you—" She glanced from one to the other in turn, then back at Worth. "Ms. Sheridan is in a coma. And she won't look like herself. She's badly bruised. Her face is swollen and her nose was broken and...just be prepared."

"Oh, dear, dear, I don't know if I can bear to look at her." Margaret rung her hands.

"You don't have to see her," Jody said. "It won't be easy for any of us."

"No, no, I must see her."

George placed one hand on Margaret's shoulder and the other on Jody's. "You two go on back to see her, then Worth can go. I'll wait for Lindsey and we'll go in during the next visitation period.''

Worth and George hovered near the doorway while Jody and Margaret disappeared inside cubicle four. Worth crossed his arms over his chest and leaned back against the wall. Neither he nor George said a word. He figured they were both trying not to think about what they'd find when they saw Faith or how savage they'd feel. Worth wanted to get his hands on the man who'd tried to kill Faith. He wouldn't have to think about what he'd do; he'd just do it. With one quick snap of the bastard's neck, he'd rid the world of a monster.

Within three minutes Jody and Margaret emerged from the cubicle. Jody held on to Margaret who was weeping uncontrollably. Tears streamed down Jody's face as they approached George and Worth.

''Must be really bad,'' George said, then moved forward to help Jody with Margaret.

''You can't imagine how horrible she looks,'' Margaret said between gulping sobs. ''The fiend who did that to Faith must be found and punished.''

''I'll take the ladies to the waiting room,'' George said. ''You go on back to see Faith.''

Worth took a deep breath, squared his shoulders and marched toward cubicle four. Before opening the door, he paused, willed himself to remain calm and in control; then he opened the door, entered the cubicle and walked straight to the bed.

He'd thought he was prepared for the worst, but he'd been wrong. Despite all the death and destruction he had encountered as an army Ranger and as a Dundee agent, nothing had prepared him to see the mother of his child lying in a hospital bed, hooked up to wires and tubes, her every breath monitored. And dear God in heaven, her sweet face and delicate body had been battered almost beyond recognition. Purple bruises covered her arms, chest, throat and face. She had a busted lip, both eyes were swollen, and her nose had been broken.

Worth stopped dead still. If the police didn't find the Greenville Slayer, he would—if it was the last thing he ever did.

Forcing himself to move, Worth eased to the bedside. Except for the rise and fall of her chest, Faith appeared lifeless. Unconscious. In a coma. Without even thinking about what he was doing, Worth touched her slender hand, lifted it a couple of inches off the bed and held it tenderly.

"Oh, Blue Eyes. This shouldn't have happened to you." Emotion lodged in his throat. "You're going to be all right. It'll take time for you to recuperate, but I'll be here with you. And when you get to come home, I'll care for you and nurse you back to health. I promise that you can count on me. You and Hope."

God, how he longed to lift her into his arms and hold her. He wished that he could take away all the suffering she had endured. If it were within his power, he'd gladly suffer for her.

"I'm here and I'm staying. Do you hear me, Faith? I'm not going to leave you."

He hoped that on some level she understood him,

that somehow she knew he was here with her, making her promises that he intended to keep. Faith needed him. Perhaps even more than she'd needed him in Subria. And Hope needed a father.

Worth Cordell wasn't the kind of man who shirked his duties.

Jody Crenson entered the ICU waiting room carrying a bag from the downstairs deli. Worth Cordell sat slumped in a chair by the windows, his arms crossed over his chest, his eyes closed. Jody had wanted to hate the man who'd broken Faith's heart, but seeing his devotion to Faith these past two days had softened her attitude toward him. The guy hadn't left the hospital in forty-eight hours; he'd been cleaning up in the rest room and eating from a vending machine. He looked like hell. His clothes were rumpled and his face was darkened with beard stubble.

As she approached him, Worth opened his eyes and stared at her.

"Hi," he said. "How's Hope doing?"

Jody set the bag down on the table beside his chair. "I called Lindsey as soon as I got off from work to check on Hope. She's doing all right. But we all figure she's missing her mommy. She's not sleeping good and her pediatrician has already changed her formula again." Jody nodded in the direction of the ICU. "Any change in Faith's condition?"

Worth shook his head, then got up and walked across the room to the coffeepot on the table in the corner. "Want any coffee?"

"Sure, fix me a cup, please. Black." Jody pointed to the paper sack. "I brought you a sandwich and some chips."

"Thanks." Worth poured two cups of coffee, handed Jody a cup, then sat and held his cup with both hands.

"If you want to shower and shave, you're welcome to come to my house or—"

"George has already offered to let me stay with Lindsey and him, but I'd rather wait until Faith comes to. I don't want to leave. Not yet." Worth sipped on his coffee.

"Sooner or later, you'll have to leave," Jody told him. "Faith could stay in a coma for weeks. The doctors don't know for sure when she'll come out of it."

"She squeezed my hand, you know. Last night."

"Yes, I know, but—" Jody stopped herself before she said something negative. By nature she was a pessimist, so she always expected the worst—of people and of situations. But there was no reason for her to take away Worth's hope that Faith would recover.

"The local police don't have enough staff to post an officer here 24/7," Worth said. "That means I'm not leaving her here unprotected."

"Unprotected? What are you saying? How is she—? Oh, my God, you think the person who did this to her might come after her here in the hospital."

"Local TV and newspapers have reported that she's alive and in a coma," Worth said. "If this guy thinks she might identify him when she wakes, then he very well could come after her.''

''I've been so caught up in Faith's condition and everything going on here at the hospital that I never thought about… Oh, Worth.''

''The police don't think we have anything to worry about.'' Worth finished off his coffee and set the cup on the table. ''The other two victims who survived couldn't ID the guy. They said they never got a good look at his face because he came up from behind them, knocked them out, then kept them blindfolded and tied up while he—'' Worth swallowed hard.

Jody laid her hand on Worth's arm. ''I'm really glad you're here.''

''Even if I am a year late?''

''Better late than never. Besides, Faith needs you to be her protector again. From what she told me, you're very good at the job.'' Jody pointed to the sack. ''It's roast beef on whole wheat. Eat up.''

Worth glanced past Jody to the door. Jody followed his line of vision. One of the ICU nurses entered, a wide smile on her face. Nurse Malone.

Worth shot out of his chair. ''Has something happened?''

''It most certainly has,'' Nurse Malone said. ''Faith has come out of the coma. She's awake.''

Jody let out a deep breath, grabbed Worth and hugged him. Worth lifted Jody off her feet and swung her around several times.

''What's she saying? How is she?'' Jody asked.

"Did she ask about Hope? Does she want to see me? Does she remember who attacked her?"

"Dr. Tracy is with her," the nurse told them. "We've telephoned the police to let them know she's conscious. Right now, Faith seems to be slightly disoriented, but that's not unusual in cases such as this."

"When can we see her?" Worth asked.

"Dr. Tracy will come out and speak to y'all after he finishes his examination. I'm sure he'll allow y'all to see Faith very soon."

The minute Nurse Malone left, Jody rushed to the pay phone on the wall, then glanced over her shoulder. "I'll call Lindsey and George, then Margaret. They'll be so thrilled to hear the good news."

"I'm sure they'll want to see Faith," Worth said. "But you should probably tell them that you'll call them back after we see Faith and give them an update."

"Yeah, sure. We can take turns caring for Hope and staying here at the hospital. And with one of us here all the time, you could go home and shower."

"Do I stink?" Worth grinned.

"No, you don't stink, but you do look pretty grungy."

Jody lifted the receiver, but before she could dial the number, Worth clasped her shoulder. She glanced up at him.

"Do me a favor, will you? Tell the others that if after the police talk to Faith, they still don't post a guard at her door, I want to call in one of my Dundee co-workers to come to Whitewood and share bodyguard duty with me until Faith is released from the hospital.''

''You really are concerned about this guy coming after Faith again, aren't you?''

''Yes, I'm concerned. And I've learned from experience that it's better to be safe than sorry.''

''Okay, I'll tell the others. I don't know what hiring a bodyguard will cost, but together we should be able to cover the expense.''

''I'm picking up the tab,'' Worth said. ''Faith is my responsibility. I'll take care of her.''

Jody stared quizzically at Worth. ''Is that all Faith and Hope are to you—a responsibility?''

''Don't put words in my mouth.''

''Whatever you do, don't tell Faith you'll take care of her because she's your responsibility. She'd kill me if she thought I told you, but…under these circumstances, I think you should know.''

''Know what?''

''Faith is still in love with you.''

Worth followed Jody into cubicle four. Dr. Tracy had told them Faith appeared to be suffering from temporary amnesia, which was fairly common in patients who had received head traumas similar to hers. He estimated the amnesia would eventually clear up entirely and her memory would return in bits and pieces. His prediction was that within a few weeks Faith should regain most, if not all, of her memory. But in the meantime, she didn't even know her own name.

Jody neared Faith's hospital bed. Worth held back, staying just inside the doorway.

"Hi, there," Jody said. "Dr. Tracy tells me that you're having a problem with your memory."

Worth inched a little closer to the bed, close enough so that he could see Faith. Her swollen, bruised eyes were open and she stared at Jody with complete puzzlement.

"Do I know you?" Faith's voice sounded incredibly weak.

"Oh, Faithie." Jody swallowed her tears. "I'm Jody Crenson. I'm your best friend. We've been buddies since we were kids."

"Jody? You're my friend."

"That's right."

"I've had an accident," Faith said. "The doctor told me that I'm going to regain my memory and he told me that I had two friends waiting to see me."

"Yeah, that would be me and Worth."

"Worth?"

Jody motioned to Worth, then said to Faith. "Yeah, this guy hasn't left the hospital since they brought you in. He's been awfully worried about you. We all have."

As Worth came up beside Jody, Faith asked, "Are you my husband?"

Jody gave Worth a concerned look.

"We aren't married," Worth said. "Not yet."

"You're my fiancé?"

"Something like that." Worth reached down and

took Faith's hand. "It's good to see you awake, Blue Eyes. You've been asleep for days."

"Blue Eyes?"

Worth chuckled. "That's what I called you when we first met. Well, actually I called you ma'am at first, but once I got a good look at those beautiful blue eyes of yours—"

Faith squeezed his hand. "Your voice seems familiar. I've heard it somewhere before."

"I've been talking to you while you were unconscious," Worth told her. "Maybe you heard me."

"What—what kind of accident did I have?" Faith looked up at Worth. "Was I in a car wreck?"

"Not exactly, but I don't think now's the time for you to worry about that. You just concentrate on getting well and regaining your memory. Don't worry about anything else. I'm going to take care of you."

"Because you love me," Faith's voice was a mere whisper.

"Yes, because he loves you," Jody answered for him. "We all love you. The whole family."

"Family?"

"You'll meet them later," Jody said. "There's George and Lindsey, who are like…well, they're like your aunt and uncle. Then there's Margaret. She's like your…sort of a grandmother to you. And there's—"

"There's plenty of time later to talk," Worth interrupted. Now wasn't the time to tell a woman who had no memory that she was the mother of an infant. He knew that despite her amnesia, Faith's maternal instincts were probably undamaged and the minute she heard she had a kid, she'd go nuts worrying about the child.

"Yeah, Worth's right. You need to rest and get well." Jody backed away from the bed. "I'm going to call the family and give them a current update."

Worth stayed with Faith, her little hand wrapped securely in his grasp. "You're going to be all right and your memory will return. I know it has to be frightening for you, but trust me to take care of everything. Whatever you want, whatever you need, I'll make sure you get it."

"I'm so tired," Faith said. "And I hurt. I ache all over."

"I'll see if they can up the dosage on your pain medication."

When Faith grasped Worth's hand tightly, he was amazed by her strength. "Don't go," she pleaded. "Don't leave me."

He leaned over and gently kissed her bruised forehead. "I'll stay right here until the nurses run me out."

Someone behind him cleared their throat. Worth glanced over his shoulder and recognized Nurse Malone and Detective Rollins standing in the doorway.

Chapter 4

"Dr. Tracy said that I could speak with Ms. Sheridan," Detective Rollins said.

"He's allowed five minutes." Nurse Malone followed the policeman into the room. "I'm to stay with him while he questions her."

Faith clung tenaciously to Worth's hand. "Why do the police want to question me? Is it about the accident?"

Worth could see not only the fear and uncertainty in Faith's eyes, but he could sense how nervous and upset she was. "Don't worry. Remember that I'm here and I won't let anyone hurt you." Worth eased Faith's hand from his, then turned to meet Detective Rollins.

"Would you mind stepping outside, Mr. Cordell?" the policeman asked.

"Yes, I would mind," Worth replied. "I'm sure you've been told that Faith has amnesia. She's not going to be able to tell you anything. Not now."

"I understand, but I need to speak with her all the same." Rollins was somewhere in his late thirties, with a short, stocky frame, dark hair and mustache and a professional manner about him. "If you want to stay, Cordell, it's fine with me."

Rollins came forward, Nurse Malone at his side. Worth rounded the foot of the hospital bed and took a stand. Faith's gaze sought and found his. He offered her a supportive smile and when she returned his smile, an odd sensation hit him square in the gut. Faith didn't remember him, didn't know him at all, yet on some instinctive level, she trusted him. It was as if her subconscious recognized him as her protector.

"Ms. Sheridan, I'm Jerry Wayne Rollins, a detective with the Whitewood police department and I need to ask you a few questions."

Faith looked to Worth. He nodded. She turned to the detective. "All right."

"Ms. Sheridan, do you remember what happened to you?"

"You mean the accident?"

"Do you think you had an accident?"

"I don't know. I—I assumed that since I'm badly injured and in the hospital, I must have... Wasn't I involved in a car wreck?"

Rollins glanced at Worth. He knew she had to be told, but why now? Couldn't it wait? It would be different if she could remember anything, but she couldn't.

Rollins looked to Nurse Malone. "The doctor said it was all right to explain things to her."

"Yes, it's all right," the nurse replied.

"Ms. Sheridan, you weren't in a car wreck," the detective said. "You were assaulted, kidnapped and severely beaten."

Faith's blue eyes widened in shock. Her mouth opened in a silent gasp. Then her gaze collided with Worth's.

"Worth?" She held out her hand to him. He rushed to her side and took her hand. "Is he telling me the truth? Is that what happened to me?"

"Yes, that's what the police believe happened," Worth told her.

"Who would do such a thing to me?"

"We don't know for sure," Rollins said. "That's one reason we were hoping you could remember something…anything that might help us."

"I'm sorry. I don't know." Faith frowned, a worried expression forming on her face. She glanced around the room nervously, then tried to lift herself into a sitting position.

Nurse Malone rushed to Faith. "Please, don't move around. You need to lie still and rest." The nurse turned to Rollins. "Perhaps you should go, Detective. I'm afraid Faith is becoming agitated."

Worth followed the policeman out into the main area of the ICU.

"Rollins?"

"Yes, Mr. Cordell?"

"Want to fill me in on what's happening?"

Rollins gave Worth a curious stare. "Such as?"

"Such as why you're here questioning Faith and not somebody from the Sparkman police department? Why you don't have a guard posted here at the hospital? Why—"

Rollins held up a restraining hand. "The Sparkman P.D. and the Whitewood P.D. are working together, along with the Greenville P.D. and the state Bureau of Investigation, but since Dr. Tracy informed us that Ms. Sheridan has amnesia, we saw no point in having anyone other than our department do the initial questioning. And at present, we see no need to post a guard. If the Greenville Slayer is the one who attacked Ms. Sheridan, then she's probably safe. He's made no attempt to harm either of the other two women who survived his brutal attacks. Not while they were recovering or since."

"You're taking a chance with Faith's life on the assumption he won't seek her out while she's here at Memorial. I'm not willing to risk it. Either I or another agent from Dundee's will stay near Faith 24/7 while she's in the hospital."

"That's fine with me, Mr. Cordell. She's your girlfriend and you feel a need to act protective. My job is to do all in my power to find the guy who nearly killed her. If she can remember anything about what happened to her, it might help us."

"When her memory starts coming back, we'll be in touch."

Before the detective was out of sight, Worth heard Faith calling his name. Repeatedly. He rushed back into cubicle four to find Nurse Malone physically restraining Faith.

"Please, see if you can do something with her," the nurse said. "If you can calm her, I won't have to give her a sedative."

Worth all but shoved the nurse aside as he leaned over Faith's bed. She reached for him, one slender arm hooked up to tubes and wires. With the utmost tenderness, Worth encompassed her fragile body in his embrace as he jerked the side rail down and sat on the edge of the bed. Lying there, cuddled against his chest, her fast, erratic breathing began to slow and return to a steady rhythm.

"Don't leave me," Faith pleaded.

Worth rubbed his chin across her temple then kissed the top of her head. "I'll stay right here with you, if you promise you'll relax and rest."

"I promise."

Worth's gaze connected with Nurse Malone's, who smiled and nodded, then left the room. When she returned fifteen minutes later, Faith was asleep, cocooned in Worth's arms.

A week later Worth sent Domingo Shea back to Atlanta. The Dundee agent had swapped out twelve-hour shifts with Worth during Faith's hospital stay, but today Faith had been dismissed from Memorial. Her cuts were beginning to heal and the bruises had faded to pale yellow. The doctors had told Worth and

Faith's "family," it was a miracle that neither of her legs or arms had been broken, only her nose, considering the severity of her beating. She had suffered several cracked ribs, which were also healing nicely.

While the nurse's aide wheeled Faith out to the canopied hospital entrance, Worth pulled his rental car to a stop, hopped out and rounded the hood. He and the aide filled the back seat with the flowers Faith had received once she'd been moved from ICU to a private room. Then Worth swept Faith up in his arms and placed her in the front seat of the car. After securing her seat belt, he thanked the nurse's aide, then returned to the driver's side.

"Ready to go home?" he asked.

"I don't even remember where home is," she said. "But yes, I think I'm ready."

"Everyone's going to be there," he told her. "By everyone I mean—"

"Jody and Margaret and Lindsey and George."

"You've memorized their names."

"Yes, and I can put each name to a face. They've been visiting me every day since I came out of the coma."

Worth pulled onto the street and headed toward downtown Whitewood. The family had agreed that Faith should be told about Hope before she came home and Worth had decided that since he was Hope's father, it was his place to tell Faith about their child. It had been a unanimous decision to wait until Faith had recovered to some degree before telling her that she was a mother.

"You're going to stay with me, aren't you?" Faith asked.

"Yes, I'm staying. We've been over that several times, haven't we? I'm not going anywhere."

"I'm sorry, Worth, but for some reason I can't get over this irrational fear that you're going to leave me."

Was her reaction simply gut instincts or was it a hint of returning memory? Worth wondered. Right now Faith depended on him, needed him, wanted him. But how would she feel once her memory came back and she realized he wasn't the knight in shining armor she thought he was? He had taken her virginity, gotten her pregnant and hadn't shown up for the most important date of her life.

Worth pulled the Camry into Faith's driveway and killed the motor, then turned to her. "There's something I need to tell you."

"Something bad? I'm not sure I want to hear anything else bad. It's been difficult enough coming to terms with the fact that someone nearly beat me to death and that this person might be a serial killer called the Greenville Slayer."

"This isn't bad news," Worth assured her. "It's actually good news."

Faith cocked her head to one side and smiled. "If it's good news, why do you look so somber?"

"Jody and the others have planned a welcome home party for you. Nothing elaborate, just them and us and..." Worth reached out and caressed her cheek.

"There's someone else in your life, someone very important."

"I don't understand." Faith's nose crinkled when she frowned. "Jody told me that my parents are dead, that I have no brothers and sisters, that she and I grew up at the Whitewood Girls' Ranch. Is this important person another friend, someone who couldn't come to the hospital to see me?"

"No, not exactly. You see…you have a…we have a… Hope is our child. She's four months old and—"

"I have a baby? I'm a mother?"

"Yeah. Her name is Hope."

"And she's our child? Yours and mine? She was born four months ago and we aren't…we didn't get married? Why didn't we marry?"

"It's a long story and we'll eventually get around to it," Worth said. "But for now, you need to know that there's a baby in there waiting for her mama, waiting for you."

"Oh. I—I can't believe I have a child and I don't even remember her. What sort of mother am I?"

"You're a good mother. The best. It isn't your fault that you're suffering from temporary amnesia."

"I'm beginning to wonder if it is temporary." Faith sighed heavily. "It's been over a week since I came out the coma and so far, I don't remember anything."

"Not consciously, but I think you do remember a few things subconsciously. Not memories exactly, but feelings."

"What if when I see my child, I don't feel anything? What if I don't feel like a mother? She'll know. She'll sense it and… Oh, Worth, I'm scared.''

''I'm pretty scared myself,'' he admitted. ''You see, Faith, I don't know our daughter and she doesn't know me. I haven't been around since she was born, so I'll be getting to know her for the first time.''

''You weren't with me when she was born?''

Worth shook his head.

''Where were you?''

''You and I had ended our relationship before you found out you were pregnant with Hope.'' Worth knew that he owed it to Faith to be as honest with her as he could be, without undermining her confidence and trust in him. ''I got it in my head that you were better off without me, so I did what I thought was best for both of us.''

''You told me about how we met in Subria, when I was working as a nanny for a billionaire's daughter and how you were part of the rescue party who freed me. Was that when our daughter was conceived, when we were in Subria?''

Worth nodded.

''But we barely knew each other. Somehow it doesn't feel right. I don't know why, but I feel as if I'm not the sort of woman who'd go to bed with a man I just met and I wouldn't have a child without a husband.''

''That's exactly the kind of woman you are—the good girl kind who gets married first,'' Worth told her. ''But when we were hiding out in Subria, waiting for the rescue chopper, we both knew we might not make it out alive. We had sex…made love because we thought it might be our last night on earth.''

''We didn't love each other?''

Worth couldn't bear the look of disappointment and regret in Faith's big blue eyes. ''Maybe not then, but later…''

''Later we fell in love?''

''Yeah, something like that.''

''But you didn't know I was pregnant and you left me because you thought I was better off without you?''

''Yeah.''

''And we have a baby together and you've come back because…'' She glared at him. ''When did you come back?''

''What difference does it make when I came back? I'm here now and I'm staying to take care of you and Hope.''

Worth caught a glimpse of the front door to Faith's apartment easing open. Jody peeped outside.

''They're waiting for you,'' he said. ''Are you ready for your homecoming party?''

''I thought I was, but… What if I don't remember how to take care of a baby?''

''You won't be alone. I'll be here and Jody lives next door and Lindsey and Margaret are only a few blocks away. We'll manage. After all, how difficult can it be to take care of one four-month-old baby?''

Worth got out of the car, lifted Faith into his arms, and carried her up the sidewalk, onto the porch and through the open front door. Jody closed the door behind them, then followed them into the living room. Margaret sat on the sofa, Hope in her lap. Lindsey and George hovered in the doorway leading to the kitchen.

"Welcome home," they all called out in unison as Worth seated Faith on the sofa beside Margaret.

Everyone held their breaths as Faith studied Hope, looking her over from curly red hair to pink booties. When Faith held open her arms to her child, a collective sigh reverberated throughout the room. Hope gurgled and gooed when Faith took her and held her.

"She's beautiful, isn't she?" Faith looked from one person to another and each person smiled and said that yes, Hope was the most beautiful baby in the world. "She looks like you." Faith's gaze rested on Worth, who stood only a few feet away. "She has your eyes, your chin and..." Faith wound one of Hope's red curls around her finger. "Was your hair this color when you were a baby?"

Worth grinned. "Yeah, it stayed that color until I was about ten, then it started turning darker."

"Hello, Hope, my precious baby," Faith said. "I wish I could remember you. I wish I could..." Tears gathered in the corners of Faith's eyes.

"Hey, we've got supper ready," Lindsey said. "And for dessert there's ice cream and a cake. Anybody hungry?"

"Why don't we go ahead and put the food out?" Margaret suggested as she rose from the sofa. "Then we can make ourselves scarce for tonight. I think Faith and Worth and Hope need some time alone."

"No, please, y'all don't have to leave," Faith said. "I'm sorry if I'm not making y'all feel welcome. It's just that I—"

"It's okay, Faithie," Jody said. "It's going to take you time to adjust. Having a houseful of people on your first evening home was probably a bad idea. Margaret's right—you need some time alone with Worth and Hope."

"We'll be nearby if you need us," George said.

Suddenly everyone disappeared into the kitchen, leaving Worth and Faith alone with their child. Worth sat beside Faith.

"Lindsey left us a to-do list," Worth said. "Things like how to fix Hope's bottles, her regular nap times, her pediatrician's phone number. Stuff like that."

"How could I have forgotten this precious child?" Faith hugged her daughter to her and Hope grasped a strand of Faith's long, dark hair.

Worth put his arm around Faith and pulled her to his side. "You'll remember her. If not tomorrow or the next day, then soon."

"What if I never—"

"Dr. Tracy said it's temporary. You might not ever remember all the details about your attack, but you will regain almost all your memory. Just give it time, Blue Eyes, and it'll come back to you."

"I don't know why, but when you call me Blue Eyes, I get a funny feeling. It's almost as if I can remember that I liked your calling me that."

The foursome emerged from the kitchen. When

Worth started to stand, George motioned for him to stay put.

"Supper's warming in the oven," Lindsey said. "There are four bottles already prepared and in the refrigerator."

"We're heading out now," Jody said. "Remember, I'm right next door, if you need me."

Their company left in a whirlwind and when they were gone, utter silence filled the apartment. Then suddenly Hope began whimpering.

For a split second, Worth wanted to call the others back, to ask them not to leave him. What the hell did he know about taking care of a woman recovering from severe injuries and a helpless little baby? Heaven help him, he was out of his element playing nursemaid and daddy.

"She's hungry," Faith said as she loosened her robe and began unbuttoning her gown. She stopped abruptly, her hand hovering over her left breast. "Did I breast-feed Hope?"

"Yeah, I believe you did."

"But I don't have any milk. It must have dried up when I was in the hospital."

"I'll get her a bottle." Worth jumped up and headed for the kitchen. His heart beat ninety to nothing. What was wrong with him? Why was he letting one fragile, petite woman and one tiny baby scare the hell out of him? He'd taken care of wounded comrades, had rescued people in great danger, administered first aid when a medic wasn't available. He'd been a Ranger, a tough guy through and through.

Why did the thought of being totally responsible for Faith and Hope put the fear of God into him?

Don't think about it, he told himself. Just do what you have to do. He couldn't deal with the reasons that were staring him right in the face. Emotions were a weakness he hadn't allowed himself since he'd been a kid. Caring about somebody meant risking being hurt and rejected. He had to find a way to take care of Faith and Hope without getting in over his head in some touchy-feely quagmire of sentimental feelings.

Chapter 5

With each passing day Faith regained her strength, but Worth insisted she not overdo. Lindsey, Jody and Margaret took turns bringing over home-cooked meals, so all Worth had to prepare was their breakfast each morning. He'd become a whiz at scrambled eggs and toast. He did all the chores, even though Faith kept insisting she could help. Keeping the apartment clean and the laundry done had been a piece of cake compared to caring for Hope. It hadn't taken him more than twenty-four hours to realize a four-month-old needed something almost continuously. He'd lost track of how many disposable diapers they'd been through in five days, how many bottles Hope had gulped down and how many miles he had walked holding her in his arms, usually in the middle of the night.

With a towel wrapped around his waist and tucked into his jeans, Worth stood at the sink, one hand supporting Hope's back while the other maneuvered a small washcloth over her soft, chubby body. She gurgled and laughed and slapped at the water in which she sat. Worth had learned the hard way that when giving Hope her bath, he'd better prepare himself for a bath, too. Her plump, dimpled hand reached for the yellow rubber duck that he'd discovered was a necessity during bath time. As he rinsed his daughter with lukewarm water, he wondered if all infants loved water the way Hope did. His little girl was definitely part fish.

"Need any help?" Faith stood in the bathroom doorway.

"Hey, there, Mommy." Worth glanced at Faith and smiled. "We're almost finished here. How about getting our towel for us?"

Faith lifted the folded hooded towel from the vanity, opened it and held it for Worth. He slipped Hope's head into the hood then wrapped her in the terry cloth and handed her to Faith.

"Can you manage her okay? She's a chunk."

"She weighed nine pounds when she was born," Faith said as she took her child and carried her into the bedroom.

Worth let the water out of the sink, dried off the vanity and set the rubber duck back in the mesh bag of bath toys hanging on the wall. When he joined mother and daughter, Faith had Hope lying on the bed with a diaper on and was struggling with the wiggling infant as she tried to pull on her one-piece pajamas.

Worth placed his hand on Faith's shoulder. "Do you realize you just remembered something else?"

"I did, didn't I? I remembered Hope weighed nine pounds when she was born." Faith sighed. "My memory is coming back in bits and pieces, not whole chunks. I recall unconnected, independent facts and incidents."

Worth squeezed her shoulder. "But every day you seem to recall more and more of these tidbits. Pretty soon those whole chunks of memory will return."

"I hope so." Faith managed to finish dressing Hope, then sat on the edge of the bed and placed Hope in her lap. "I've started keeping a list." She nodded to the dressing table under the double windows across the room. An ink pen lay atop an open notebook. "Every time I remember something, I write it down."

"That's a good idea." Worth sat beside Faith. "Doing that should help you see how much you're recovering."

"It's odd what I remember and what I don't. I remember Jody and Margaret, but my memories are of them from years ago. But I don't remember anything about Lindsey and George. Or you." When she looked at him with those luminous blue eyes, Worth could not control his reaction. From the first moment he'd looked into her eyes in a country halfway around the world, he'd felt an unbidden attraction and an instant desire to protect her.

"You've known Jody and Margaret most of your life. Those memories are returning first."

Faith shook her head. "I know Dr. Tracy said it wasn't unusual to remember my childhood first, but I've had flashes of memory about more recent events. I remember giving birth to Hope, how much she weighed, how happy I was. And I'm having quick bursts of thoughts. I see myself sitting on a park bench and it's snowing."

"I'll go to the kitchen and warm Faith's bottle." Worth rose to his feet. He wasn't sure he wanted her to remember that night.

"I should ask Jody about it—about my sitting on a bench in the snow—because I hear her voice calling my name while I'm sitting there. I wonder if it's a real memory."

"It's real," Worth said. "Let's get Hope down for the night and I'll tell you what I know about that memory."

Faith smiled. "All right."

She smiled more and more often these days; and every time she focused one of those brilliant smiles on him, he wanted to kiss her. Actually, he wanted to do a lot more than kiss her. After the first time he made love to her, he'd become addicted to Faith; and during their brief affair over a year ago, he'd made love to her several times. But Hope must have been conceived the first time, in the cave where they'd hidden from the Subrian soldiers—the one time he hadn't used a condom.

In the past year, since they'd said goodbye at the

airport in Golnar and she had concocted a plan for them to rendevous at the square in Whitewood on Christmas Eve, Worth had tried to forget Faith. He'd lost track of how many times he had fought the urge to pick up the phone and call her. And each time he had stopped just short of dialing her number. He'd convinced himself that they were better off without each other.

But for now, until she fully recovered, and he was sure she was in no danger from the maniac who had nearly killed her, Worth knew he was needed here. Faith needed him. And so did Hope.

Faith studied Worth Cordell as he laid Hope down in her crib and stood over her, a gentle, loving expression on his face. If only she could remember this man. She must have been very much in love with him. After all, they shared a child. And even without any memories of him or their love affair, Faith felt an undeniable attraction to the big man who took such good care of Hope and her. Every time she looked at him, butterflies fluttered in her tummy. His every word, every deed, every tender touch seduced her.

Not once had he mentioned loving her—now or in the past—but his actions spoke to her heart. He acted like a man in love. Why else would he be here, caring not only for his child, but for his child's mother? Sometimes when he thought she wasn't looking, Faith would catch a glimpse of Worth staring at her, a hungry longing in his eyes. Whenever he touched her, either on purpose or by accident, she felt an instantaneous connection. When she questioned him about why they weren't married, she sensed his reluctance to discuss any details of their past, so she hadn't pushed him. Soon enough she would remember everything, or so the doctor kept telling her.

Faith eased up beside Worth and placed her hand on his back. He tensed, then relaxed. It was as if her touch burned him.

"She's so very precious," Faith said as she gazed down at her sleeping daughter. "I want to remember everything about her, from the moment I knew I was pregnant."

Worth slipped his arm around Faith's waist. "When you do remember, I want you to share those memories with me. I wasn't around to share them with you."

Taking the opening he'd given her, Faith asked, "Will you tell me about my memory of sitting on the bench in the snow? There has to be a reason that it seems to be so important to me, some reason that it's my strongest memory."

Worth picked up the baby monitor, then led Faith out of the bedroom, leaving the door open behind them. When they reached the living room, he set her down on the yellow-and-blue striped sofa sleeper, where Worth slept every night. Before joining her, he placed the monitor on the oak end table to his left, then lifted his arm and spread it out across the sofa back behind Faith's head.

"When I left Golnar, you returned to your job as the nanny for Phila Constantine, to work out a two-week notice.'' Worth lifted his arm off the sofa, then rubbed the tops of his thighs nervously. He purposely avoided making eye contact with her. Faith concluded that what he was going to tell her must be difficult for him. ''At the airport in Dareh, Golnar, we said goodbye, but you came up with an idea that would give us both time to think about our feelings.''

''What sort of idea?''

''Actually it was a plan to give me time to sort through my feelings,'' Worth admitted. ''You were pretty sure of your feelings.''

''I was in love with you,'' she said, and realized she knew without a doubt how she'd felt about him. Not exactly a memory, but a certainty coming from an inner past knowledge.

He nodded. ''You said that if I—if we decided we loved each other, we'd meet in the Whitewood town square at eight o'clock on Christmas Eve. You showed up. I didn't.''

''You didn't meet me?''

''No, I...uh...I couldn't meet you. I'd gotten shot on an assignment and wound up in the hospital. I didn't regain consciousness until Christmas Day.''

''Then you called me and explained and—''

He shook his head. ''No, honey, I decided that Fate had played a hand in my decision, that I'd been right about your being better off without me in your life.''

''You didn't meet me and you didn't call me later to explain.''

''I thought I was doing the right thing,'' he told

her. "I had no idea you were pregnant. If I'd known... I'm sorry, Faith."

"Was it snowing that night, the night I waited for you?"

"Yeah, Jody said it snowed that night."

"It must have been very difficult for me. I must have expected you to show up. I had the most wonderful news to tell you, didn't I?" A vague, cloudy memory surfaced, then gradually became clearer. "I couldn't wait to go to the square that evening. It was raining, but I didn't care. I walked from the house to downtown. I knew you'd be there because I believed you loved me as much as I loved you."

Worth looked directly at Faith. "Are you actually remembering that night?"

"Yes, parts of it. I remember how I felt. I remember being very happy. And I remember the snow. It was terribly cold and I could hear the church bells chime out the hour."

"You shouldn't have waited," he told her.

"But I did wait. I waited and waited, but you didn't come." Anger combined with sadness and Faith understood she was experiencing the same emotions she'd felt that night. "I loved you so very much." Her gaze locked with his. "Did you love me? Did you love me even a little bit?"

"Faith...I..." He sat there beside her, staring at her, his mouth open, but no other words came out.

"No, you didn't love me, did you? And you don't love me now. You're here out of some misguided sense of obligation, not love."

She felt his rejection as keenly as she'd felt it that night and the pain spread through her at an alarming speed. She didn't think she could bear sitting here, so near to him, seeing the truth in his eyes.

Faith surged up off the sofa and ran toward the bedroom, then she remembered her sleeping child and turned back toward the kitchen.

Knowing she was going to cry, she didn't want to risk waking Hope. But before she reached the kitchen door, Worth caught up with her. His big hand clamped down on her shoulder. She froze instantly.

"Faith, please..."

"Please, what?"

When he grasped her shoulders and began turning her to face him, she thought about rejecting him, but something within her succumbed immediately. He didn't say anything, just looked at her. Why was it that, if this man had been little more than a stranger to her in the past and was no more than that to her now, she understood him so well? He wanted to say the right things to her, but he was afraid to speak, afraid he'd say the wrong thing and hurt her even more. He might not love her, but he cared. She was important to him—very important—whether he realized it or not.

"All my memories aren't going to be happy ones," she told him. "Some of them are bound to hurt me. Especially if...when I remember about the attack. You can't protect me from the truth." She lifted her hand and caressed his cheek. "I know you want to protect me, want to cocoon me in some safe place where I can't ever be hurt again.''

Worth said nothing for a moment, and then, as if giving into some inner struggle, he lowered his head until his lips met hers. Faith held her breath, uncertain and yet expectant. When he kissed her, she responded without giving a thought to the consequences. On some instinctive level, she remembered the feel and the taste of this man. His body heat seeped into her skin; his passion consumed her. Giving herself over to the moment, she dissolved into Worth, becoming one with him as sensation alone dominated their actions.

She could feel everything; all her senses were heightened. His mouth was warm and moist, his kiss powerful and demanding. Her body longed to know his complete possession. Whimpering, she opened her mouth, allowing him admission. His tongue thrust inside like a velvet-tipped hot poker, exploring as it raked softly against the smoothness of the interior. Tingles spiraled upward from her feminine core. Her nipples peaked. Her body pulsated with need.

It had been this way before, this overwhelming desire to be with him. With Worth. Only with Worth. He was the other half of her, a part of her soul.

But he doesn't love you, a taunting inner voice said.

Yes, he does. Yes, he does! Her heart defended him. *He loves me. He just doesn't know it yet.*

Suddenly Worth ended the kiss and gently pushed Faith away from him. After taking several deep breaths, he said, "I'm sorry, honey. I shouldn't have let things get out of hand."

"It wasn't your fault. I wanted it to happen just as much as you did."

"Yeah, I figured that out." He shoved open the kitchen door and held it for her. "How about something to drink? Some tea or cocoa or—"

Faith laid her hand on his chest; he went rigid as a stone statue. "You want to make love to me, don't you?"

"Faith…"

"Don't you?"

"Yes."

"I want us to make love," she told him. "I don't know if it's right or wrong. All I know is that…I love you. With or without my memory, my feelings are the same. During the time we've spent together, I've fallen in love with you all over again. Don't you see, that must mean we're meant to be together."

"Faith, honey, you're not fully recovered, physically, mentally or emotionally. If I took you to bed now, I'd be taking advantage of you."

She rubbed the palm of her hand over his chest, caressing the cotton material of his sweater, when what she longed to touch was his naked chest. "What are you so afraid of?"

"I don't know what you mean." He lifted her hand from his chest and gently released her.

She smiled to herself. This was the way he'd acted once before…in the cave, when she'd asked him to make love to her. He'd been afraid then, too. Afraid of her.

"I remember," she told him. "The first time we made love, I asked you and you said no, at least you did in the beginning."

"You remember?"

She nodded. "Not everything, just how reluctant you were. You were afraid to make love to me then just as you are now. You're afraid of the way I make you feel, afraid that you might love me."

"Don't do this. Don't build up some imaginary fairy-tale romance around you and me. I'm no Prince Charming, believe me. I'm the last guy a sweet, gentle, loving woman like you needs."

"Why do you say that?" She wanted to put her arms around him and hold him close, but she sensed his need to keep some physical distance between them.

"Faith, you don't know me. The real me. You never did. You have no idea what I'm capable of doing. I was a soldier, a special forces soldier. Do you know what that means? I've killed people. Men and women…" He swallowed and glanced away, focusing his gaze on the floor. "And children. Do you hear me—on my last assignment for the Rangers, I was part of an ugly battle between our guys and the native rebels. They came at us from all sides—men, women and children, some of them no more than ten or eleven."

"Oh, Worth, how terrible for you. You're such a

kind man. That type of brutal killing must have been very difficult for you.''

When she reached out to him, he grabbed her wrist and hauled her up against him. ''Damn it, Blue Eyes, don't you understand—I've been a hard-ass son of a bitch all my life. I'm a white-trash redneck from Arkansas who knew how to hot-wire a car by the time I was twelve. I'm not good or kind or caring. I'm none of those things.'' He cupped her face between his big hands. ''But God help me, I want to be. For you. And for Hope.''

''I wish you could see yourself through my eyes,'' Faith said. ''To me you are all those things—good, kind, caring, gentle and loving. Ever since I woke up in the hospital and I saw your face, I somehow knew that as long as you stayed with me, I'd be all right.''

''You see something in me that no one else ever has.'' He kissed her forehead, her cheeks and then her lips. Sweet, tender kisses, his passion held in check. ''Maybe love *is* blind.''

''I see you perfectly, Worth Cordell. I accept that you have flaws. Everyone does. Just look at me.''

''I am looking at you,'' he told her. ''All I see is how wonderful you are.''

Just when Worth's lips touched hers again, the doorbell rang. They halted before they actually kissed. Worth groaned, then slowly released her. Feeling slightly unsteady on her feet, she leaned back against the door frame.

''I'll go see who it is,'' Worth said.

She waited for him to get to the door before she

walked across the living room and came up a few feet behind him. He turned on the porch light, glanced through the peephole and then opened the door. Detective Rollins stood on her front porch.

"May I speak to you and Ms. Sheridan?" Rollins asked.

"Come on in." Worth nodded, indicating a welcome.

"Thanks." Rollins entered the living room; Worth closed the door. "I've got some bad news and I wanted to deliver it in person."

"What kind of bad news?" Faith asked as she inched her way closer to Worth.

"You might want to sit down," Rollins suggested.

"Oh, God…" Tremors shivered through Faith's body.

Worth reached out, slipped his arm around her waist and pulled her to his side. "Out with it. Can't you see you're scaring Faith."

"Sorry, ma'am. It's just I hate like the devil to have to tell you this." Rollins inhaled and exhaled deeply. "The Greenville Slayer's second victim, Gloria Clemmons, who survived the ordeal, just as you did, has been found murdered in her own home."

"How was she…" Faith's voice trailed off as tears lodged in her throat.

"Blunt trauma to the head," Rollins replied.

"Any suspects other than the obvious?" Worth asked.

Rollins shook his head.

"Why would he kill her?" Faith asked. "She couldn't identify him."

Rollins stuck his hands in his coat pockets and rocked back and forth on his heels. "We figure he came back to finish the job."

"That means...oh, Worth—" Faith buried her face against his chest as he wrapped his arms around her. "He's going to come after the other woman who survived, isn't he? And he's going to come after me."

Chapter 6

After Detective Rollins's visit three days ago, Worth and Faith had discussed the precautions they would take to keep Faith safe, but she had been adamantly opposed to leaving town with Worth. He'd wanted to whisk Faith and Hope out of harm's way and take them back to Atlanta with him. But in the rational part of his brain, he'd known what Faith had pointed out to him—that if the Greenville Slayer wanted to kill her, he'd find her no matter where she went. Rollins had hinted at using Faith as bait to catch the killer, but Worth had dismissed the idea before the detective had been able to fully explain it to Faith. She had told Rollins that she would seriously consider the idea, but no way was Worth going to let Faith put herself in more danger.

This morning they'd driven into town to finish

Christmas shopping and purchase a live Christmas tree. The big day was coming up in less than a week—Hope's first Christmas. She wasn't old enough to understand the concept of Santa Claus, but it really didn't matter. Faith and Worth were knee-deep into the Jolly Old Saint Nick fantasy. They'd practically bought out the local toy store.

This afternoon Worth had gotten up on a ladder and strung white lights across the edge of the front porch roof, as well as around several large shrubs in the front yard. Since Jody was on Christmas holiday break from her job as an elementary schoolteacher, she'd volunteered as a baby-sitter while Worth and Faith put up the tree and decorated it.

Faith stood across the room and surveyed their handiwork. "It's beautiful. All it needs is the angel on top." She lifted the tree topper from its cushioned bed in the box, then walked across the room and handed the golden-haired angel to Worth. "When I was a little girl I thought all angels had blond hair and blue eyes."

Worth leaned down from his perch on the ladder, took the angel in one hand and clutched Faith's chin with the other. "Some angels have blue eyes and dark-brown hair."

Coming in from the kitchen, with Hope on her hip, Jody cleared her throat. Faith jumped away from Worth as if she'd been caught doing something naughty.

"Oops. Sorry. Was I interrupting something?" Jody asked.

"Not a thing," Worth replied. "I was just getting ready to put the finishing touches on the tree." He placed the blond angel in the flowing white gown atop the tree. "Is she straight?"

"Perfect," Faith said.

"Hey, I was wondering if y'all want me to order pizza for supper?" Jody asked. "It's nearly five and I'm starving."

"Is it that late?" Faith checked her watch. "The day has gone by so fast." When Faith held out her arms, Hope came to her immediately. "You order the pizza and I'll fix Hope's bottle."

"We like cheese pizza," Jody said. "What do you like, Worth?"

"Meat Lovers Supreme," he said. "Order one of each. I can eat a medium all by myself."

Jody sized him up, from head to toe. "I don't doubt that for a minute."

When Faith disappeared into the kitchen, Worth stepped down off the ladder, folded it and put it away in the closet. Jody lifted the receiver and dialed the phone on the end table by the sofa. While Worth gathered up empty boxes in which Faith stored Christmas ornaments, Jody ordered supper.

Worth picked up the remote, turned on the television to check the local news and weather and laid the remote on the sofa arm. The forecasters had been predicting snow for today, but none had materialized. No snow, sleet or even rain.

"She's doing great, isn't she?" Jody plopped down

on the sofa by Worth. "She's regaining more of her memory every day."

"Yeah, she's recalling more and more about her past, her friends, Hope and even me. But she still can't remember anything about the day she was attacked."

"Maybe it's better if she never remembers," Jody said. "It's not something I'd want to remember."

"If she could ID her attacker, I'd want her to remember. That guy needs to be stopped before he kills someone else."

"I know you're concerned about what happened to that other woman, another of his victims who survived. But Faith has you to protect her. Or is that the problem—are you getting tired of hanging around, playing knight in shining armor?"

"I thought you and I had buried the hatchet," Worth said. "You still don't trust me, do you?"

"I trust you to protect Faith, but I don't quite trust you not to break her heart again."

Before Worth could reply, Faith emerged from the kitchen.

"When she finishes her bottle, I need to give Hope a quick bath and change her clothes before we leave." She handed Hope and her bottle to Worth. "I'll go get things ready, so when she's through, bring her into the bathroom."

"Where are y'all going?" Jody asked.

"We're taking Hope to the mall this evening to see Santa Claus and get her picture made with him," Faith replied. "Why don't you come with us?"

"Sure, I'd love to." Jody glanced at Worth. "That is unless I'd be a third wheel. After all, a trip to see Santa is sort of a family thing, isn't it?"

"You're family. You're Hope's Aunt Jody," Faith said as she headed toward the bedroom.

"Faith's right," Worth added. "We want you to come along."

Suddenly Worth heard the television announcer mention something about the Greenville Slayer, but since he had the sound turned down low on the TV, he didn't catch exactly what had been said. Readjusting Hope in his arms, he reached for the remote on the sofa arm, then upped the volume for the television. Before focusing his attention on the TV screen, he glanced over the sofa to Faith, who stood dead still by the open bedroom door.

"The Greenville Slayer has struck again and this time it's another repeat attack," the announcer said. "Lois Helton, the Greenville cosmetologist, who survived a brutal attack two months ago, and her husband were both shot and killed in their home today. Police estimate the murders occurred around three this afternoon. The police officer guarding Mrs. Helton was critically wounded and is not expected to survive."

"Oh, God!" Jody gasped.

"He's killed both women who survived," Faith said. "It's only a matter of time before he comes after me."

Worth checked Hope's bottle. She'd drunk three-fourths and was still guzzling away. With Hope in his arms, Worth stood and went over to Faith. He looked directly at her, his gaze demanding her eyes to meet his.

"We'll cancel the trip to see Santa," Worth said. "Next year, Hope will be over a year old and she'll enjoy getting her picture made with Santa more than she would have this year."

Faith nodded. "Does this mean I'm going to be a prisoner in my own house? I've been remembering what it felt like to be held captive in that horrible basement in Subria when I was abducted with Phila Constantine last year. It's a terrible feeling. Not one I want to experience again."

"I wish I could say that it won't be necessary to curtail all your normal activities even more than we have already, but we can't take any chances," Worth told her. "Not with your life on the line."

"It'll be only temporary. Just until the police catch the killer," Jody said, as she jumped up off the sofa and looked back and forth from Faith to Worth. "And you have a big plus the other women didn't have— you've got your own professional bodyguard right at your side."

"You're right on both counts." Faith reached out and took Hope from Worth. "I am lucky to have my own bodyguard. And this insanity isn't going to stop until the killer is caught and put behind bars."

"I know what you're thinking," Worth said. "For-get it. I won't let you do it. Do you hear me, Faith?"

Snapping her gaze back and forth from Worth to

Faith, Jody asked, "What's he talking about? What won't he let you do?"

"The police suggested setting a trap for the killer and using me as bait." Faith pressed a tender kiss on top of Hope's head.

Jody gasped. "I'm with Worth on this one. No way, Jose!"

"Can't you both see that it's the only way!"

"No it's not the only way," Jody said. "You're getting back more and more of your memory all the time. You'll probably remember the attack and be able to ID the attacker—tomorrow or the next day or—"

"Or never." Faith turned away and walked into the bedroom.

"Hell! Do something," Jody told Worth. "I know Faithie, and when she's determined, nothing can stop her."

Worth and Jody followed Faith into the bedroom. She sat down in the white rocker beside Hope's crib, removed the empty bottle from the baby's mouth and set it on the floor; then she rocked back and forth as she crooned a soft lullaby.

"You can't do it," Jody said.

"Sh— Be quiet," Faith whispered. "I don't want to discuss it. My mind's made up."

"Then unmake it," Worth told her. "Think about Hope. Think about your friends...your family."

"I am thinking about Hope and about my family. You can't guarantee me that he won't try to harm Hope. And with your standing between him and me, he could hurt you. This man won't stop killing until someone stops him.''

''Why does it have to be you?'' Jody asked.

''Because I'm the only one left. If I don't do all I can to stop him, he'll kill again and again.''

''We need to talk about this before—'' Worth said, but was interrupted by the shrill ring of the telephone. ''I'll get it.''

He stormed across the room to the phone on the nightstand, then picked up the receiver. ''Cordell here.''

''Mr. Cordell, this is Detective Rollins. I have some more bad news.''

''Yeah, we already know. Your bad news is being broadcast on all the local TV stations.''

''We're going to send a patrol car to stay outside Ms. Sheridan's apartment, around the clock, starting tonight,'' Rollins said.

''Who is it?'' Faith asked.

Worth placed his hand over the mouthpiece. ''Detective Rollins.''

''Tell him that we're coming to the police station first thing in the morning to discuss his plan.''

''No, Faith.''

''Yes, Worth.''

After removing his hand from the mouthpiece, Worth said, ''Rollins, Ms. Sheridan and I will see you in your office in the morning. She wants to discuss your plan to capture the killer.''

Worth heard Rollins's indrawn breath, then silence for a couple of minutes. ''If she agrees to do this—

to put herself directly in the line of fire—I swear to you, Cordell, I'll do everything in my power to keep her safe.''

''She's not doing this unless you agree that I'm part of the team. I want to be there, close by, participating. Not in the background.''

''I believe that can be arranged.''

Worth hung up the receiver, then turned to Faith. ''We'll have to arrange for someone to take care of Hope until this is all over.''

''I can—'' Jody said.

''No.'' Faith shook her head. ''I'll pack some of her things in the morning and we'll take her to Lindsey. She can stay with Lindsey and George until…'' Faith looked at Jody. ''You're in the apartment next door. If this guy finds out where I live, I don't want Hope anywhere around here.''

''You're right,'' Jody agreed. ''The best place for her is with George and Lindsey.''

The doorbell rang. A collective gasp filled the bedroom, then utter silence.

''You two stay here,'' Worth said, then left the bedroom and headed for the front door.

He peered through the viewfinder and saw a teenage boy carrying two boxed pizzas. A relieved sigh swept from his lungs to his lips.

After paying the delivery boy, he carried the pizza into the kitchen, then called out, ''Pizza's here. Let's eat.''

Worth ate. Jody and Faith nibbled. They tried to engage in idle chitchat, but it took more effort than it was worth to keep up the pretense of a normal evening. At eight, Jody hugged Faith and said goodnight. At eight-thirty Faith and Worth gave Hope her bath, then Worth gave her a bottle and rocked her to sleep while Faith showered and got ready for bed.

By nine-thirty Worth was sacked out on the sofa bed in the living room. The latest David Baldacci bestseller he was trying to read wasn't doing much to help take his mind off the reality of Faith's situation. He wasn't Faith's husband, but did that mean he didn't have a right to be part of the decision making? He cared about Faith and the thought of her dying scared the hell out of him. Hope needed her mother. Faith's friends needed her. The whole world needed a kind, caring person like Faith.

And you need her, an inner voice told him. *Faith has become very important to you, as vital to you as the air you breathe.*

Worth slammed the book shut and tossed it aside, then slid down until his head hit the pillows. After turning out the lamp on the end table, he pulled the covers to his neck and stared up at the dark ceiling. He lay there listening to the quiet sounds of night. Solitude. Loneliness. He felt both, despite being a part of Faith's life. He had lived with solitude and loneliness since he'd been a kid. When his mother died and his father remarried, he'd been alone. He might have lived with his father and stepmother, but he'd never been a part of their family. The only family he'd ever had was his half sister and he'd lost her years ago. A drug overdose at a wild college party. He hadn't loved anyone since he lost Norma.

He hadn't meant to care so much about Faith, but little by little he'd fallen under her spell. And she had turned to him these past couple of weeks for protection and emotional support, just as she'd done when he'd rescued her in Subria. She'd called her feelings love then and she believed herself in love with him now. But Worth had his doubts. Somewhere in that gentle heart of hers she had confused hero-worship with love. Faith needed him; but did she really love him?

And then there was Hope. His daughter. He'd never thought about fathering a child and had been careful to always practice safe sex—except that one time with Faith. Maybe he should regret the fact that he'd gotten Faith pregnant, but how could he? That tiny baby girl had wrapped him around her little finger. Whenever he looked at her, his heart swelled with love. He was glad to be Hope's father. He loved her and wanted to be a part of her life from now on.

But what about Faith? *Admit the truth,* he told himself. *You want to be a part of Faith's life, too.*

An earsplitting scream surged from the bedroom and reverberated through the house. Worth bounded out of bed and raced toward the bedroom, his only thought was to reach Faith and Hope. Hope's whimpers burst into gulping cries. With his heart racing like mad, he skidded to a halt when he saw Faith sitting straight up in bed, a look of sheer terror on her face. He rushed to her, grabbed her shoulders and shook her gently.

"What's wrong?" he asked.

She flung her arms around him. "A nightmare. A terrifying nightmare."

Worth soothed her, stroking her back and whispering reassurances. "It's okay. It's okay."

The phone rang. Hope cried louder and louder.

"You get Hope," Faith said. "I'll answer the phone."

When Faith picked up the phone, Worth headed toward Hope's crib in the corner of the bedroom. As he lifted his daughter into his arms and placed her on his shoulder, he heard Faith reassuring Jody that everything was all right, telling her that she'd simply had a nightmare. Worth walked the floor with Hope, humming to her as he patted her back. His big hand covered her upper torso. She was tiny and helpless— and his. Did every father feel this way—loving, possessive and protective?

In his peripheral vision he noticed Faith get out of bed and head for the bathroom. He laid Hope in her crib and rocked her back and forth until her droopy eyelids closed.

"Go back to sleep, sweetheart. Daddy's here and everything is all right." He bent over the crib and kissed his daughter's forehead. "I need to take care of your mama now."

He met Faith as she came out of the bathroom, her face moist and her hair slightly damp. "Are you really okay?"

She nodded. "A splash of cold water in my face helped."

"You should go back to bed and try to rest."

She crawled into bed, then held out her hand to him. "Stay with me. Please."

"Faith, I'm not so sure it's a good idea."

She smiled faintly. "I seem to remember your saying something like that once before, or is my memory wrong?"

Worth sat down on the edge of the bed. "Do you remember that night?"

"Most of it. I remember how dark the cave was and how cold I felt…until I curled up to your back. Then I got hot pretty fast."

"You were a regular hussy." He reached out and pushed several loose strands of her hair away from her face. "Want to tell me about the dream?"

"He killed me. In my dream, he killed me."

"Faith…" Worth scooted over in the bed and pulled Faith into his arms. "He's not going to kill you. Whatever happens, I'll be there to take care of you."

She wrapped her arms around his waist and snuggled close, burrowing her nose against his neck. "How could you have ever thought I would be better off without you?"

"We shouldn't let this happen again," he told her, but made no move to release her. "You were afraid of dying that night, when I made love to you for the first time. And now, tonight, you—"

"Hush." Lifting her head from his shoulder, she

placed her index finger over his lips. "I seem to recall that we made love several times after we were rescued. We couldn't get enough of each other. Those memories are coming back to me now and I know how much I loved you then...and how much I love you now."

"But Faith..."

She tapped her finger on his lips. "It's all right. You don't have to say you love me. For some reason, you find it difficult to say the words. But I know how you feel. Your actions—in the past and in the present—have proven to me how much I mean to you."

She brought her arms up and around his neck, then pressed her body to his. He couldn't deny that he cared about her because he did. And he couldn't turn away from the need he saw in her eyes. She wanted him the same way he wanted her.

He spread kisses in her hair, over her face, down her neck. "I'll try to be gentle. I don't want to hurt you."

She sought his mouth, then whispered against his lips. "Don't hold back. Make love to me the way you did before. I know you won't hurt me."

He laid her back into the mattress and came down over her, bracing himself with his knees as he kissed her. The kiss grew hotter, wilder and more intense. They devoured each other, hunger urging them to take everything, to enjoy every millisecond of their passion. Faith's fingers skimmed his chest with inquisitive touches, acquainting herself with every inch of flesh, every muscle. With unsteady hands, he reached between them and unbuttoned her pajama top, then spread it apart to reveal her small, high breasts. When his lips suckled one tight nipple, she moaned; when he licked and stroked the other nipple, her hips rose off the bed. With her mound pressed against his erection, she wriggled and squirmed, rubbing herself up and down in an enticing manner.

"Keep doing that and I'm going to lose it before I'm inside you," Worth murmured against her ear, then grasped the waistband of her pajama bottoms and tugged.

She lifted her hips enough for him to easily maneuver the pajamas down her legs and over her feet. As he tossed the pajamas to the foot of the bed, he kissed her again. Deeply. Savagely. And when she gasped for air, he painted a trail from mouth to breasts. She whimpered and writhed beneath him. His tongue slid over her rib cage, down her belly to her navel. She held her breath. He moved southward, pausing at the edge of her triangle of dark hair. When his mouth captured her tenderness, his hands covered her breasts and kneaded, then tweaked her nipples.

Faith keened deep in her throat when his tongue delved and retreated, then delved deeper. He found her most sensitive spot and stroked her, harder and harder, until she clutched his head and held him in place while he finished the job. He felt her body tighten; he worked harder and faster. Faith cried out as her climax splintered through her. While she was in the throes of fulfillment, Worth rose up and over her, took her slender hips in his hands, lifted her and thrust his sex to the hilt within her.

As he hammered into her, seeking his own satisfaction, she clung to him and within minutes began undulating to the rhythm he'd set. When the moment came, his ears rang and his body trembled from the force of his release. But before the pleasure subsided, Faith reached the pinnacle a second time. As the aftershocks rippled through them, Worth fell exhausted into the bed beside Faith, pulled her into his arms and lifted the sheet and comforter to cover them. She snuggled against him.

"I love you," she whispered a moment before she fell asleep in his arms.

Chapter 7

They dropped Hope by Lindsey and George Dawson's before heading out to the police station. Worth had done everything in his power to dissuade Faith from offering herself as bait in the police's trap, but she'd been unmovable in her conviction that it was the only way to regain control over her life. He understood how much that meant to Faith, especially since her captivity in Subria last year. Nothing made a person want to exert control over their life as much as having all power taken from them.

Detective Rollins met them at the door to his office and welcomed them, then ordered coffee.

"Detective MacMillan from Sparkman, Detective Roberts from Greenville and Agent Colter from the state bureau will be working with us on this plan," Rollins said. "I'm expecting all of them here by ten this morning. I'd rather wait until they arrive before we discuss the details.''

''That's fine with me,'' Faith said. ''I—'' She glanced at Worth. ''We don't mind waiting.''

''None of us like the idea of using you to lure this guy into our trap,'' Rollins said, ''but we admit that the law enforcement of three towns and the state of South Carolina are no closer to nabbing the Greenville Slayer now than we were right after the first murder.''

''I intend to play a vital role in any scenario that requires Faith to risk her life.'' Worth reached across from his chair to Faith's and grabbed her hand.

''You'll have to humor him.'' Faith squeezed Worth's hand. ''It's the only way I could get him to stop fighting me about my decision. If Worth isn't involved, then neither am I.''

''Your assistance isn't needed and won't be appreciated.'' Rollins's gaze met Worth's. ''But I've given you my word. I'll explain to the others that your involvement isn't debatable.''

''I'm not exactly a civilian,'' Worth said. ''I know how to conduct myself under dangerous conditions.''

''I had you checked out, Cordell. I know your background.''

One of the police officers brought a tray laden with coffee cups into Rollins's office and offered a cup first to Faith and then to Worth.

Rollins glanced through the open doorway as he lifted his cup from the tray. ''I see our team has arrived a little early.''

Worth and Faith followed Rollins's line of vision. Three men in plainclothes stood outside the office. Rollins motioned to them.

"Come on in. Ms. Sheridan is already here."

The threesome entered, Rollins made introductions and once they were seated, Agent Carter laid out a simple yet potentially dangerous plan.

"There's a good chance this guy is already keeping tabs on Ms. Sheridan," Carter said. "If he is, he's aware she's never alone, that you're with her at all times and a police car is stationed in front of her apartment."

"Lois Helton's husband was with her when she was killed," Worth reminded them.

"Lois Helton's husband was sixty-five years old," Detective MacMillan said. "If this guy's gotten a good look at you, Cordell, he's probably been intimidated by your size alone."

"Bottom line is we have to make it appear that Faith is alone," Agent Carter said. "It's probably the only way to bring him out into the open. And we believe if she goes alone to Toddle Town on some pretense, he'll be less suspicious than he would if it appeared you'd left her alone at her apartment."

The minute Worth heard the details, his survival instincts kicked in. He didn't like the sound of it. It wasn't a bad plan and the odds were they'd catch their guy; but there was a downside—they couldn't give Worth a hundred percent guarantee they could keep Faith safe.

"You want me to go to Toddle Town alone?" Faith asked.

"We'll send a policewoman with you," Detective Roberts said. "She'll wear street clothes and you two can act like a couple of old friends. We'll have Toddle Town under surveillance and our men will already be in place when this guy follows you there."

"What makes you think he's watching me? And if he is, why do you think he'll follow me?" Faith looked around the room at each lawman.

"We don't know for sure, and it might take more than one try for this plan to work," Rollins explained. "If you'll go to Toddle Town every day at the same time, stay for say two hours and then go home, it will set up a routine and make our killer less suspicious. If he's watching you—and the odds are that he is— he might keep tabs on your activities for several days or even a week or so before he strikes. And by setting the trap at Toddle Town, we know it's a place he's familiar with. It's where he abducted you the first time."

Faith turned to Worth. "What do you think?"

"It's too dangerous. I don't like it."

"Other than that, what do you think? It's a good plan, isn't it?"

"If we don't factor in the possibility that you could get killed, yeah, it's a good plan."

Faith looked at Rollins. "When do we start?"

"How about late this afternoon?"

"That soon?" Faith sucked in a deep breath. "All right. Let's do it."

* * *

Six days until Christmas. On day one, Faith and policewoman Dale Carruthers drove up in Faith's SUV, parked and headed straight to Toddle Town's front entrance. They carried on a conversation, both appearing perfectly natural; Faith even managed a realistic-sounding laugh. Once inside, they set about taking down Christmas decorations and straightening up the individual rooms. They spent two hours trying to act as if they weren't waiting for a killer to strike. Since the high temperature for the day was supposed to be thirty-four, it had been easy enough to hide the bulletproof vests they wore beneath bulky sweaters. SWAT team members were stationed across the street in the upstairs of a dry cleaners and various police officers joined the downtown Christmas crowds on Hickory Avenue. Disguised as a city work crew repairing a broken pipe line, Worth, Rollins and Macmillan stood around in coveralls and thick jackets, their bulletproof vests and their 9 mm weapons well out of sight.

After two hours, Faith and Dale locked the front door and walked to the SUV. No sign of their guy. Five minutes later, the fake work crew got in a city truck and drove away. Worth didn't like the fact that there would be a good fifteen minute interval when he wouldn't be with Faith. He knew that Officer Carruthers was well trained to defend Faith, but his gut instincts warned him that no one, not even the entire SWAT team, could protect Faith the way he could. Hell, it wasn't personal to anyone else.

And the fact that it was personal for him was as much a disadvantage as an advantage. The minute he saw Faith in imminent danger, not only would his trained instincts kick in, but so would his natural emotional instincts. It was as basic as the fact he would be protecting his woman and not a client.

Day two came and went in pretty much the same manner as day one, without even a hint of their killer being in Whitewood, let alone him following Faith.

Day three. Saturday. Another no-show. Tensions mounted for everyone involved. Worth could see how nervous Faith was and how valiantly she tried to hide it. They took a day off on Sunday. Worth attended church with Faith and Hope, which was a strange event for him. He hadn't been inside a church since his mother died when he was six. After church they ate lunch at the Dawsons', joined by Margaret and Mr. Tippins, as well as Jody and Jody's on-again/off-again boyfriend, Tommy Kenyon. Old Horace, the Dawsons' beagle, slept soundly in front of the fire the entire time.

Later on at home, while Hope took a late afternoon nap, Worth made slow, sweet love to Faith. Although Hope had stayed with Lindsey for the past few days, Worth and Faith decided to bring her home with them today. Each moment they shared together as a family became more precious with each passing day. Tomorrow afternoon, they would return Hope to the Dawsons. Three days of nerve-racking waiting had taken a toll on both Faith and Worth. He wasn't sure how much longer either of them could endure the uncertainty.

In the aftermath of lovemaking, they lay in bed together, naked and sated. Worth idly stroked Faith's slender hip.

"I remember so much about my life," Faith said. "Almost everything."

"But not the attack?"

"I remember everything that day, up to when I locked the door to Toddle Town and walked toward the parking area. Then it's all a blank until I woke up in the hospital."

"What about everything before then—from your childhood up to that day?"

"I still have a few holes in my memory, but not many. It's odd, but I still can't recall everything about the night I waited for you in the square. I remember going to the square. I can hear the church bells and even see the snow, but I don't remember leaving the square and going home. I've lost several days there, maybe even a week or so. I remember being in the hospital after Christmas. I think I had pneumonia. Is that right?"

"Didn't Jody tell you about—"

"Jody told me she thought it was best if I waited for my memories to return instead of her filling in the blanks."

Worth pulled Faith to him and kissed her. "Jody's right. Give it a little more time. You'll remember."

He hoped she never remembered all the details of the night she had waited for him for four hours. He couldn't bear the thought of her experiencing that kind of emotional pain again. If her memories of that night remained vague, he knew that sooner or later, he'd have to tell her. But selfishly, he wanted it to be later. A part of him feared that when she recalled all the details, she would hate him and not be able to forgive him for disappointing her.

Three days to Christmas. Faith spent Monday morning wrapping presents and trying her best to pretend her life was normal. She'd put on a CD of *All Time Favorites* and the mellow voice of Bing Crosby crooning "White Christmas" filled her apartment. The aroma of gingerbread cookies baking in the oven wafted out of the kitchen and a spicy scent permeated the air. Worth sat on the pallet on the living room floor with Hope, watching her waver back and forth as she shook the rattle in her hand. Faith loved seeing Worth with his daughter; she could tell by his every action that he adored their child. But her big, strong, macho guy couldn't put his feelings into words. She knew, in her heart of hearts, that Worth loved them. Even if he didn't know it yet; even if it took him a while longer to come to terms with emotions alien to him.

Worth lifted Hope into his arms and stood, then walked over to the sofa where Faith sat with a gift box half-wrapped in bright-red paper. "If this afternoon's stint at Toddle Town is a bust, I want you to put an end to it. We've all given it our best shot. This guy has eluded the law for months now, which means he's not stupid. He's probably suspicious about why I'm letting you go to Toddle Town every day without me.''

''We can't give up.'' Faith clipped off a piece of tape and used it to secure the folded edges of her package. ''Today could be the day he shows up. Or tomorrow.''

''Or next week or next month? Honey, you can't keep doing this day after day. It's going to wear you down.''

''What's our alternative?''

''I get Dom Shea back here and we keep you and Hope under guard 24/7 until the police nab this guy.''

Faith placed the wrapped gift atop the stack she'd made in the floor in front of the sofa. ''For how long? We can't live that way indefinitely. Besides, I'm not doing this just for myself, you know. I'm putting myself out there as bait so we can stop this lunatic before he kills another woman.''

Suddenly a loud singsong siren went off. Faith stilled instantly. A smoke detector. The kitchen? Were the cookies burning? Then she realized it wasn't her smoke detector. The sound wasn't loud enough.

''That must be Jody's smoke detector,'' Faith said. ''You'd better go check it out. I'm pretty sure she spent the night with Tommy last night and probably isn't home yet.''

''You stay here.'' Worth handed Hope to Faith. ''I'll check it out. Where's your key to Jody's apartment?''

''I don't have a key,'' Faith said. ''Jody keeps an

extra taped to the back of the wreath on the front door.''

''I'll have to talk to her about leaving a key where just anybody could find it.'' Worth went to the closet, got his jacket, then checked the pocket for his Glock. After slipping into the jacket, he headed for the door. ''Lock the door behind me and don't open it to anyone except me. Not even Officer Deloney out there.'' Worth nodded to the unmarked vehicle across the street.

''Do you think—''

''I don't think anything in particular,'' he told her. ''Just lock the door.''

As soon as Worth went outside, she closed the door behind him and locked it.

''Well, Miss Sweetie Pie, let's go check on those cookies while your daddy's gone.''

Faith entered the kitchen, placed Hope in her bouncy seat in the middle of the table, then picked up her oven mitts and put them on. Just as she bent over to open the oven door, she heard a loud crash. Her first thought was that Worth had broken something next door. Gasping, she jerked around to check on Hope. In her peripheral vision, she caught a glimpse of the back door to her apartment. Something had shattered the glass pane.

Oh, God! Oh, God! Faith dashed toward Hope, grabbing her, just as a hand reached through the empty space where the glass had been. The gloved hand twisted the doorknob. They kept the door deadbolt locked and the key was on the kitchen counter.

With her heartbeat thundering in her ears, Faith started to run toward the living room. A gunshot rang out. A bullet whizzed over her head and entered the wall. Faith dropped to her knees, cradling Hope in front of her. Another shot ripped into the floor not a foot from Faith. She began crawling on her knees, trying to place herself out of the shooter's line of vision.

Worth stood in Jody's kitchen gazing at the open back door when he heard the crash. He was halfway out the door when he heard the gunshots. Damn! Racing outside onto the back porch, his thoughts jumbled with fear, recriminations and pure rage, Worth saw the man shooting through the broken pane in Faith's back door. Then he heard the scream! His blood ran cold. Faith screaming in agony.

Worth pulled out his Glock, prepared himself for battle and charged. The guy spun around, his eyes wild as he scowled at Worth.

"You're too late. She's dead," the gunman said. "And you're next."

An evil, crazed grin spread across the guy's face as he pointed his pistol at Worth. Thank you, Worth thought. Thank you for making it so easy for me to kill you, you son of a bitch!

Before the killer got off another shot, Worth aimed and fired. The bullet hit the guy right between the eyes. He reeled backward and fell onto the porch in a dead heap. Worth barely glanced at him as he rushed past and into the house. When he saw Faith sprawled out on the floor, facedown, his heart stopped.

No, please, God, no!

He ran across the room, dropped down on his haunches and grasped Faith's shoulder. She grunted, then rolled over, Hope still secure in her arms. Hope yelled at the top of her lungs.

"Where are you hit?" Worth asked. "Just lie still. I'll call 911."

"I'm all right. I don't know how he kept missing me, but he did. He didn't shoot me." Faith held Hope out to Worth. "Take her while I stand up."

A sense of unparalleled relief washed over Worth, a tidal wave of thankfulness. With one hand he lifted Hope up and braced her on his hip, then reached down, grabbed Faith's arm and pulled her to her feet. He wrapped mother and daughter in his arms.

Officer Deloney came running around the side of the house, his pistol drawn. The minute he saw the dead man sprawled out on the porch, he skidded to a halt.

"Is everybody okay?" Deloney asked.

"We're safe," Faith said as she clung to Worth. "Finally, we're safe."

Chapter 8

The police, an ambulance and a fire truck showed up after Officer Deloney put in a 911 call. Before the first emergency vehicle pulled into the driveway, every neighbor within two city blocks showed up in the yard. Although Faith insisted she was perfectly fine, Worth demanded she allow the paramedics to check her.

"Really, Worth, I'm all right," Faith insisted, but her voice quivered slightly. If Worth didn't have his arm around her waist, she wasn't sure she could stand.

"Either you let them check you out or I'm taking you straight to the hospital right now." She gazed up at Worth and realized how deadly serious he was. His tense, strained expression told her he was fighting to control his emotions.

Worth kept gently jostling Hope in an effort to

soothe her. Her yelping cries had softened to sobbing whimpers.

"All right," Faith agreed. "But first, let me sit down before I fall down."

George and Lindsey Dawson came rushing in the back door, allowed entrance by their nephew, one of Whitewood's policemen.

"Merciful heavens," Lindsey said. "Are y'all okay?" She glanced from Faith to Hope to Worth. "Give me that baby and you see to Faith. She looks like she's about to keel over."

Without hesitation Worth handed his daughter to her honorary grandmother, then caught Faith in his arms just as she swooned in a faint.

"Damn," Worth cursed under his breath.

"Poor thing," George said. "She's been through so much. That child deserves nothing but happiness for the rest of her life. Nobody should have to experience so much tragedy in one lifetime."

Worth turned to the two paramedics standing in the kitchen. "I'll put her in the ambulance and ride along with y'all. And I'd suggest we get going before she comes to." He turned and looked at Hope nestled securely in Lindsey's loving arms. "Take care of—"

George slapped his hand down on Worth's back. "No need to tell us to take good care of Hope. We'll bring her on to the E.R. and wait with you until the doctor checks Faith out."

"Thanks. I don't know what Faith and Hope would do without you two."

Worth carried Faith through the house and out onto

the front porch. Suddenly the throng of neighbors congregated in the yard quieted and every eye focused on them. Inquiries buzzed from various lips. "Is she all right? Was she shot? What can we do to help? We'll pray for her. We care so much about Faith."

Just as one of the paramedics opened the back doors to the ambulance, a sleek, silver sports car skidded to a halt on the street in front of the duplex. Jody jumped out of the Corvette and flew across the yard, parting the crowd like Moses parting the Red Sea.

"Faith, Faith, Faith!" Jody screamed. "Oh, God, Worth, what happened? Is she—?"

"She's all right," Worth said. "She fainted. I think she may be suffering from a mild case of shock. We're taking her to the E.R. to get checked out. Lindsey and George are bringing Hope."

"What the hell happened?" Jody asked, her voice tinged with hysteria.

One of the paramedics interrupted. "Sir, we're ready to go."

Worth crawled into the back of the ambulance, laid Faith on the gurney, sat beside her, then looked back at Jody. "Get Tommy to bring you to Memorial and I'll fill you in on the details. But don't worry about the guy who tried to kill Faith. He's dead."

Jody's mouth gaped open. "Oh. You—you—?"

"Yeah," Worth replied just as a paramedic closed the ambulance door.

When the ambulance was only minutes from her apartment, Faith roused and looked up at Worth. "Where's Hope…what—?"

When she tried to sit up, Worth grasped her shoulders, forcing her to stay put. "Lie still, Blue Eyes. Hope's fine. She's with Lindsey and George. You've had quite a scare. You need to relax and stay calm."

"Me?" Faith smiled. "Worth Cordell, you're the one who needs to relax and stay calm."

"I am perfectly calm," Worth said through clenched teeth.

"No, you're not, so don't try to lie to me. I can see the expression on your face and in your eyes. I know you well enough to be able to read what those brown eyes of yours are saying."

"Damn it, Faith, what do you expect? I'm not going to fall apart on you just because I'm still shaking like a leaf inside. When I realized there was no fire in Jody's apartment, that somebody had gotten into her place and set off the alarm as a distraction to get me away from you—" Worth clutched his knees tightly as he leaned over the stretcher on which Faith lay. "If anything had happened to you…" He swallowed hard and glanced away.

Hope lifted her hand and laid it atop his on his knee. "You saved me…again. It seems to be your fate to be my hero. I guess I'm just one of those women who needs her own personal protector."

Worth gazed deeply into Faith's blue, blue eyes. He'd never cared as much for another human being as he did Faith and the intensity of his emotions scared him. He'd never been in love, not really. Just a teenage infatuation that had gone bad. He wasn't sure he knew what being in love was all about. What he felt for Faith was the most powerful emotion he'd ever known. Possessiveness, protectiveness and a huge dose of pure male lust. When he was near her, he wanted to look at her, touch her, taste her, absorb her. No matter how many times he made love to her, he wanted her again. He realized that he could never get enough of her. But was what he felt real love? Hell, if it wasn't, it was the closest thing to love he'd ever felt.

"You've gotten awfully quiet," Faith said as she lay there looking up at him. "You're not worrying about me, are you?"

"Just thinking," he replied.

"About what?"

"About us."

"Oh."

"Be quiet and rest until we get to the hospital. We'll have plenty of time to talk later." When she nodded, Worth took her hand in his. "Everything is going to be fine."

"As long as you're with me."

A tinge of uncertainty alerted Worth to his deepest fears. Did Faith love him or was she mistaking her need for a protector with genuine love?

In less than ten minutes the paramedics unloaded Faith and carried her into the emergency room at Memorial Hospital. Worth followed, staying as close to Faith as possible. By the time the doctor had given Faith a clean bill of health, Jody and Tommy, Lindsey and George, with Hope, as well as Margaret had arrived at the E.R. and were congregated in the waiting area.

"I'm perfectly all right," Faith announced as she held out her arms for Hope.

"That's just what we wanted to hear," Margaret said.

When Faith brought Hope close and kissed her rosy cheeks, Worth put his arm around Faith.

"Y'all are coming home with us," George said. "We've got plenty of room in our big old house and we can go get anything you need from the apartment."

"Oh," Faith sighed. "I guess we can't go home right now, can we? Do you suppose the police are still there?"

"They might be," Worth said. "But even if they aren't, there's no way we'll be going back to that apartment."

Faith shivered. "You're right. I don't think I can ever go back into the kitchen without thinking about…"

"Let's get you to the house," Lindsey said. "I have a nice pot roast cooking and I made a fresh sweet potato pie this morning."

George chuckled. "My wife thinks all of life's problems can be solved with a good, hardy meal."

Lindsey glanced around at Margaret, Jody and Tommy. "Y'all are invited to come to supper, too. After a day like this, we should all be together."

An odd sensation seeped through Worth, a bittersweet realization that for the first time since he'd been a small child, he was part of a family. Faith's family. And he didn't want to lose that good feeling, didn't want to lose Faith and Hope.

Faith doesn't need you now, an inner voice reminded him. *She got along for the past year without you and if you left today, she'd get by just fine.* But what about Hope? Every child needs a father. But he couldn't use Hope as an excuse to remain in Faith's life.

"What are we waiting for?" Margaret asked. "I've got my car here. Faith, you and Worth and Hope can ride with me." She turned to George. "Get Hope's car seat for me."

In no time at all the entire group arrived at the Dawsons' home. Cars lined their driveway. Faith was seated in a big recliner in the den and Hope stayed in her mother's lap while the other ladies put supper on the table. Just as George brought Worth and Tommy a bottled beer apiece, Detective Rollins showed up at the front door and asked to speak to Worth.

Worth stayed in the foyer, keeping his voice low during their brief conversation.

"We'll need you to come down to the station. Later tonight if possible," Rollins said. "There's no doubt in anyone's mind that you killed the guy in self defense, but—"

"I understand," Worth replied. "I've been through this before. In my profession, being willing to kill to protect a client is part of the job."

"How's Faith doing?"

"Truth be told, I think she's doing better than I."

Rollins nodded. "It's rough on a man to see the woman he loves at risk. Thank God you were there with her."

Worth walked the detective out to his car, then joined the others in the dining room for a late supper.

"We'll all have Christmas here," Lindsey said. "George and I will bring your gifts from your place over here and put them under our tree tomorrow."

"This is Hope's first Christmas, so I want everything to be perfect," Faith said.

Margaret patted Faith's hand. "We'll make sure the day is perfect for Hope."

Worth noted that Faith hadn't touched her meal. She had simply moved the food around on her plate. She was such a tiny thing, slender and delicate. Something in him—that caring, protective part of him—wanted to spoon-feed her, but he knew she'd veto the idea.

Later that evening while Faith settled into bed in the Dawsons' guest room, Worth helped Lindsey give Hope her evening bath.

"Why don't you settle down in that rocking chair with her?" Lindsey suggested. "I'll warm her bottle and bring it to you."

An hour later, long after Hope had finished her milk, Worth sat in the semidark room, slowly rocking his daughter and humming softly to her. Faith had fallen asleep within minutes of going to bed, her sleep the results of a mild sedative given to her in the E.R. Worth rose from the rocker, placed Hope in the crib that Lindsey kept at her house, then walked down the hall to find his hosts.

Undoubtedly everyone else had gone home; he found George and Lindsey alone in the den. When he entered the room, they both glanced up at him.

"Are our girls asleep?" George asked.

Worth nodded.

"I've made up the bed for you in our elder son's old room," Lindsey said.

"That's mighty kind of you," Worth replied. "But I won't be staying tonight. I've got some things I need to do."

"You aren't leaving," Lindsey said, alarm in her voice.

"Now, honey…" George cautioned her not to interfere.

"I'll be back," Worth said. "In the morning, tell Faith that I'll see her tomorrow night. Tell her to meet me in the town square at eight o'clock."

"Oh, my." Tears gathered in Lindsey's eyes. "You're going to…oh, Worth, what a sweet thing to do."

"I have a great deal to make up for…to Faith and to Hope. Tomorrow night, we'll start all over again. And this time I'm going to do it right."

With Hope bundled in a pink snowsuit, Faith entered the town square at seven-fifty. She knew that her family was across the street, waiting and watching from the storefront windows at Margaret's Goodies. Faith's heart beat wildly as she headed toward the bench where she'd sat and waited for Worth a year ago tonight. As she drew closer, she saw him approaching from the other side of the square. Worth Cordell was the best-looking man on earth. Big, tall, rugged. And about as masculine as a man could be. The closer he came, the more erratic her heart beat. She increased her pace, as did he, until they were practically running toward each other. When only a couple of feet separated them, they both stopped abruptly; their gazes locked and held.

"Hello, Blue Eyes."

"Hello."

"You told me that if I realized I loved you, then I should meet you here tonight," he said.

"Yes, I did, didn't I?"

"Well, I'm here. And I love you, Faith."

She swallowed tears of happiness. This was the moment she had been waiting for, dreaming of, for what seemed like a lifetime. "You know I love you. I have since that first night we were together."

Worth delved his hand into his coat pocket and brought out a tiny jeweler's box, flipped open the lid and held it out to Faith.

The marquise-cut diamond solitaire shimmered in the muted glow from the streetlights in the square. For a split second, her heart stopped.

"Will you marry me?" he asked. "Marry me as soon as possible."

"Oh, Worth. Yes, yes, I'll marry you."

When Worth opened his arms, she walked into his embrace. He slipped the glove off her left hand, then removed the ring from the box and slid it onto her third finger. With Hope snuggled between them, Worth leaned down and kissed Faith. Hope squirmed and whimpered.

"I think she's trying to tell us that we're smothering her." Faith laughed.

Worth chuckled as he took his daughter, held her up so that her cheek lay on his shoulder; then he draped his arm around Faith's waist and led her through the square. Just as they neared the street, snowflakes began falling. Tiny flakes at first, but they soon grew larger and more dense. By the time they walked across the street, the snow had already begun to stick to the grass.

"This is the happiest moment of my life," Faith said.

Worth halted, kissed Hope's cheek, then kissed Faith again. "Mine, too. And I promise you that I'm going to do everything I can to make sure the rest of your life is filled with happiness."

"How could it be anything but happy, with the three of us together. And who knows, maybe by this time next year, we could give Hope a baby brother."

"Are we planning on having a large family?" Worth asked.

"How does three children sound to you?"

"It sounds just fine to me. I've found out with Hope that I like being a daddy."

Faith snuggled against Worth, then whispered, "Margaret has a little party planned for us at her shop, but act surprised when we walk in and everyone is there.''

''Sounds like your family was pretty sure of me.''

''Oh, Worth, my darling, everyone, including me, knew that you loved me. You were the only one who seemed to be clueless.''

''I always was a slow learner,'' he said. ''But once I learn a lesson, I never forget it.''

Worth, Faith and Hope entered Margaret's Goodies and found their family waiting to celebrate with them. They drank hot chocolate, sang Christmas carols and stood by the windows watching a white blanket of new-fallen snow cover the town of Whitewood.

This Christmas was only the beginning, the first magical moments of happiness destined to last a lifetime.

* * * * *

THE THIRD CHRISTMAS
Margot Early

* * *

PROLOGUE

Santa Barbara Harbor
December 6
Three years past—the year without Christmas

DIVE CONDITIONS were bad. Immersed in the murk, his view constrained by the edges of his scuba mask, he watched the dark unidentifiable shadows beneath the ship and the docks. There was nothing there, neither shark nor mariner's ghost nor the other thing, and yet he watched, afraid it would come back. Watching helped him forget the tangible threat, the police diver at his elbow. But that was all he could forget.

Behind his eyes, the colors came—brown mostly. Stormy charcoal green. Red. His heart started screaming again, and his breaths grew shallow.

The scene changed, a bad cut, and through his mind reeled the old scratchy film of unwanted remembrance, set against an unchanging backdrop. The arctic seascape that haunted his dreams. Icy abyss as far as he could see. Cold, so cold. *Full fathom five, thy father lies....* And mother.

And now, thought David, my lover. Skye—my wife, my hell.

The shriek rose inside him again, and he quelled it. He concentrated on trying to drive some warmth into his limbs. Even underwater, he knew it was December. The temperature of the harbor was indifferent to shock and horror, and he was cold, but he wouldn't leave while the divers worked under his ship, while they might find something.

Listening tensely to the whooshing and bubbling of his regulator and the endless creaking of the docks, he sought another distraction. The dark void with its specters and its taunts offered too little, and too much, and her voice wouldn't leave him.

Death is a wild night, David, and a new road. I'm not afraid of death.

God, she should have been, with her damned Emily Dick-inson quotes.

He should have been.

David peered through the soupy water at the police team searching the three-foot screws beneath his ship. They had found something.

Physically, he felt no reaction. His heart had never stopped pounding, nor his mind racing, not for hours. Psychically, he felt a flicker of fear.

He was twenty-eight years old, and today he had become a veteran of an ugly war. Whatever was in the props couldn't be worse than what he'd already seen. But he didn't want to see any more.

Still, he kicked toward the blades.

Immediately one of the divers turned, holding up two hands. *Stay back.*

He stopped, wondering what they would do if he suddenly dove. He knew the harbor better than they did. He could get away. Maybe.

But he had no intention of fleeing, nor of spending his life as a fugitive. Chris needed him, this minute and for years to come. For now, David was glad Jake had taken him down to the marine supply, away from the cops. It was Saturday and Santa Claus was on hand at the wharf, but

Chris had received that news with apathy. David didn't blame him.

What goes through a three-year-old's mind at a time like this? he wondered. Nothing that would be improved by seeing his father handcuffed and marched away.

David doubted that would happen, but he hadn't been willing to chance Chris's witnessing such a drama. He'd already seen more than anyone ever should. For a moment, David envisioned detectives grilling his son and felt impotent rage. Could it happen?

They have nothing, he told himself again. Not even a body, and they wouldn't get one. He wasn't a prisoner, and he wouldn't be.

The anger surged through him again, mingling with other emotions he didn't want to touch with a ten-foot pole. *How had it happened?*

The panic returned, a baseball-size thing in his throat, alien to him as fear. The colors came back. The shape in the water coming at him.

A diver at the keel was swept to one side by the power of the current, and David refocused on the police operation, his view now unobstructed.

He saw what they were removing from the screws.

MINUTES LATER, on the gusty aft deck of the ship, a diver handed the evidence bag to the technician from Forensics. "That's all we found." He shrugged. "You might get an order from the judge and put her in dry dock, but I don't see the point. There's no body—or parts. Frankly, it's hard not to doubt his story."

Struggling to hang on to the blowing piece of paper on his clipboard, the tech tagged the bag. "This is something, anyway." He eyed the dark sky, the gray-green water and the masts of the sloops rocking in the next marina, their stays banging in the whistling wind. "Those boats make a racket in this weather, don't they?"

No one answered. Keough from Homicide, his Lieutenant Columbo coat flapping like a sail, watched a red tinsel garland loosen itself from a nearby dock piling and drop into the water. It reminded him of party decorations on the morning after—though Christmas was still almost three weeks off. For the living.

Reaching to his throat to ease an extra inch of breathing room into the reindeer tie his daughter had given him years earlier, Keough glanced incuriously at the evidence bag. True, it was something—but not nearly enough.

Keough was far more interested in David Blade, across the deck, who was staring at a woman on the stern of a cabin cruiser two slips away. The woman was shedding her scuba tank beneath a canopy strung with colored lights. Seeing her scrub brush and scraper, Keough decided she was a bottom-cleaner. Unusual line of work for a woman. Blade might be thinking the same thing, but probably not.

He would have other things on his mind. His son, maybe.

Or his wife.

Or the uniforms all over his ship.

Without looking at his colleagues, he asked, almost rhetorically, "So, what do you give the wife who has everything?"

The diver was the one who answered.

"A push."

CHAPTER ONE

December 3
Three years later—the third Christmas

DON'T THINK OF YOURSELF as a bottom-cleaner, Jean. You're *a slime warrior, ridding boats in the Santa Barbara Harbor of a disgusting scourge. It's a noble calling.*

Jake Doherty's words had cost him an extra fifty cents a foot, Jean reminded herself as she scrubbed thick slime from the keel of his Chinese junk, *Lien Hua.* Slime warrior. Her arm ached, a scumlike film clouded the view through her mask, tar clung to her hair, and her forehead throbbed. The slime warrior should be home studying for her cetacean-development final—unless she wanted to spend her life cleaning boat bottoms. And despite her dean's list standings, that was looking like a possibility.

Baby nuzzled her cheek as though attempting to kiss away her headache, and Jean, drawing as deep a breath as her ancient regulator allowed, ran a gloved hand over the dolphin's smooth underside. *Baby,* she thought, *you make this worth it.*

Baby was the best thing that had ever happened to her, and this filthy job kept them together. It seemed to Jean they were two of a kind: Baby, dishonorably discharged from both the U.S. Navy and Marineland and ostracized by her own kind; Jean, unable to find the diving work she coveted yet hating to work on land—and always feeling so different for it.

Baby slid along her side in an affectionate caress as Jean attacked the last square foot of slime on *Lien Hua*'s keel. Minutes later, holding Baby's dorsal fin, she gratefully accepted a lift to the surface.

At the top, she dropped her mouthpiece, breathed the tar-scented winter air and reached her arm around Baby, brushing her lips over the dolphin's smooth, warm skin. "Thanks for the ride, sweetheart." Reluctantly releasing Baby, she inflated her vest and pushed back her mask, in no hurry to haul herself out of the water at the dock. There was no diving ladder on the *Lien Hua*—more justification, Jean told herself, for charging two dollars a foot.

Still, she took a moment to rescue one of Jake's holiday decorations from the drink—Baby's work undoubtedly. Since Thanksgiving, Baby had been disarranging Christmas trimmings all over the harbor. Anything that looked like it might make a good toy was irresistible to her, and this time the casualty was a string of bells made from red and green pop cans. The bells had been draped along the starboard side of the *Lien Hua,* clinking faintly in response to the breeze, but Baby had been dissatisfied with the intermittent effect. Earlier, Jean had seen her attempting to ring them herself by hitting them with her snout. Now the entire string was floundering near the surface of the water. Jean gathered up the cans and slung them over the gunwale, then left the side of the junk and made her way to the dock, Baby chattering beside her.

Jean whistled back, mimicking Baby's clicking sounds as best she could and knowing it was a sorry attempt at communication. Swimming backward as Baby nosed her face, Jean said, "You're my best friend in the world, pretty thing."

Her tank bumped the dock, and Jean turned clumsily to reach for weathered wood. Instead, she grabbed a worn running shoe—with a foot inside. A warm, full-grown male foot and not Jake Doherty's.

"Sorry." Moving her hand to the dock, she squinted up at the tall figure standing over her, a black cutout against the cloudless sky. As he crouched beside the water, blocking the afternoon sun, Jean's heart gave a lurch.

David Blade, head of the Blade Institute of Marine Exploration.

"Jean."

The shadows hid his eyes, but Jean knew what was there. Small lines etched in the corners, telling of days spent on the sea watching distant horizons; irises of deep brown, shades darker than his sun-tipped hair and closely trimmed beard.

Today a long-sleeved rugby shirt hugged his broad shoulders, and the long legs of his canvas pants were splattered with old paint, dried splotches of white that suggested he did his own maintenance on his ship. Staring through dripping lashes at the promise of muscle beneath the worn fabric, Jean thought stupidly, *He knows my name.* And an instant later, *Why is he here?*

"I need a diver. Would you like to work on my ship?"

She set her scrub brush on the dock. "Bottom-cleaning?" It always was.

"Bottom-cleaning," he said. "I'll help you, and we'll get her scrubbed as fast as we can. I'm leaving for Baja the week before Christmas."

With a team of divers, no doubt, thought Jean. Why couldn't she find that kind of work? Once she had suspected the episode in Mexico of damaging her credibility, but it had happened years ago—and the story couldn't have reached the ears of *every* employer to whom she applied for diving work.

She didn't respond immediately and David said, "I hope you can help. Everyone else is working salvage."

He was more candid than tactful. Jean said, "I charge a dollar-fifty a foot." Her voice was shaky—fatigue, of course. *It's just like any other job,* she thought. *The only difference is he heads the Blade Institute.*

It was a big difference. The small but prestigious research institute founded by David's father, the late undersea explorer Christopher Blade, had once led the field in oceanic research. Though the institute had dropped in size and prominence over the past few years, it was still highly respected.

David said, "Can you start tomorrow?"

"I have a cetacean-development final at noon. I can come after that."

"You're a student."

"I'm a student till tomorrow. Then I graduate in marine biology with an emphasis in cetaceans." She sounded like a talking résumé, but David didn't seem to notice. Probably all marine-biology students spewed their credentials at him on first meeting.

Jean was wondering how to mention summa cum laude and the K. L. Sayles Award when Baby nosed up beside her, pushing an inflatable ring imprinted with the image of a Christmas wreath. Putting her beak through the wreath, Baby tossed it at David's feet. It bounced off his shins, hit Jean in the face and plopped back into the water.

Jean was grateful that if anyone had to witness the dolphin's playful mischief it was David Blade. Who better to understand Baby's antics and her constant demands for attention than a man who had written two books on cetaceans? For once, Baby might prove a career asset.

But David hardly glanced at the animal. Scooping the wreath from the water, he dropped it onto the dock beside him and asked Jean, "Want a hand up?"

Jean considered. If she said yes, he might think she was weak. If she said no, he would think she was hard to work with. The fact was, she welcomed the help. "Um. Yes. I can do it myself, but—"

"I know you can."

Jean let him take her arms, and he lifted her from the water and sat her on the edge of the dock. In his shadow, Jean stripped off her tank and fins, stood up and tripped over the inflatable wreath. She crashed into David and clung to his arms to steady herself—and to keep from tumbling into the harbor. Jean heard his quick intake of breath and felt the heat of him and the hardness of his muscles before he set her back from him—as one might a dog who had rolled in dead fish. The contact left his clothes wet, smeared with slime and tar.

"I'm sorry," Jean said at once. "Would you like me to wash them for you?" It sounded absurd, but it was the best reparation she could envisage on the spot.

"No." The word was curt and decisive.

Flushed, Jean peeled off her diving gloves. David Blade was taller than he'd seemed from a distance, and she felt small beside him. Fine hairs all over her body rubbed the inside of her wet suit as his gaze absorbed her.

As the only female diver working in the harbor, Jean was used to getting the once-over from employers who seemed to wonder if she had the muscle for the job. She did. At five-six and 115 pounds, she was no linebacker, but she was a strong swimmer, an experienced diver and a second-degree black belt in tae kwon do. Quick and agile enough to stand on a dock without falling over her own feet and slamming into the nearest man.

David Blade's scrutiny felt unforgiving. Imagining the grimy picture she made, Jean turned toward the water to squeeze out her thick, sun-singed braid. Tar was clumped in the loosened golden strands. She was a mess, and she wanted to get away from David Blade's eyes. It was impossible not to think of his sleek, beautiful, debutante wife, now three years dead. No one would have caught Skye Haverford Blade covered with slime and tar.

Baby rolled onto her side and waved a flipper at Jean. As Jean halfheartedly waved back, David frowned at the dolphin. "Your diving buddy?"

Jean heard the criticism and knew she deserved it for violating the number-one rule of scuba safety: *Never dive alone.* Of course, with Baby she wasn't exactly alone, but the dolphin wouldn't be much help if her equipment failed. On the other hand, at only ten or fifteen feet below the surface, how bad could things get? She shrugged. "It's just bottom-cleaning."

The reaction was all in his eyes, which darkened. "I must have misread my dive manual. I don't recall any special clauses regarding bottom-cleaning."

Coming from a man who'd logged more hours underwater than the *Nautilus,* the comment was scathing.

Before Jean could reply, he added, "No one dives solo from my ship."

Jean smiled stiffly. "It will be nice to have your company." Like diving with a twelve-foot shark.

David did not return the smile. Instead, he picked up the wreath at his feet and pulled the plug, releasing the air from inside. As he deflated it, evoking a whistling chatter of complaint from Baby, he glanced again at the dolphin and said, "They don't make good pets."

Jean was speechless. Baby was not a pet, and David Blade, of all people, should know that. Reading his books,

Jean had perceived him to possess a sympathy with marine mammals that bordered on mystical. He was wise, aware and compassionate. He was a kindred soul.

He was folding the inflatable wreath into fourths.

Watching her toy shrink, Baby cried loudly.

Jean nodded at the wreath and asked David, ''Is that yours?'' His ship, the *Skye,* was berthed less than a hundred yards away in the next marina, which could explain how Baby had retrieved the ring so quickly.

''It belonged to my son.''

Belonged? The past tense implied that either his son was history or the wreath was. Since as far as she knew, the little boy she frequently saw sitting on the deck of the *Skye* was alive and well, David must mean he planned to confiscate the wreath. For what? Letting Baby have it?

David reached for her tank. ''I'll take your gear to the *Skye,* since you'll be working there tomorrow. That will save you lugging it to the marine supply and back.''

Jean was surprised he knew her habits. But then, he also knew Jake Doherty, who ran the marine supply. She said, ''Thank you. You don't have to do that.''

He reached for her mask. ''When's your final over tomorrow?''

''I'll be here by three-thirty.''

''Marina D. I'll meet you at the gate.''

''Okay.'' Jean looked toward the *Lien Hua,* a study in flea-market Christmas decor. Her diving bag and beach towel were on the junk, and she had to retrieve them before heading home.

She turned back to bid farewell to David Blade, but he'd already left. The gate at the top of the dock clanged shut behind him as he strode down the boardwalk toward the next marina. Gone.

Jean stared after him, stunned by the abrupt departure.

He hadn't even said goodbye. Marking the cold, purposeful strides of his retreating figure, Jean told Baby, "I think I should have charged two dollars a foot."

Baby whistled and dove, then leapt from the water and landed with a splash. Her late-afternoon exuberance was predictable as clockwork—like the cries that would follow Jean when she left the marina. Both were pleas for her to stay. *Pay attention to me, Jean.*

Oh, Baby, thought Jean. The dolphin seemed so vulnerable in her solitude. It was always hard to leave her. Jean knew she should be home reviewing the embryonic development of *Globicephala scammonii* and other cetaceans, but instead she sat down on the edge of the dock and slid back into the water. At least David had saved her some time by taking her gear to his ship. She could spend that time with Baby.

David Blade. No wonder she didn't feel like studying. He was a distraction to ruin anyone's grade point average. As Baby surfaced near her and blew a long sighing breath from her blowhole, Jean said, "He's even better up close, isn't he, Baby? Mean, but cute."

Baby lifted her head from the water and released a faint whistle.

Jean echoed the sound and reached her arms around the dolphin to hug her, but she was still thinking of David, of the times she'd surfaced in the harbor after a dive and found him watching her and Baby from the deck of the *Skye*. And of the other times they'd passed each other on the waterfront and his eyes had lingered on her as though he wanted to speak.

She told Baby, "Now we know what he wanted to say, don't we? *I must have misread my dive manual.* That was so embarrassing, Baby."

Especially because he was right. Baby was a genius at

chasing off diving partners, but that was no excuse for going down alone. And Jean couldn't blame David for resenting her recklessness. Nobody wanted to drag a body out of the harbor, and he'd already suffered his share of that kind of grief.

Three years earlier, a few weeks before Christmas, Jean had been on one of her first diving jobs when the *Skye* pulled into the harbor with a police escort. Curious spectators had crowded the dock as David Blade and some other divers entered the water at the *Skye*'s stern. Jean and her diving buddy had taken more trips to the surface than usual to watch the commotion, and soon the owner of the boat they were working on, just three slips away from the *Skye*, came back to fill them in. Jean still remembered the tremor in the man's voice.

"That's a homicide team. His wife fell overboard out at the islands."

Jean and her partner and their employer had watched until the divers surfaced, David Blade with them. On the *Skye*'s diving platform, he'd dropped his tank and pulled off his mask, turning at the sound of two different camera shutters. On his feet instantly, a tall and bearded Poseidon in neoprene, he had snarled at the photographers, "Get off my ship."

The shutterbugs fell over each other getting out of his way.

Feeling like another spectator, Jean had cleared her mask as another diver surfaced at the stern of the *Skye* with something in his hand. A plastic bag. Forensic evidence.

From the newspapers the following day, Jean learned the divers had removed a grease-coated bikini top and some strands of dark brown hair from one of the screws. The story was on every front page on the south coast and many across the nation, beneath macabre headlines,

PUBLISHING HEIRESS SKYE HAVERFORD
DISAPPEARS FROM SHIP
HUSBAND QUESTIONED

David Blade told police he had seen his wife fall from the bow and had cut the engine as soon as he could. The details were sketchy, as though the papers had found the story in its entirety too ghastly to print, and Jean's mind wouldn't let go of the questions. Had Skye been sucked under the ship and killed by the propellers? The possibility was horrifying. She had seen the props on ships the size of the Blades', and she knew their effect on the water and everything around them. And if her body had gone into the screws, the man at the helm probably would have felt it— and the sensation would stay with him till his dying day. Jean didn't know how anyone could live with it.

The articles taken from the propeller that day were all that ever surfaced of Skye Haverford's remains, and with no body there were no answers. Free to go, David Blade had left Santa Barbara for an expedition near Fiji, then gone on to a long project in Antarctica. And two and a half years later, when the *Skye* at last returned to her berth, Jean noticed David again. His reappearance was the most intriguing change in her life of diving and study and tae kwon do since the day Baby showed up at her favorite surfing spot.

Now Jean asked Baby, "Do you think all that time at the south pole made him so…glacial?"

Baby responded with a series of clicks.

Jean said, "True. Someone should thaw him out, and it should be me."

How many times had she imagined he would ask her to clean the *Skye*'s hull? Too many to count. But her version had never included David's hefting her onto the dock like a net of fresh catch or her tripping and falling on him and smearing slime and tar on his clothes. Remembering the look on his face when she'd offered to wash them, Jean gave a quiet moan that faded to bubbles as she let herself slide briefly under the water.

None of it was supposed to happen that way.

In her imaginings of their meeting, she was always ready to go down for a dive, though not in her usual guise. Her hair long and loose, she would look like something assembled from the pages of *Professional Diver,* the *Sports Illustrated* swimsuit issue and *Elle.* Cool, collected—and somehow both chic and sexy, like her sister Cecily. David Blade was always shirtless—as she'd occasionally observed him from a distance—and he always opened their conversation by confessing, "I've been watching you for months. You do things for a wet suit I didn't think were possible."

Later he would suggest she accompany him on a year-long expedition to some distant, exotic diving location. Sometimes it was to see the giant squid of the Humboldt Current, other times to the reefs of the Red Sea. Always she impressed him with her competence as a marine biologist and her sensitivity as a woman. After long afternoons diving, they would lie on sandy beaches in little clothing, and he would say things like, "I never dreamed I would fall in love with a research assistant. I have to tell you, Jean. No woman's ever made me feel this way." *This way* meant possessed of insatiable desire for her, a desire they would repeatedly attempt to quench.

The recollections and her encounter with David now seemed mortifying. She'd better get home and study. She was not David Blade's research assistant, lover or consort. She was still the Goddess of Slime, and like every other oceanic explorer around, David Blade apparently thought scraping hulls was the upper limit of her employment potential.

"Tomorrow," she told Baby, giving the dolphin a last stroke before climbing from the water, "I'm going to prove him wrong."

ERIKA BLADE WATCHED her brother remove a bottle of tequila from a high locker behind the bar, uncap it and take two quick swallows. Then he stood staring out the salon's one clear-paned starboard window at the next marina. He took another drink.

She said, "Good day?"

David started, then stared at the wheelchair that had soundlessly entered the salon. Meeting Erika's eyes, he said, "I'm going to put sleigh bells on that thing."

"Why not?" Erika laughed, setting the brake. "'Tis the season." There were few secrets between them, and she nodded at the bottle he held. "Speaking of which, is that why? The holidays?" Or the time of year, she wondered. It was almost St. Nicholas Day—again.

"You know better."

Erika wasn't sure of that, but she let it slide. "Individual glasses are more sanitary, unless you're planning to finish it."

He turned the label to face her. In black permanent marker, across José Cuervo's imprint, was scrawled the word "mine."

Erika smiled. "My brother the lush." He wasn't, fortunately. David cared too much for his son to damage any of their lives that way. And he had too much self-control. Still, as he capped the bottle in his hand, Erika wondered if it wasn't some sort of anesthetic for him, a quick fix for difficult moments in the day. There was pain there.

Watching him tuck the bottle back into the locker and secure the door, Erika changed the subject. "What happened to your clothes?"

He looked away. "I was helping a diver out of the water."

Erika did not ask which diver. She had eyes. And so did her brother—for the harbor's prettiest bottom-cleaner. She suppressed a smile, imagining a host of scenarios that could be responsible for the tar on his clothes. Any of them would be good for him.

David asked, "Where's Chris?"

"Reading. Number five or six of *Hank the Cowdog*. I think he wants to live on a ranch."

"I hope not." David smiled. "Next you're going to say he wants a horse for Christmas."

Erika recognized a perfect opening. "No, but I've been thinking about a puppy or a kitten."

David drew back almost imperceptibly. Then he reached for an object lying on top of the locker and unfurled it for Erika. The deflated wreath. He told his sister mildly, "Let's work on getting him to take better care of his toys for now."

Erika said, "My God, David. He's a kid. Surely you're not upset because he was playing with that dolphin. It's probably good for him."

"I doubt it. And we've covered this before. No pets." He started to leave.

Slam, thought Erika. The door was closed. That was David. One minute warm and almost loosening up, the next shut down, maximum security, closed for the duration. In the last few years, he'd become a master of protection, building barriers around all three of them. Too late, reflected Erika. We're already damaged, and David is broken.

He paused over the hatchway that led to the galley. "I have a diver coming tomorrow. We're going to work on the keel."

"Good," Erika said pleasantly. "Is there anything I can do to help?"

David's back was to her, and he closed his eyes. What it must cost her to say that, to say it so sincerely and serenely when he knew as well as anyone that she must long to be in the water, too, even bottom-cleaning. He forgot to answer. He wanted to tell her he loved her, that he wanted her to have the use of her legs again as much as she wanted it—maybe more. But Erika knew that.

When his silence became long, she said cheerfully, "I'll keep Chris out of the way. How's that?"

David turned swiftly, remembering her question. He met her eyes. "You do help. Every single day."

And because his throat suddenly hurt from the truth of the words and because he couldn't look at her any longer without seeing himself, he started below to the galley.

"David."

He looked back.

Erika's eyes were steady, but she chewed on her bottom lip for a moment before she continued. Instinctively he realized whatever she had to say was going to be bad.

"You know I'm going into rehab over Christmas."

"Yes." He faced her, unconsciously bracing himself on the edge of one of the lockers.

"I don't think I'll come back—here, that is."

His insides felt as if they were falling a mile. Not come back? When he spoke, it was an incredulous whisper. "Erika."

She looked unhappy, undoubtedly for giving him pain. "It's not you," she said. "Or Chris. You're the only family I have. But this is for me. I think I've leaned on you as long as I should."

Stalled two steps down the companionway, David backed against the locker on the starboard side of the stairwell. His eyes were keen. "Or maybe you mean I've leaned on *you* as long as I should."

Erika threw him a tender smile, the beauty of which her crooked incisors seemed only to enhance. She said, "Maybe I do, David."

His heart sank. It must be hard as hell for her to take this step. But if she walked away, she was going to leave a mess behind. His mess, which she had politely waded through for three years. He thought of Chris and all Erika had provided for him. A female role model and a great caretaker when David was working. What was he going to do now? Chris was only six.

Erika read his thoughts. "Get a nanny. You can afford it, and it will be good for him."

"A nanny?" David straightened up. The idea made him feel as if he was choking. He asked Erika, "Should we get one who'll decide to cast off while we're away from the ship like that girl down in Newport? Ten thousand dollars worth of damage to the boat. Remember? Or maybe we should get one like—who was it—the Averys' nanny, down in Baja. Went off with her boyfriend, and the kids burned down the condo."

Erika rolled her eyes. "I'm sure there's more to that story than we've heard. You and I both know that even on a bad day Chris wouldn't play with matches. And Jennifer Avery—"

She didn't finish, but that was Erika. If she couldn't say anything nice, she shut up. This time, David wished she'd continue. Jennifer Avery's husband, Michael, was a marine-biology professor at the university and had recently applied for a grant from the Haverford Trust. David had mixed feelings about the proposal and would have liked to know more about the man.

In any case, Erika was right about the nanny story, which he'd heard secondhand. There was probably more to it.

But a nanny for Chris!

Lost in thought, he murmured more to himself than to Erika, "A nanny." He couldn't picture it. *He'd* never had a nanny, and neither had Erika.

But they'd had a mother.

He became conscious of Erika watching him. Her smile was long gone, and he knew she was worried. Not about Chris, but about him, about how he'd get along without his big sister on board.

He turned and met her eyes gamely. "A nanny. Good idea." Before she could suspect his true feelings, he turned again to go below.

"David."

"Yes." He paused, but didn't look back.

"A wife might do as well."

"No, thank you. I can always fire a nanny." He dropped into the galley and hurried to his cabin.

CHAPTER TWO

THE NEXT AFTERNOON Jean found him waiting in the sun on a bench outside marina D. He was leaning against the window of the boardwalk espresso shop, which was painted with a holiday scene—a sailboarding Santa Claus whose saucy wink seemed to say, *I see you when you're sleeping; I know when you're awake—thinking about David Blade.*

Jean was nervous, a state that worsened as David, his expression remote, stood up to greet her.

She said, "Am I late?"

He glanced at his diving watch. "No."

Jean looked down at her short denim skirt and white sweatshirt, sorry she wasn't already suited up.

He said, "You can change on the *Skye.*" Crossing the boardwalk, he opened the gate with his key card and ushered her into the marina.

The dock seemed gloomier than those surrounding it. All the boats were deserted, many were covered with tarps, and not one was decorated for the season. Swinging her dive bag beside her, Jean scanned the water for Baby, but the dolphin was nowhere in sight. David said nothing, and only the slapping of rigging on masts and the splash of waves accompanied their footsteps as she followed him down the dock to slip 23.

There, the black-and-white hull of an eighty-foot ship loomed over them, a colorful array of flags streaming from her mast on the fly bridge. Following David down the narrow walk alongside the berth, Jean read the name printed in utilitarian block letters on the side of the bow: *Skye*.

The infamous ship that had killed the woman who bore its name. *Sad,* Jean thought, remembering. In her musings the previous night, she had wondered if perhaps unhealed grief was behind David's gruffness.

Her pale green eyes lifted to his, but he had already jumped aboard. He held out his hand, and Jean took it. Clasping his long, strong fingers, tanned brown and hardened by work, she allowed him to help her onto the ship. The gangway was narrow, and she balanced precariously between David and the ship's railing as she held her dive bag clear of the immaculate sides of the cabin.

"Careful." David steadied her, then dropped her hand and led the way to the aft deck. Her stomach flooded with heat from their close proximity, Jean took a deep breath before she followed. He was an occupational hazard.

It was a relief to turn her attention to the ship.

There was varnished wood trim everywhere, from decks to doors, unusual on a vessel used for scientific expeditions. But the *Skye* was legendary. Steel-hulled, she boasted powerful twin engines and a false nose, which housed an underwater observation chamber, a feature that interested Jean immensely.

Yet every utilitarian quality was matched by something rare and lovely. A diving platform at the stern gave way to a teak deck, and several of the triple-paned cabin windows protected stained glass. As she followed David aft, Jean saw a hammerhead shark captured in one frame, narwhals in another. Two colorful wind socks blew beneath the canopy, and a Jolly Roger waved over the stern, grinning insolently at the star-spangled banners on other boats.

Jean had noticed the pirate flag in the past. She was occasionally a reader of pirate fiction, and the emblem attracted her, hinting that David possessed a romantic soul—

or at least a good sense of humor. In the past twenty-four hours, she'd ruled out the latter. As for the former—

A small boy peered around the edge of the cabin, grounding her flight of fancy.

"Hi, Chris." David reached out to touch a head of fine hair the same wet-sand color as his own. "Jean, this is my son, Christian. Chris, this is Jean. She's going to help me clean up *Skye*."

Ah, thought Jean. The owner of the wreath.

The boy, whom she judged to be about six, melted against his father's side, buried his face, then chanced a look at Jean with solemn dark eyes. She was surprised by his shyness. Often she had seen him sitting on the aft cushions of the *Skye* watching Baby, usually in the company of a woman in a wheelchair Jake Doherty said was David's sister. Jean told David, "He looks like you."

David glanced down at Christian, and the two made identical faces and simultaneously shook their heads. "We don't think so," David said. "But thank you."

Jean met Christian's dark brown eyes, so much like his father's. "Hi, Chris." She realized her heart was beating faster than normal. It was ridiculous that the appearance of a child should make her anxious, but it did. Had her mother been right? Had that disastrous time in Mexico said something about her she wasn't prepared to face?

At least David's son seemed well behaved. In fact, Christian Blade appeared unusually reserved for a boy his age, not that she had much basis for meaningful comparison. He was wearing a black turtleneck and blue jeans, a sober ensemble that matched his demeanor.

David asked him, "Where's Erika?"

His sister, thought Jean. Jake had said her name was Erika.

Christian detached himself from his father's leg and shrugged, nodding toward the cabin. His eyes never left Jean.

David squinted at the sun dropping below the canopy and turned to her. "I'll show you where you can change. We don't have much daylight."

Baby's cries answered his words, announcing her arrival at the *Skye*'s berth. Jean whistled to her, then felt the sudden heat of David's gaze and remembered what he'd said about dolphins as pets. Blushing, she said, "I'm ready."

Without a remark or so much as a glance, David opened the nearest cabin door and steered Jean inside. Christian raced away to the stern and settled on the aft seat to look at Baby as his father let the door swing shut behind Jean.

Thinking again of the inflatable wreath and wondering what had become of it, she said, "Your son's quiet."

"Very." David indicated the enclosed area where they stood. "This is the diving alcove."

Jean noted scuba tanks, a compressor and a locker marked Masks and Fins. Two surfboards were mounted to a rack on the vestibule wall.

He opened another door, and Jean followed him down stairs carpeted in plush blue to a spacious cabin sensibly furnished. The chairs and matching couch were understated and looked comfortable; even the koa end tables blended rusticity with elegance. Along both sides of each clear window were stained-glass images, now dramatically lit by the sun and framed in the same rich, dark wood as the bookcases and cabinets that edged the walls. The bar and stereo console were mounted to withstand the high seas, as were two globes, one on each of the forward lockers: the Earth and the moon.

"The salon," said David. He continued below to the galley, but Jean paused to admire a watercolor hanging over the aft companionway. The portrait showed a striking brunette with brilliant blue eyes standing in a tide pool.

Skye.

Jean remembered pictures of the heiress in the news after her death. Now she stared at the portrait, captivated by the woman's half smile, until David spoke from the galley. "The engine room's beneath your feet. The access is under these stairs." He indicated the ladder down to the galley.

Her eagerness to see the vessel momentarily triumphed over her curiosity about Skye Haverford. Abandoning the watercolor, Jean followed David into the depths of the ship.

The galley was soled in teak. By the time her sneakers touched the wood, David had ascended another set of steps to a door labeled USE OTHER DOOR. Jean glanced around as she crossed the companionway. The galley was shipshape and well equipped yet homey, with a child's drawing of a rather unhappy-looking snowman taped to the refrigerator and a note on the espresso maker—FIX NOW. At a spot low on the wall, eye level for a six-year-old, hung a pasteboard advent calendar with the first four doors opened, revealing seasonal images. The offering for December fourth was a pair of silver skates.

When Jean reached the top of the stairs, David propelled her into a sunlit teak-and-koa cabin. "This is my cabin. You can change in here."

The room was masculine, tasteful and personal. A quilt appliquéd with dolphins and whales covered the queen-size berth, and a rag throw rug brightened the teak sole. Bookshelves, map table and a mounted rolltop desk—all of exotic woods—lined the walls beneath the windows. Like the windows in the salon, the clear panels of these were edged by stained glass. The lockers were tightly secured, the space immaculate.

"Come out whenever you're ready." David nodded toward a set of steps aft. "That door will put you in the wheelhouse. The hatch goes to the deck. Do you need anything?"

Turning, Jean shook her head at him. In the close quarters, it was hard not to stare and harder not to admire the details of him, particularly his eyes. The whites were immaculate, almost supernaturally clear, the irises dark as black walnut. He was an extraordinarily handsome man.

He said, "I'll meet you on deck. I'll take care of the tanks." And he left.

Alone, Jean kicked off her sneakers and peeled off her clothes as she pored over the photographs on the walls. She recognized Christopher Blade in one, David's son, Christian, in another. Examining the photo of his father, she remembered that Skye's death had not been the first major tragedy in David's life. At nineteen, he was sole survivor of the wreck of the *Siren,* his father's scientific-research vessel, which hit an iceberg near Greenland. He had lost both parents and the ship that had been the family's home, then gone on to revitalize the Blade Institute until it rose like a phoenix from its briny grave.

As she pulled on her black tank suit, Jean looked for a photo of Skye Haverford Blade but found none. In fact, there were no photos of women in the cabin, only the images in the four stained-glass panels. A mermaid, a geisha, a dark-skinned island beauty and a golden-haired pirate's wench. The words of an old song played through her mind. *In my ship I've sailed around the world, looking for a woman like you….*

As she examined the windows, Jean noticed a word etched into the wood beneath the mermaid: "Skye." There was something tortured in the crudely carved letters, and her heart twisted. Jean wished she'd paid more attention to the news three years earlier, but Christmas had been depressing enough that year. With her own parents dead only sixteen months, she had identified with what David and his son must be suffering. She'd avoided the media coverage and tried to tune out her classmates' morbid jokes about the mishap.

Realizing she was lingering too long in the cabin, Jean hurriedly zipped up her purple-and-black wet suit. Then she piled her clothing into her dive bag and carried it with her as she retraced her way through the boat.

David was in the salon, his wet suit peeled to his waist, and with him was the woman in the wheelchair. For the first time, Jean saw a second door from the deck to the salon, this one equipped with a ramp. Another ramp created a second companionway leading aft.

Pausing in the shadows at the foot of the galley stairs, Jean found her gaze riveted unwillingly on David's lean, muscled torso—and a long, symmetrical, crescent-shaped scar on his back. It was a deep, ugly, sinister-looking thing, and Jean had seen another like it in a diving magazine. Shark bite. Undoubtedly she would find its mate on his chest when he turned around.

Brother and sister were too deeply absorbed in debate to notice her presence, and as Jean sensed the tension in the room she became loath to announce herself. Instead, she listened, not intending to eavesdrop, as Erika said, "David, he belongs in school."

"He doesn't want to go, and I don't want him to. He's three levels above his class academically—more in some subjects—and there's nothing he can get there that he won't get here. Except a lot of grief."

Erika's voice was calmer than his. "He's lonely, David. He needs friends."

"He's growing up the way we did."

"Wrong. You and I had each other. He has no children in his life, and you won't even let him have a pet."

"He went to school, and they made fun of him. I love him, Erika. Do you think this is easy for me?"

"No, but I think it's indicative."

"Of what?"

"Of your wanting to protect everyone."

David said, "This is a bad time for this conversation, Erika." As he spoke he saw Jean hanging back in the unlit galley. Instead of answering Erika, he glared down the companionway at his new contract labor. Her pale green eyes were so wide she reminded him of a kitten ready to bolt. She'd probably heard plenty, and the possibility embarrassed him. He growled, "Are you ready?"

"Oh, David," said Erika, plainly exasperated.

"I'm ready." Jean tossed her dive bag up onto the sole of the salon and scrambled up the stairs. "I hear Baby outside making a racket."

Smiling, Erika pushed her wheelchair forward. "Baby? Is that the dolphin? She's so beautiful."

David pulled on the sleeves of his wet suit, his eyes flashing away from Jean's. Next Erika was going to want to get Chris a dolphin for Christmas.

"I'm Erika, by the way. David's sister."

Jean grinned. "Jean Young. Slime warrior."

Erika laughed, more heartily than David had heard her laugh in weeks. "I don't envy you. No, scratch that—I do." Before Jean could respond, she said, "I love watching you and that dolphin. They are the most spiritual animals."

"Sensual, anyhow," interjected David.

Erika laughed. "David says I think brine shrimp are spiritual."

"You do."

Still smiling, Erika sat back in her chair and said, "Jean, I have to confess, you're even prettier up close than you are from a distance. Frankly, for months now I've been dying to paint you. Say you'll sit for me. I'll pay you."

David cast his eyes away in disgust, then back. Clenching his teeth, he watched Jean's gaze gravitate toward the watercolor over the stairwell.

She didn't speak, and he didn't plan to. Damn Erika. He hoped she did move out, the sooner the better.

At last Jean said, "Thank you, Erika. That's very flattering." She glanced at David, then indicated the painting. "I'm sorry about your loss." Hastily she added, "I mean, I know it was a long time ago...."

"Not long enough." He looked away. "Shall we dive?"

Jean turned to take leave of Erika. "I'm glad to have met you."

Erika said, "Me, too. I meant that about painting you, Jean. And I probably pay better than the slave driver here."

David threw them a last glare of impatience, and Jean hurriedly claimed her dive bag and followed him up to the diving alcove.

CHRISTIAN WAS still sitting on the aft cushions watching the dolphin, and Jean would have smiled when she saw him, but her rush of pleasure was too short-lived. She couldn't enjoy the child's interest in the animal without thinking of what she had overheard inside. No school, no friends, no pets, no life. No wonder he was so withdrawn.

David frowned at Baby. "We're going to have company, I see."

David Blade wasn't going to win any maritime congeniality awards, Jean decided. But there were things he should know about Baby. Fins and mask in hand, she said, "I'm glad you're able to dive with me today. But I want to warn you that Baby can be possessive."

He looked at her.

Unintimidated, Jean explained, "She's careful of breathing apparatus—"

"As careful as a possessive four-hundred-pound female can be."

Straightening, Jean said, "I didn't invite Baby into my life, but I feel privileged to know her. We made friends when I was surfing, and now she finds me whenever I'm in the water. Wherever I'm in the water."

"You encouraged this relationship, then."

Jean met his eyes and was unprepared for their impact. Her voice trembled. "I've had some concerns, but yes. And now it's too late." She paused. "You're not the way I thought you'd be."

Spoken aloud, the words sounded childish, and Jean wished she'd kept them to herself. The silence that followed seemed huge.

David selected a mask from the locker. "And just how did you think I would be?"

All right. You asked, I'll answer. "I thought you'd appreciate the beauty of this kind of kinship with a marine mammal—with any creature of the sea. And I thought you'd have more respect for a dolphin who's been used by humans for their war games and to entertain them in public aquariums."

"And now, apparently, to accompany them on solo dives." David spared her a cool glance. "Your naiveté is truly remarkable. Believe me, I have enough respect for Baby to know her limitations. As a diving partner, she's criminally inadequate." He nodded toward Jean's regulator, the weakest part of her diving ensemble. "And I wouldn't stake my life on your equipment, either. I hope you don't dive anywhere else with that thing." Pushing open the door of the diving alcove, he walked out into the afternoon sun. "Let's get on with this, unless there's anything helpful you can tell me about your possessive friend."

There wasn't. Gritting her teeth, Jean trailed after him and joined him in the sun.

Lifting the aft railing, David stepped down to the diving platform and crouched by the water. Watching Baby peer up at him with one liquid eye, Jean said, "Hi, you pretty thing."

If David had a drop of humanity, his hand would itch to touch the animal, Jean thought. Dolphins were irresistibly tactile, seductive to touch; surely David Blade knew that. But instead, he stood up. "Let's get to work."

As he and Jean put on their fins, he smiled at Christian. "What are you going to do with yourself, Chris?"

His son shrugged, eyeing Jean distrustfully. He turned

away from both of them, effectively erasing David's smile, and concentrated on the dolphin.

Seeing David's reaction to his son's withdrawal, Jean felt sympathy for him. It wasn't easy to be responsible for another person, for needs emotional and spiritual, as well as physical. And with Chris's mother gone, the emotional part had to be tough—for father *and* son.

While she and David donned the rest of their equipment, Jean tried to remember if Christian had been on the *Skye* at the time of the accident. It was possible and could account for a lot. From the corner of her eye, she watched Chris crane his head over the railing to get a better look at Baby.

Good. Maybe he can keep her busy. Jean knew she'd rather not see David's reaction to Baby's more vexatious behaviors. She doubted patience was his strong suit.

Fortunately Baby did seem happily preoccupied. As Jean and David entered the water and cleared their masks, the dolphin stayed near the surface with Chris. Only when the divers had grabbed scrapers and brushes and dropped down along the hull did Baby join them, nosing against Jean for a caress. *Good girl,* thought Jean. *Be good. Please.* Knowing how Baby craved touch, she stroked her smooth, soft belly before setting to work with the dolphin swimming peacefully nearby.

The water was tepid, thanks to El Niño, the warm-water current flowing through the channel, and before long Jean was sweating in her wet suit. Never stopping her work, she glanced over at David scrubbing the slime that clung to the black hull. Beneath the close-cropped beard his jaw looked intractable, and Jean reflected that already she'd seen evidence of a temperament to match.

Why didn't he want his son in school? Why no pets? Why had the children made fun of Chris? He was a handsome child and apparently quite intelligent. None of it made sense. Certainly none of it agreed with the man Jean had always believed David Blade to be.

Jean's scraper paused momentarily on the hull. David had already made clear that he wasn't what she'd once perceived. He had called her naive. Thinking of the way he had spoken to her—chewed her out, really—about her diving habits and her equipment, Jean flushed behind her mask and resumed scraping. No wonder she hadn't been able to get a decent job. But even without the things David had criticized, that incident in Baja four summers earlier was a strike against her. And so, probably, was Baby.

Feeling her nearby, Jean glanced over to find the dolphin turning mischievous. Helpless, she watched Baby push between David and the ship, sliding her body against his. But Jean's annoyance gave way to mystification.

This wasn't Baby's usual behavior around strangers. It was more like the way she treated Jean, and Jean was stunned. Baby had accepted David.

He was oblivious to the compliment. Dumbfounded, Jean watched him continue scrubbing the hull, indifferent to Baby's show of affection. Sorry for her friend, Jean reached out to touch the dolphin's back as she swam by, but Baby had found a new curiosity and gamely rubbed David's legs, then lingered beside him blowing bubbles, a certain attempt at communication. She was ignored.

A little hurt by Baby's desertion, Jean returned her attention to the boat. She and David worked side by side, only the sounds of their regulators, the occasional shift of the dock overhead, and their brushes against the hull breaking the stillness.

Baby was not discouraged.

Still receiving no response, she made another pass along David's side and shoved him against Jean. Arms and shoulders bumped, then hips and legs. Jean almost dropped her mouthpiece and was annoyed when Baby pushed her into

David again. It was a bad situation, but safety soon became a secondary concern.

She chanced a look at David to see how he was handling Baby's antics.

He'd been watching Jean, waiting for her to meet his gaze. Now, eyes flashing behind his scuba mask, he pointed toward the surface.

Jean's exasperation took a turn toward resentment. *Darn it, Baby. You're about to cost me a job.*

WHEN THEY SURFACED, David dropped his mouthpiece and pushed back his mask. "That's possessive?"

Jean grabbed a rung of the swimming ladder. "That's not what she usually does." Pulling off her mask, she saw that Christian had deserted the deck. She and David were just inches apart in the water, and his hand was against hers on the ladder.

Conscious of the contact, Jean moved her hand so they weren't touching, and he drew back, as well.

Emerging beside them, Baby touched Jean's cheek with her tongue, as if to say, *Hi, Mom. Here I am. Did you miss me?*

It took all Jean's willpower not to respond. Hopeful because he hadn't fired her yet, she asked David, "Shall we try again?"

"In a minute."

Holding her breath, Jean saw him search her face.

"This is why you dive alone."

"Not exactly this." Jean wished she could stop the heat rushing through her. "Baby doesn't usually do this. She does...other things. I think she likes you."

Baby nudged David's arm with her flipper as though agreeing, and rubbed against his side. David tensed.

Jean caught the reaction. Uncertain what to make of it, she ventured, "Maybe if you just touched her, she'd be satisfied and let us be. She probably thinks you need some affection.'' Jean bit her lip. What imp had inspired that remark?

"I don't.'' He pulled his mask over his eyes and cleared it. "We're wasting time. I'll touch your dolphin if you think it'll make her go away.''

Jean cleared her own mask. "Oh, she won't go away.''

Eyes dark, David took his mouthpiece. They went down without another word.

ENFOLDED IN THE COMFORT of the water, the sounds around him familiar and soothing, David watched the big dolphin approach and braced himself to touch her as she glided by.

His mind was reeling with a dozen thoughts, a dozen excellent reasons he wanted nothing to do with Baby and less still with Jean Young. Yet, here he was, giving this warm, sensual being a long fluid caress, feeling her slide against his chest in response. He traced her dorsal side with his hand, and Baby nuzzled his jaw with her beak. He thought, *Go away, Baby.*

She didn't. She hung beside him like a shadow, like another shadow in his life, and he kept feeling an urge to turn and find the silver shape in the misty green. When she swam near him with a swish of her tail, it stole his attention and broke the rhythm of his work. But he found her more than a profound annoyance. She was incalculable, and tolerating her presence jeopardized the tenets by which he lived—and by which he sheltered his son. For Chris he wanted to build a world of certainty, and befriending a dolphin was a bad risk.

But he had to put up with Jean's example or find a new bottom-cleaner, of which there was none.

He focused on the hull, but the turbid harbor water was perilous in its own right just for the memories it brought. His body tight with tension, David felt the cold seeping into his wet suit—a December cold, a cold of the mind that was impervious to the effects of El Niño. The recollections began to close on him, and he swiftly redirected his thoughts, knowing the remedy was to concentrate deliberately on something else, something clean and whole and sane.

Jean was convenient. Working peacefully and competently beside him, she seemed interested in nothing but the hull and Baby, blowing bubbles beside her. The long rope of her braid swung behind her in the water as she worked, and David made himself imagine what it would look like unbound. The best hint was in the tendrils escaping near her hairline. Soft, springy waves in the water.

He began to relax.

Idly he let his gaze continue its remote assessment, taking in her whole body. Her breasts weren't centerfold material, but they filled that purple wet suit. The legs he'd seen earlier beneath the hem of her denim skirt were all muscle and length, as far up as he'd been able to see. David realized he'd like to see farther, all the way to the top.

Unwillingly he had a vision of his hands sliding her panties down over those narrow hips. Pink cotton panties. French cut.

His own wet suit was growing uncomfortable now. As a handpicked distraction, Jean had been a poor choice and he tried to change channels, but all that came to mind was his own concern for her safety. She ought to lose her scuba certification for diving solo. She could lose her life.

Again David tried to redirect his thoughts, telling himself Jean Young was far down on his list of pressing concerns.

Christmas shopping was higher.

And Erika's moving out.

The realization that she was leaving came over him again as it had a dozen times in the past twenty-four hours. What was he going to do?

The question was a welcome diversion. He took refuge in thoughts of keeping order in the wake of his sister's desertion, and his only other thought of Jean was a swift calculation of how fast they could finish the keel so he could get her and that dolphin out of his way.

CHAPTER THREE

THE SUN WAS TOUCHING the horizon later that hour as Jean dragged herself up the ladder and onto the platform. As David followed, she removed her mask and tank and reached over the stern to pet Baby.

Unzipping his wet suit, David said, "I'm glad Christian isn't hanging around to see your friend."

Squeezing water from her braid, Jean looked up at him.

David said, "Since he's gone, this is as good a time as any to tell you I'll discourage an attachment between him and that creature any way I have to. Dolphins who seek the company of humans have one thing in common—short lives." With a directness Jean was learning to expect from him, he added, "You seem to know something about my wife's death, so I'm sure you're aware of what Chris has already been through. I'd appreciate your cooperation in not adding more tragedy to his life."

Recalling the conversation she'd interrupted in the salon, Jean suspected the present tragedy in Christian Blade's life was an overprotective parent. She asked, "Is that why you took away the wreath? So he wouldn't play with Baby?"

David couldn't have looked more affronted if she'd asked the balance in his checking account. He said, "I did not *take away* the wreath. Chris gave it to Baby and lost it. However, it has been returned, with the hope it will soon reach its natural end. Ephemeral as the season."

And we're a lover of Christmas, are we? thought Jean. Glad to know he wasn't a man who went around sticking pins in inflatable toys, she watched the water drip from David's beard and the dark hair on his chest. As her eyes faltered to his scar, he grabbed a beach towel, wrapped it around his shoulders and folded his arms across his chest.

It was all Jean could do to mask her interest. Though disfiguring, the scar made him more intriguing, more a warrior. More a pirate. She asked, "How did that happen?"

"The usual way. Recklessness and stupidity." Setting his tank and fins on the deck, he tossed over his shoulder, "Keep track of your share of the keel, and I'll see you back here in the morning. You can leave your gear in the alcove."

Jean decided she was going to have to get used to abrupt leave-takings. "What time in the morning?"

"Nine." As though reading her mind, he murmured with the most forced courtesy Jean had ever heard, "I have dinner plans, so I hope you'll excuse me." From the deck, he dropped the aft railing into place and pointed to it. "Don't forget this. There's a child on board."

After he had taken his tank and disappeared into the alcove, Jean spent a few minutes more at the water's edge with Baby, murmuring inanities to the dolphin in a hushed voice. "Doesn't he have a nice dockside manner? Yes, from now on we charge *three* dollars a foot to people with personality disorders. Also to pirates. What do you think, Baby, is that Jolly Roger for real?"

Baby reared up in the water, clicking agreeably.

Jean grew thoughtful. Despite her jesting, she knew David's behavior must be the result of the loss he'd suffered three years ago. Running over his wife in an eighty-foot ship was bound to make anybody cranky.

Remembering, Jean winced. The books he had written, books that had affected her deeply, showed a man of sensitivity and depth. It was hard to believe that one incident, however horrifying and tragic, could completely change a person. Somewhere under that barbwire exterior was the real David Blade.

Maybe, thought Jean. And maybe I'm naive, like he said.

In any event, she couldn't help wondering about the nature of his dinner plans. There had to be a woman on the agenda. For a moment she entertained a vision of David Blade scowling through a dinner interspersed with caustic remarks. It was difficult to imagine him as a charming dinner companion. A rock would be more engaging—and more sensitive.

But what if he's not like that with everyone? she wondered. Suppose there was a woman with whom he relaxed—someone who understood. Someone who rubbed his shoulders and massaged his scalp and listened to his troubles.

It seemed distinctly possible. And a little disheartening.

Jean was unaware of any movement behind her, so she jumped when a slender arm reached out beside her, and a small hand touched Baby. Christian had lifted the guardrail and joined her on the diving platform.

As Jean watched him, she recalled his father's clearly expressed wishes concerning Christian and Baby. If David should find his son befriending the dolphin, he might fire her. And Jean wasn't sure she'd blame him. David might be overprotective, but that was better than the reverse. Experience had taught her that. Besides, he must know his own son's vulnerabilities.

Yet Jean couldn't bring herself to tear the solemn little boy from his new pastime. And Chris had remembered to put on a life vest, which meant either he was extremely well trained or one of the other two adults on the ship had sanctioned this adventure. If so, it wasn't David.

Jean asked him, "Have you touched a dolphin before?"

Christian shook his head almost imperceptibly.

"Watch out for her blowhole," Jean cautioned. "It's like

a nostril, so she won't like to be poked there. She likes her tummy rubbed.''

Christian experimented with this technique and was rewarded with more attention from Baby, who turned in the water to look at him.

Nervous that David would reappear, Jean suggested, ''I'd better get dressed. We should let Baby go home.'' Wherever Baby's home was, which Jean wasn't sure.

Standing, she searched for a question that would draw even a single word from the child. He didn't go to school, so that was a bad subject. Same with pets and friends. As Chris gave Baby's head a last pat and climbed up on deck, Jean ventured, ''How old are you?''

Six fingers. Erika called his name from below deck, and he turned apologetically and retreated to the cabin.

A nice little boy, she thought. But very quiet.

She undressed in the diving alcove, pulling her clothes on over her swimsuit. David didn't reappear, so she hung her wet suit on a hook in the alcove, stashed her equipment in a locker and departed without saying goodbye.

She left the marina at a slower pace than usual. For four years she'd been on the run to classes or the library or the gym. Tonight she had nowhere to go but home and nothing on her hands but time—and a university degree.

Elation was absent. Completing her studies felt like weight off her shoulders and little more. Even the K. L. Sayles Award had seemed like a minor accomplishment, jumbled in with the other awards given at the ceremony that morning, far less meaningful than her belt rank advancements in tae kwon do, for instance. And Jean was almost past hoping the award would help her secure the kind of work she wanted. She was still scrubbing keels, and every interview she'd wangled for better work had turned out the same. A very, very brief chat, followed by the offer of a lab position in a coastal facility, or of administrative work, or sometimes no offer at all. Never fieldwork.

Though she had graduated with highest honors, she knew she wouldn't attend the commencement ceremonies later in the year. Cecily, if she was in the country, might come to see her graduate in a cap and gown, but the fact that her parents, particularly her father, wouldn't be there made the prospect too painful. She'd rather skip it.

Wandering past the docks and the breakwater, she followed the beach west. One mile down was the property she and her sister had inherited when their parents passed away. The sun had nearly dipped out of sight as Jean reached the stairs that led up to the rambling adobe where she had lived since childhood.

For a moment she paused on the beach, absorbing the familiar smell of tar, the cool sand beneath her bare feet, and the waves rushing to the shore under the orange-and-lavender sky. The swell was good, and several figures in wet suits floated on boards beyond the breakers. Jean waved to them, and someone waved back. Watching one surfer wipe out in a spray of foam, she turned to climb the sandy, tar-spotted stairs to the house on the cliff.

She checked the mail first. A notification from a marine institute in Florida that the job she'd applied for had gone to someone else. And a brief letter, *par avion,* from Cecily in Paris, dashed off in her graceful, feminine hand:

Dear Jean,
Shooting will keep me busy till 23 Dec., I'm afraid. Jean-Claude has asked me to St. Moritz for Christmas (he has the most precious *enfants;* they call me Tante Cecily in the dearest voices), and it makes more sense than trying to come home. Anyhow, where is home? I'm becoming more European daily. I think I was meant to be French.

I've been taking French cooking evenings, creating the most incredible dishes. Monsieur Renault thinks women should not be chefs, but I am changing his

mind. *Bon appétit!* Can't wait to cook for you, but it
may be as late as February. I do miss you. I know this
is bad news, but I hope the holidays have special
things in store for you, *ma chère soeur*. Look for a
huge package in the post.

                                                    Love,
                                                    Cecily

Jean held off the tears suddenly steaming behind her
eyes. She'd half expected news of this sort, and last year
had been worse, when the Caribbean country where Cecily
had been modeling someone-or-other's summer line had
become politically unstable overnight. Nonetheless, as she
put down Cecily's letter Jean spontaneously leveled a half-
hearted kick at some boxes stacked near the kitchen
counter—the artificial tree and Christmas ornaments she'd
brought out of the garage that morning for the first time
since her parents' death. She'd planned to decorate that
night.

Her kick toppled the box on top, and she grabbed it,
rescuing what was precious—Christmas past. Christmases
when people came home.

Feeling a sudden kinship with David Blade in his sen-
timents about the season, Jean hurried to her room and
changed into shorts and T-shirt, then returned to the living
room she had long since adapted to her own needs. All
furniture was pushed to the walls, clearing the hardwood
floor. In her mother's lifetime, practicing martial arts in the
living room would have been unthinkable; winter or summer, Jean and her father were banished to the patio to spar.
Now, seeing her mother's enormous Christmas cactus
blooming near the sliding glass doors, like an embodiment
of the woman who had prized it, Jean felt a familiar guilt
at violating the Sanctuary, as her father had called it.

But tae kwon do was as sacred to her as the room had
been to her mother.

She knelt in the center of the floor, facing the long orange line of the sun's reflection setting on the sea, and sat back on her heels to meditate. But peace did not come. Only hurt and emptiness and anger at her younger sister.

After a workout that left her calmer but lonelier than before, she ate the last two slices of a frozen pizza for dinner, then curled up on the living room couch with a pirate romance she'd bought at the campus bookstore—a graduation present to herself. But she didn't crack the cover. Instead, she stood up and went to the bookcase across the room and selected a book about whales by David Blade. It made sense to bone up—in case he considered her for more serious work than slime removal.

She opened it to a section in the middle on gray whales, but time after time, her eyes strayed from the page. Listening to the waves hitting the beach, she stared at the black-and-white photo on the back of the book jacket. In this picture David had no beard, instead sporting a gorgeous, incredibly rugged chin and jaw that, for the sake of her sensibilities, Jean was glad he disguised. She turned the book faceup. David Blade was a bad choice for an unrequited passion.

Still, her encounter with his family had left her curious. A sister in a wheelchair, a son whose classmates had made fun of him for reasons unknown. And what had Erika said about David? *You want to protect everyone.* Jean could empathize with that. After her parents' death, her own protective instincts had come out, focused on Cecily.

But Ceci, seventeen at the time and already making waves on the international modeling scene, did not appreciate being protected. And the last thing Jean had ever wanted was to hold back her sister. On the contrary. She wanted Cecily to have every opportunity she would have had if their parents were still alive—maybe more. And Cecily had proven time and again that she could take care of herself.

Jean turned her thoughts back to the Blades.

Did David protect Erika, as well as Chris? With mixed emotions, Jean recalled Erika's offer to paint her, and David's displeasure, and her mind's eye conjured up the portrait of Skye. The watercolor was well executed, the style familiar. It seemed possible Erika was a professional and Jean had seen other pieces of her work without knowing who she was.

What had happened to Erika that she couldn't walk? Illness? Accident? Something stirred in her memory, and she reopened the whale book, leafing through the pages until she found what she was looking for.

A photo of a suntanned brunette standing on the fly bridge of the *Skye,* pointing at a humpback whale spouting in the distance. The tails of the work shirt she wore over her swimsuit were whipping away from her, blown by the breeze, revealing a tall, strong body. The caption did not identify the woman, but Jean knew her. It was Erika Blade.

Swiftly she paged to the front of the book to check the copyright date. Only four years earlier.

Jean turned back to the photo, noted Erika's muscular legs, her long hair, her laughing expression. Remembering the woman she had met that day, still spirited and beautiful but now confined to a wheelchair, she wondered again, *What happened?*

"AH, FREE AT LAST."

David, completely in agreement, loosened the bow tie at his throat, then removed it, folded it and stuffed it into an outside pocket of his tuxedo jacket. He'd needed to attend the dinner, but the combination of University Center food and black-tie attire was always hard to stomach. Unfastening the top button of his shirt, he paused beside the information desk to glance at a student newspaper abandoned there.

The professor who had left the banquet hall beside him paused, as well. "Any trips planned this winter?"

David picked up the paper. "Baja. Whales." He glanced at the row of four student photographs above the masthead, started to flip the paper to see the lower half of the page, then stopped.

It was her, in a yearbook photo that made her look even younger than usual. *Jean Young. K. L. Sayles Award for outstanding work in marine biology. B.S. Marine Biology. Summa cum laude.*

For a moment he was stunned. She had said her last final was today. Remembering their meeting outside the marina that afternoon—and Jean, obviously fresh from her exam— he thought, *I didn't even ask how it went.*

David glanced at the professor. The man was looking toward the exit but going nowhere, undoubtedly waiting to see if they would walk to the parking lot together. *The Haverford Trust,* David thought. Everyone wanted a grant, and his was always the deciding word. The responsibility was huge, but so were the benefits to the Blade Institute. Skye's will had made those benefits possible, though no easier for him to accept. Once, the institute had stood on its own.

Impulsively he turned to the professor and pointed at Jean's picture. "Do you know her?"

Absently unclipping his tie, the other man nodded. "I recommended her for that award."

David replied with only an expression of vague surprise.

The professor seemed to take his measure. "If this is professional interest, I would recommend her absolutely."

David regarded him coolly, with a direct gaze that tended to freeze speculation in its tracks. "She's doing some work for me," he said. "She's a bottom-cleaner."

"I know." The professor nodded with a slight smile of amusement—and respect for Jean. "Though I didn't know she was working for you."

He paused, reflective, and David sensed he was debating further revelations. What? he wondered. *I would recommend her absolutely* had sounded like unqualified approval.

At last the professor said, "She's a neighbor of mine. Her parents were friends of my wife and myself."

"Were."

"Killed in a car accident. It's just her and her sister now, though her sister spends a lot of time abroad. She's made it big in modeling."

David said nothing, but his conscience was talking plenty, and so was his heart. Both shouted an uncomfortable message—that somewhere along the line he had stopped behaving like the man he wanted to be. His mind said he'd had reasons, but David could no longer accept that excuse. As he listened to the warring parts of himself, all he could think was that today Jean had finished earning her degree and won an academic award, and he had treated her like something they'd scraped off the keel.

THE WATER WAS SO DEEP she couldn't see the top, but Jean wasn't afraid. Her partner's brown eyes watching her from behind his scuba mask made her feel as though she was in the grip of nitrogen narcosis. She wouldn't leave for anything.

Except the toll of the doorbell. It broke into her dreams, and Jean blinked up at the green shade of the reading lamp glowing over the back of the couch. The bell rang again.

She sat up and peered at the digital clock on the VCR. It was 10 p.m.

Groggy, she stood and went to the door, squinted through the peephole and saw a man in a delivery jacket. He held a bouquet.

For Cecily, thought Jean. Someone doesn't know she's out of the country.

She briefly considered not answering—after all, Ceci would never see the flowers. Then, thinking she could at least drop her sister the card, she shrugged and opened the door. The van parked at the curb bore the name of a Montecito florist.

"Jean Young?"

She nodded, still only half-alert.

He smiled and handed her the large vase. It was overflowing with orchids, two or three dozen at a glance, and weighed a ton. She needed both arms. Cecily's beaux were never cheap.

Absently she said, "Thank you," and shut the door with her foot.

She carried the vase into the kitchen, examining it as she walked. The orchids were spilling over the edges of a blued-copper urn in the shape of two dolphins. The vase was exquisite and had to be worth a pretty penny. Possibly a big-name designer was behind the gesture. It had happened before.

As she admired the abundance of color and species in the arrangement and the silver-and-gold holiday bows cascading down the front, her eyes fell on the envelope with the name *Jean* scrawled on the front.

The words of the man who had delivered the bouquet echoed in her mind. *Jean Young?*

Jean, not Cecily.

Her heart pounded as she set the vase on the table. She didn't have to open the envelope. In her heart she knew.

A copper vase. Orchids delivered at 10 p.m., when florists were closed.

She could think of only one man with the wealth to arrange it. Only one man.

Unconscious of doing so, she clasped the envelope briefly to her thundering heart before slipping the card from within. No ordinary floral card, this pictured a watercolor of a girl beachcombing. It was an Erika Blade print. Jean sank into a chair at the table before opening it.

Masculine script, too natural for any florist-written card:

"Congratulations on your academic achievements. David."

FOR DAVID the dawn was bound by ritual. Coffee, brief reflection and an hour of ancient fighting drills steeped in two thousand years of Eastern tradition. When he was done, he ran. Running was a good remedy for the aftermath of bad impulses—like his of the previous night.

But he hadn't counted on running into Jean.

She was standing in the packed sand at the water's edge, peeling off a black wet suit that had seen heavy wear, and her surfboard lay on the beach beside her. Seeing her, David drew to a halt, then wondered if he should have kept running. Against the morning fog and the dark gray-green channel, she seemed as exotic as the orchids he wished he hadn't sent.

Jean looked stunned to see him, so he spoke first, neither warmly nor coldly. "You're an early riser."

Her hair was loose, hanging halfway down her back and front like spiraling tangles of kelp, and her eyes reminded him of the sea. Yesterday, the Mediterranean; today, the channel. Between her hair and her eyes and the fact that she stood before him in only a black swimsuit, David found it impossible to see her as anything but a pretty woman in very little clothing. She was…well arranged.

Hesitantly she said, "Thank you for the flowers. They're beautiful, and so is the vase."

"You're welcome."

She said, "It's been years since I've gotten flowers."

"It's been a long time since I've given any."

They both fell silent, and David was about to excuse himself to continue his run when she said, "I live up there." She nodded at the stairs to the cliff top.

David thought about the address he'd hunted in the phone book the night before. He said, "I know."

Jean blushed, something he noticed she did often.

She said, "It's the house I grew up in. My sister and I own it. Our parents died a few years ago...."

David straightened. She wasn't telling him anything he didn't know, but he was unexpectedly touched that she was telling him. He said, "I'm sorry." A moment passed during which they heard only the waves. At last he said, "Well, you live on my favorite beach."

"Mine, too."

Shivering, Jean dropped her wet suit on top of her surfboard and wrapped her beach towel around herself. Her swimsuit would have said function-not-fashion on another woman, but Jean had assets the cold and wet only more sharply defined. Trying to secure the towel around her body—a good idea, he thought—she said, "How was your date?"

"My date?"

"Dinner. You had to go to dinner. I assumed it was a date."

Lingering when he'd intended to leave, David asked, "Why do women always think it's a date when you have a dinner engagement?"

Jean looked startled—even alarmed. "Not because they're hoping to go on one with you, if that's what you're thinking."

David was surprised to feel the corners of his mouth twitching. "Do you always say what you think?"

"This time I didn't think what I said. I'm sure women do want to date you." She threw him a wary glance. "I'm sharper after coffee. Have you had breakfast?"

David couldn't remember the last time he'd had an urge to tease a woman other than his sister. "Are you asking me on a date?"

Her apprehension turned to dismay. "No. And I wasn't asking you to breakfast. We're going to start on your boat in an hour, and I was just wondering if you'd eaten. You look...hungry," she finished lamely, pulling her eyes away from his body.

Suddenly David found it hard to believe she didn't want to go out with him. Surprising himself for the second or third time that morning, he said, "I am hungry."

An expression of panic crossed her face. She was deliciously easy to tease, much better than Erika. David said nothing, waiting to see what would happen next.

Meeting his eyes in a no-nonsense fashion that seemed completely at odds with the quivering pulse at the base of her throat, she said, "Do you think if you stand there expectantly I'll invite you for breakfast?"

"Would it help if I fainted?"

Jean paled slightly. "I think we've already established that you don't have to grovel for dates."

"And that this isn't one," he added.

"Of course it isn't. I haven't invited you!" She clamped her lips shut, as though determined not to be roped in.

David said, "I think I should taste your cooking. I need a galley slave for my next expedition."

At once he wished he hadn't said it. Jake Doherty had told him Jean's career was her Achilles' heel. David wondered what she'd actually do for it. Granted, there were some things he wouldn't ask, however seductive the prospect, but if she could cook... Or care for a child?

He rejected the idea. Meals were one thing, Chris was another. It was a bracing thought. What was he doing here, anyway? Flirting with the bottom-cleaner, a woman he wanted nothing to do with, that was what. He hadn't had this kind of conversation in years, hadn't wanted to. Possibly hadn't been able to.

As Jean stood biting her lip, David glanced at his watch and started to excuse himself.

Jean blurted out, "What do you like?"

His heart played tug-of-war with his mind. He echoed, "What do I like?"

"For breakfast."

He could leave now. This was his chance. He *had* been joking about tasting her cooking.

But he said, "Oh, anything. Are you sure this isn't an imposition?"

Rolling her eyes good-naturedly, she turned away.

While he waited, stretching in the cool, foggy air, she took her wet suit to the water and rinsed it in the breakers, soaking her towel in the process. The way it clung to her legs and rear end was sexier than if she'd been wearing nothing. Watching her clutch her wet things as she stooped to pick up her surfboard, David decided they'd both be better off once she was dressed.

When she rejoined David, he took her surfboard without asking and accidentally dislodged her towel. It fell off, and she pulled it clumsily back around her body, spreading sand all over herself. The sand was much paler than the bare skin of her legs. Unexpectedly her eyes lifted and met his. Her lips were parted, her nipples erect, and David understood the vulnerability in her eyes. She knew what she did to him and that he knew he did the same to her.

For David, the knowledge was life-affirming. Like flirtation, it hadn't happened in a long time and was vaguely painful, analogous to pushing muscles that had grown slack from disuse.

She was only inches away, and he said softly, "This feels dangerous."

Hugging the towel around her shoulders and breasts, leaving her legs exposed, Jean turned and walked in the direction of the stairs. Her voice shook only slightly as she said, "A perceptive remark from a man who's never tasted my cooking."

The comment distracted him. She had deliberately misunderstood him, and David wondered why. Perhaps the invitation he'd cajoled *was* an imposition.

Or maybe she had a boyfriend.

Falling into step beside her, he offered, "I could make breakfast."

Jean paused, then started toward the stairs—fast. "And miss the opportunity to taste my cooking? Don't think of it." Stopping at the foot of the steps, she pointed out, "I invited you, after all. I'll scare something up. You just sit and relax." She lifted her chin slightly. "I've cooked before."

"How reassuring." David smiled again. "Shall I make out my will?"

Jean laughed, but inside she suddenly felt a little hollow. She couldn't hear David mention death and money without thinking of Skye Haverford Blade.

CHAPTER FOUR

WHAT WAS SHE GOING to feed him? A man like that could probably really put it away. He was all muscle, but suddenly even his lean build made Jean think of a ravenous lion. And she could barely cook! Was he really looking for a galley slave? Or something else?

This feels dangerous. Her heart still hadn't settled from that comment—or from anything else that had happened on the beach. He'd been flirting with her. Unmistakably. Somehow, in the past twenty-four hours, she had won David's acceptance. Had he learned about the K. L. Sayles Award? That could explain the flowers. That and the way they'd been eating each other up with their eyes moments earlier. As she opened the patio door and led him into the living room, Jean felt a stirring of excitement. Months of silent glances on the boardwalk and across the harbor were actually leading to something.

To making a fool of myself, she thought. As far as she knew, the Pizza Palace didn't deliver at eight in the morning, and a large, thick-crust Vegetarian Dream probably wasn't David's idea of breakfast.

But at least the house was neat. Receiving his flowers had woken her from her lethargy, and she'd opened the boxes of Christmas ornaments. Because setting up an eight-foot tree had seemed like overkill for a woman living alone, she'd brought inside her mother's only surviving bonsai, a miniature olive tree. Jean had hung some of the smaller, lighter ornaments from the limbs and set the tree on the coffee table, then taken the rest of the boxes outside. Now, she was glad she'd made at least that concession to the season. It was good to see some of her family's ornaments again. Together the bonsai and the flowering Christmas cactus made the house more cheerful.

So did the presence of another human being.

Leaving David in the living room, Jean went to her bedroom to change into a sweatshirt and shorts. When she returned, he was sitting on the edge of the couch staring at the bonsai Christmas tree. Jean was relieved; perhaps he wouldn't wonder why his book was lying on the table beside the pot—next to her pirate romance with its no-holds-barred cover.

David said, "You must be good with these. This tree looks old."

"It's older than me," said Jean, "but only by luck and the care my mother gave it. After she died, it took me less than a month to kill a Japanese boxwood and a scrub oak. And that little monster—" she indicated the olive tree "—has had every kind of professional help but psycho-therapy."

David laughed. Their eyes met for a moment, and Jean thought of the two plants in the room, the ancient bonsai and the gargantuan cactus, and all they represented. Little of it was good.

Take care of children? Jean, I wouldn't trust you with my houseplants for the summer. You're never home for more than a few minutes at a time—

The memory of her mother's words stopped abruptly as she realized David's attention had turned to the books on the table. She felt compelled to explain why his was there. Stepping around the bar to the kitchen, she said, "I was reading up." *Reading up and gazing at your face on the cover.* "What would you like to drink?"

"Whatever you have." Bypassing his own book, he picked up her pirate romance.

Watching over the bar, Jean wished she'd had the presence of mind to stuff that particular volume under a cushion.

David perused the back cover. "Reading up on what?"

"Mating habits." *Bad, Jean,* she thought. *Any old lie would have done.* She opened the refrigerator door, prepared for the worst. There were eggs, a few vegetables and a pitcher of water.

"Mating habits?" Setting down the romance, David trailed after her into the kitchen. The flowers were still on the table, and he glanced at them disinterestedly.

Jean slammed the refrigerator door, not wanting him to see what wasn't inside. "Mating habits of gray whales. The book is about whales. You know that. You wrote it." *An omelet,* she thought. Omelets were made from eggs.

She paged through three cookbooks while he wandered around the kitchen, examining prints on the walls and photos of her and Cecily, most of which had hung in the same places when her parents were alive. David paused beside one framed picture. "'Mean Jean and Ceci-la-belle,'" he read.

Jean swallowed. "My dad called me that. It was affectionate." The nickname had been part and parcel of the bonds between them—diving, surfing, tae kwon do. Still, Mean Jean struck a deep and sometimes stinging contrast to Ceci-la-belle, particularly when Jean remembered the different inflections her mother had put on the two names. She'd never needed to spell it out. Cecily was Ceci the sought-after, universally desired for her womanly qualities, while Mean Jean was the self-absorbed, pleasure-seeking tomboy. It was a perception Jean was still trying to live down.

As she leafed through the cookbook, she felt David's silence behind her and imagined he was looking at Cecily's modeling shots.

"You're a black belt." He sounded shocked, and Jean

glanced over to see him staring at a five-by-seven her father had taken of her executing a flying side kick. "In?"

"Tae kwon do. Popularly known as Korean karate."

David stared at the photo for a moment more, his expression neutral. Then, unexpectedly, he turned and gave her a very slight, circumspect bow.

Eyes on his, Jean returned it reflexively, then looked away, discomposed. It wasn't a gesture she was used to seeing from anyone but other tae kwon doists. Why had David done it?

Embarrassed, she said, "We only do that in the gym." But when her father was alive, the two of them had followed the same formal courtesies whenever they practiced together at home. She told David, "I've gotten away from it lately."

"Why?"

"School, mainly. And Baby." She could imagine what David thought of that and wished she'd kept it to herself. He'd probably have more empathy with her strongest reason—avoiding memories of her father.

But he said nothing.

Jean found an omelet recipe, retrieved the vegetables from the hydrator and set to work at the cutting board with the cookbook open in front of her.

Behind her, David asked, "What are you attempting?"

"An omelet. Vegetarian." She looked at him.

"Sounds wonderful."

He was brave, Jean decided. It was bad news when someone needed a cookbook to make an omelet. Sloppily she broke an egg over a cast-iron skillet. "So who watches Chris while you run?" She fished an eggshell from the pan.

"Erika. I should probably give them a call, now that you mention it."

"Go ahead." Jean nodded to the phone.

David went to the wall phone, lifted the receiver and

punched in a number. "Hi. It's me. I stopped for break-fast."

Jean noticed he didn't say where. She heard the soft tones of Erika's voice at the other end.

David said, "That's bad. Can you manage for an hour?"

Erika's reassurance was audible.

"Good. And yes, I'll buy more Christmas bulbs." A pause was filled with more words from Erika. "Not the kind that blink. Not the kind that make the others blink. Not too many red ones. I understand."

Jean looked up as he replaced the receiver.

"They turned off the dock power this morning to repair a line. Now our generator's down." In a tone of resigna-tion, he added, "Erika likes to do the whole Christmas thing. With lots of lights."

It sounded unsafe. But then so was this meal. And David would be home soon to help with the lights, if he didn't die from her cooking.

She picked up another egg to break it.

"Jean."

She turned to find him inches away, so close she could see his skin through a tiny, worn hole in the arm of his T-shirt. He smelled like the ocean and very male. Jean thought it nearly unnatural for a man to smell that good in the morning—and after a run.

Oblivious to the overwork he was causing her circulatory system, he stepped past her to the sink and turned on the water to wash his hands. He grimaced. "I can't watch this any longer. Go sit down."

Jean slowly met his eyes.

"I mean it. Sit down. I'll cook."

Jean wasn't sure whether she should be mortified or overjoyed, but one thing was clear—she wasn't in the run-ning for galley slave. Retreating to the counter, she sat down on a bar stool. Unhappily she thought of her mother forever saying, *The way to a man's heart is through his stomach.* To Jean, it had always sounded like an arduous way to win a man's love. But as David diced an onion in record time, she asked, "Can I do anything to help?"

"Talk to me. Did Baby join you surfing today, or were you out there alone?"

Here we go, thought Jean. That sounded like the David Blade who had hired her to scrub his ship. She told him, "Baby was with me this morning, but there were people, too, if that's what you're getting at. I know lots of surfers, and we look out for each other."

"Isn't there anyone you can dive with?"

You. Especially since Baby had actually allowed them to work the previous day.... "Baby's made nothing but enemies among my diving buddies, I'm afraid. She swims into them, knocks brushes out of their hands, pins them against whatever keel we're cleaning. And, of course, lately she likes to steal Christmas trimmings." Jean paused and decided to chance it. One thing she could depend on from David was candor. Trying to keep her tone even, she said, "I've sometimes wondered if Baby is why I can't get decent diving jobs. You must have been amused to see me leap at the idea of being your galley slave."

Was that guilt in his expression? He said nothing.

Jean told him, "The fact is, I'd settle for nearly any kind of work on an expedition. I'm happy to start at the bottom—no pun intended—but I can't even get out of the harbor. I'm a deep-water diver, and I've been a lab assistant at school, but I can't get even an internship on a research vessel. And none of the salvage companies will take me. I've applied to places on both coasts, but nobody seems to think I'm fit for more than scrubbing boats in the harbor."

David shook his head. "Wrong."

"Then what is it?" Her mind stirred uneasily. Did he know? The Baja story had certainly made the rounds at the university, but that was years earlier. And she'd never heard it mentioned on the waterfront, not even by Jake Doherty, who knew everyone's business better than his own.

David set a green pepper on the cutting board and sliced it expertly. "No, I'm sure they just think you're a little too young—"

Choking down her relief, Jean pointed out, "I'm twenty-three."

"—and a lot too pretty," he finished, "to be at sea for months on a ship full of men." His eyes drifted to hers. "Twenty-three?"

He had called her pretty. Heart hammering, she asked, "How old are you?"

"Thirty-one. Look, to address your problem, I know how I'd feel if I got an application from a twenty-three-year-old woman straight out of school."

Jean remarked, "We make great slime warriors."

David glanced at her, then back to the stove. After a moment he took a breath and said, "I'll make you a deal."

Jean looked at him.

"Ever handled a camera in the water?"

"Some." Her heart started pounding again—hard.

"What else can you do?" He adjusted the heat under the skillet. "Typing? Computers?"

Jean nodded without expression. Office work would take her away from Baby. But if the job was with the Blade Institute, wouldn't it be worth it?

"How would you like to work on my ship?"

Gripping the edge of her stool, she attempted poise. "Very much."

He smiled. "There's a catch. A few catches."

Jean wondered if the catches would make a lifetime of slime removal look attractive.

"I don't need a full-time diver, but I could use a secretary—and someone to help look after my son occasionally. Erika's going into rehab this Christmas, and she doesn't plan to return to the *Skye*."

Jean was surprised by the news. The transition had to be harder than he was making it sound. As far as she knew, his sister had lived with him since his wife's death.

David said, "I'm booked on a trip to Baja over Christmas, a whale project in Scammon's Bay. We're trying to observe mating, actually. The trip's been in the works for almost a year, but I wouldn't dream of being apart from Chris over the holidays. Needless to say, I can't look after him while I'm working." He reached for the pepper shaker. "Do you have plans?"

Jean's thoughts spun. David Blade wanted her to look after his son? Over Christmas? Light shone ahead onto the bleak holiday she'd been anticipating. Instead of spending Christmas alone in Santa Barbara with only memories of her family for company, she would be in Baja with David Blade.

And his son. Jean drew a long, shallow breath.

She couldn't let this offer slip by! She'd studied cetaceans for four years but had never been to Scammon's Bay to see the birthing and mating place of the gray whales. She couldn't imagine a finer way to spend Christmas.

But looking after his son—

Take care of children? Jean, I wouldn't trust you with my houseplants....

David said, "I know it's a family time. I suppose, if you like, your sister could come. There's room, and then you'd be together."

Jean said, "She's out of the country."

"For Christmas?" He seemed surprised, but Jean's thoughts were elsewhere—on the offer he'd made. And the fact that she couldn't lie to him about her past.

But on the other hand, if he didn't ask, she wouldn't *have* to tell him about Baja. Hadn't her own career counselor at school cautioned her, *If I were you, I just wouldn't mention any of that, Jean. It's unrelated.*

To marine biology, yes, thought Jean. But not to caring

for Christian Blade. And she doubted David would care that what had happened in Baja wasn't her fault.

She noticed he was starting to look irritated that she hadn't leapt at his offer. And Jean saw it slipping away, the *Skye* sailing without her.

Her acceptance escaped her lips in an unexpectedly throaty question. "Sure I'm not too young?"

David made a sound that might have been a laugh. Or he might have been choking. "No."

Too pretty? wondered Jean. Apparently she wasn't. He was hiring her.

And she was letting him.

Courtesy, integrity, perseverance, self-control, indomitable spirit. The tenets of tae kwon do, drilled into her since she was a child, came to her now. *Courtesy. Integrity...*

David left the stove and came to her, meeting her eyes.

"Here's the bargain, Jean. If you work for me, you must promise you will never under any circumstances dive alone. Ever. And Baby doesn't count."

Jean held his gaze, telling herself discretion was not deceit. In this case it was self-preservation. She told David, "That's fine. I don't like to dive alone."

"I'll be with you." He returned to the stove and fell silent, watching the skillet. Finally he said, "There's something else I don't know if you've picked up on. Sometimes people don't." He paused as though the next words were hard for him. "Chris doesn't talk."

Jean listened to the sputtering of the frying pan. *Doesn't talk?*

"Not since his mother died."

In a flash, Jean glimpsed the sore, still open and unhealed, of Skye Haverford Blade's death.

"He knows sign language, but he doesn't use it much. He's just damned...quiet."

The revelation shook Jean. She wanted the job, but knew she shouldn't take it. The incident in Baja aside, she was lousy with children. She told David, "You should find someone else."

David lifted his eyebrows and stirred the onions in the skillet. "Why is that?"

Jean tried to center herself. If she let this chance escape, she might never have another. At last she said, "I mean there are people trained to be nannies, and you could certainly afford to hire one." Her face felt hot as she said this. "I like kids and I like your son, but I'm not sure I'm cut out to be a nanny." She *knew* she wasn't. She told David, "Even my mom said I'd probably never be a very good mother."

David's expression was well masked. After a moment he remarked dryly, "No one's asked you to be a mother."

Jean's face burned. "That isn't what I meant."

"Or a nanny," David added. "As it stands, this is a temporary arrangement. After the Baja trip, we'll see. If you want the job."

"I want the job."

Switching off the burner, David stepped back and leaned against the counter. After reflecting for a moment he looked at her. "I'll take you provisionally, but I'd like references. Five. At least one academic, two employers, no relatives."

Five? It seemed extreme for a temporary job, but she was prepared for extremes. There were five references on her résumé, and she would give them to David immediately after breakfast. *He's giving me a chance,* she thought in astonishment. *He's actually giving me a chance.*

Silently she vowed he wouldn't be sorry he had.

AFTER BREAKFAST, as they walked back along the beach toward the *Skye,* she said, "Perhaps it would be best if you tell me exactly what you expect of me with Christian. I understand he doesn't go to school." She said the last cautiously, remembering the subject was touchy.

"No," David answered. "And you're not responsible for

his schooling. As for what I expect—I don't expect you to hover over him. There are rules on the *Skye,* and he knows them. He shouldn't be on the diving platform without a life vest and an adult present. The same goes for the foredeck while we're under way.''

Jean guessed the reason for that. Nonetheless, the ship had a bow rail, and it was a mystery to her how Skye Haverford could have managed to fall off. No wonder the police had doubted David's story. But Jean never had.

David said, ''Just be yourself with Chris. Keep him company. Play with him a few hours a day, and let him have some time alone.''

''Sounds like a nanny.'' When David looked at her sharply, Jean said, ''David, your son is important, and a ship can be a hazardous place for a child, as you pointed out yesterday. I think we need clear communication on this. When is he my responsibility, and when is he yours?''

The question both jarred and impressed him. He paused on the beach and found her eyes directly on his, clear and focused with a sobriety he admired.

''As I said before, looking after him is only part of your job,'' David answered. ''I'll tell you whenever he becomes your responsibility. Otherwise he's mine.'' Noting the tension in her shoulders and wondering again at her mother's influence on her self-confidence, he added, ''The words will be, 'Jean, watch Chris.' Clear enough?''

She had wrapped her arms around herself as though she was cold—even though the sun had come out. She told him, ''Perfectly.''

THOUGH ELECTRICITY from the dock hookup was restored by the time they returned to the *Skye,* the generator needed to be repaired before the ship sailed for Baja. Because that project and Erika's holiday decorating plans promised to keep David busy most of the morning, bottom-cleaning was out of the question, and he assigned Jean another task.

"You may as well clean the office."

Sliding open a door in the galley, he led her down a spiral companionway to a dark, dusty cabin. David flicked the wall switch, and a single tracklight overhead illuminated the chamber.

It was an office, but not of the utilitarian variety Jean had anticipated. The work space had once been lavish. Now cobwebs and dust dulled everything, and the place had an eerie, stagnant feeling.

There was a cherry-and-leather executive chair, a large desk of cherry burl, its top littered with dust-covered papers, and a wall crammed with photographs. File folders, photos and more documents lay strewn on the floor beside the desk, as though they had slid there when the ship was at sea and no one had bothered to pick them up. Sheets of paper lay half-torn and crumpled in balls as if savaged by someone in a rage. Even the blotter on the desk had slid far to one side.

Two filing cabinets stood against the wall, and they, like everything else, were shrouded in dust. The handles shone where fingers had opened the drawers, and footprints tracked through the dust on the sole.

The disorder was in complete contrast to the rest of the ship, and as she joined David at the foot of the stairs Jean endeavored to hide her shock.

He admitted, "Out of sight, out of mind. The washer and dryer are behind those folding doors." He indicated the koa doors beside another spiral stairway. "I come down here to wash clothes, and that's about it."

Nodding toward an elegant floor lamp mounted to the wooden sole near the desk, he told her, "I'll get you a bulb for that. Just...do what you need to. The mops and brooms are by the dryer. Make yourself comfortable, and throw out anything that doesn't relate to the business or have obvious legal significance. There's nothing else down here I want."

Jean nodded, her throat dry.

David waited a moment for a reply, then mounted the stairs and ducked through the door, leaving her staring helplessly at what she knew had been Skye Haverford Blade's office.

HE DIDN'T WANT to make the calls from the ship, not with her on board. The obvious choice was his office at the marine supply, where he could pick up Christmas bulbs and parts for the generator and telephone Jean's references.

Four of them, anyway. The other was Jake Doherty.

As he left the marina and hurried down the boardwalk toward the wharf, he studied the names she'd given him. He knew four of the people on her list: Jake; the professor who had recommended her for the Sayles Award; the owner of a local dive shop; and Frank Smith, who ran the martial-arts center.

The last was a neighbor.

The professor had already given a recommendation. David knew what Jake thought of her. And sooner or later he'd run into Frank and could quiz him about his student.

Spontaneously David crumpled the list and tossed it into a nearby trash can. For form's sake he would ask Jake a couple of questions, but the bottom line was he trusted her.

"JUST THROW EVERYTHING out, eh?" Jean murmured aloud, guardedly approaching the desk. Lying on the floor beside it was a framed photograph of David and Skye. The glass was cracked, a long, jagged line dividing the two subjects, but Jean couldn't stop herself from bending to pick up the frame.

The couple must have been on their honeymoon. They stood against a blue sky, and the light in their eyes as they smiled at each other, embracing, was that reserved for lovers. David looked young.

Swiftly Jean calculated the years. Christian was six, so David and Skye must have been married at least four years.

A good foundation, she thought. They would have lived out their days together, perhaps had more children.

How David had changed. In the photo, he looked as though he held everything he'd ever wanted right in his arms. His wife was beautiful. Not pretty or cute or attractive, but exquisite, with skin like buffed porcelain and eyes the color of her name. High cheekbones gave way to dimples and a nearly impertinent grin. Reflecting that Skye could have made a second fortune as a model, Jean lay the photo on the desk. Definitely David didn't mean to get rid of that. The broken glass could be replaced.

Finally she crossed the room and opened the folding doors. Besides a washer, dryer and ironing board, she found cleaning supplies, heavy-duty garbage bags and two empty cardboard boxes. The last two would come in handy.

Assessing the task ahead of her, Jean allowed herself a small groan. Regardless of David's instructions, she was not about to discard his wife's personal effects. Probably he found it painful to see her things, but someday he would want them. Taking the boxes and a rag, she went to the desk and set to work, first dusting the chair, then sitting.

On the blotter lay an engagement calendar turned to December 6, and Jean wondered, *Is it the sixth already?* But it wasn't. She stared, immobilized, realizing the calendar was three years old.

And Skye Haverford Blade had died on St. Nicholas Day.

It came back to her. The eerie gray weather. The holiday decorations on the docks fighting the wind and losing. The huge Christmas wreaths swaying from cables over State Street and the wharf.

Had nothing in the office been touched since Skye's death?

Oh, David, Jean thought. *Is it that bad?*

But it would be, she decided, remembering the healing she had gained from dressing her parents for burial. A friend had made the suggestion, pointing out that caring for the dead had once been women's work. Jean had gone through with it, though Cecily had declined, and now she knew that helping the funeral director care for her parents' bodies had helped her with her own grief.

But David had never even seen his wife's body.

Reassessing the chaos of the office, Jean wondered, Had there been no one to help with these details when Skye died? Erika couldn't have made it down the stairs, but surely there was some friend, someone David trusted. On the other hand, if there was, why had he waited three years and assigned the task to a virtual stranger?

Involuntarily she recalled sitting at her father's and mother's desks, going through their papers, their address books, everything marked with their familiar scripts. All the details came back. The funeral director, their bodies, the settling of the estate—and the sense of life on hold, of unfinished business. The argument with her mother over the catastrophe in Baja was responsible for that.

Jean shook off her memories. This wasn't her parents' office, and she could spare David some pain.

She began separating the paper and other odds and ends into personal and business categories, discarding trash. There were opened letters she glanced at to determine their nature, then filed in their rightful stack. She came across a few letters from David to Skye, probably written while he was at sea and she at home in Santa Barbara, because many bore foreign postmarks. Love letters, concluded Jean, biting her lip as she tossed the envelopes into the box of personal items.

After clearing the desktop, she tried to pull open the drawers, only to find them locked. She located the keys in the bottom of the letter caddy, unlocked the top middle drawer and slid it open. Inside lay more cards and letters and photos, packed so tightly it was a wonder the drawer had opened at all.

Sighing at the sorting ahead of her, Jean reached for a photo on top. It showed Skye in a bikini, embracing a mustached blond man whose lips were dragging sensuously over her hair. Puzzled, Jean turned over the photo and found bold, masculine writing on the back.

In love in the Bahamas—with you. Homeless Shelter Fashion Shoot with my favorite model. It was dated four years earlier, during Skye and David's marriage. So Skye had modeled—for charity. The blond man must have been her photographer.

Doubting David would want it, Jean tossed the snapshot into the trash and continued working. Beneath a jumble of postcards, she unearthed vials of pills and examined the labels with interest, but she knew too little about medicine to determine what Skye had been taking or for what. Only that they were Skye's pills, from a variety of doctors, mostly marked No Refill.

More letters then, from David and other people. Leafing through a stack of postcards, Jean was surprised to find one showing a stone relief she recognized from one of her tae kwon do books. The photograph showed two giant figures poised in tae kwon do stance carved in the tower wall of a Buddhist temple in the ancient city of Kyongju. Two thousand years old, the carvings were considered evidence of the antiquity of the martial art.

Until that point Jean had refrained from reading Skye's mail, but when she turned over the postcard and saw it was from David, she could resist no longer.

Dear Skye,
I used to visit this place often when I lived here. It feels the same now, as though the deepest part of me were born here. The other parts came from the sea. Where did you come from? I need to know, and so do you. I love you deeply.

                                                        David

Jean felt as though someone had stuffed a rock in her windpipe. For a moment she sat frozen, holding the postcard. Skye had been so young, and they were in love. They had a child, the ultimate symbol of their love for each other.

Trying not to puzzle over his words, which led her nowhere but to the final message of love, Jean, instead, pondered the news that David had lived in Korea. It made her think of his bow to her in her kitchen that morning. Knowing he had lived in the Far East, she found the gesture less surprising. What did surprise her was that he used to visit the temple at Kyongju, a place Jean would never have heard of but for her study of tae kwon do.

Long seconds passed before she at last put the postcard with his other letters and reached for the keys to unlock one of the bigger, lower drawers.

The drawer opened slowly, and her efforts were met with the clinking of glass. She had discovered Skye's private liquor stash. Grasping two nearly empty bottles by the necks, Jean pulled them out. Grand Marnier and Irish cream. Next came a half-empty gin bottle, another mostly gone cognac and a glass containing a decomposed olive. In the back of the drawer were two broken bottles, a half-drunk fifth of tequila and one decayed lime. The inside of the drawer was sticky with spilled alcohol.

Wondering how much Skye had drunk and why she hadn't used the bar in the salon, Jean debated over the bottles. She wasn't sure three-year-old liquor was still good or if there was enough in the bottles to merit saving.

At last she placed the bottles in the garbage bag, then began picking the broken glass out of the drawer. A sound at the top of the stairs startled her, and she jumped, slicing her hand on a jagged piece of glass. Wincing, she saw Christian looking down the companionway.

Her hand was bleeding, and she grabbed the dust rag to put over the cut, but she could feel glass in the wound. Hurriedly she stood up. "Chris, your dad asked me to clean this office and I cut myself. Can you show me where the first-aid kit is?''

He nodded, and when she got to the top of the stairs, Jean showed him her wound. The cut was more than an inch long, and she couldn't tell how deep. Taking charge, Chris reached for her other hand and led her into the galley.

The galley steps had been raised and latched overhead, revealing the open door of the engine room. Leaving Jean in the galley, Chris went into the engine room and emerged a moment later. He was opening a locker beneath the sink when David appeared, his hair tumbled across his forehead, his slacks stained with engine grease.

''Chris said you cut yourself.''

''It's nothing.'' She clasped the dusty rag to her hand. ''I'll just clean it out.''

David ducked into the galley. ''Show me.''

Jean lifted the rag. ''See? Nothing.'' Her heart was hammering.

''Chris, thanks for getting me. I'll take care of Jean.'' David stepped to the sink and took the first-aid box from his son. ''You did just the right thing.''

As though reading something unspoken in David's eyes, Chris hurried up the steps that led to his father's cabin and went inside, closing the door behind him.

Jean asked, ''Is he okay?''

''Shouldn't he be?'' David's glance was incisive.

Jean reflected that she'd been sitting at Skye's desk when Chris appeared at the top of the stairs. Had the sight stirred up memories of his mother? She said, ''He left quickly.''

Without reply David led her to the sink and held her hand under a cold stream of water. ''There's glass in that cut. What from?''

His jaw was taut, and Jean trembled. She could feel the heat from his body.

''Just...some broken bottles.'' Jean tried to sound nonchalant, but the admission discomfited her. She'd never known anyone who kept a bar in a desk. Did David even know which bottles she meant?

Apparently, because he was silent as he washed his own hands and shut off the water. Leading her back to the dining booth, he gestured for her to sit down. He sat beside her, his thigh against hers, and with tweezers from the first-aid kit began to remove the glass from her hand.

"I can do this," said Jean.

"With your left hand? I don't think so."

They sat in silence for nearly a minute, and Jean stared absently at the advent calendar on the wall. Another door had been opened to show a stocking hanging by a hearth. The fifth, she thought as a glass sliver pricked her wound.

She shuddered, and David's arm slid around her shoulders over her braid. "Sorry. Just another minute." His hand squeezed her shoulder through the cotton of her sweatshirt as he extracted the sliver, then set to work on another. "Bottles," he remarked. "I'm sorry I asked you to do that. If there's broken glass, leave it for me, all right?"

"I didn't mind." Jean could think only of his arm around her. She could feel his heart beating against her side.

Again a sliver dug into the cut, and she gasped involuntarily.

David pressed her shoulder gently.

Recklessly Jean looked up, and her pulse lodged in her throat. "Sorry I'm such a baby."

David shook his head. "It's nice to— Speaking of babies, where is she?"

Nice to what? Hold her? It took all Jean's concentration to think of Baby. The dolphin had appeared soon after she and David reached the *Skye,* but Jean could no longer hear her outside. She shrugged. "I guess she knows we're not diving today. Baby doesn't hang around begging for attention." She said this guiltily, because Baby would do exactly that if given the slightest encouragement.

"That's good," said David. "At times I've suspected she's very emotionally dependent on you."

"At least you see she has emotions," Jean answered, sidestepping the remark. "Most scientists won't admit to that."

"As a scientist I won't, either. As a human—" he plucked the last sliver from her hand "—I can't believe anything else. And that kind of emotional attachment with a wild animal is a mistake." He inspected her hand under the light. "Did I get it all?"

"I think so." Jean studied his face, pondering his remarks about Baby. How could loving her be wrong?

But David seemed finished with the subject—and her hand. He doused the wound in betadine and closed it with a butterfly bandage. "Good as new," he said, holding her finger slightly. "Leave the glass for me, now, okay?"

The touch was too much. To Jean, it felt hot and sexy and forbidden, yet she knew it couldn't be affecting him that way or he couldn't sit there so calmly. Good grief, he was her boss.

Abruptly he dropped her hand and stood up, and Jean felt a shaft of disappointment run through her as he murmured a dismissal she couldn't make out and disappeared into the engine room.

Left behind at the table, she gazed at the closed doors of the calendar, all the unknown days until Christmas. Imagining the anticipation Chris must feel before opening each door, Jean realized she was looking ahead to the coming days with similar excitement, for what each might reveal about David. Yet she was apprehensive, too. This morning he had begun to thaw, and she, without meaning to, had begun to care—and to understand.

David was a man with grave responsibilities, including a disabled sister and a mute son. Thinking of his shifts in mood, the shell of coldness replaced by warmth, Jean knew he was scarred, badly, by the death of the woman he'd loved.

IN THE ENGINE ROOM David rested his chin in his hands and stared sightlessly at the generator.

He'd touched her.

Quite a bit, for him. Keeping his hands off was going to be a problem, and unfortunately not the only one.

Over breakfast and since, he had begun to perceive that Jean was both uniquely independent and highly unpredictable, qualities that attracted him but made her a dubious choice for a shipmate. A crew member could be either part of a ship's operation, a cog in the wheel or a separate force, disrupting established patterns, shaking things up. Like Skye.

Like Jean.

Big mistake, hiring her. The offer had been impulse, and he was rarely impulsive. But Jean continued to surprise him, and part of him could not resist surprises. For instance, the knowledge that she studied tae kwon do. He'd dived headfirst into hot water with a black belt who read romance novels and was a klutz in the kitchen and thought she was bad with kids. And he'd forgotten what a ship's close quarters could accomplish unasked.

David heard her tread on the companionway, then a thud from the galley and the clanking sound of bottles hitting each other.

He made his way out of the engine room and into the galley.

Jean had set a cardboard box on the table. On top was a photo of him and Skye. Letters and open papers lay underneath.

David said, "What's that?"

"I thought you might want these things."

"I don't." And he had told her so. "Throw it out."

Jean looked up at him. Now her eyes were the same color

as her sweatshirt—sage. From her expression, David knew he was going to get an argument.

She said, "Her family might want these things. Or Chris might. There are diplomas, letters—"

"Thank you for going to that trouble, but this ship's not big enough to keep everything. You can throw those out." He said the last in a voice he hoped would convey how little he liked repeating himself.

Jean toyed with the tail of her braid and regarded him with a frown. In the manner of someone uncomfortable offering unsolicited advice, she suggested, "You must have a safety-deposit box or something. Why don't you just…take a few of your letters—for Chris."

Giving her a brief, icy stare, David washed his hands at the sink and returned to the box at the table. He reached for the stack of letters, flipped through them and selected a few of the older ones, stuffing them into the pocket of his canvas shirt. He tossed the rest in the box and told Jean, "To the Dumpster."

She said, "You're making a mistake."

He had to hand it to her—she had nerve. David clenched his teeth and enunciated with cool precision, "Throw out the box." He pulled the letters from his pocket and tossed them on top of the rest. "And take those too."

Jean took a step back, and David realized in disbelief that she had no intention of following his orders. She said quietly, "If you want to throw those things out, you can carry them to the Dumpster yourself. You couldn't even bring yourself to tell me it was your wife's office."

"You figured it out."

She moved toward the sink as though she was avoiding him. If so, she had good instincts. He wanted to throttle her.

But when there was more distance between them, she turned to meet his eyes. "You have no right to be angry at me. You should have looked through those things yourself. That's the only way to deal with death—to look it in the face.''

David felt momentarily light-headed. She'd called him a coward. He said, ''How dare you. You don't have a clue what I've seen.''

She looked as though he'd hit her. Her features were white, stricken, her eyes huge with an expression of self-blame and sorrow David found infuriating. ''My God, I'm sorry,'' she whispered.

He didn't reply. She was shaking things up all right. David did not like to be shaken.

Jean turned her back on him and leaned against the counter, overwhelmed by the realization of what David actually might have seen, not just when his wife died but also when the *Siren* went down. And she'd self-righteously accused him of refusing to face death—as though he'd had a choice.

Watching her back, David locked his arms across his chest, primarily so he wouldn't touch her. The thought that he might made him treat her coldly. ''Pull yourself together. I didn't hire you to come apart at the seams when I give you a simple order.''

Jean wheeled where she stood, fighting for control as she thought of his ''simple'' order—to throw out his wife's belongings. She glanced at the box, then at him. ''I am not coming apart at the seams, and that order was not simple or reasonable. You have a son to consider. Those things belonged to his mother.''

''Don't tell me about my family.'' Face tense, eyes mad with emotion, he stepped toward her.

Jean drew back, her hands flat, facing him. Two palms that could easily curl into fists. She said, ''Stay back!''

Her voice was strong enough, her stance sure enough, to give him pause. But the look in her eye charged him, and a small knot somewhere inside him unraveled. He said, ''No.''

CHAPTER FIVE

SHE DIDN'T WANT to hurt him, only keep him away. Without time to think it through, to think more than that he was nearly upon her, she delivered a glancing side kick, pulled so as not to hurt him. Faster than she could blink, David blocked the blow and counterattacked.

Jean hit the sole of the galley like a sack of laundry, for a moment uncertain what he had done. Belatedly she realized she had met one of her own.

She said, "You bastard."

"We're not done." As she began to spring up, he easily shoved her rest of the way down, slipping a hand beneath her head so it didn't hit the teak sole and at the same time covering her body, pinning her ankles to the floor. Then, he kissed her.

Jean froze. Because she didn't want to fight, she closed her eyes. In a kind of quiet trance, she absorbed the brush of his beard, the feel of his muscles, of his mouth, of his hand on her braid. He was tense, but gentle. And for a fraction of an instant, in a dark corner of her mind where wild concepts roamed, Jean wondered if he was frightened.

Abruptly David moved off her and sat up. Pulse erratic, body still, Jean stared up at him.

He drew a long breath and leaned back on his hands as though signaling that if she wanted to hit him he would allow it. He said, "That was inexcusable. I'm very sorry." He met her eyes. "I know you pulled that kick. Are you hurt?"

Sitting up, Jean shook her head. "Not how you mean."

He looked interested. "How do *you* mean?"

Jean said, "It's just not how I dream of being kissed."

David shut his eyes, and she knew the words had cut, primarily because they were deserved.

After a few seconds, he opened his eyes and met hers. "May I try again?"

Jean's breath quickened. In the past minutes she had wondered many things about him, but never if he would physically hurt her. Her attempt to keep him from touching her had been only that. They had both been wildly upset.

With a slight tilt of her chin, she nodded.

David moved closer to her on the floor. His eyes flickered over her, and then he touched the corner of her mouth.

Jean's lungs squeezed closed. It was hard to look into his eyes, and yet she wanted to and sensed he wanted her to. They were dark and full of so much. She had seen him rude and cool and remote and now angry, but she knew that ultimately he was deep. So deep, she wondered if she could even scratch the surface.

Jean held her breath as he stroked back a lock of her hair loosened in their tussle and searched her face. Then he fitted his mouth to hers.

Jean was unprepared for her own response. Her throat tightened, and her heart felt as though it were going to jump out of her body. The artery in her neck pulsed so violently she knew David must feel it. He did, because he put his hand there as he kissed her.

It was a simple kiss and an incredibly complicated one. When he drew her closer, Jean acquiesced without struggle. She pushed nearer, feeling the muscles in his arm and the wall of his chest. His thigh pressed against hers. She felt his breath and discovered it was as uneven as her own.

Her lips parted and she felt, as she'd hoped she would, the touch of his tongue, tasting, experimenting. He clasped her more tightly to his body, and Jean wondered if he wanted to lie down as badly as she did.

When he finally pulled away, she felt mildly disoriented. He unwound her arms from his neck and set her hands in her lap—away from him. Then he stood and offered her his own hand. Jean took it and rose, as well, wondering if he would embrace her.

He didn't. He let go of her and bowed.

Meeting his eyes, Jean returned the courtesy and offered her hands.

He took them. *"Kamsa hamnida."* Thank you. "Let's not do that again."

Kissing? Jean wondered as they released hands. Or spontaneous sparring?

She thought of the postcard of the Kyongju temple and his bow to her that morning. She wanted to ask him why he hadn't told her he'd studied tae kwon do, but David spoke first. Directing her attention to the box on the table, the catalyst that had set off their argument—and everything else—he said, "Please get rid of that. It's the last time I'm asking. And believe me, I won't be so patient again."

Jean recognized a warning. She said nothing.

"You can take it to her lawyer's office. It's at 51 Coast Village Road. Peter Barnes. Tell him I'll call him about what to do with it."

As Jean chewed on the realization that this particular order was a compromise, he took some keys from his pants pocket and dropped them in her hand. "Take my car. It's in space three beside the café."

Jean stared at the key ring.

David said, "Can you drive a stick?"

She nodded.

"Go get some lunch, but be careful. It's a fast car." He ducked into the engine room. "You can take the top down."

Her eyes followed him. "Do you want anything?"

He turned and looked at her, his own eyes like two sentinels guarding a dungeon that might hold monsters—or treasure. "I want you to go."

Nodding toward his cabin, the exit she should take, he disappeared into the engine room.

Jean looked down at the letters he'd tossed on the box and wondered if he planned to call the lawyer and tell *him* to throw them out. Impulsively she removed his letters, placed them on the table, then picked up the box and the garbage sack. David might have looked death in the face, but love was harder.

As she carried the bulging garbage bag and the box to the parking lot, Jean played back everything that had occurred in the galley—argument, anger, takedown, kisses.

She was far from blameless. When he'd stepped toward her, she'd overreacted—almost as though for a moment a part of her had wondered if he *had* killed his wife.

But that wasn't it at all. The thought had never crossed her mind. The simple fact was he affected her as no man ever had, and she'd lost all semblance of composure and forgotten the basis of her tae kwon do training—self-control.

Apparently so had David.

Jean didn't know what to make of him or of what he had done. She'd seen a gamut of responses in him, all unrestrained as though something inside had snapped.

Which was possible. Their dispute had been intense and, for him, highly personal. Part of her wished she could take back things she'd said. It was mentioning Chris that had sent him over the edge. Or maybe Skye.

Don't tell me about my family.

As she neared the boardwalk, a sight on the other side of the marina gate jerked her from her thoughts. Jake Doherty, who ran the marine supply, sat outside the espresso shop.

Bad timing, thought Jean. For her, not Jake.

Six foot six, with a waist-length mane of auburn hair, Jake lived in the harbor on his Chinese junk, the *Lien Hua.* Jean knew vaguely that his past included college basketball, an engineering degree and time spent doing practically nothing in places like Jamaica and Thailand. But for the past six years he'd been in business on the wharf, and now he was a harbor institution, respected for his mechanical savvy and his omniscience. He knew everything that had happened on the Santa Barbara waterfront in the past decade and much before that, and he lived to learn new things daily.

Before Jean reached the marina gate she saw his eyes light up, more with curiosity than pleasure. He stood to help her with the gate, glancing with apparent disinterest at her box and the heavy-duty garbage bag.

Jean wasn't fooled. Like Santa Claus, Jake missed nothing. Right now, he was as welcome as the bad fairy at a christening.

She said, "Hi, Jake," and walked past him through the gate.

"Hi yourself, stranger. Let me give you a hand with that." Before she could protest, both items had been lifted from her arms and Jake was striding down the boardwalk beside her, peering into the box he was hefting. "Where to, gorgeous?"

"The Dumpster for the garbage. I'll take the box," she said, reaching for it.

He held it out of the way. "I wouldn't hear of it." He eyed the photo of Skye and David at the top of the box. "So David let you clean the shrine?"

Jean felt a new respect for Jake's powers of deduction. It was hard to fathom how he had known exactly where the contents of the box had originated. She said, "The shrine?"

Jake grinned at her. They had reached the nearest

Dumpster, and he handed her the box and tossed the garbage bag inside. It landed with a loud shatter of glass, and he chuckled at her expression. "Skye's medicine chest?" He winked. "The babe had some great parties."

Jean thought of the tequila and cognac and unmarked vials of pills. Jake sounded as though he'd had personal experience with Skye's parties—and her "medicine chest." Briefly she imagined him and Skye sitting together in the office, laughing and enjoying drinks. It was a strange picture, two unlikely people linked by a common thread— David. At a loss for a suitable reply, she said, a little ironically, "Thanks for carrying the trash."

"No problem." Jake started to take the box, but Jean moved away.

She said, "I'll carry it." She wasn't sure why she felt as she did about the box. A glance inside could tell nothing, yet Jean felt compelled to protect the contents, almost as though she was protecting David and Chris and even Erika, the people Skye's death had touched.

Jake didn't quibble over the box, in which he now seemed genuinely uninterested. He said, "I hear you've been promoted."

With a start Jean remembered she had listed Jake among the references she'd given to David that morning. David must have spoken with him, and Jean wondered what he had asked—and how Jake had replied.

"He wanted to know if you have any secrets."

Jean almost dropped the box, and Jake rescued it. When she didn't object, he assumed the burden, remarking, "A royal flush, eh?"

Jean said nothing. His words were as good as an admission that he knew nothing about Baja, but that didn't stop her heart's frantic knocking. The last thing she wanted was for David to hear that story. If even her own mother had doubted her, how would he react? David, who was so protective of his family.

Jake shrugged. "Like I told him, everyone has secrets. Including David, by the way." He jostled the box. "Where does this go?"

"David's car." Jean's breathing had almost returned to normal, but her mind was racing. What were David's secrets?

Jake eyed the car keys in her hand. "The 'Vette." He smiled sideways at Jean as they walked around the espresso shop. "Don't feel too special. I think he secretly hopes someone will total it and he'll be relieved of the responsibility."

Jean's eyes darted toward his. "What do you mean?"

They had reached space three, and Jake set down the box and began stripping the cover from a long, low sports car. "See for yourself. A 'sixty-five roadster. Low miles, totally cherry. The thing's priceless. Rich people—people richer than David—buy cars like these and park them in their garages and drive them on Sundays. David parks his here. At the waterfront. Nothing's ever happened to it, but like I said, I think he's hoping."

Jean hurried to the side of the car to help with the cover. She was of a mind to march back to the *Skye* and tell David Blade she wouldn't drive his car as far as the next parking space. Priceless? What if she wrecked it? She asked, "Why does he have the car if he doesn't like it?"

"Skye," said Jake, rolling back the cover to reveal a sleek black hood.

Jean looked at him.

Catching her glance, Jake said, "The woman was a mindblower, wanted to control everyone she met. She couldn't control David, so she married him. Some people are like that. The big challenge in life is to crack the whip. If Skye had ever figured out how to control David she would've left him. Hell," Jake added, "she's working on it even now. Voilà. The will. The car."

Jean blinked at him, not understanding.

Jake took the car cover and folded it neatly, his eyes on hers. "She left him a seven-digit life-insurance plan—and more—provided he'd take the car. She'd been trying to buy him a fast car the whole time they were married. He used to drive this VW squareback with the roof torn off. It was a classic in its own realm, but Skye hated it so much she finally totaled it. *Whammo.* Then, she leaves David a vintage Corvette of untold value in her will. He's got to take it—or else." Jake pantomimed cracking a whip. "The state the Blade Institute was in, he didn't have a choice. He would have lost his ship—everything."

Jean tried to look as though she knew just what he was talking about. The Blade Institute in trouble?

"Note the vanity plates. They came with."

Jean looked. The California license read PRESENT.

"I mean, you're a woman, Jean. What do you think when you see a guy who looks like David driving a car like this with plates like that? You think he's the favorite toy of some rich babe, and she bought him a hot car to show her appreciation."

Jean reddened. "I—I don't—"

"Of course not. You're still an innocent. But trust me, Skye knew what she was doing. You know what I think those plates mean?" He tucked the car cover under his arm. "I think they mean she's present, even now. She's here. You're on that ship sometime at night, you'll know what I mean. You can feel her, teasing him. They say the soul of a drowned person never rests." Jake shrugged. "But what do you care? It's just a job, right? And better than slime war, eh, babe? By the way your check for the *Lien Hua* is at the marine supply. You were so gaga over David's offer you forgot to collect." He gave her a teasing smile, then looked at the car. "You want the top down on this monster?"

Jean nodded, relieved to see the conversation change

course. Together, she and Jake lowered the top of the convertible.

WHEN JEAN RETURNED to the *Skye* after her errand and a quick lunch, Chris was lying on the aft deck, his arms stretched out under the railing, trying vainly to touch Baby. The deck was much too high.

Jean longed to take him out onto the diving platform, but it would violate one of her own Baby policies and result in a host of undesirable behavior from the dolphin, all stemming from a need for attention.

Besides, David had been clear about Chris and Baby, and what he'd said about the life spans of lone dolphins was true. More than once, Jean had been kept awake by fears that Baby would be hit by a speedboat in the harbor. If Christian became as attached as she was to Baby, the dolphin's death could devastate him.

She paused on the aft deck. "Hi, Chris."

He looked up, but did not smile.

Embarrassed by his ambivalence toward her, Jean moved toward the cabin, wondering if Chris was safe lying on the deck that way. It was easy to see him reaching farther and farther to touch Baby—

She turned around. "Chris, that's not safe. Sit up on the cushions or stand against the railing."

He glanced at her but didn't move.

Again Jean felt a sense of her own failure with children. How could she take care of Chris if he wouldn't obey her?

A circle of fear tightened her throat, and she pushed it away. He *would* obey her.

She walked over and crouched on the deck beside Chris, meeting his eyes. It was a nerve-racking experience. His eyes were so like David's.

Swallowing, Jean said, "I guess your dad didn't tell you this, but he hired me to help look after you. I'm going to make the same decisions for you I would for a child of my own, and I hope you can help with the decision-making.''

Chris shifted his eyes, watching Baby, but she kept talking, feeling her way. "Right now you have a choice. You can get up and sit on the cushions, or I can go get your dad. He's not crazy about you playing with Baby, anyhow."

Chris didn't move. It wasn't working.

Jean stood up and turned away, but when she looked back from the diving alcove, Chris had moved to the cushions.

She released a breath she hadn't known she'd been holding.

DAVID AND ERIKA were in the salon, surrounded by strings of Christmas lights. An artificial tree stood in one corner of the room, and David lay sideways beneath it, bolting the stand to the sole of the cabin.

Seeing him again, Jean stiffened slightly, both anticipating and dreading the moment he would turn and see her.

Erika said, "Jean! I'm so glad you're here. We need another pair of hands."

"We need to get rid of some lights is what we need." David did not look up as he spoke. He'd hoped to be gone when Jean returned, but Erika had waylaid him.

"Scrooge," accused his sister. "I'm glad Jean's going along to Baja with you, to make sure you don't ruin everyone's Christmas with your whining."

David stood up. "I never whine. I make practical suggestions." Bracing himself, he turned to Jean. "I finished the office for you. There's a new bulb in the floor lamp."

"Thanks." She didn't quite meet his gaze.

"I left a W-2 form on the desk for you."

That got her attention.

He said, "You passed."

He meant the references, Jean thought dimly. She was

hired. With confusion she remembered what had happened before lunch, and as she caught David's expression she wondered if he was remembering the same thing.

"Can you two do business later?" Erika asked. She told Jean, "If I let David get away from this now he won't come back."

"That's true," he agreed.

Erika wheeled through a path between the lights and picked up a bunch of mistletoe from the floor. She handed it to Jean, instructing, "You find a place for this, and David can tack it up. I have to go find the star." She sped down the aft ramp.

Jean looked down at the mistletoe in her hand, then scouted the salon for somewhere to hang it. David scooped up a couple of thumbtacks from a box beneath the tree.

She asked, "Where does this usually go?"

"Usually?" He glanced indifferently at the mistletoe. "We haven't had the stuff around for years. I'm surprised Erika bought some." Catching Jean's inquisitive glance, he explained, "Let's just say she and I are both a little cynical."

"Cynical?" said Jean. "Erika?"

"You'll understand when you know her better." He eyed Jean distantly. "I notice you didn't question *my* cynicism."

Jean smiled faintly. "You must have hung the mistletoe somewhere before you turned cynical."

There followed an uncomfortable silence in which his eyes spoke volumes. B.C.—before cynicism—must have been before Skye's death. David wouldn't want to hang the mistletoe where he had kissed his wife and lover many times.

Jean hastily suggested, "Let's put it in the galley, so the cook and the dishwasher get lots of kisses."

At David's look of speculation, she remembered that was where they had kissed, and her face flamed to her hairline. "Or maybe…over the stairwell."

His eyes slanted toward hers. "Maybe we should just hang it in my cabin and be done with it."

Jean stammered, "Let's put it over the stairwell. The aft stairwell." The one farthest from his cabin.

David took the bough from her hands, his fingers grazing hers. "I like the idea of putting it in the galley. Come on." He gave her a gentle push toward the galley stairs. "You can help me hang it straight."

She didn't move. David looked at her for a moment, then stepped around her to descend the companionway. After a moment Jean followed.

When she entered the galley she saw the table was clear. The letters she had left were nowhere in sight, and she wondered what David had done with them—and if he would mention this violation of his orders.

Not immediately at any rate. He was tacking up the mistletoe. His expression did not invite company, and Jean hung back by the table.

Finishing, he looked at her and said rather remotely, "Go ahead and help Erika for now. Then suit up so we can tackle the hull again. I'll meet you topside in—" he glanced at his watch "—one hour."

His change of mood baffled her. Chewing on her lip, Jean wondered if it was because she had hesitated in the salon. Tentatively she moved toward him.

David shook his head at her. "You were right." Without another word he started up the stairs to his cabin and disappeared inside, shutting the door behind him.

Jean wasn't sure what to feel. Did this mean he intended to keep their relationship strictly business? That was wise, but disappointing. Casting a last glance at his closed door, Jean started up the other companionway to the salon.

Erika's voice called to her from aft. "Where'd you put the mistletoe?"

"In the galley near the sink."

Erika wheeled up the ramp, a stack of ornament boxes in her lap. "Where's David?"

"In his cabin." Hoping her inner turbulence didn't show, Jean focused her attention to the lights on the carpet. "Have these been tested? Should we string them yet?"

"Sure. I'm a little concerned about Chris," admitted Erika. "I haven't seen him for a while."

Jean climbed to the salon door and looked through the windowpane and the windows of the diving alcove to the aft deck. David was there. He must have gone out through the wheelhouse. Jean watched him hoist his son on his shoulders.

The comfortable display of affection tore at her somehow, and her voice was less than even as she told Erika, "I think David's taking him to town."

"Good." Erika frowned at the lights. "Yes, I think these are ready to go up. Let's plug them in one more time."

Jean fitted the plug into the nearest socket, and the bulbs sprang to light.

"Hooray!" said Erika. "Always a happy sight."

Jean smiled. "It's fun to do this in a family environment. My sister—" She stopped, but Erika looked interested, and Jean found herself confessing what her last Christmas had been like.

Erika nodded understandingly. "David and I spent the holidays apart, too, for a couple of years after our parents died. Money was the problem. I was studying in Australia when the ship went down, and David insisted we use the life insurance to continue paying for my education. He was living in Korea, fishing, and airfare seemed like an extravagance."

Korea again. Had David studied martial arts in the Orient?

Erika said, "And then, the year Skye died was another story. David just forgot about Christmas. No tree. No Santa Claus. It just didn't happen." She told Jean, "I meant that about being glad you're going to Baja with him. He tries to make the holidays nice for Chris, but he gets pretty black, too. Those two really need a woman around.''

Jean liked the sound of the words. They seemed to imply that she, a woman who had killed two out of three bonsai trees and couldn't cook breakfast, possessed the nurturing qualities to bring out the Christmas spirit in an unhappy widower and his somber little boy.

But if Erika knew how much David and Chris needed a woman, why was she moving out? It seemed sad that she would spend Christmas alone at the rehab center.

As Jean unplugged the lights and gathered up the string, Erika asked, ''Do you mind if I get my book and sketch you while you do that?''

Shaking her head, Jean began clipping lights to the tree branches as Erika retrieved a sketchbook and pencils from a drawer in the end table. Arranging the lights, Jean peered across the room to the painting over the stairwell. Skye's silvery turquoise eyes and bewitching smile seemed to follow her every move.

Seeing Erika watching her, Jean said, ''It's a beautiful painting. Can you make me look that good?''

Erika laughed. ''Skye would've hated that. Sort of like the queen in *Snow White*.'' Her humor faded. ''I shouldn't have said that. It sounded terrible.'' Brow creased, she said, ''Skye truly was 'the fairest of them all.'''

Jean longed to ask questions. Erika was clearly a remarkable person. She handled her disability with courageous optimism and always seemed full of kind words for others. What had she thought of David's wife? Jean said, ''I saw Skye's photograph. Her eyes really were as blue as you painted them.''

Erika nodded, subdued, and Jean wondered what she had felt toward her sister-in-law. She said, ''I'm sorry, Erika. That was insensitive of me.''

Erika cut her short. ''Don't apologize, Jean. Just because

things are unpleasant doesn't mean we should never speak of them.''

Jean relaxed, reassured. She liked David's sister more than ever.

Erika drew a line on the paper. ''I was just thinking of a conversation we had—David and Jake and me. You know Jake, don't you? He's served as our first mate on many shorter expeditions, even before he and David opened the marine supply. I think he's going to Baja.''

This was all news to Jean, and she asked herself why Jake had never mentioned that David was his partner. *Probably a silent partner,* she reflected.

''Anyhow,'' said Erika, ''Skye had been dead just a month or so. We were sitting around here when Jake started telling this absolutely beautiful Chumash myth about souls going to Šimilaqša.''

Jean listened with interest. The Chumash were the Native Americans who had inhabited the south coast before the Spanish settlement. Their rock art was painted on the walls of many caves in the area, but the tribe was nearly extinct, destroyed by the scourges that came with the settlers.

''Jake said some Chumash believed that after death souls traveled west toward the sun, where they were born again. Others thought they went to Šimilaqša, the place where they never grew old, like a Christian heaven. On the way the soul encountered many dangers—a woman who could sting with her tail and ravens who plucked out the eyes. But then the soul picked poppies from the ground and placed them in his eye sockets and could see again. When he reached Šimilaqša, the soul was given eyes of blue abalone.''

Erika shut her eyes briefly, then reopened them. ''But David interrupted Jake and said the Chumash also believed the soul of a drowned person wandered the sea forever and never reached the land to the west to be born again. I'll never forget how David looked just then. He said, 'Skye's eyes were like blue abalone when she was alive. And I don't care if her soul rests or not. You think mine does?''' Erika looked down at her drawing paper. "I don't know why I'm telling you this. The whole thing was awful." She gave a shake of her head like a shudder. "I've just never forgotten the way he talked about her eyes."

He had talked like a lover, thought Jean. She wondered exactly what Erika meant by awful. What had happened out in the channel? Jean wished David would talk about it, but she imagined it was something he discussed rarely— and only with those closest to him.

Still, unable to stop herself, she nodded out the window toward the islands and asked Erika, "What really happened out there?"

Erika lifted her shoulders in an exaggerated shrug. "Ask my brother. You might get further than I ever did." Releasing a long breath, she said, "I suppose it's only fair to warn you that tomorrow's the anniversary of her death."

Jean straightened. December sixth. Of course.

Erika said, "Don't worry. He probably won't ask you to work. He usually takes Chris out to the islands. There's a marker on one of them, and they leave some flowers." She explained, "I just wanted you to know that if he seems touchy, that may be why."

Jean thought of their skirmish in the galley. As she rearranged a section of light cord, her eyes again caught the painting of Skye. Bending an uncooperative tree bough, she asked, "Erika, don't answer if this is too painful, but...what was she like?"

Unexpectedly Erika laughed. When Jean looked over at her, she said, "That's a big question, and I'm probably not the person to answer it." She glanced at Jean. "Why did you ask? Do you like David?"

Jean was sure her face gave her away. Squeezing behind the tree and taking the light string with her, she said, "I probably don't have to answer that."

Erika smiled but said only, "Let's see. What can I tell you about Skye?" Thoughtfully she remarked, "She went to two different European universities. I'm not up on that sort of thing, but David has said they're famous schools. I think he envied her that—he's never been to school at all, and he reads like a fiend." Erika looked faraway, as though recollecting her sister-in-law. "God, sometimes she used to make me laugh, Jean. Her sense of humor was hilarious. She was so mean and so funny all at once. And creative. She made that beautiful quilt on David's bed."

Jean noticed Erika had managed to make meanness sound like a positive attribute. Like being clever.

David's sister fell silent, then shrugged gracefully. "As for the rest, I guess it would suffice to say she was no angel. But she didn't marry one, either."

Jean peered at her through the branches of the tree. "That sounded like a warning."

"I'm not sure I meant it that way. David's a complicated man. I think he could be a lot to handle."

No kidding, Jean thought.

Erika smiled. "And shut up so I can sketch your mouth, all right?"

Jean answered with a grin, knowing the instruction was Erika's playful way of saying the discussion was over.

Under Erika's guidance, she decorated the salon and the tree, tying the ornaments to the branches so they wouldn't shake off at sea. It was a disturbing task. She was charmed by the gold sand-dollar ornaments and other slightly damaged treasures Erika said dated back to her father's life and had been salvaged from the *Siren.* There was even an aluminum ornament David had made as a child. But also, nestled in protective layers of tissue, were the inevitable personalized trinkets: *David and Skye—Our First Christmas Together; Skye's Silver Skate; Christian's First Christmas.* There was even a photo of Skye nestled in a pearly ball.

Jean asked, "Does this go up?"

"Oh, no." Erika wheeled forward to take it. "And don't put up any of the ones with her name on them."

Jean reflected that the ship still had her name on it. And her portrait hung on the aft stairwell.

Perplexed, Jean watched Erika grab a shoe box from the floor and hastily stuff the Skye ornaments into it, then shut the lid as though she were locking up a shameful secret— or something dangerous, like a loaded gun.

CHAPTER SIX

WHEN DAVID SAW HER an hour later, she was leaving the aft head in a teal swimsuit, her clothing tucked under one arm, a coffee cup in her other hand. The mug had been Skye's and bore a cartoon of a chatty-looking woman and the quip, *If you don't have anything nice to say about anyone, sit right here by me.*

David had never been able to bring himself to get rid of it.

Seeing her just feet away in the narrow hall, he slipped back into the doorway of the darkroom, which he had been restocking.

Jean didn't see him at first. The hall was in shadow, and when she made out the tall figure in the doorframe, her heart stopped.

He said, "You need to wear more clothes around here."

Unconsciously she clutched her stack of clothing and the coffee cup against her front. She said, "My wet suit's in the diving alcove. I'm sorry."

"It wasn't a criticism." In the dimness, he let his eyes take swift inventory of her figure, then made a decision. Inclining his head toward the bow, he said, "Your cabin will be the crew's quarters—since you're my crew. You can get there from the foredeck or my cabin or the office. And please use the forward head and showers." After a pause, he added, "You and I share."

Jean nodded, picturing walking in on him in the shower some morning. Then the reverse.

David said, "Soon there'll be half a dozen men on this ship. And you. So this is the best arrangement." He asked, "Do you get seasick?"

She'd never been out in rough weather. "I don't think so."

"The bow's the worst for that, but it can't be helped. That's where I want you."

Accessible to him and no one else, Jean thought. But it made her feel protected and cared for as she hadn't been for years. She said, "Okay."

He was looking at her coffee cup, the one Erika had said was fine to use—"None of our cups are important." The one Jean knew had been Skye's.

Now it was empty, and David reached for it. "I'll take that to the galley for you. It's on my way. I'll see you on deck."

Their hands did not touch as she handed him the mug.

JEAN WAS ZIPPING her wet suit when he stepped out of the salon. He was wearing a pair of blue trunks and nothing else. He was sinew and suntanned skin, hard and scarred, a man who'd been shark-bit.

He made Jean's heart thunder, and as he took his wet suit from where it was hanging, she said, "You need to wear more clothes."

David cast her a look that was both amused and grudgingly respectful. "Touché. And thank you. I will." His eyes lingered on hers for a moment, as though silently measuring her. Then he began pulling on his wet suit. Nodding toward the diving platform, he said, "Let's see if we can finish the keel in the next few days. We have a lot of other work before we leave for Baja."

Jean thought of the next day, the anniversary of Skye's death. So far, David hadn't mentioned a break in their schedule.

They readied for the dive in silence and emerged on deck

to find Christian kneeling on the aft cushions, holding the end of a cotton rope. On the other end was the inflatable wreath in which he had interested Baby. Recalling David's hopes for the wreath's demise, Jean glanced his way. But he was watching his son.

When Jean and David reached the stern, Chris looked up and signed something to his father—his first use of sign language in Jean's presence.

David's face showed little expression as he turned to her and said, "Chris would like to go swimming with Baby."

The look in his eye made Jean think of a stick of dynamite with the fuse lit. She said nothing, and Chris watched his father hopefully.

With a dark look at Jean that said, *This is your fault,* David told Chris, "You may swim. Wear your wet suit. And bring your snorkel, so you can help us."

As Chris leapt off the cushions and raced toward the cabin, David said, "Walk."

When the child had disappeared inside, he turned to Jean. His voice and features were even and uninvolved, but his eyes told her a different story. "I don't appreciate any of this."

Suspecting she heard a veiled reference to the letters she'd left on the galley table, Jean tugged nervously at the rubber strap on her mask but made no reply.

David went aft and lifted the railing. "Go away, Baby."

The dolphin nestled up to the platform, lifting her head for a stroke.

David stepped down to the platform and looked back at Jean. He said, "I told you to take everything in that box to Skye's lawyer. You need to follow instructions. Consider yourself warned."

WITHIN AN HOUR Chris was enjoying "rides" through the water as he clung to Baby's dorsal fin. Jean and David watched him with help from Erika, and Jean wondered what David felt when he saw his son's delight in the animal. How could he feel negative about something so obviously healthy for Chris?

Whatever his feelings, he didn't confide them. Whenever they were topside he said little, and Jean realized he was still angry. Justifiably. But his demands had opposed the instincts of her heart. And the boundary between personal and professional now seemed blurred and indistinct, as though part of it had been erased.

Which it was, Jean thought, earlier today. *Whether he likes it or not.*

The water had begun to darken when her scrub brush uncovered something engraved in the black hull near the propellers. Serial number, Jean assumed. But as she continued scrubbing, she realized she was wrong. With rigid muscles, she cleaned away the grime, her eyes watching each letter grow clear.

For all at last returns to the sea. SKYE HAVERFORD BLADE. December 6—

Jean stopped scrubbing and stared at the words, forcing herself to breathe evenly. She had known David loved his wife, but for some reason the cenotaph, like the postcard she'd read and the incident with Skye's coffee cup, brought the fact to vivid life. She felt illogically as though she had just walked into a room and found him in bed with another woman.

Silly. Not only was this woman his wife, she was dead. Gone forever.

And he's your employer, Jean, she reminded herself, but the thought rang hollow. Right or not, David was more to her than an employer. On a strictly private plane, she felt involved with him and his family. She liked his sister and was concerned for his son. Christian's feelings for Baby matched her own, and Jean longed to find other common ground with the silent boy.

Moreover, somewhere so deep inside she barely ac-

knowledged it, lurked the desire to help Chris heal so he
would speak again. Yet that seemed a laughable goal for a
woman with her history with children.

Baby nosed against her, and Jean turned in the water.
David was behind the dolphin, and he pointed topside. But
his eyes were on the cenotaph, and even the soupy harbor
water could not veil the emotion exposed in his face. In a
blink of time Jean glimpsed how vulnerable he really was.

WHEN THEY REACHED the surface, Chris was sitting on the
diving platform holding the inflatable wreath, which
seemed to have lost some air. As Baby surfaced, he leaned
over the water to touch her head. Ignoring the action, David
pushed back his mask and nodded at Jean's regulator.
"That piece concerns me. You should have something better."

"It was my dad's," Jean explained, then wished she
hadn't. She could guess David's feelings about sentimental
attachment to inferior diving equipment. "I'm used to it,
so it's hard to part with."

"Like Baby." His eyes were cool with irony. "That's it
for today. Take tomorrow off, and I'll see you the next day
at nine."

There it was, the locked door to his past. He was ex-
cluding her from the family ritual. As was appropriate, Jean
knew.

Fighting a sense of hurt and sudden loneliness, she
grabbed the rails of the dive ladder and started up, removing her tank once she was on the platform.

David did not follow. He remained in the water with
Baby and began explaining the dolphin's physiology to
Chris. Listening while she removed her fins and mask, Jean
suspected he was trying to reduce his son's emotional involvement with Baby by treating her like an object of scientific interest.

She watched as he answered a question Chris had signed to him.

Seeing her eyes on him, David translated, "Chris wants to know if Baby's in danger from sharks." He shook his head at his son. "A big shark maybe, but I don't think so. Dolphins are more dangerous to sharks than the reverse. Of course, Baby would be much safer with her own kind. Dolphins protect each other from predators like sharks. But here in the harbor she's at greater risk from fishing lines and nets, boats with propellers, and polluted water. Of course, for an orca Baby would be easy prey, loner that she is. I can't picture any orcas swimming into the harbor, but if Baby continues to follow Jean up and down the coast, anything could happen."

Jean said, "I think you're slanting things a bit. No shark is going to bother Baby, and no orcas, either. Killer whales are unusual here, and the ones who come are only passing through." She'd told herself so repeatedly.

Giving her a look that said he wished she'd shut up, David answered, "You may be right. I was just pointing out to Chris that he shouldn't be surprised if Baby washes up dead on the beach someday."

Jean was tempted to retort that the same thing could happen to any of them. In deference to Chris, she said only, "Well, Baby has been a victim of circumstances, but we're all lucky to know her." She crouched beside Chris to stroke Baby's skin, enjoying the sweetness of the eye that watched her from the water. "She really likes you, Chris, or she wouldn't have stayed so close to you today and let you ride on her fin."

Chris looked doubtful—and slightly distrustful.

"She shies away from most people," Jean explained, "and to others she's downright mean."

"Let's not attribute our own feelings to her, Jean," said David. "As scientists."

"As scientists?" Jean bent over the water and exchanged

kisses with Baby, then forced a smile as she stood up. "I thought we agreed to be human, instead."

David's eyes followed her as she lifted her tank and gear to the deck and swung herself after them. "As humans we'd be doing her a favor to return her to her own kind."

Jean toyed with the zipper toggle on her wet suit. "She's free, David. I don't think she'd go to her own kind, and I doubt they'd have her—even if this were a part of the ocean where her species abounds."

David rested his arms on the top step of the diving ladder. "We could take her there."

Chris began signing at his father with great urgency. His face was worried, and David gave Jean a look clearer than language. *See what you've done?*

JEAN'S THOUGHTS were still on David's inexplicable attitude toward Baby when Cecily called from Paris that evening. Her sister asked, "Is the connection good at your end?"

"Yes." Jean bent along her outstretched legs to hook her hands over her feet. Ceci had caught her readying to go to the first tae kwon do class she'd attended in weeks, and Jean had grabbed the receiver from the floor. "Can you hear me?"

"Basically. It's a little scratchy," said Cecily. "I just wanted to talk to you and find out if you'd like to come here for Christmas?"

Jean was surprised by the offer—and pleased. Sometimes she wondered if Cecily cared as much as she did about their relationship. She felt genuine regret as she said, "I'd love to, but I've made plans, and they're important."

"Tell," said Ceci.

"Do you know who David Blade is?" Jean didn't want to wait for an answer. "Anyhow, he's a pretty big-time marine explorer, and first he hired me for bottom-cleaning, then he asked me to work on his ship. It's not a real diving job, but it's getting closer." Jean hesitated. "He wants me to watch his son."

"*Ee,*" said Cecily expressively. "Did you tell him—"

"No," answered Jean.

"David Blade," said Cecily. "That name's familiar." She gasped. "*Click.* I just made the connection. The Blade Institute, right? He killed his wife." The last was uttered in a tone of bewilderment. "You're working for *him?*"

"He didn't kill his wife," said Jean.

"So he says. I remember that story, and it sure looked like the perfect crime to me. Don't take any boat rides, Jean."

Jean heard the warning, incredulous. Whatever David's problems, she couldn't believe him capable of murder. In her heart she believed he really hadn't recovered from Skye's death. Painfully she remembered how he had taken the coffee cup from her hand that afternoon, as though it was something precious to him. She told her sister, "Well, I am going on a boat ride. I'm going to Baja with him."

"With other people," said Cecily. "Say yes."

"Yes. And I don't think he killed her."

Cecily said, "Just do your Korean karate thing if he gets too close. *Hi-yah!*"

Jean bit her tongue. That method had already failed.

Suspiciously Cecily asked, "Are you falling for him or something?"

"Yes."

Cecily said, "Tell me more. You never fall for anyone. This is interesting."

Jean told Ceci about Chris and Erika and about David's ambivalence toward Baby. She didn't tell her sister he had kissed her. Or that Chris couldn't talk.

"Well, does he like you?" Cecily asked.

Jean wondered what "like" meant. Want to sleep with? Or want to love? Was throwing a woman to the galley floor and kissing her as an encore to anger a sign of affection?

Hesitantly she revealed, "He sent me flowers for graduation." *Orchids.* She bent her left knee, tucking her leg to the side, and stretched forward again.

Cecily gasped. "Oh, God, graduation! Jean, I blew it, didn't I?"

"It's no big deal." She stretched, thinking what a difference those flowers had made.

"It is too a big deal. *Damn,*" said Cecily. "Well, I don't feel as bad as if no one had sent you anything. Tell Monsieur Blade *merci beaucoup* from *moi.*"

Jean tried to imagine herself saying, *My sister says to tell you thank you for doing her the favor of sending me flowers, David, because if you hadn't no one would have.*

She asked Cecily, "Isn't this phone call costing you a fortune?"

"It's been worth it. Did my box come?"

"No." Jean reminded herself to send Cecily's presents the following day.

"Well, if you have a hot date, open the one from the London shop early. It'll keep you warm so you won't have to rely on the arms of a suspected murderer."

Jean wondered if her sister guessed how appealing was the image stirred by her flippant comment. David keeping her warm. She knew he could be gentle from the way he'd held her when he kissed her. She knew he wasn't a murderer.

And she was glad to get off the phone and turn her attention to her martial art. Spending the evening at Frank's class would clear her mind.

"MR. BLADE."

"Mr. Smith."

Jean's head was touching the floor of the gym when she heard David's name. When she heard his voice she nearly lost her balance. What was he doing here at Frank Smith's tae kwon do class? She stared between her spread legs at him, upside down. He looked easy and relaxed as he bowed to Frank.

Without moving Jean watched in fascination as David rose first from the bow, a sign he was the senior black belt. Then she noticed his belt itself.

Jean knew a well-used black belt was the hallmark of a dedicated warrior of the *do,* the way. David's belt looked as if it had seen years of practice and many launderings. Considering its condition—tattered and faded to charcoal, the ragged cotton showing white in places—she felt less chagrined by her own loss of control that morning.

And more astonished by his. Using martial arts to steal a kiss was *not* exemplary black belt behavior.

Jean straightened up from her stretch, and a teenage girl working on her black belt came over and asked her a question about pattern Choong-Moo. Jean showed her, deliberately not looking at David. She wished he would leave, but he was dressed for tae kwon do, so it seemed unlikely.

Frank clapped his hands, calling the class to order. Because she wasn't officially a member of the class, Jean moved to the back of the room with David. He nodded to her. She didn't feel like bowing, but she did, in case Frank was watching. The instructor was half-Korean and ran a traditional martial-arts class, steeped in formality. Nonetheless, as she took her place beside David, Jean couldn't help murmuring, "It *was* inexcusable, sir."

David smiled slightly, and Jean realized with shock that he was embarrassed.

The senior student said, *"Cha-ryot!"*

As THEY SALUTED the flag, then dropped to the floor for meditation, David remained aware of Jean. She was gorgeous, and he regretted coming. He hadn't expected to see her there, and he'd wanted to talk to Frank about her. The two men had known each other more than ten years, long enough for David to be able to count on Frank's candor—

and discretion. Though the questions would be professional, his reasons for asking them were personal.

Unfortunately his showing up at the gym when she was there was awkward. He could imagine a host of uncomfortable scenarios.

Frank nodded to him across the room, and David moved to the front, reluctantly.

"For those of you who do not know him, this is Mr. David Blade. He is a fifth-degree black belt and a master instructor. You may address him as *'Sabumnim'* or 'Mr. Blade, *sir.*'"

Everyone bowed. Jean had never met a fifth-degree black belt before David.

Frank said, "Mr. Blade practices tae kwon do on his ship. A martial-arts historian would tell you this is not as unusual as it sounds. During the Ch'ing dynasty, students of the *hung gar* style of kung fu were forced to train in secrecy to avoid persecution, and many of them practiced in junks and sampans in the ports of southern China. Confined spaces and low ceilings forced them to make adaptations in their style." Frank smiled. "Tonight we may have the opportunity to observe Mr. Blade's unique and formidable fighting style."

As Frank spoke, Jean watched David. His manner was quietly dignified and he exuded the presence of a warrior, but Jean suspected he would have preferred less attention.

She would have preferred to be absent. Whenever she recalled how she'd kicked David that morning—and been felled like a tree for her efforts—she wished the floor of the gym would open and swallow her. Now, when she longed to redeem herself and prove her competence, she felt, instead, the impact of her erratic class attendance since her parents' death. And the reality that nearly five years had passed since she'd advanced to second *dan*.

Toward the end of the evening, the black belts took turns free-sparring, and her partner was a high school senior she had never fought before. He was well focused, while Jean was nervous and conscious of David's presence. She took a painful blow to the ribs before Frank stopped them and looked at David, as though inviting his comment.

Sure that his presence was at least partially to blame, David said nothing. He was glad when Jean and her partner bowed, shook hands and sat down on the other side of the room. Then, by prearrangement, he stepped forward and invited Frank to spar.

Watching, Jean understood the subtleties of the proposition. For Frank to extend the challenge would have meant that Frank must spar at David's level. She sat back, silent.

They began.

As Frank and David exchanged kicks, punches and blocks, Jean's sparring partner muttered, "That guy has *ki* in spades."

True, when he moved David appeared to be wielding not only his own strength but an additional unseen energy operating beyond the laws of physics—and in concert with them. Jean remembered what Frank had told her long ago. *Ki is everywhere. Everyone has it. The trick is learning to use it.*

Nonetheless, observing David's skill, she was both mesmerized and dispirited. Before she'd known him, he'd seemed unattainable, miles above her realm. Writer, explorer, pirate of the seas with his own vessel to command. Now she was beginning to know him, yet he seemed further out of reach than ever.

She felt like crying, and the minute everyone stood up and clapped at the end of class, she bowed to Frank and to David and to her sparring partner, and headed for the wall where her sweatshirt lay. In a minute, she was out the door.

"JEAN."

David's voice reached her in the night, and her heart started hammering. *I'm going to have a cardiac condition when this job is over,* she thought. Did workman's comp cover emotional duress? She turned to look at him.

Standing over her, the security light in the parking lot shining behind him, he asked, "Where's your car?"

Jean said, "I walked. On the bike path."

David could imagine which one. It was isolated, and the waning moon shed just enough light to make her visible to someone who might hurt her. He said, "I'll drive you home."

"Okay. Thanks."

Deciding to take up the topic of basic safety at another time, David asked, "Don't you have a car?"

"I still have my dad's car, but I don't drive it often." Hastily she said, "I'm a good driver. Don't think I was dangerous in your car."

She was going to be in his car again, this time with him, and David smiled at her choice of words. As she glanced toward the parking lot where the Corvette was parked, he said, "Give me a minute. My clothes are inside."

He looked her over as she followed him back toward the gym, and Jean wondered if he was thinking about her uniform and the fact that she was still wearing it. Ceci's call was to blame in part for her lack of street clothes. Dressing at home was always faster than getting a locker at the gym. But she was breaking a philosophical code by wearing her uniform in transit. Seeing her black belt, potential adversaries would be alerted to her skills—and might even view them as a challenge.

David said nothing about it. As they reentered the lobby, he told her, "I'll be right back."

Soon he was, dressed in a pair of toffee-colored canvas pants and a thick, black rugby shirt that had faded to dark gray. His uniform was folded in his hands, his belt with it, and he told Jean, "Let's go."

In the parking lot, he unlocked the passenger door of his car, his body brushing her shoulder briefly. At the contact,

Jean couldn't stop herself from looking up at him, and for a moment their eyes met in the dim glow of the parking lamps.

From the walkway that led to the street, Frank Smith called, "Don't go home with that man."

David looked up and replied, "She's taking *me* home." He winked at Jean and opened the door for her.

Seconds later, when he had slid behind the wheel and closed his own door, Jean asked, "How do you know Frank? And why have I never seen you here?"

David fastened his seat belt and started the car. "I train at a place in Ventura. It's—" he searched for the right word "—low profile." A converted storeroom on a back alley. The master was a seventh-degree black belt with whom David had never exchanged a word of English. David told Jean, "I met Frank in Korea. He was visiting family. I used to live there."

"Is that where you learned tae kwon do?" Even as she asked, Jean knew it couldn't be the whole answer. David must have a good twenty years of training.

He said, "I've had many teachers. Actually my father was the first. He was very good." He backed out of the parking space.

Jean said, "My father was my sparring partner."

David heard the sadness in her voice and understood it better than she would ever know. They had been about the same age when they lost their parents. Another parallel, like their interest in tae kwon do. If he'd believed in such things, he would have wondered if she was his soul mate, come to him at last.

He didn't believe in such things.

He said, "Have you eaten?" It was nine-thirty.

She'd had only a peanut-butter-and-jelly sandwich, which she didn't care to confide. She said, "I eat light before class."

"Want some dinner?" They were at the exit to the parking lot, and he waited for her answer.

Jean couldn't believe her ears. "That would be great." Then she remembered she didn't have any money with her. She told him so.

David looked at her and shook his head, as though at a charming but appallingly ignorant child. "I'll pay," he said. "Always."

HE TOOK HER to Sulphur Springs Tavern in the Santa Inez Mountains. It was a tavern in the truest sense, with a bar next door that was the haunt of college students and bikers alike; yet the restaurant itself, located in a separate building, was considered one of the finest in the area, with a reputation for superb food, from seafood to wild game to a natural California cuisine. Pricey but informal.

The drive took nearly half an hour, and Jean loved every minute of it. It was too cold to have the top down, but riding in the Corvette on the highway was like being in a rocket. Pulling the elastic band from the end of her braid, she loosened her hair and leaned back in the seat, shifting to ease the pain from the kick she'd taken.

David caught the motion and remembered the blow. He said, "Go ahead and take off your belt. This place can be rough, and drunks sometimes see a black belt as an invitation to fight. Better to look like a pastry chef."

Jean laughed at the image. She had two *doboks*—one all white, symbolizing purity, and another trimmed in black, symbolizing the dignity of a black belt. Without a belt, the all-white uniform she was wearing did resemble a chef's outfit. Appreciating the way David had cautioned without criticizing, she untied her belt. "You haven't been in a fight here?"

He shook his head. "I run fast. I've never been in a fight anywhere." His eyes hit hers briefly. "Except with you."

Dropping her belt on top of David's uniform between

the seats, Jean smiled, unsurprised. Avoiding unnecessary violence was part of the martial way. Yet she knew if David's family was threatened he would stand his ground.

David fell silent, suddenly wondering what he was doing. He should have driven her straight home. Or taken her somewhere in town. This impulse to feed her at the best restaurant in Santa Barbara County was stupid. Now she was practically lying down in the passenger seat, her hair all around her, like a woman who'd just gotten out of bed— or was on her way there. She looked happy and relaxed and as though she'd love to be ravished. By him.

And he wasn't looking forward to sitting through dinner with a hard-on. He didn't even have anything to say to her.

She said, "Is Erika with Chris?"

"Yes."

She said, "I'd better learn some sign language so I can understand him."

David nodded, relieved she had chosen a simple topic. "He writes, too. Extremely well. But I'll teach you a couple of signs at the restaurant."

When they pulled up in front, there were rows of motorcycles parked on both sides of the mountain road in front of the log tavern, and university students in fraternity sweatshirts were spilling outside. Rock and roll blared from inside the building, where neon beer signs blinked in the windows, offering holiday slogans.

Before getting out of the car, David tugged a heavy, navy blue sweater on over his head. Jean pulled on her sweatshirt, opened her door and stepped out into the night. She locked the door before she shut it, then shivered. It was a pristine night. The white Christmas lights on the roof eaves of the tavern buildings seemed a pale imitation of the stars winking through the towering evergreens.

David said, "Come on." He didn't move toward her or touch her as they crossed the road to the restaurant.

When they were seated in the rustic dining room at a

table ornamented with a spray of holly and a single red candle, David ordered a bottle of wine, then proceeded to show Jean some sign language as promised.

"This is Hank the Cowdog. Do you know about Hank?" he asked.

Jean shook her head.

"Chris will tell you," David told her. "I think I'll leave it to him." His hands moved. "This is SR-71 Blackbird. That's his favorite plane. And Corvette. His favorite car." Then he showed her some practical signs, but when Jean tried to copy them, he stopped her. "Don't. You talk. Let him sign to you. I want him to talk."

Abruptly David fell silent. That was something he never said to anyone, never uttered aloud. To cover the revelation he showed Jean some other words. "Bow. Stern. Fore. Aft. Locker. Stateroom." He moved faster, teasing her until she laughed.

She said, "I can't remember all that."

"You'll catch on. And there's this one, of course."

Jean watched the movements. He didn't say anything afterward, just lowered his hands and gazed toward the kitchen.

Jean said, "What's that one?"

His eyes shifted to hers. "I love you." Then, he reached for his water glass and looked at his watch, as though wondering where the waitress was so they could order and eat and leave.

SHE WAS ASLEEP when he pulled up to the curb in front of her house and killed the engine. The wine, thought David. It was excellent, but he should have ordered a couple of glasses of the house, instead. He and Jean were both pretty loose by the end of the meal, and he'd put his hand on her shoulder on the way to the car. Three or four times she'd given him a look that said plain as words, *I want you to kiss me.*

He wasn't going to do that again.

But he thought about it as he watched her sleeping in his car, his sweater over her legs. He thought of kissing her. He considered starting the car again and taking her to the ship. He briefly envisioned making love to her in the car, at the curb. Finally he clapped his hands, the sound she would have heard at the beginning of every tae kwon do class.

She blinked and looked at him, momentarily disoriented.

He said, *''Cha-ryot.''*

Attention. Jean winced, then rubbed her eyes.

"You're home." David scooped up a black belt and dropped it into her lap. "I'll see you to the door." The lawn was dark and tree-shaded, the moon now shrouded in fog. Not liking the fact that Jean came and went from this place alone at night, he opened his door and got out.

Groggy, she opened the passenger door and stood up, clutching the belt and David's sweater. She set his sweater back on the seat, then looked up to realize he was holding the door for her. When she stepped away from the car, he shut it.

Jean led the way through the side gate and across the lawn to the patio and the back door. The house towered over them like a monster of the night. She had left the back light on but was glad for David's presence. Had she actually fallen asleep in the car? Yes. She could still feel the effects of the wine.

Watching her fit the key into the lock, David reflected that he should come in and check the house for her. But if he did he would never leave. He kept quiet.

When the door was open, Jean snapped on a light, then turned to him with a smile. She gave him a small, sweet bow.

It was too much for him.

Instead of returning it, he reached for her. She seemed momentarily stunned, then came near, holding his arms. He rearranged her, wrapping her arms around him. She hugged tightly.

Good, thought David. It was what he wanted.

His mouth started out against her hair, then hungrily worked its way to her face and her lips. Already he was as hard as could be and had to pull her close to him, closer, had to take everything he could from the mouth he'd been watching all night. His hand found her breast, small and high and taut. She pressed nearer to him, plainly returning his desire.

David relaxed some, continuing to draw her near, fit her against his body, learn the feel of her mouth. If a kiss was all that was going to happen—and it was—he planned to enjoy it and extend it. But he wanted so much more. He wanted her hands on him, places no one else touched. He wanted to touch her, undress her, put his mouth on her everywhere, taste her, come inside her. But he only kissed her and wrapped her hair around and around his hand.

The hair was the mistake. Holding her hair.

The colors came back to him, the fluid red, the shape in the sea, and he backed away so fast that Jean lost her balance and nearly fell. He caught her and set her toward the door.

His desire was gone, snuffed out. A heartbeat earlier she had been the source of his need, the whole of his focus, but now he couldn't even touch her. The life force inside him had died and rotted. Images still swam at the edges of his consciousness, threatening, and he wanted to be alone to deal with them, banish them if he could. He said, "Good night."

She said, "Thank you, David."

He nodded and waited until she went in and closed the door. Then he went back to his car and waited there, listening, because he hadn't checked her house and knew he should have.

And because he couldn't bring himself to return to the ship.

AFTER LOCKING UP, Jean went into the living room and hurled herself onto the couch, tossing down the black belt she held. Her emotions were a tumult, her body still hot from holding him.

David had ended the kiss abruptly, but Jean thought she understood. She'd felt his excitement, and he was being decent to her, which she appreciated. She wasn't sure she was ready for much more than he'd given, but she knew if he had tried to take her to bed she would have gone.

He's nice, she thought in wonder as she had so many times that evening. He'd been a good date. Attentive. Not especially talkative, but never rude, either. Not tonight, anyhow.

Her mind flashed back to the sign language he'd shown her, to his eyes on hers when he said, *I love you.* He was just translating, but for a moment it had felt almost as though he wasn't, as though he had found a way to tell her something he didn't feel ready to say more plainly.

Jean squelched the notion. It had been a beautiful one— she and David knowing immediately they were right for each other and being unable to help falling in love.

But then she remembered Skye Haverford Blade and that the following day was the anniversary of her death. The thought upset her. She didn't want David to still be mourning his wife.

He's not for you, Jean. You're a good student and a diver and a black belt, but his wife was sophisticated and apparently brilliant. Two European universities.

Which schools? Oxford? Cambridge? It hardly mattered. Undoubtedly the heiress had been a match for David. If someone asked him, he would probably say in an understated way, *Yes, Skye was smart.* And behind the words would be a backlog of memories.

Jean cut off the thought. She was torturing herself, and she knew it. He had kissed her tonight with dizzying thoroughness, and that should be enough.

Idly she reached for the black belt at her feet, preparing to roll it, and felt with shock the texture of frayed edges beneath her fingertips. It was his.

CHAPTER SEVEN

WHEN SHE ARRIVED at the *Skye* two mornings later he was already on deck in his wet suit. Jean asked, "Am I late?"

She was uneasy.

David looked wary. He shook his head and nodded to a coffee mug sitting on a locker beside him. "I'm just waiting for the fog to lift."

The twofold reply encompassed the weather and the early hour. It was a chilly morning with a smell of salt rather than tar in the air.

Jean wondered how the previous day had gone. She had thought of little but David and Chris as she went about her own chores, Christmas shopping and gift wrapping. What were they thinking about? What did the marker for Skye look like? Did Chris remember his mother?

Did David cry?

His belt, still on her couch, was a constant reminder of their dinner together and the kiss at her back door. Although she knew he had handed it to her accidentally, the belt reminded her of a man leaving a hat in a woman's closet so he'd have an excuse to see her again.

But of course David didn't need an excuse. He was her boss.

As she joined him on the aft deck, Jean told him, "I forgot your belt."

David shrugged. "You can keep it for a while. I've been using yours." He didn't add that Erika had noticed, not just the belt switch but Jean's initials. *J. Y. Do I know someone whose initials are J. Y.?* David had thought he'd never hear the end of it, but he liked the idea of Jean having his belt. For a while.

Pleased that he was in no hurry to have his belt back, Jean remembered an idea she'd mulled over the day before. She didn't know how to ask. David was staring out over the stern at a spot in the water, and she tried to imagine what his reaction might be.

When he looked up she bowed. "Would you please teach me?"

Teach you what? He hoped she didn't ask other men that question with those trusting green eyes. She must mean tae kwon do. For a moment he studied her. Then, unsure of his voice, he said, "If you like. We can work out together, and I'm sure we'll both benefit. I start at five-thirty every morning." Hearing himself, he wanted to wince. What was he getting into?

Jean Young. Ready-made diving buddy and sparring partner, albeit light and small for the latter. They'd both have to be careful.

He nodded at her jeans and sweatshirt, pointing out that she wasn't suited up. "Let's get to work."

OVER THE NEXT FEW DAYS they fell into a routine. Jean arrived at 5:25 each morning, after walking from her house in the dark. David usually seemed restless when she arrived. He was always stretching on the deck, eyes alert as though he'd been watching for her arrival. Jean changed in the crew's quarters, and then joined him on the aft deck or in the salon.

Only the first day was different. Jean had worn her uniform to the harbor, carrying a change of clothes in a day pack, and David met her as she boarded the ship. In the gray-blue light before dawn, he drew her aft, and in the dimness under the canopy he stepped close to her and began untying his black belt from around her waist. Meeting her eyes, he said, ''I think we'd better trade back.''

Jean didn't move, only watched his hands as he took the belt. A moment later he reached for hers, which had been lying on a chair nearby where she hadn't even noticed it. He tied it around her waist, his eyes on hers as he knotted the ends. Jean felt like a pirate's captive who'd just been tenderly bound to be enjoyed later. She couldn't talk and was both relieved and crushed when David stepped back and bowed to her.

Moments later Baby started calling to them from the water, and David said, ''She's a distraction. Let's go below.''

It was a new relationship, different from diving with him and taking his orders, different from the times they'd kissed. Tae kwon do was mental, physical and spiritual. It was combat and honor and integrity. Jean had not sparred so regularly with any one man since her father's death, and sometimes she felt almost as though she had been passed from her father's hands to David's.

And David was a master.

But he didn't kiss her again.

He seemed to have neatly compartmentalized his treatment of her, following different rules in different situations. For work, it was cool professionalism; for tae kwon do, formal courtesy. She was ''ma'am.'' He was ''sir.'' *Sabumnim.* Master instructor.

Whenever he touched her during sparring or teaching, the courtesy was a wall between them, but Jean knew it was also a channel. The silence of meditation, the challenge of drill and the intensity of fighting all reinforced a common philosophy and mutual respect. When they met each other's eyes, bowed to each other and clasped hands after sparring, Jean was always reminded of a favorite saying of her father's. *Respect is love in plain clothes.*

She loved David.

It was useless to tell herself she barely knew him. It was also increasingly untrue. His character permeated his life and his actions. He was a good father and brother, a hard worker, a shrewd businessman, and a gentleman. And he intrigued her endlessly. Jean could not imagine wanting a different man—or ever having this one. When days passed and he made no mention of kissing her or eating dinner with her, she realized they were operating in a professional mode and likely to remain that way. Tae kwon do, "the way of punching and kicking," became intimacy. Work became a means of knowing David better.

As the days passed, she helped him with maintenance and cleaning and began to assume the role of personal secretary. Trying to focus on furthering her career, Jean tirelessly swabbed the decks, filled the water and composed business letters, and she sensed she was winning David's approval. When she took the time to recoil a disarranged line on the deck, she could feel him watching her, and she knew it was what he would have done.

And then there was Chris. Jean had never believed a child could really like her, and it shocked and thrilled her to learn she was wrong. After her first morning workout with David, she was on her way to change clothes in the crew's quarters when she came upon Chris in the galley, opening the eighth door on his advent calendar. When he saw her black belt, his eyes grew huge—which surprised Jean, because his father was a black belt, too. A master.

But his reaction provided an opportunity for communication, and she asked him about the calendar. Was it his? One nod. Did Erika give it to him? A shake of his head. His dad? Big, emphatic nod. Stunned by that, Jean asked what was in the eighth door, and he showed her. An angel. Then a game began. What did he think was in the next door? Shrug. An elephant? He shook his head, and Jean tried to think of something more ridiculous. A squashed peanut-butter sandwich? For a moment, she thought he would giggle, but instead, she saw only a silent expression of merriment, laughter without sound. But every morning thereafter, when she and David finished their workout, Chris was waiting for her to play the calendar game and count the days until Christmas.

Three days after the anniversary of Skye's death—the ninth on the calendar, marked by a candy cane—David asked her to watch Chris for the afternoon. Eager to prove herself, Jean took him to the park and to the library, where she found a book on Christmas crafts to make with children. They spent the rest of the day making ornaments from macaroni, yarn and bottle caps and cutting out paper snowflakes, which Erika hung all over the ship until David said it felt like Ellesmere Island.

But he seemed quietly pleased, and later that same day he suggested Jean teach Chris some beginning tae kwon do techniques. So every afternoon she took Chris to the East Beach lawn for a lesson. He clearly loved it. Jean caught him in moments alone practicing elementary kicks and punches, and she knew he longed for the uniform David said he *might* get for Christmas.

On their third day of lessons, Jean glanced up from teaching and saw David sitting on a boardwalk bench watching. She told Chris, ''There's your dad.''

Chris looked at him and waved, then returned his attention to her, waiting for his next instructions.

Jean said, ''Shall we show him the Very Best Method of Self-Defense?''

Chris nodded.

With a mock roar, she leapt toward him to tickle him.

Grinning, Chris darted away and ran to the bench where his father sat. David smiled in approval, complimented him on his escape, and sent him back.

Because they'd been at it for forty-five minutes, Jean told Chris, ''Time to call it quits, sir. *Cha-ryot.*''

After a brief meditation, they walked over to the boardwalk, and David stood up from the bench. He touched Christian's hair, but his eyes were on Jean.

She sensed he wanted to talk and was glad when he took fifty cents from his pocket and handed it to his son. "Salt-water taffy. We're right behind you."

Giving a small leap in the air, an unusual show of exuberance, Chris skipped ahead of them down the boardwalk toward the wharf. David and Jean followed at a slower pace.

David said, "I like what you're doing with him."

Jean let herself feel the sun on her face, the light breeze in her hair, the pleasure of walking beside David and hearing him—or anyone—tell her she was doing the right thing with a child. But a concern had come to her more than once when she was working with Chris, and though she knew the problem couldn't be helped she felt a need to share it. Her only hesitation was in giving David pain—and in knowing he must already be aware of the obstacle. But she spoke.

"David, he can't *ki-hop*. I know that's obvious, but the loud yell is such an important part of self-defense, of tae kwon do." She didn't add what David knew, that besides adding force to blows, the *ki-hop* gave the practitioner a powerful physical and psychological advantage. She glanced at David's face and wished she'd said nothing. His features were quiet, but she sensed a storm in his heart. She said, "I'm sorry. I know you can't do anything about it."

He stared ahead on the boardwalk, watching his son turn onto the wharf and pause to investigate something on the planks. He found himself admitting, "A few months ago, after a series of speech therapists failed, I tried to teach him to *ki-hop* as a means to get him to speak." When she glanced up at him, he avoided her eyes but said, "Christian ended up in tears, and so did Erika." And so had he, though not until later. Taking a small breath, he said, "But if you want to try, be my guest."

Jean realized he was giving her permission to do whatever she could to help his son speak, even at the price of Chris's eerie, silent tears. It was a tremendous sign of trust. But Jean said, "I think the problem's out of my league."

"Join the club." They had reached the wharf, and David watched Chris, still ahead of them, pause for a long look at a pelican sitting on a piling. Then he glanced at Jean, whose eyes were also on Chris. She was watchful, as though she half expected him to slide beneath the wooden railings that edged the pier. He said quietly, "I think you'd make a very good mother."

Jean drew in her breath, tasting the salt and tar in the air. Her chest felt full, swelling, and she remembered telling him her mother had said she'd make a bad mom. She knew David had said what he had because he, too, remembered. Waves of emotion scattered through her, and it was a moment before she could formulate a reply. She said, "That's the nicest thing anyone's ever said to me."

David looked at her and put his hand on her back over her braid as they walked. A moment later he dropped his hand to his side and shoved it into the pocket of his pants as though to keep from touching her any more.

AFTER THAT DAY, he asked her more frequently to watch Chris, and Jean loved it. The only drawback was Baby. The more time she spent on shore, the less Jean saw of the dolphin. Often, when she'd been working on deck and had to go below to complete a different job, Baby cried to her from the water. Every evening Jean swam with her in the ocean, but she sensed the dolphin's sadness, and she couldn't forget David's saying he suspected Baby was dependent on her. Now, whenever work absorbed her, Baby was lonesome.

To make amends, Jean began to spend her breaks and lunch hour with Baby. On the afternoon of the sixteenth, three days before they were scheduled to depart for Baja,

Jean was playing with Baby when David came to the aft deck with a thick manila envelope and asked her if she'd look at a grant proposal someone had sent him for the Haverford Trust.

Jean threw the deflated Christmas wreath to Baby one last time and stood up on the diving platform to climb back on deck. Erika was there sketching her, and Jean wondered whether David would have offered her a hand if his sister hadn't been present. When they were alone or with Chris, he sometimes did.

But now he stood holding the envelope and watching Baby retrieve the wreath. Scrambling onto the aft deck, Jean said, "I don't know anything about grants."

David stepped behind her, directing her toward the salon. "You're going to learn. I read a lot of them, and so will you."

It was a promising remark, the first hint Jean had heard from him that her position on his ship might be leading to something permanent. It wasn't diving, but Jean felt confident that would come.

David told Erika, "Sorry for taking your model."

"I'll do Baby," said Erika. "She'll appreciate the attention since you're keeping Jean so busy. If I didn't know better, David, I'd think you were hoping Baby would go find a different friend." Her tone was ironic—and challenging.

Jean paused, struck by the words. She hoped David would answer his sister, but instead, he put his hand on her own shoulder, urging her toward the cabin.

Compliantly Jean went below. Only when David had followed her into the salon did she speak. "Is what Erika said true? Are you trying to keep me from Baby?"

"I'm trying to keep Baby away from my ship. Yesterday she showed up with a tinsel garland she'd taken off someone's boat. She's mischievous, noisy and demanding, and none of us have time for her."

Jean took a step back. "We could have time for her. Instead, you send me into town and over to the park with Chris to keep us from being near her."

David heard the "us." He found it threatening. "That's my prerogative. Where Chris is concerned at any rate. Where you work and for whom is your choice, of course. We have no contract, *ma'am*," he added.

Jean heard that as a subtle reminder that she could be dismissed with a word. And that the coaching he gave her in tae kwon do was a gift. That was the "ma'am" part.

Jean thought it graceless of him to mention it. Graceless, but clever. Carefully concealing all sarcasm, she said, "Your point, sir."

"Thank you." Shifting the manila envelope, he said, "Let's look at this in my cabin. The light's better."

His cabin. Thoughts of Baby evaporated as she followed him down through the galley and up to his room. But when they went inside, David left the door open.

The top of his desk was rolled up, and stacks of paper, manila folders, account books and correspondence covered the writing surface. Until that moment, Jean had never appreciated how much paperwork he must have to do. What he sent her way was the light stuff.

Indicating that she should sit in the chair, he took the edge of the berth, the only other seat, and briefly explained his obligation to the Haverford Trust. Each year he had to select a number of scientific and academic grants to award.

Jean's curiosity simmered like a pot on a stove, and as soon as he had said that much, she asked, "The Haverford Trust? Is that…yours?"

David looked at her, first startled, then amused. "I didn't know that my holdings interested you."

Jean reddened. "I didn't mean it that way."

David was sure she did. "The answer is, no, the trust is not *mine,* as you put it. I am one of several trustees, and the Blade Institute is one of several beneficiaries. The other trustees take care of many tasks I dislike.'' He met her eyes for a moment. He wanted to tease her more and wondered if it would be a mistake. With Jean, the verbal sparring was trickier than anything they did during their morning work-outs. He was more likely to lose his balance.

But she was still blushing.

He said, ''There's a copy of last year's income-tax re-ceipt almost right under your nose.''

Jean looked deliberately away from the desk, her color deepening. He must know how nearly irresistible an invi-tation that was. Her feelings for him had nothing to do with his financial worth, but that didn't mean she wasn't curious. Lifting her eyes to his for a moment, she said, ''You're very mean.''

''Very rich, too,'' said David, eyes warm on hers. ''More than rich enough to keep a woman in wet suits and diving equipment for the rest of her life.''

Jean swallowed hard.

Seeing her throbbing pulse and the wide green eyes that could never hide anything, David cursed himself. What in God's name had prompted him to say something so insane? Realizing he now had little choice but to add something that might hurt her, he no longer felt playful. He felt only self-disgust. He muttered, ''I shouldn't have said that. Please don't read anything into it.''

''Of course not.'' She folded her arms across her chest and blinked at the manila envelope, which lay against his knee. ''Tell me about the proposal.''

David watched her reaction. It was on the tip of his tongue to say something that would soften his comment, but he held back. He'd been honest, and that was what he had to be.

Trying to put the indiscretion out of his mind, he reached for the envelope, removed the bulk of paper from inside and set the proposal on his desk. ''The applicant is a man you probably know. He's a professor of marine biology at the university. Michael Avery.''

Jean felt faint.

David said, ''He wants to go to Antarctica to study krill.''

Krill, thought Jean stupidly, trying to focus. The tiny shrimplike krill were a major food source for many arctic animals. She asked David, ''What do you want me to do?''

He nodded at the proposal. ''Read that and tell me if you think we should award the grant. I have my own ideas, but I'd like a second opinion.''

Jean considered suggesting Erika provide it. She wasn't sure she could be objective.

But David had stood up. ''That will take you some time. Look for me if you want to talk about it. I have to meet with some board members this afternoon, and I'd like to tell them something.''

For several minutes after he'd gone, Jean sat motionless at his desk. Was this fate, come to collect payment? Did David *know* Michael Avery?

She rested her elbows on David's desk and buried her face in her hands. She had to tell him what had happened in Baja.

If she could.

WHEN JEAN EMERGED FROM his cabin more than an hour later, David was nowhere in sight, but Erika was in the salon inspecting the matting and frames on some of her paintings, which were going into an exhibit that weekend. There were pictures on the couch and on all the chairs and leaning against two walls.

Erika said, ''There you are. I was beginning to wonder if my brother had locked you in the cargo hold.'' With a quick glance at Jean, she said, ''Don't read anything into that.''

I shouldn't have said that. Please don't read anything

into it. David's words echoed through her, and Jean shut them from her mind. Seeing Erika reminded her of her dispute with David over Baby. Perhaps Erika would have some insight into her brother's attitude. Postponing her search for David, Jean asked, "What do you think he has against Baby?"

Erika looked at her, eyes direct. "What do *you* think, Jean?"

Jean gave a helpless shrug. "I know he doesn't want Chris becoming attached to her."

Erika nodded. "In David's experience, loving something that can die is a hazard. I think he would prefer for Chris—and himself—to love only the more permanent things in this world. The ocean. The sun. Ideas. The things he thinks can never be taken from him."

Jean found Erika's choice of words telling. The ocean had been taken from her. She said, "But, Erika, a person can't go through life like that. David loves Chris—and you. He can't help that."

"But he can help loving Baby. And he thinks he can stop Chris from loving her."

Jean said, "I suppose that explains it. I'd wondered if maybe he just doesn't care for animals—or if that shark attack affected him."

Erika shook her head. "No. David likes animals, but he keeps an emotional distance. They can die, you see."

"Like Skye," murmured Jean, hardly knowing she spoke.

"Not just that," said Erika. "Our parents' death was awful for him. Apparently, when the *Siren* started sinking, Dad ordered him to ready the life raft. Mother went below to get something. And that was the last David saw of either of them."

Jean was shocked. It was easy to imagine the scene. David inflating a life raft on the icy deck, waiting for his parents to come, then searching for them. And finally realizing he would lose his own life if he didn't leave the ship.

Erika changed the subject. "Are you interested in David's shark bite? You must be," she said without waiting for an answer. "You're a diver. You need to watch some unedited Blade-family home videos." Wheeling across the salon, she opened a locker containing rows of videotapes. She found the right one in moments and closed the locker. "You won't want to watch this whole thing. It's uncut footage from our series on sharks," Erika explained, turning on the monitor and popping the tape into the VCR. "David was seventeen and very playful with the sharks."

Jean badly wanted to watch, but she remembered the proposal on David's desk. And what she must tell him. Her stomach pitched at the thought. She told Erika, "I'm supposed to talk to David."

"He went to the marine supply."

To see Jake? Jean reminded herself again that Jake didn't know about the Averys; he had as much as told her so.

Erika gestured to the floor. "Take a load off, woman. David would want you to. He might not want you to see this," she admitted, laughing as she pushed the play button, "but he would want you to have a break."

Christian slipped up the companionway into the salon and joined Jean on the carpet in front of the screen.

Erika laughed. "Chris likes to watch his dad pull the shark by the tail."

Jean remembered how David had said the bite had happened: *recklessness and stupidity.*

As the tape reeled, she rapidly became engrossed, her attention glued to the first test shots on the deck of the *Siren,* Christopher Blade's famous research vessel. Jean had seen the Blade shark series on public television years earlier, but it was entirely different to see the footage as a "family home video." These were people she knew: Erika walking the deck in a wet suit, her hair bound in a jaunty ponytail. A much-younger David, his brown eyes untouched by years and experience. Most intriguing, however, was the patriarch and captain, Christopher Blade, his hair salt-and-pepper gray, his body young and fit.

Watching her father help toss a shark cage overboard, Erika remarked, "David was very close to Dad, which I think is why resurrecting the Institute was so important to him. Unfortunately the bad publicity around Skye's death almost destroyed us. The Institute's just me and David now. We have an office in Washington that handles mailings and book and video sales, but we'll never have the reputation we once had. Some blows are just too devastating."

Remembering that Jake had mentioned David was in danger of losing his ship at the time of Skye's death, Jean wondered what blows she meant. But her attention was drawn back to the screen as Christopher Blade explained that Erika would film the sequence from a separate cage while he and David manned the larger one and chummed the water to attract sharks.

"Where is this?" Jean asked.

"Hawaii." Erika smiled. "When the paramedics came, one of them said David had received a great blessing from Kama-Hoa-Lii, the shark king, and would be reincarnated as a shark in his next life. David was losing lots of blood at the time, and Dad was just furious at the remark. The next-life bit, especially."

Jean watched David and his father descend in the shark cage and begin to chum the water with fish.

"We were trying to provoke a feeding frenzy," Erika explained. "The blood in the water drew them, but they just fed calmly, and we all got impatient. We'd picked Hawaii rather than another locale because we were short on funding just then, but the sharks had been disappointing."

David opened the cage door, and he and his father swam out.

"See that device in David's hand? It produces a beating sound that attracts the sharks."

Jean glanced at Chris, and he smiled at her. He had lost a tooth just the previous day and had been left a silver dollar by the tooth fairy. Unable to stop herself, Jean reached an arm around him and hugged his shoulders, and Chris settled comfortably against her.

Jean watched David approach a shark twice his size and latch onto its tail. Flabbergasted, she asked, "What species is—"

The animal turned and bit David's side around his chest and shoulder. Jean watched David push back the shark's snout with the sound-maker while Christopher Blade came wielding a big camera.

"The cameras were our best protection," Erika explained as another shark narrowed on them and attempted to bite David.

Jean was frozen in place, her heart racing. *He lived,* she reminded herself. *You know he's safe.*

Yet David and his father were yards from the cage, and sharks surrounded them, swimming faster as streams of David's blood clouded the water. Barely breathing, Jean followed the Blades' long journey back to the cage and the fight to keep the big sharks from joining them while smaller ones slipped between the bars. Then the camera cut to the deck and David's young body, bleeding. A man his father's age pressed a blood-soaked towel hard on the wound, stemming the flow, and said, "That'll be two inches deep, and you're lucky he didn't take a piece of you with him."

David, white, looked at the camera and said, "Erika, do you have to take movies? I might be dying."

Laughing, Erika shut off the VCR. "My favorite line. He went into shock a few minutes later. There's more— mainly family stuff with his wound and his stitches—but it's not that interesting."

For you. Jean was hungry to know more about David,

even the smallest things. Feeling wan, she smiled down at Christian. "Do you think your Dad's brave?"

Chris nodded earnestly.

Jean wondered what else lay in the Blades' home-video collection. Seeing a younger Erika reminded her that David's sister hadn't always been disabled. What had happened? No one ever talked about it.

When Chris had gone to play with Baby, Jean asked, "Erika, do you swim?"

"Sometimes," Erika admitted. "And I swim vicariously, watching you dive every day. There are so few women divers courageous enough to find employment in diving. I know cleaning boats is dirty work, but when I see you out there with Baby— Suffice it to say I'm envious."

Jean wanted to ask the details of her disability but felt her questions wouldn't be welcome. She'd observed that Erika never walked and seldom put weight on her legs. Yet her legs appeared to be intact.

Jean suggested, "Why don't you come swimming with Chris and Baby and me this afternoon? It's sunny, and the water's warm."

With some persuasion, Erika joined them. Jean helped her from the deck to the diving platform, and the three spent an hour in the water, Baby befriending Erika as she had the other Blades.

Erika's eyes shone as she hung on to the swimming ladder and tossed the flattened Christmas wreath to the dolphin. Jean felt a strong empathy for David's sister. Erika had been a diver, too, and it was easy for Jean to imagine herself in the other woman's shoes, deprived of the undersea world she loved. Jean admired David for making it possible for Erika to enjoy a life on the ocean, however altered from the one she had known. Surely it had been costly and difficult to make the *Skye* even partially accessible to a wheelchair.

They were still swimming when David returned from his

errands. He reacted with pleasure seeing Erika in the water, and his good mood spread over the ship like the warmth of a Santa Ana wind. From the water, Jean watched Chris, still dripping, run to his father and embrace him.

David said, "What's this running on deck? Down, Hank."

Chris performed a frolicsome cowdog imitation, based on the hero of his favorite series of books, then proceeded to challenge David to a wrestling match. Clutching the edge of the diving platform, Jean laughed as David succumbed dramatically on the aft deck, pinned. A minute later, he flopped his son over and returned the favor.

There was love shining in his eyes, and Jean realized again, more potently than ever, that Christian was the center of his world, the thing most important to him, most carefully guarded. Soberly she watched them as they lay on the deck together, Chris signing at his father and David looking as though he had all the time in the world, which Jean knew he didn't. He had a board meeting to attend.

And she had something to tell him.

SHE WAS DRYING HERSELF in the diving alcove fifteen minutes later when David finally approached her. He'd just helped his sister out of the water and seen her inside, and he told Jean, "Swimming's good for Erika. Thanks."

"Thank Baby." Jean unzipped her wet suit.

Glimpsing her swimsuit and the curve of her breast, David reached for her zipper toggle and pulled it back up, hiding her body from his own eyes. "In your cabin."

She stared down at his hand. David withdrew it and turned to leave the alcove before he could touch her again.

She asked, "David, what happened to Erika?"

"Car accident." He opened the door.

"What, exactly, is wrong?"

David paused. She had a right to an answer. He said, "I don't know. It's been three years, and the doctors say it's all in her head. Psychological. Any physical problems are healed, but when she tries to make her legs work she's only frustrated. She says she has no sensation.''

Jean studied him for a moment. "Three years. Was that before or after—'' She stopped, looked away.

David knew how the question ended. Before or after Skye's death. "Before.'' He watched her eyes dart up. Holding the doorframe, reminding himself he needed to leave, he asked, "Did you finish your reading?''

Jean nodded, her face pale, and he waited for her to say what she'd thought of the proposal. At last she did. "It seems expensive, but it might be worth it.''

Just what David had thought. It didn't help, except as flimsy proof that Jean's mind worked somewhat like his own. He said, "Thanks.'' His eyes lingered on her body, and he remembered what had happened the night they'd met at the gym. Right now she seemed as desirable as she had when he'd kissed her that night—until the colors came. The horror locked inside him.

Would the nightmare ever stop?

He watched Jean thoughtfully as she shivered in her wet suit. She seemed preoccupied, as he was, and he wondered what was on her mind.

Deliberately David called up the darkness inside him. For a moment the ghastly images and sensations filled his mind, and then he choked them down and let himself see Jean. She was blameless, unconnected with his pain. Neither of them could help it that he wanted her.

He knew he shouldn't be afraid.

He told himself he wasn't.

As she shivered again, he touched her. His hand fell to her hair, then slid against her neck to cup the underside of her jaw.

She shuddered faintly at the touch and moved nearer.

Lightly, he let the length of his body meet hers, then wrapped his arms around her and hugged her close. How had she ever come to him, this woman who lived in a wet suit and sparred in a black belt? Like a cat burglar, she had penetrated the outer barriers, eluded the guards.

A part of him wanted to let her in deeper.

The larger, more combative part wanted to snarl at her for how close she had already come.

But now his mouth was beside her hair. He said, "Jean, how would you like it if I were to begin to feel seriously about you?"

CHAPTER EIGHT

JEAN DIDN'T TRUST her voice, but she answered, "Very much."

He moved back a little, enough to see her eyes. Then he kissed her.

The heat and gentleness of the action disconcerted her, highlighting her own deception. But Jean knew she could no longer risk the truth. The stakes had suddenly become much too high.

Was it possible David could love her?

Panic raced through her. His question had suggested he could turn serious feelings on and off like tap water, which seemed possible. He'd probably had practice. Jean hadn't. If she could have stopped loving him, she would have already. Emotionally the man was as accessible as a shredded document.

Except when they kissed. His mouth conveyed more as it touched hers than it ever did through speech. She felt the ever-present tension in him, but also something else, something deeper than desire. Need. And darkness. And some quaking emotion she couldn't quite make out. It reminded her that he could hurt her.

Against his lips Jean whispered almost inaudibly, "I haven't had a lot of relationships, David."

David stiffened almost imperceptibly, but he didn't pull away. He said, "Neither have I. And let's not call this one."

Jean looked up, and David felt himself relax slightly at

her expression. He said softly, "I think, in this context, a relationship implies something that doesn't work out."

Jean felt as though she were dreaming. He *was* serious.

Her heart thudded against him, and David, feeling it, experienced a mixture of pleasure and apprehension. He said, he hoped gently, "It also implies something I'm not ready for."

She met his eyes. "I'm in no hurry, either. I've only had one lover, David. It was a long time ago."

He couldn't help his reaction. Everything inside him recoiled—not from what she said but because the admission was intimate. His desire to be close to her warred with three years of survival instincts—and lost.

David released her and stepped back, and Jean's heart plunged.

He saw her expression, and he wished he could reassure her. But he already felt as though he was coming apart just at the uninvited glimpse into her sexuality. He responded the only way he could. "That's not my business."

He turned and left the diving alcove, shutting the door hard behind him as though locking an ungovernable animal inside.

LEAVING THE SHIP and the marina, David crossed the breakwater and climbed down the tar-coated rocks to the sand. He had an appointment in forty-five minutes, but for now he needed to be away from the ship, away from Jean, away from everyone.

No one was on the beach, so he tore off his clothes and went into the water. The cold was bracing, but even swimming felt like madness. He had somewhere to be, and he'd have to return to the ship to shower and wash the tar off his body.

He didn't care. He swam out far past the breakers, hoping it would make him tired. The afternoon sun was setting, and he seemed to have the stretch of water to himself. With every stroke he heard her repeat that whispered confession. And he heard his own brutal reply.

Why had she told him? He hadn't asked her to sleep with him, and he wasn't sure he ever would. Naked and inside her, where could he hide? If the colors came— If she was to look in his eyes and really see— And what if he—

As his throat closed on the thought he couldn't finish, the water parted beside him, and a glistening silver shape appeared and took a breath through a blowhole. Baby's eyes cleared the surface, and she looked at him.

David stopped swimming. "Go!"

Baby pushed against his chest, and the heat, the strange contact from one of another world and yet his world, set his nerves tingling. He did not pet her. He turned back toward shore and started swimming.

Baby followed, sliding against his side like a woman trying to seduce a man. Treading water and attempting to dodge her attentions, David said in a tone that had shades of affection he hadn't intended, "You little tramp, get out of here."

She clicked at him and touched him on the arm with one of her flippers.

David said, "Go find Jean. I don't want to be friends. Go!" He pointed toward the islands.

She cried at him softly.

David swam away from her. She didn't follow him, but her sorrowful cries did as he rode the waves to the shore.

He had never in his life felt so cruel.

THE SANTA ANA WINDS came in that night. They were a gift from the mountains, a breath of summer in the midst of December, and they made Jean wish she was doing something more exciting than going to the library to re-search the death of Skye Haverford Blade. But she honored the warm weather and the approach of Christmas, now only nine days off, by dressing in an outfit Ceci had given her for her birthday, a multicolored ribbon-weave tank top and gauzy, tricolor, wraparound column skirt. The outfit, which Ceci had modeled in Paris, made her feel feminine, freed from the image of the androgynous athlete whose biggest fashion decision was which wet suit to wear.

Nonetheless, Jean felt conspicuous as she approached the reference desk at the library and filled out request slips for several issues of the *South Coast Sun* from just after the heiress's death. No one could guess her purpose, yet she couldn't stop thinking of David and what he might feel if he knew what she was doing. As she went to the microfiche viewers and set to work with the first film sheet, she was filled with shame. But she couldn't stop.

She had to know, not just to satisfy her own curiosity but to try to understand what had made David so...

Terminally repressed, thought Jean, flushing again as she recalled his telling her that how many lovers she'd had was none of his business. As this was none of hers.

The first paper she examined featured a photo of David taken at the harbor the day of Skye's death. Jean stared at his image, the face she now knew well, and tried to discern his emotions from his expression. She couldn't. He looked handsome and unapproachable. For a moment she reached out to touch his face on the screen, then hastily withdrew her hand, glancing behind her to see if anyone had noticed. The area was deserted.

Scrolling down to the article, Jean began to read. The most apparent fact was that David's story was the only one anyone had—and would ever have, unless Chris, three at the time, came to remember the accident. The more Jean thought about it, the more unlikely that seemed. Three was very young to recollect much of anything.

What interested Jean was the doubt the police had shed on David's version of the accident. An officer called it ''improbable''; another said ''hard to swallow.'' According to

the paper, David claimed Skye had fallen from the bow
while the ship was cruising full throttle in the middle of
the channel. He'd been making a small repair to the fly-
bridge railing, and it took him a few seconds to reach the
helm and kill the engine. When he did, he saw blood in the
water behind the ship. After taking his distraught son below
deck, he put on a mask and dove beneath the hull looking
for Skye. Finding nothing, he returned to the deck and ra-
dioed the Coast Guard, who arrived in minutes. The wind
and the seas had begun to rise, impeding their investigation
under the ship, and they were forced to return to the harbor.

Jean knew what had happened there.

Finishing the article, she wondered why the police found
his story incredible. Did they doubt that a twenty-seven-
year-old woman could have fallen from the bow of a ship?
Something in the article didn't ring true, and Jean suspected
that certain important details had been omitted from the
story. But if so, what? The *Sun* had the sensibilities of a
local paper, but usually it gave the facts.

Dissatisfied, Jean shifted the position of the microfiche
until she found a glowing editorial obituary praising Skye's
education, beauty and generosity, and naming a number of
charity events she had organized and hosted. The final
words were, "The South Coast will miss this great lady."

A pair of hands closed on her bare shoulders, and Jean
tipped her head back, half expecting to see someone from
school or an old diving partner.

"Hi." David smiled down at her, and Jean saw the progress of his eyes from the ribbon-weave curving over her
breasts to the tullelike film clinging to her legs. When their
eyes met, Jean decided his repression probably wasn't ter-
minal, after all. He said, "You look like an ad for somewhere I'd like to go."

Heart racing, Jean fumbled for the switch to turn off the
viewer. While she was still trying, David's hands slid from
her shoulders and he stepped back.

Jean stood up, jerked the microfiche from the viewer and clumsily returned it to its envelope while David watched aloofly. She said, "What brings you to the library?"

"Returning books." His gaze drifted to the microfiche in her hands, then back to her face. "Are you done?"

Jean nodded, sick inside. Judging by the look in his eye, he knew what she'd been doing. Did he feel betrayed?

He said, "Let's go somewhere."

Jean felt a confusing mixture of misery, misgiving and anticipation. She wanted to be with him more than anything, yet it occurred to her that he was going to fire her. Subdued, she said, "Okay. Let me take these back to the desk."

Minutes later, as they walked outside into the warm, caressing breeze, David asked quietly, "What were you researching?"

Damn, Jean thought. Trust David to waste no time. Holding her skirt down to keep it from flying open in the breeze, she said, "I wanted to know what happened to your wife."

He didn't answer, and Jean thought of the blood in the water. He had seen Skye's blood. She wondered if her curiosity pained him.

The wind rustled palm fronds in the trees above and pushed on a large tinsel wreath hanging from a guy wire over the street. David nodded toward the far curb, where his car was parked. As they crossed the street he asked, "Want to come home with me?"

With David, that could mean anything. There'd never yet been any reason for her to spend the night on the ship, but Jean wondered if that was what he was suggesting now. She thought of her cabin on the *Skye*—and his.

What *had* he meant? Wasn't he angry? He didn't seem so.

And the warm, heady magic of the Santa Ana night was seeping into her veins, intensifying all her feelings for him. She said, "I'll come."

Without reply, David led her to the bare-topped Corvette and opened her door.

The *Skye* was dark, but David offered no steadying hand as he led her through the salon to the galley, where a night-light burned over the sink. Jean knew that Erika was home and that Chris was asleep in his stateroom, but the ship seemed deathly quiet. Even the things most familiar and comforting, the snowflakes she and Chris had cut out and the advent calendar with its sixteen open doors, looked different at night.

David said, "Let's go in my cabin. Would you like a drink before we go up? Or coffee?"

"Sure. Anything." Jean began to relax. David's mood was serious but not ominous. Perhaps he would tell her, at last, about his wife's death.

He said, "What do you drink?"

Jean shrugged. "I hardly ever drink." She remembered the bottle of wine they'd shared at the restaurant.

David seemed to be remembering it, too. With the first smile she'd seen since his initial appearance at the library, he said, "I can believe that."

He fixed two café mochas with Irish cream and carried them up the companionway. In his cabin he turned on a banker's lamp on his desk, then raised the hatch overhead, letting in the warm winds. The lamp lit the room with only the most mellow glow, and the dimness was inviting. David pulled out his desk chair and held it for Jean. He sat on the bed, and Jean thought of the last time they had sat like this, before she'd read Michael Avery's proposal.

Now his eyes were warm but distant. Careful. He asked, "Did you try your coffee?"

Jean sipped at it, remembering the bottle of Irish cream in Skye's desk drawer. Undoubtedly David had done this before. "Delicious," she said.

"Good."

They sat in silence, seeming to have nothing to say to

each other, and as the pause extended, Jean began to wonder why he had asked her there. She said, "Are you mad?"

David didn't ask about what. He said, "No. You were curious, and I'm grateful you didn't ask me."

Jean wondered if he knew that answer would hurt. Trying to tell herself that his experience probably became no easier to relate upon repetition, she nonetheless felt shut out. They were close enough for honesty.

But you haven't been honest with him, an inner voice pointed out.

David took a drink of his coffee, his eyes on hers. He said, "I can see the wheels spinning. What are you thinking?"

Jean cloaked her feelings. "That I wish I knew you better."

"It takes time. You know me better than you think you do." He paused. "Better than I know you."

Jean thought of the Averys. He might be right.

David said, "I'll tell you what. We'll trade personal questions. You ask one, I ask one. Then we're done, for now. Sound fair?"

It sounded like Russian roulette, but Jean nodded.

He said, "Go ahead."

Wanting to ask him about Skye, she shook her head. "You."

David took another drink of his coffee, wishing it contained something stronger. All he could think was what she had told him that day—one lover, a long time ago.

Questions knotted inside him. How was it? Who was it? Did she love him? He didn't know which to ask. So he said, "Why only one lover?"

She choked on her coffee. He didn't blame her, but he didn't withdraw the question. It was some time before she answered, and when she did she didn't quite meet his eyes. She said, "It ended badly and...and I haven't met anyone else I want to be that close to."

David imagined sliding his hand under her clingy skirt to test her words. He said, "Really?"

Jean flushed. "Is it my turn now?"

He gave her a long look, then began to laugh. "I guess it is. Ask away."

Jean was soothed by the warmth in his eyes, a guarded fire. Now it was her question, but before she could decide what to ask, an unholy scream erupted in the night. David rose at once and moved toward the door.

Jean was momentarily paralyzed. She opened her mouth to ask what it was, but David said, "Chris. He makes all his sounds at night." He pulled open the door and went below to the galley.

Jean stood up and followed, but he was already out of sight, and she had to find her own way back up the companionway and across the salon in the dark. Under Skye Haverford Blade's icy blue gaze and secretive smile, she slipped past the unlit Christmas tree and navigated the aft stairs, following the screams to a starboard stateroom near the stern. When she reached the door David was sitting on a narrow bunk holding the crying child. Seeing Chris's crumpled face, hearing his tearful sobs, Jean felt her heart shake in her chest.

There was a sound from across the hall, and David called, "Don't get up, Erika. I'm here."

Erika's voice murmured, "So am I if you need anything."

Jean stayed against the wall as David held his son and attempted, unsuccessfully, to quiet the screaming rage. Standing in the shadows, she realized she had seen only the tip of the iceberg when it came to the impact of Skye's death on the lives of her family. As Chris screamed in the dark, it seemed unbearably cruel. Aching inside, Jean watched David bury his head against Chris's, clutching the small body against his chest.

The episode lasted only a couple of minutes, but when

Chris at last quieted and dropped back onto his pillow, Jean's heart was racing, her breath short. Tae kwon do had made her used to loud yells, but not of this kind.

David pulled the blankets over his son and tucked them around him, then stood. He ushered Jean out the door and back up to the salon, saying, "We've driven neighbors out of their berths before, but the harbor master's very understanding. Now we have no neighbors—just boats."

As David bent over to plug in the Christmas-tree lights, Jean asked, "Has this been going on long?"

"Three years." The room sprang to light. "Do you play chess?"

Jean nodded. "I used to—with my dad."

David opened one of the lockers to retrieve a chess set from inside. "Will you play?"

"Sure." She settled on the carpet across from him and helped arrange the pieces. "Has Chris seen a doctor? A psychiatrist?"

"Psychologists, psychiatrists, neurologists, hypnotists. He's seen them all. They agree he's having night terrors, though they're unusual in a child his age. It happens about once a week, sometimes more."

Jean asked, "Did he see her fall?"

"Yes."

Jean knew if she wanted details she would have to ask for them. She remembered the one personal question she was allowed but found herself unable to ask. David had as much as said he didn't want to discuss his wife's death.

They played a long chess game, which he finally won, and by then it was nearly midnight.

As he put away the set, he said, "You're staying, aren't you?"

Jean nodded, sorry to see the night end. In a moment, she would go to her own cabin and David to his.

He interrupted her thoughts. "Want to walk off some of

that coffee before we turn in? Chris won't be up again tonight.''

THEY LEFT the *Skye* and walked up the dock to the marina gate. Sailboat rigging chimed in the wind. Together with the splash of the water and soft creaking of the docks, it made a quiet music, the song of a harbor night. Lights burned on several boats, all on other marinas, and from across the water Jean heard the faint sound of a carol playing:

Sleep, my love, and peace attend thee
All through the night....

It made her think of Chris and of what David had said about their lack of neighbors. Now, the waterfront seemed deserted except for a homeless person drinking from a thermos on the bench outside the espresso shop. Holding the gate for Jean, David greeted him by name and remarked, ''Nice night.''

''Beautiful,'' the man answered. ''I've been watching the stars. Can't bring myself to move. Scorpio was spectacular earlier.'' He said, ''Hey, David, thanks for those sleeping bags. We really needed them a few nights ago. That was a great St. Nicholas Day gift.''

As the gate clanged shut behind Jean, David said, ''Forget it.'' Nodding to the man, he led Jean down the boardwalk toward the breakwater.

Thinking of what she'd just learned, Jean remarked, ''You know everyone.''

Casting her a glance, David said, ''Street people were one of Skye's big causes. She raised a lot of money for them nationally.''

It occurred to Jean that giving sleeping bags to homeless people on the anniversary of her death might be something he had done in her memory. As they crossed the breakwater and paused to take off their shoes and socks, she remembered the photo she'd found in Skye's desk of her and the blond man—Homeless Shelter Fashion Shoot. In her mind, she pictured the man's lips caressing Skye's hair and wondered if David had ever seen the photo and how he would have felt if he had. The more she knew him, the less she believed he would like it.

Her conversation with Jake days earlier had made her curious about the kind of woman Skye Haverford had been; so did this new thought.

Under the stars, David set his running shoes and socks beside a rock and gestured toward her sandals. "We can leave these here."

In the dark, his eyes looked black, and Jean felt the intimacy of being alone with him on such a warm, beautiful night. As they trudged across the beach toward the white breakers and followed the wet sand at the water's edge, Jean tried to think of a way to draw him out.

David asked, "Want to swim?"

Jean surveyed the dark cliff and the empty beach, noting the absence of moonlight. David was little more than a tall black shape beside her, but she glimpsed his even white teeth as he spoke.

They hadn't brought swimsuits. Thinking of this, she said, "I always thought that wasn't safe. Because of sharks."

Not responding, David stripped off his shirt. His pants followed, and he kicked them into a pile with his shirt. As Jean wondered if he was going to remove anything else, he said, "Don't let me drown," and started toward the sea.

Watching his tall, muscular form in the black night, Jean said, "I won't be able to see you."

"Then you'd better come."

Recklessly she took off her skirt and top and dropped them to the sand. Shivering slightly in her pale blue panties and bra, she followed David into the velvety darkness.

The water was cold, but the breakers were old friends. David was a couple of yards away, and Jean felt him glance over at her. Ignoring him, she held on to her underwear as she fell into the tossing foam, the current ripping beneath her. Ignoring the cold, she swam under a wave and emerged beyond the first set of breakers, feeling the freedom of her loose hair sweeping around her shoulders in the water. It had been months since she'd been in the ocean without a wet suit. The adrenaline sent her blood rushing fast, and she was glad when David emerged near her. Another wave was coming, and they both stroked toward it, watching it rise over their heads.

Jean gasped, "This is crazy," and dove under the wave, trying not to think about sharks as she swam through the dark, cold sea, feeling the force of the swell over her. When she came up, she was beyond the breakers. David was swimming toward her. Jean had warmed up, and for a moment she floated, enjoying the buoyancy of the salt water. Her cotton underwear clung to her loosely, and she hoped it wouldn't come off.

She stopped floating and tread water, letting the ocean hide her body when he neared. David seemed so much more *male* than anyone she'd ever known. Her eyes fell on the dark hairs curling wet on his chest and the scar tracing over his shoulder.

David said, "Not so bad, is it? No sharks, just me."

He looked a lot more threatening and unpredictable than a shark, but Jean nodded, enjoying their closeness. "It's fun." Her leg brushed his under the water, and she moved back. "Sorry."

He smiled at that.

"What?"

"Nothing."

He was near enough to touch and seemed much bigger than she was, a dark, wild stranger of the sea. But now, in the night and the water, she could feel his affection for her and his desire.

He came closer.

Jean gasped as the water moved beneath her and something rose between them, a warm, gray body. She cried out, afraid, and then released a breath that sounded like a sob and a laugh. "Baby."

As the dolphin slid against her chest, hugging Jean with her flippers, David said, "I suppose she has no context for the expression 'fifth wheel.'"

Jean laughed. Stroking the dolphin's side, she said, "Baby, you're nice and warm." She hugged her and laid her cheek against Baby's soft skin. Jean's senses had never felt so alive. She wanted to share her bliss with David, but when she slid away from the dolphin to turn to him he was watching her with a look she recognized. A look like a storm bulletin.

Baby came over to nuzzle him and he ran a casual hand down from her beak. "Hi, Baby." He told Jean, "Let's go in."

"But Baby just got here. We'll hurt her feelings." Jean touched her, but Baby was more interested in David. She brushed along his front, and he backed away, starting for the shore.

With regret Jean gave the dolphin a final stroke and followed.

Baby swam with them, calling in the night, pleading for them to stay, and Jean ached for her. Baby was alone out there, without friends, tragically solitary and desperate for love. Why didn't David understand that?

Jean caught a wave and rode it into shore, then spent a moment rinsing the sand from herself as best she could. Standing up in the shallow breakers, she forgot about Baby as she realized how much her underwear and bra revealed in their dripping state. After readjusting both, she folded her arms across her chest and walked to where she and David had left their clothes.

David was zipping up his pants, and he reached for his shirt when he saw her. Keeping her back to him, Jean scooped up her clothes. When she stood David stepped near her and slid his shirt over her head. The thick cotton tumbled around her body, dropping to midthigh, and Jean gratefully slipped her arms into the long sleeves. "Thank you," she whispered, looking up. "You're not cold?"

"No. Put on your skirt and we'll walk back." He wondered if she wanted to take off her wet underwear. Then he wondered if she'd like help. Cooling the thought, he turned away as she finished dressing. Together they walked back toward the breakwater to retrieve their shoes.

As Jean bent to pick up hers, she said, "Thanks, David."

"For what?" The chance to see her in transparent underwear, her breasts slick with water and swaying ever so slightly when she moved? He should thank her—or curse her.

Jean said, "For the swim."

"Sure," he made himself say. "It was nice."

The words sounded heartbreakingly casual, and Jean couldn't escape the feeling she'd made some mistake. She wanted to undo it, but since she didn't know what she'd done, that seemed impossible. His mood had changed when Baby joined them.

In tune with her thoughts, David said, "Look, Baby belongs with other dolphins. Perhaps if you left her alone, she'd find her own kind."

Jean didn't believe that, but she was glad he felt empathy for Baby's plight. As they crossed the breakwater, she said, "Baby would never be accepted by a school. Their social order just doesn't work that way. To the best of my knowledge, they don't take strangers."

"No one knows that for sure."

Jean fell in step beside him on the boardwalk. "I can't

believe you really think Baby would choose the company of any person over that of other dolphins.''

''I don't see why not. You prefer her to humans.''

Jean stared up at him, suddenly remembering the moment in the water when Baby had come between them. She said, ''You sound jealous.''

She half expected withdrawal, but instead, he smiled—almost. ''Your point, ma'am.''

Once they'd returned to the *Skye,* David led her through the wheelhouse and his cabin and slid open the door to the landing that separated their quarters. Then he walked her to the crew's quarters, and when Jean switched on the light he idled in the doorway, looking at the walls.

Jean loved her cabin, had from the first time she'd seen it. A high, double-wide berth of Hawaiian koa was nestled against the forward hold, and the space beneath contained drawers and cupboards with footholds for climbing to the bunk. David had suggested she bring from home whatever she felt would brighten the place, and Jean had chosen three photos and a net strung with shells she'd collected with her father.

Now the net hung against the bulkhead like a tapestry, and David smiled when he saw it. Jean watched his silent examination of the three pictures—she and her father sparring, Ceci mugging, and an underwater shot of Baby. Of the last, David asked, ''Yours?''

Jean nodded, her eyes clandestinely tracing the lines of his shoulders and the ropes of muscle on his stomach, with its dark hair tracing downward in a seductive line.

''You've got a steady hand.'' He turned to meet her eyes, only inches below his. ''Sleep tight.'' Briefly he let his mouth touch hers, then stepped carefully back.

Jean recalled her question. If she didn't ask now, she might never have the chance. As he began to leave she said, ''David, don't I get to ask you something?''

He turned toward her again, his eyes clear and cool, a wall hiding his soul. "Ask."

She said, "I want to know what happened to your wife."

David paused. There were a number of replies that would be equally correct. He chose the most succinct.

"Skye killed herself."

CHAPTER NINE

Skye killed herself.

Jean whispered, "How?"

"One question, remember?" He looked at her, and now Jean saw emotions she couldn't identify. He said softly, "What you read in the papers was close enough. Please don't ask me again."

Jean said, "It's better to talk about it."

David felt as though there were an earthquake in his chest. "Not for me."

That could be true. Nonetheless, she hurt for him.

Seeing what looked like indecision in her eyes, David told her, "You might not know there's a tae kwon do philosophy suggesting that one should honor the requests of one who is five or more years older than oneself."

David was eight years older. *How convenient for you,* thought Jean.

David's eyes smiled faintly, as though he knew what she was thinking. Then he turned and left, shutting the door behind him.

A moment later Jean heard the door of his cabin shut, as well.

She awakened in the darkness to the sound of the shower running. Seeing the portholes beside her bunk, she recognized her surroundings and recalled what had happened the night before.

It must be David in the shower.

Sleepy, she reached for her diving watch hanging on a hook and pressed the button that would illuminate the dial. Three twenty-three. Hanging the watch back in place, Jean reclined against her pillow, listening to the shower shut off. What was he doing up? Had her questions about Skye interfered with his sleep?

The idea was painful, and it started a carousel of questions in her brain.

Had Skye really killed herself?

Jean could hardly believe it, yet it made an unlikely lie. All the information at her hands, everything she had read and heard, came rushing back at her. They were the same questions she'd asked herself when David had left her in her cabin earlier, and Jean wished she had some answers. The one he'd given her had only raised more doubts.

Why had the paper never mentioned suicide? And what of the "seven-digit" life-insurance policy Jake said David had received—by accepting the Corvette? Had David told anyone else that Skye had killed herself? He must have told Erika, and he should have told the authorities. To withhold that and then collect Skye's life insurance was fraud. Jean could not picture David compromising his integrity that way.

But hadn't Erika and Jake both said the Blade Institute was floundering at the time of Skye's death?

Lying in her berth, Jean listened to David leave the shower room as she played through her mind what she could be reasonably sure was true.

Skye must have jumped from the bow. David had implied as much by saying that the story in the papers was "close enough." But what kind of woman jumped from the bow of a cruising ship—with her husband and son looking on? Jean had asked if Chris had seen her fall, and David had said yes. *Fall*, Jean thought. He hadn't said anything about her jumping then.

Had Skye shot herself first? Jean disliked herself for even

trying to guess. Whatever Skye's manner of death, David must blame himself—whether or not he would ever admit it. His wife had killed herself and his son had witnessed it. Little Chris, whose child's mind had mercifully locked away the memory where it couldn't plague him.

Chris, who no longer spoke.

Added to the fact that David had been unable to stop the ship in time, the tragedy was enough to keep a man awake all the nights of his life.

Jean listened to the silence of the ship. She was wide-awake now and thirsty. She got down from the bunk.

She'd slept in David's shirt, and before sliding open the door to her quarters she took a pair of faded gym shorts from her locker and pulled them on. Then she stepped out onto the landing.

No light shone under David's door. Was he back in bed? Restless and walking the deck? Concluding that he must have gone out, she slipped soundlessly down the companionway into the office, black in the night.

Skye's place. How could a woman with so much have killed herself?

But anyone could be unhappy. Remembering the pills she'd found in the desk drawer, Jean wondered if Skye had been depressed. Scars from childhood? Abuse could happen in the best of homes, and its consequences were sometimes far-reaching.

Hurrying through the office, Jean felt for the stair railing in the dark and crept up the companionway to the galley. As she slid open the door, she sensed motion near the sink, and David snapped on the small light over the stove and looked at her. He was wearing a pair of well-worn blue jeans and nothing else, and his hair was wet and uncombed. He ran his hand through it as he saw her.

Jean said, "Sorry. I wanted a glass of water."

"Don't be sorry. You live here—basically." He lifted a

glass from the shelf and filled it from the cold-water tap in the freezer door.

Stepping into the galley, Jean took it from his hand. She drew it to her mouth, wondering if he expected her to leave.

He said, ''I hope I didn't wake you.''

She shook her head, eyes on the muscles in his upper arms, sleek and tanned. She wanted to touch him.

David said, ''You slept in my shirt.''

He didn't sound bothered, just interested, but Jean wished she hadn't done it. Her reason was that she hadn't been prepared to sleep on the ship; she had only one change of clothes in her locker. And—her secret reason—she'd wanted to absorb David's scent as she slept. She said, ''I didn't think you'd mind.''

''I don't. Just don't let my sister see you or she'll be wishing us joy. You look like I've made you mine.''

Jean's legs felt unsteady. Hesitantly she asked, ''Are you going back to bed?''

He seemed restive at the question. ''No. I don't need a lot of sleep.''

Jean silently calculated. He'd had two hours at the most and didn't appear remotely rested.

David turned away and opened the freezer to take out a bag of coffee. From the corner of his eye, he saw her lift the water glass to her mouth again. She didn't appear to be leaving. He said, ''What I told you last night is confidential.''

''Naturally.'' But it wasn't natural at all, she thought. Why the secrecy? It reeked of shame and darkness. She thought of the life-insurance policy and knew she wouldn't ask. Some lines should not be crossed, and on the *Skye* those lines surrounded her.

David was a time bomb. She didn't want to be the detonator.

Her eyes fell on the calendar on the wall, and she counted the closed doors. Chris would open the seventeenth when he awoke in a few hours. On the nineteenth they would leave for Baja. Then, just a few days until Christmas. Somehow it was hard to believe it would ever really feel like Christmas on the *Skye*. For David and Chris, the season could only mark the passing of the years.

Growing impatient with her presence and yet also somehow glad of it, David asked, "Are you up now? I'll make you breakfast if you are."

"I never refuse a meal," said Jean.

David smiled, remembering their breakfast at her house. Leaving the coffee bag on the counter, he opened the freezer door again, removed a can of frozen orange juice and handed it to her. "Read the directions if you're confused."

Knowing she was being teased, Jean pressed her heel lightly on his instep.

He murmured, "So you want to spar at my level now." With two quick moves he took the can from her hand, deposited it on the counter and pulled her where he wanted her—under the mistletoe.

Jean's hand and arm were twisted behind her, and with her free hand she slapped her leg, a silent request that he let her go.

He released her arm and drew her against him. He didn't kiss her immediately but murmured, "What have we got on under here?" and lifted the hem of the shirt she wore to slide his hand beneath. As he felt the silk of her skin he told her, "Say no if you want me to stop."

She closed her eyes and let her forehead rest against his throat as his hand moved up to caress her breast.

David could feel her heart keeping time with his own. Fast and hard. He pressed his hips lightly against her, acquainting her with the need she'd awakened. He touched her nipple, thinking of the galley stairs and wanting to latch them overhead so no one could come upon them. There was only Chris and Erika, but he wanted utter privacy. And he didn't want her in his cabin.

His mouth fell on her hair, tracing her hairline, and Jean put her lips to his throat. When she whispered his name there was a plea in it.

He said, "Okay?"

"I'm fine."

He could barely hear her. He kissed her mouth and touched her other breast. He couldn't remember ever wanting a woman so badly, not even Skye.

Skye.

He tried to forget the thought, but it was too late. He drew his hand out from under her shirt—his shirt—and hugged her close with both arms, vowing he wouldn't back away till he was ready. The images were there, but he was prepared this time. He could accept their presence with hers—at least like this. Holding her.

Jean's arms stretched around him, feeling the muscles in his back. She respected his strength and his tenderness. There was a power in size that made a man's gentleness toward a woman a quality by which she could most esteem him.

David was gentle.

But why had he stopped touching her breasts?

Closing her eyes, Jean let her cheek and nose sink against the base of his throat, nuzzling his skin. She wished it were so easy to touch his heart and mind. When he'd told her of Skye's suicide, David had made a chink in the wall that divided them. His kissing her tonight was another chink. Perhaps in time the crack would widen and she could see inside. Yet she feared the smallest misstep on her part could threaten their newfound closeness. *Trust me, David,* she thought silently. Her heart cried that she loved him.

His hand beneath her hair, he tilted her head back again and kissed her once more. Kissing him back, Jean knew the caress was extending longer than he'd intended. She sensed he didn't want to release her.

But eventually he did. He stepped back against the counter and let his eyes rest on her. They conceded nothing.

Jean said, "If that's sparring at your level, I think I could get used to it."

David picked up the can of orange concentrate and handed it to her. As it slid into her hand, ice cold and wet, he nodded to a locker overhead. "There's a pitcher up there."

LATER THAT DAY David suggested she take the Corvette home and pack what she needed for Baja. He planned to take Erika to her rehab center in Los Angeles early the next morning, leaving Chris with Jean, so it made sense for her to spend the night on the ship again. And the day after that they would leave for Baja.

Jean and Chris had made exhaustive plans for their day together—a visit to the natural history museum, then Christmas shopping. Jean was looking forward to it, but she felt the weight of responsibility. David would be leaving his son with her for more than twelve hours while he went out of town, and as she packed for the trip and closed up her house she could think of nothing else. Nothing else except the fact that she'd never told him about working for Michael and Jennifer Avery in Baja.

Most of the time Jean could forget the fiasco—or convince herself David would understand. But at home, in her own house, she heard the echo of her mother's voice and saw her skeptical stare, and she knew she could expect no better of David.

Even the houseplants accused her—or at least the Christmas cactus did. The bonsai olive tree was too needy to accuse. It seemed to cry to her, *Don't leave me for two weeks. The neighbors might not water me.*

But the cactus played tapes from the past.

Ceci's our nurturer. Jean's a little too self-involved. I don't know what kind of mother she'd make. For one thing, she's never home.

Small wonder, thought Jean. She looked at the flourishing olive tree, and another tape began to play.

You must be good with these. This tree looks old.

I think you'd make a very good mother.

Tears stung her eyes. Quickly she went to the kitchen table where paper and gift tags lay. She scrawled a card to the professor who'd recommended her for the Sayles Award and his wife, then collected a gift bow to stick on the cactus planter. She opened the front door, then returned to the cactus and hefted it into her arms to carry across the street.

Briefly she wondered what Ceci would think of her giving their mother's Christmas cactus to the neighbors. But then it occurred to her that her sister was seldom home and never noticed the plant when she was.

And later, as she carried the bonsai to the Corvette to take with her on the *Skye,* Jean remembered the olive branch was a symbol of peace. She knew she would never look at the little tree again without hearing David say she was good with plants and would make a very good mother. And without seeing Chris waiting in his pajamas for her to watch him open the next door of the advent calendar.

That was peace—unbroken but for the shadow of her lie to David.

WHEN SHE AWOKE the next morning to a heavy knock on the door of her cabin she was momentarily confused. David had said she and Chris should sleep in. He and Erika would be gone when they awoke.

But it wasn't Chris's small hand on her door. It was David's, and David's voice saying, "Sorry, Jean. Chris is up. Just throw something on and come out."

She was wearing her turquoise flannel pajamas, another

of Ceci's selections, and she climbed out of bed and opened the door at once. David was on the landing, waiting. He was alone.

Seeing her, David remembered the feel of her skin two nights earlier. He hadn't touched her since. But now her hair was down and uncombed, and her pajamas looked loose and soft and easy to remove. He wanted to feel the curves beneath them so badly it took him a moment to remember why he was there.

He said, "Chris is pretty upset about Erika. Would you like me to take him with us?"

Jean was surprised by the question. It wasn't like David to give in to his son's tears. But Erika's departure must be traumatic for both of them.

She said, "If you think that's the best thing." As David frowned at her answer she asked, "Where is he?"

"Out in the salon with Erika." Jean nodded and started to turn down the companionway, but he said, "Wait a minute," and touched her sleeve.

Jean paused, looking up.

David felt something give inside his chest, another tie coming unbound. He said, "A day seems like a long time not to see you." He meant only to touch her shoulder, but somehow, instead, she was in his arms. He pressed his mouth against hers, kissing first her bottom lip, then the top, then both, for much longer. Against her he said, "Jean," and felt her stir, trying to get closer. David knew how close he wanted to be—naked and inside her.

He envisioned it for a moment, sliding inside her, melting any resistance, hearing her whimper and cry out. Though she might not.

It ought to be simple, but it never would be. It would be complicated and intense—or a nightmare.

For a moment he saw blood.

Jean sensed his tension and wondered what he was thinking. "Are you all right?"

"Sure." With a hand on her back, he guided her down the companionway ahead of him, and as they descended into the darkness of the office he asked, "Do you have enough money?"

Jean couldn't help laughing. The night before, he had given her a hundred dollars, a major credit card and the keys to the Corvette. He was taking the Blade Institute van. She said, "What do you think we're going to do?"

David smiled in the darkness. "Order pizza."

Apparently he'd given up the idea of taking Chris with him. Jean was glad. Erika's leaving was going to be a hard adjustment for Chris, and she wanted to help ease it—if she could.

When she and David came up from the galley they found Chris sitting in Erika's lap in her wheelchair, his arms around her neck. He was still wearing his pajamas and was crying hard, but without sound.

Jean felt a hollow cracking sensation inside her, like a glacier breaking off a cascade and falling a thousand feet.

Erika looked up at Jean and shook her head, pain in her eyes.

Chris followed her gaze.

Jean said, "Hi, there. Calendar time?"

Chris sniffed and rested his head back against Erika's chest. He stared at Jean but made no reply.

Jean's heart fell. Giving Christian, Erika and David a compassionate glance, she said, "I think I'll have some coffee." She felt stupid. Chris's whole life was changing. Why would he care about his calendar now?

As she hurried down into the galley she heard David say, "Come on, Chris. Erika can't sit like that too long."

"Oh, let him stay, David."

Jean ached inside. She wanted to be able to comfort Chris. His tears always seemed more pitiful for being un-accompanied by any sound but sniffling and gasping breaths. If he had come to her, she would have held him as long as he wanted, till the sobs stopped.

She took the lid off the espresso maker and turned to fill the pot at the sink, only to bump into Chris. Jean hadn't heard him come down to the galley, and when she said his name in surprise, he signed something to her. He was still drying his eyes and his expression was serious, but he looked apologetic.

Jean knew David or Erika must have made him come down.

She crouched on the sole beside him and put her arms around him. "You don't have to be nice, Chris. I know you feel rotten."

He pressed his cheek, still wet, against hers, and held on to her hair.

FIVE MINUTES LATER David called down from the salon to tell them he and Erika were going out to the car. Jean and Chris stood in the center of the galley floor, where she was rearranging his walking stance and low block. She said, "Okay, now this arm comes up like this, and this one comes up this way, so you can step and *punch.*" She demonstrated.

Chris copied—almost.

"Your fist and your wrist twist here. Relax, then… *punch.*"

Chris tried again.

David smiled, admiring the techniques of both—Chris's athletic, her interpersonal. Unable to stop himself, he came partway down the stairs and leaned around the door to see Chris's calendar. The eighteenth door was open, revealing a dove.

Jean looked up.

David said, "We're leaving."

Chris waved disinterestedly and returned to starting position again.

Jean told him, "Let me say goodbye to Erika, and we'll do it again."

Chris signed something at his father.

David said, "That's fine." As Jean climbed the stairs he told her, "Chris already said goodbye."

And so had they to each other, but during the second they were alone in the salon, David put his lips against hers again, felt her hair brush his skin. Then, not wanting to speak, he went ahead of her onto the deck.

A HUNDRED DOLLARS and the fact that it was a "special occasion" justified breakfast downtown before embarking on the day's missions. With Chris beside her in the Corvette, Jean drove to one of her favorite breakfast spots, a natural-foods café on a downtown side street. As they ate baked goods and drank fresh-squeezed orange juice, they finalized plans for the day. Museum, then shopping.

For Jean, Christmas gifts for the Blades presented a dilemma. Erika had been the easiest. The previous night, Jean had given Erika her gift, an artist's smock batiked with dolphins. David's sister had been delighted, and Jean felt certain she could please Chris just as easily.

For him, she had bought stickers, colored glue, a hacky sack, a collection of plastic bugs from the natural history museum, a simple balsa airplane model, the newest adventures of *Hank the Cowdog* and a children's tae kwon do book. It was a lot. When she realized how much she'd chosen for the six-year-old, Jean wondered how she would find the courage to give him the presents under David's eye. One gift should have been enough, and Jean was afraid David would think she was assuming something that wasn't there. Family ties. She wasn't Santa Claus, after all.

But Jean had put the problem out of her mind to confront later. The purpose of this day's shopping trip was to choose gifts for David, a complicated task. Jean wanted to give him something, and she wanted to make sure Chris found something to give his father that would be satisfying to both.

As they wandered downtown together, looking in shop windows, Chris seemed as much at a loss for ideas as she was. Things were complicated by the ever-present language barrier. Jean had spent some evenings studying sign-language books, but her understanding of Chris was clumsy at best. Sometimes he signed at her almost frantically, and she couldn't read a word. When they went downtown, she prepared herself, taking a pen and notepad. As David had assured her, Chris could write well for his age, a skill that helped them over many hurdles.

They had been window-shopping without result for nearly a half hour when Chris tugged on her arm and pointed at the store they were passing. It was a photography studio.

Jean said, "A photo of you? Chris, that's a good idea. I bet there's nothing he'd like better."

Chris was shaking his head and pointing to both of them.

"No," said Jean. "You're his son. I just work for him."

Chris signed at her. Jean didn't understand him, but she wondered if he'd seen David kiss her that morning.

He frowned.

She told him, "My camera's on the ship." She'd packed it to take to Baja. "Let's go home and get it. We can shoot a roll of film and take it down to the one-hour photo shop. Maybe they'll do an enlargement for us today."

Chris nodded agreeably, and they hurried back toward the Corvette.

Jean said, "We'll do the photos, and you can make him something, too."

Chris looked at her as though she'd suddenly grown antlers. *What?*

"Whatever you think he'd like," said Jean.

Balancing on one foot on the curb, Chris frowned in dissatisfaction.

"I have a really good idea," Jean told him. "Something I did for an art class in high school. Do you mind getting your face gunky?"

Chris shook his head and pointed at her.

"I have a gunky face?" Jean guessed.

Chris shook his head.

"You want my face to get gunky, too."

He nodded enthusiastically.

Jean said, "Deal."

A voice broke into their exchange. "Squiring around the prettiest girl in Santa Barbara? Gimme five, Chris." Jake Doherty, just emerged from a sandwich shop, crouched to exchange high fives with David's son. Eventually he stood and turned to Jean. "Where's David?"

Jean explained that he'd taken Erika to rehab.

Jake said, "Erika's got it tough. David will do penance on that one for the rest of his life."

For Erika's accident? He made it sound as though David had been driving. Jean longed to ask for details, but not with Chris standing near. It was too tempting to rely on the fact that he couldn't talk.

Her eyes drifted to Chris, and Jake's followed. He shrugged at Jean. "I'll see you tomorrow. Bringing party clothes?"

Party clothes? Jean said, "I'll be working."

Jake snorted lightly and made a dismissive motion with his hand. "You'll be playing, too. Didn't David tell you?" Shaking his head at his own question, Jake said, "He wouldn't think about clothes. He owns four or five tuxes, and Skye had evening gowns in every locker."

"Evening gowns?" said Jean. She didn't own one, and it seemed both presumptuous and highly inappropriate to pack such a garment for a scientific expedition.

Jake said, "There's an annual holiday party at Cabo San Anselmo. We do it every year."

Cabo San Anselmo. On Baja. Jean carefully did not react,

nor ask precisely where on the cape the party was. She said, "I'm sure David plans for me to take care of Chris." At Cabo San Anselmo.

"Ah." Jake smiled. "I forgot. You're the nanny." He winked at her, and Jean told herself his choice of words was coincidental. He reached down and ruffled Chris's hair. "See you tomorrow, cowboy. Gonna help steer the ship?"

Chris nodded eagerly, and Jean knew it must be something they had done before. She began to relax, but in the back of her mind lingered the unsettling knowledge that the *Skye* would be making a stop at Cabo San Anselmo.

AFTER LEAVING JAKE, Jean and Chris stopped at a drugstore to get supplies they needed for their art project, then returned to the *Skye*. Because the light would be better later in the day, they postponed the photo session and, instead, set to work on their art project for David. In the late afternoon, refusing Baby's pleas for a swim, they left the harbor and went to the beach.

Jean took pictures of Chris standing in the breakers and building sand castles, and when he showed interest in using the camera she allowed him to take some of her. Then, carefully placing the camera on a rock, she set the timer to shoot a few pictures of both of them to have for her own. She wanted the physical memento of the time she spent with Chris.

When they had shot an entire roll, they hurried the film to the All-Night Developers, and Jean asked them to make prints and select the two best of Chris for a five-by-seven and an eight-by-ten.

After eating pizza they'd had delivered to the *Skye,* they returned downtown to collect their photos. The developer had taken the liberty of making three from which to choose, one including Jean. At Chris's insistence she bought them all, and they hurried back to the ship, eager to be there before David returned from L.A. He wasn't home yet, so

Jean read Chris a chapter of *Treasure Island,* his most recent interest, then hugged him good-night.

As she straightened up from his bed, Chris signed a phrase Jean recognized and had seen before in the Sulphur Springs Tavern.

I love you.

Immeasurably grateful and pleased, she hugged him again and whispered, ''I love you, too.''

And then he asked something else. It took her a moment, but at last she understood. *Will you sing to me?*

Without thinking she asked, ''Did your mom used to sing to you?''

But Chris only looked at her blankly, and she knew he didn't remember.

She said, ''A Christmas carol?''

He nodded.

She chose the carol she'd heard nights earlier, when she was out with David.

Sleep my love, and peace attend thee
All through the night.
Guardian angels I will lend thee
All through the night....

ON THE DOCK beside the ship David heard her voice. There was a husky, boyish quality to it that always seemed sexy to him. Now, hearing her singing in Chris's cabin, he remembered something long ago on the *Siren.* Christmas. His mother singing to him, holding his hand. How could he remember that when Chris couldn't remember three years past?

Because what Chris had forgotten was too horrible to remember.

Love alone my watch is keeping
All through the night....

He pictured Jean sitting beside Chris's bunk. Her braid would be loose now. It always was at night, like the night before when he'd found her on the aft deck watering that bonsai tree. Thinking of the bonsai, of her bringing a plant onto his ship, he tensed inside. He knew he should go inside and get it over with. Everything.

But her voice moved the memories inside him. The *Siren*'s silhouette plunging down in the icy sea. And a much older warmth.

He looked across the misty night at the Christmas lights glowing pastel in the fog. The other boats seemed faraway, their shrouds gossamer spiderwebs. Everything seemed distant but the silence he now heard from the cabin.

He realized it felt like Christmas.

And he turned and left the ship to go walk on the beach.

AFRAID TO RETIRE to her cabin for fear Chris would have a night terror and she wouldn't hear, Jean settled in the salon with her sign-language book, but it was hard to focus on the page. Repeatedly her attention wandered to the watercolor of Skye. Words and images jumbled in her mind. The photo of the newly wed David and Skye that she'd found in the office. The postcard from the Kyongju temple.

Where did you come from?

The big challenge in life is to crack the whip.

She was so mean and funny all at once.

Skye, carved on the windowsill in David's cabin.

Skye's eyes were like blue abalone when she was alive. And I don't care if her soul rests or not. You think mine does?

I love you deeply...deeply....

Suicide, thought Jean. What kind of pain had she been in?

Even with her eyes closed, she felt Skye's eyes of abalone blue watching her in the dark, and an echo of Jake's words came to her.

You're on that ship sometime at night, you'll know what I mean. You can feel her....

DAVID TUCKED the quilt from his bed around her body. He wasn't sure why he had chosen it to cover her, except that it was warm and beautiful, like her, the woman who could sleep in a chair.

Jean stirred beneath his hands and opened her eyes.

He said, "It's me. Sorry for waking you. I didn't want you to be cold."

Jean looked down at the quilt, and David saw her start. Erika must have told her Skye had made it.

Breaking the silence, he said, "Did Chris run you ragged?"

She shook her head sleepily. "He was wonderful." Recalling how they had spent the day, Jean almost jumped out of the chair before she remembered that the things they had made for David were safely stowed in Chris's cabin.

She met David's eyes. "He says he loves me."

David stared at her for a moment. "And you understood him."

Sign language. Jean wondered if he, too, was thinking of the night they'd gone to the tavern. She said, "Yes. I remember that one."

Their eyes held for what seemed like a very long time. At last David suggested, "Let's go up on deck for a while. No Santa Ana winds, but it's not too cold, either."

"Okay." Standing, Jean folded the quilt and set it on the chair.

Watching her sit down on the carpet beside the tree to put on her sneakers, David asked, "Like a nightcap?"

She shook her head, tied her last shoe and stood up.

They went up to the deck, and in the diving alcove he

silently helped her into a foul-weather jacket, sizes too large for her, to break the wind, then drew her outside into the night.

Jean paused under the canopy. "Where shall we sit?"

The cushions on the foredeck would be wet from the fog. David grabbed a towel from a hook inside the door of the alcove and said, "This way."

They went out on the forward deck under the starless sky. A filmy gray murk hung in the air, socking in the harbor. Damp wisps of fog swirled round the masts of the nearby sailboats, and the dock lights shone through a haze. David dried off the forward seat and they sat down a couple of feet apart.

"Cold?" he asked.

If she said yes, would he put his arm around her? She hesitated, but he didn't move. Jean said, "I'm fine."

"Good."

Silence fell between them, and Jean hurried to fill it. "How was your trip? I hated to say goodbye to Erika, knowing she'd be alone for Christmas."

David shared her feeling, but he said, "The research trips are hard for her. She wants to dive."

"Could she?" Jean asked.

"It's not safe. As divers we deal with certain limitations, anyhow. Without the use of her legs, Erika is doubly vulnerable." He gazed absently down at the zipper on his hooded shell, then looked up at her. "I want to ask you something. A couple of things, actually. Would you like to start with the difficult or the shocking?"

The question terrified her. Concluding that there was no point in postponing it, she asked, "Are you going to fire me?"

"God, no." He laughed, his eyes finding hers.

Jean wasn't sure she'd ever seen him so handsome.

He said, "Don't think it for a minute." Watching her,

he ran his teeth over his lower lip as though making a hard decision.

Jean said, "Then I suppose we should start with the difficult and move to the shocking."

"Okay." David appeared relieved. Stuffing his hands in the pockets of his jacket, he sat back against the cushions. "In L.A. I talked to a few people who think Baby might be accepted by other dolphins if we give her a chance. I'd like to try to get her down to Mexico with us, if she'll follow the ship. We'll probably see some dolphins of her species, and there's a possibility she'd join them."

Jean felt as though she might be crushed by the weight of his words. Baby join a school? Of course it would be best for her, but it would never work. The trip would only endanger her.

When she could trust her voice, she said, "I've read that orcas wait at the mouth of Scammon's Bay to ambush mother whales and their calves, but they'd just as soon attack a dolphin. I'd hate to expose Baby to that risk." Her voice was casual, but her feelings were not. Orcas were savage, and the thought of Baby coming to harm made her sick.

David said, "I may as well point out that I think she'll follow the ship, anyway—to be near you."

Jean had never considered that possibility. Baby's home was Santa Barbara. To lead her away from it was to lead her into risk. But the alternative—abandoning the Baja trip and Chris and David—she wouldn't consider.

David said, "Let's drop this for now. Baby will do what she wants, and I need to talk to you about something else." He paused and said very quietly, "You and me."

Jean's head snapped up. It was the last thing she'd expected, and his tone made her instantly fearful. Was he going to push her away again?

David turned his head and looked at her. "I gave our situation a great deal of thought today. An expedition can be a very intense professional situation, and obviously you and I have something personal going on.''

From David, it was a huge admission. Jean thought, *Don't say you want to end it.*

He told her, ''You should also be aware that on a ship, when two people feel a strong attraction for each other, it becomes glaringly apparent to everyone else.''

He must be thinking of Skye. Though Jean tried to ignore it, the thought pricked her like the point of a dagger. It was impossible not to imagine the lovers slipping away to their cabin in the middle of the afternoon to make love.

Sitting back, David stared aimlessly over the bow at the boats in the next marina. ''I know this job means a lot to your career. If you want to be taken seriously, it won't help for anyone involved with this expedition to suspect you're sleeping with me.''

Jean hadn't given a thought to what anyone would think. She was stunned, but at the same time she understood the message that she wouldn't be working for him forever, that at some point she would need to apply to someone else for employment.

Temporary, she thought. *All of this is temporary.* Dizzy with the implication of his words, she thought of the fact that it was David who had chosen to put her in the crew's quarters, in the one berth on the ship with easy access to his. She said, ''Perhaps I should move to an aft stateroom.'' It was the last thing she wanted.

David said, ''That's a solution and not one I'm fond of.''

Jean drew a silent breath of relief. ''What do you suggest?''

His brown eyes turned to hers in the darkness. ''I'd like to marry you.''

CHAPTER TEN

FOR A MOMENT Jean couldn't speak. When she could, she said in a fragile voice, "Marry me, as in...marriage of convenience?"

David thought of the pirate romance he'd seen in her house. If not for the gravity of the topic, he would have laughed. Instead, he shook his head. "Inconvenience. Life on a ship doesn't agree with most people. Which is why an engagement of reasonable length would be a good idea first." He added, "If you're interested."

Jean could hardly think. Of course she was interested, but what on earth could be his motive? He didn't love her. At least she didn't think so. She turned in her seat and saw him stand, clearly restless.

Jean's voice shook madly. "Why are you doing this? I don't understand. Are you talking about a real engagement? A real marriage?" Before he could answer she said, "It seems like an extreme way to protect my career."

In the fog David looked down at her. "This isn't about your career. I was wrong to start that way."

In the faded glow from the distant dock lights, Jean peered up at him, probing his eyes, wishing she knew his thoughts.

Moving away, David stared out across the water. "We have so much in common it's uncanny."

Jean wasn't sure he was going to say any more, but eventually he turned back. Despite the absence of light, Jean had the impression his eyes were as clear and candid as she'd ever seen them.

He told her, "I don't think there are two of you out there, Jean."

Jean pondered that, understanding what he meant—that he believed she was unique and somehow right for him.

He sat down again, closer to her this time. "And my son loves you. Isn't that what you said?"

You're supposed to love me, she thought, wondering how large a factor Christian's affection for her really was. Huddling in the yellow sailing slicker, she replied, "I'm not sure Chris loves me so much he wants you to marry me."

David smiled. "He probably wants to marry you himself." He put his hand on her back and touched her hair. It was loose, so thick he could drown in it in bed. He wanted to.

Why am I hesitating? Jean asked herself. *This is David sitting out here in the fog asking me to marry him.* So what if she'd known him only two weeks? In her soul she'd known him forever.

She loved him. She said, "Okay."

Because she sat beside him, David had to move his head forward to meet her eyes. "Yes?"

"Yes." Her heart was rushing. She was afraid she was going to cry. This was exactly what she wanted and yet it wasn't. She huddled deeper into the foul-weather jacket.

David said, "Sure?"

Was he hoping she'd change her mind? She said, "If you are."

"I'm not, but for grown men that goes with the territory. I think we'll do fine together." David couldn't take his hand out of her hair. It was a relief to know he didn't have to, but he wished he could see her face.

Jean said, "So we're engaged?"

Her voice sounded strange, thought David. Very emotional. He stroked her back. "Yes." Thinking of it, he said,

"Tomorrow's busy, but we can take an hour in the morning and look for a ring, if you like. Not that it's something we should rush."

Jean's throat closed. *So we won't have to return it?*

"We want something special," David said. "You'll be wearing it a long time."

Jean couldn't help it then. She turned her face against his shoulder, buried it against the yielding folds of his jacket and cried. *Don't be lying to me,* she thought. *Please don't.*

WHEN DAVID RETIRED to his cabin, two hours after he'd seen Jean to hers, he took her bonsai olive tree and his bottle of tequila with him. The tree was a surprisingly pleasant symbol of the season—and of her. The tequila was a necessity. Since he'd left her, he'd already drunk more than was good for him but not enough to make him unconscious, which was what he wanted.

He had not expected her to cry. Or to say yes.

He'd handled the moment by kissing her and touching her as long as he could, but then the strain had become too intense. He'd seen her to the crew's quarters and given her a brief kiss outside the door. It was easy to leave her in her own room, much easier than it would ever be to lead her into his. That was an eventuality he was happy to postpone.

Lying in the dark, he stared at the bonsai and nursed the bottle comfortingly, no longer minding the fire. It was making him drowsy. Good.

Oh, Jean, why did you have to say yes? Why did I ask?

Because it seemed obvious that he should. It was more than tae kwon do or diving or that she was young and beautiful, though those were the things that had swayed him where he thought he would never be swayed. When he'd thought about her on the drive back from Los Angeles, he'd realized she met and exceeded his own stringent criteria for what was acceptable in a mate. She was sober, assertive, honest and complex.

And what she had said about Chris had clinched it. *He says he loves me.*

Chris needed a mother—one who would sing Christmas carols at his bedside.

That was a huge factor, that and a casual remark from Erika, who had said, *Chris fell in love with her right away, didn't he, David? It's wonderful for him to have someone like that.*

David had seen the corollary—that it would be heart-breaking for Chris to lose her.

Which, as he'd told Jean, wouldn't have been enough by itself. She had provided the rest, with her individuality and her integrity.

David thought of her tears that night, her incredible explanation. *I never thought this would happen, David.*

Neither had he.

He drained the tequila and shoved the empty bottle onto the nightstand. Then he lay down in the darkness. Listening to the water and the docks, he remembered how her hair and her mouth felt.

He thought how different she was from Skye in every way.

He slept.

THE ALARM ON HER WATCH beeped at five-thirty, and Jean sat straight up in her bunk, remembering she was engaged to David. Hugging herself, she thought, *Yes, Jean, there is a Santa Claus.* Not only was she engaged to the man she loved, but they were leaving for Baja that afternoon to see whales. She would spend Christmas in David's arms, in Scammon's Bay, the place of her dreams.

Unfortunately Baja was also the land of her worst night-mares, but she tried to forget that. Jake had to be wrong about their going to Cabo San Anselmo, if only because everything else was so perfectly right.

Unable to sleep when David left her in her cabin the night before, Jean had used pages from her notebook to write a long letter of explanation to Ceci, which, through careful editing, had become shorter and shorter. Now, she wondered if she would even send it. What if David changed his mind?

The thought was terrifying to her, the more so because it seemed possible, even likely. Two weeks' acquaintance was enough for her, but she could hardly believe it was enough for David. Considering that the first time around he'd married a woman who had killed herself.

Jean shivered in the morning air. There would still be fog outside, and she didn't bother to lean close to the porthole and check. Instead, she climbed out of the berth, took her *dobok* and belt from her locker, laid them on the bed and looked under the door that led into the shower room. No light.

She knocked, then went in and switched on the light herself.

It was a space she liked. The showers were separated from the forward head by a door made of woven wood, bamboo and beads. David had remarked once that he was going to replace the door because it was a magnet for mold, but Jean loved the look, just as she loved the shower room's one mahogany-framed, stained-glass window. Giant sea turtles. There were two shower heads and a large sunken bath with whirlpool jets. Jean wanted to try the bath sometime, but it seemed wasteful of the ship's water reserves.

She stepped into the shower stall closest to her cabin and turned on the spray.

In the next cabin, the sound of the water roused David, though he neither noticed nor identified it. All he noticed was the way he felt.

It wasn't the worst hangover of his life or even in the

top five, but it was sufficiently unpleasant to fog the world and distract him from thoughts of the previous evening and the fact that he was now engaged. He remembered the last almost immediately, but at the moment it seemed less overwhelming than the hangover.

He hadn't done this to himself since the weeks after Skye's death, and as he kicked himself out of bed and rose naked to his feet, he wondered if asking a woman to marry him was sufficient justification for having done it again.

Yes.

He pushed open the door to the forward head and a few moments later opened the door and went into the shower room.

David realized his mistake at once. The room was full of steam and the scent of her shampoo. She was there outside the starboard shower stall, paused in the midst of drying off as she stared at him with wide eyes.

Frightened? Flustered? He didn't analyze it. He left, taking the sight of her small, long-legged muscular body and pink-tipped nipples with him.

As he paused at the sink and washed his face, she called through the door, "I'm done, David."

Which meant she'd taken her hair out of the drain, too, thought David. Conscientious. Again, exceeding the criteria.

He didn't answer. He was thinking of the glimpse of her slender hips, the triangle of hair at the top, the way she looked bent over just slightly as she dried herself.

"Mine," he murmured. His hangover seemed to ease.

JEAN DRESSED for tae kwon do and waited for him on the aft deck in the darkness. She hadn't seen him since he'd come in when she was getting out of the shower, and his silence when she'd called to him through the door was unnerving. Jean half expected that when he joined her on deck it would be with bad news—that he'd acted hastily the night before, perhaps spurred into a proposal by her announcement that Chris had said he loved her.

When David at last emerged from the cabin, dressed not in his *dobok* but in a pair of khaki canvas pants and a thick Blade Institute sweatshirt, her fears buoyed to the surface. He was going to call it off.

Jean watched him, trying to keep from showing her insecurity. He was carrying a cup of coffee and a bran muffin.

Eyes hooded with what looked like regret, he said, "Hi."

Jean stood up from a stretch but didn't move toward him.

Crossing the deck, he took a seat on a steel locker near the stern. In his condition, sparring was out of the question. He'd end up with cracked ribs or worse. He suggested, "Why don't you work on patterns this morning? I'll... coach."

Jean bowed to him and began to move the deck furniture to make room. Then, suddenly, she stopped and glanced all over the deck.

David knew she was looking for the olive tree. He said, "It's in my cabin."

Jean looked at him. "Was it in the way?"

He shook his head. "I like it. It seems like...Christmas. In a good way."

For a moment he thought she was going to cry again, but instead, she knelt to meditate. David watched her posture, her closed eyes, her tranquil expression, her even breathing, and felt his heart stir.

Again, he thought, *Mine*.

DAVID DID NOT MENTION going downtown to look for a ring. Instead, he seemed wholly focused on preparations for the trip. Even less talkative than usual, he gave concise directions, which Jean followed to the letter. But her disappointment was keen. Though he had commandeered her bonsaï tree, his "forgetting" their date to look for a ring was inauspicious. Again she wondered if he wanted to spare himself the trouble of returning it. Hiding her anguish, she played the calendar game with Chris and helped ready the ship for departure. If they finished early, perhaps David would take her downtown. There was no one to watch Chris, but they could take him along.

On the other hand, perhaps David didn't want his son to know about the engagement.

Or maybe he was waiting for an opportunity to break it.

When Jake Doherty arrived at nine, her last hopes were dashed. Jake came bearing provisions for the expedition and bad news. The cook they had hired for the trip had bailed out at the last minute and no other was to be found.

As Jean stowed the groceries in the galley, she thought how ironic it was that David needed a cook. Jean remembered her father telling her, *Look, Jean, don't worry about what your mother says. Anyone can read a cookbook. You don't need to be Julia Child.*

Jean imagined that at this point David would settle for less than a chef. She thought of the engagement ring he was avoiding, and when the cabin door opened and she saw him coming down into the salon, she leaned up the companionway from the galley and said, "David, I could cook."

David reminded himself that she was going to be his wife, and witticisms about her culinary skills should probably be kept to a minimum for the time being.

Jean saw the reservation he was striving to hide. It made her want to persuade him. Coming up the companionway to meet him in the salon, she said, "I'm a biologist. The kitchen's not that different from the lab."

She had a point, although it only underlined her unsuitability for the job. But her offer to do something he knew she disliked was endearing. He nodded at her. "Okay." Watching her eyes widen at the realization that he'd agreed, David said, "Jake's going to watch Chris for a while. Ready to go downtown?"

Jean heard his words with joyful amazement. He had remembered the ring. Her palpable fear at the thought of cooking for a half-dozen men receded.

David saw her emotions flit over her face. Her vulnerability—and her inability to hide it—touched him and made him want to take her to bed and prove his gentleness. It made him want to see the symbol of his promise on her finger.

He said, "Let's go."

As THE CORVETTE IDLED at a traffic light, Jean asked, "Have you said anything to Chris?"

He shook his head. "We'll tell him when we get home."

We. The word was a promise. She was part of his life.

The Christmas shoppers were out in force, and the first store they entered was busy with a mother looking for "something special" for her daughter, three ladies shopping for a gift for a co-worker, and a husband choosing for his wife. But the jeweler knew an engaged couple when he saw one. When he offered to show them rings, David looked at Jean, then said, "We'll browse for now."

Peering silently into cases lined with red velvet, Jean felt almost as though she were doing something forbidden. Was she really engaged to David? Were they really choosing rings together? Large diamonds winked at her from the cases. Simple settings. Ornate settings.

They left the store and stepped out into the sunshine on State Street. David asked, "Did you see anything you liked?"

Jean had seen a lot, but she wasn't even sure what she liked. She wished David would choose something.

He told her, "I'll say first that money is no object, second that you should like the ring. Those are the rules." His hand slid into hers. "Good enough?"

Jean nodded, smiling up at him. She said, "I think a ring from a gum machine would satisfy me."

David looked down at her. "Today it might. Wait till we're married, though. Everything changes then."

Jean noticed that after he spoke he looked somber, as though lost in a saddening memory.

Hand in hand they continued down the street, at home with the Spanish-style architecture, red-tile roofs under shading palms. Near the outdoor shopping plaza, a costumed madrigal group was singing renaissance carols, and as they paused to listen, David put his arm around Jean's shoulders and brushed a kiss across her temple. He bought hot apple cider from a street vender and kissed the spice from her lips. Jean felt as though she were in some other woman's body, living a dream that belonged to someone else. But it was *her* dream, the man *she* loved.

When at last they moved on to another jewelry store, David opened the door and held it for her. Jean stepped in ahead of him, wishing, not for the first time that morning, she was wearing something more stylish than faded jeans and a sweatshirt. Or at least more feminine and Christmassy.

But the elegantly dressed young woman behind the counter did not frown at her attire. Like the first jeweler, she seemed to sense they were a couple scouting for rings. Jean watched her smile broaden as she hurried toward them. Then, abruptly, the smile vanished and shock took over. For a moment Jean thought the woman was going to faint. She actually seemed to pale before regaining even a semblance of her former expression.

"David. What a surprise."

David nodded, wishing he'd chosen a different store. "Hi, Jill. I didn't know you were working."

Jean was interested that he did not add "here."

"I come in and help Daddy once in a while. Usually in the Montecito shop." The woman had recovered admirably, and now her carefully lashed eyes were busy taking in Jean.

"Today I just got lucky." She remembered to look at David. "What can I help you find? A Christmas gift?"

"A wedding set."

Jean noticed that Jill looked like a woman who had just received enough news to last her a lifetime. She turned to Jean, brown eyes wide. "Well, my goodness. Congratulations, my dear."

David studied Jean's face and doubted she recognized the cut. She was blushing. Before she could reply and give Jill further opening for ridicule, David said, "Thank you, Jill. I don't think we see anything in here today."

Jill looked momentarily taken aback. Then she said smoothly, "I'm so sorry. You used to have such luck coming here with Skye. She liked everything. I'll never forget those freshwater pearls you bought that one Christmas."

David turned Jean around and guided her to the door, then opened it.

Sensitive to David's pain, Jean hurried out, but she felt as though her own heart were breaking. She was aware of him behind her, his face a cool mask, showing nothing. For a moment he paused on the sidewalk, watching the cars pass, as though in the grip of indecision.

Waiting in the shade of the shop awning, Jean stared in the window at a display of rings lying beside some artfully arranged red glass Christmas balls.

You used to have such luck coming here with Skye.

Had he only remembered what store it was once he was inside? Or was that when the memories had suddenly become too much?

She thought of Jill's sleek style. The jeweler's daughter must have been a friend of Skye's. Jill's French twist looked unmussed, her makeup as though it had been applied by a professional and wouldn't fade by the end of the day. Despite Ceci's coaching, Jean's own experiments with makeup were always unsatisfactory. She preferred to go without, but inside the store, beside Jill, she had felt messy and unpolished.

She was certain Skye had been of Jill's ilk. Glossy and immaculate.

Jean saw David in the glass behind her. He was watching her reflection, and he put both hands on her shoulders. He said, "Would you trust me to have something made for us?"

The rings. Jean turned and looked up at him, her throat suddenly huge. She nodded.

It seemed natural that he would embrace her, but he did not. He said, "Then let's go home."

WHEN THEY PULLED into space number three in the marina parking lot, a uniformed mechanic from a nearby garage was waiting for them.

As he got out of the car, David said, "Hi, Jim. Thanks for coming to get it." He handed the mechanic the keys as he walked around the hood to let Jean out. She had already opened the door, so he shut it after her.

Jim said, "No problem to come and get this beast. I love to work on her."

David wished him a happy holiday and turned with Jean to lead her toward the marina.

She asked, "Is he going to take care of your car while you're gone?"

David nodded. "Leaving it here while I'm home is risky enough."

So Jake had been mistaken when he said David wanted the Corvette to come to harm. That seemed to debunk his insinuations about problems in David's marriage. Perhaps he was wrong about the party at Cabo San Anselmo, too.

If they were going David would have mentioned it, unless he expected her to stay home with Chris. That would have been natural at first—the job she was hired for—but

462 The Third Christmas

she was his fiancée now. If there was a party he would take her.

Jean hoped there was no party. And she hoped they would not stop at Cabo San Anselmo.

As they reached marina D and David used his key card in the gate, he said, "Jean, I think perhaps I should be alone when I tell Chris." He didn't say what he was going to tell him; they both knew.

Jean glanced up at him as she moved through the gate, wondering what had prompted the change of course. Did he think Chris would be upset? And what if Chris *was* upset, was worried or hurt or angry? Jean closed off the thoughts. "If you think that's best."

David shut the gate behind them. "I do."

Jean spent the next half hour making the office shipshape for departure. It was the perfect task because it kept her hands busy and her mind free, and it kept her out of the way of Jake and any arriving expedition members. Below, in the security of the lower cabin, there was no need to hide the worry on her face as she thought of David talking to Chris—and no need to hide her preoccupation as she replayed her brief date with David.

The final scene in the jewelry store became more painful upon mental repetition. Jill's congratulating her, as though she were the big winner. She, about to blunder her thanks while David chivalrously accepted the courtesy. How different it must have been for him with Skye.

Numbly she imagined him choosing those freshwater pearls, a Christmas surprise. Or had Skye gone with him? Had they lingered over the cases together? Had he shaken his head at her choices or she at his? Had they found together what they liked and David said, *Those, please?* What a contrast to today. He had asked to see nothing, not even to have her sized, and Jean doubted now it was because nothing had pleased him.

She was distracted from her musings and her work when

the door at the top of the stairs opened, letting light shine in from the galley. She saw Chris's small silhouette and David's larger one behind him. They stepped onto the landing, and David closed the door as Chris started down the companionway.

His progress was laggard, and Jean was reminded of the withdrawn child she had met two weeks earlier. His behavior had changed so much since then, and the reversion was worrisome. Was learning of his father's engagement to her the cause? If Jean had doubted it, she would have seen the answer in David's eyes. He seemed lost in thought, absently focused on Chris and almost unaware of her.

Chris came to stand near the desk where she was working and signed a phrase at her. Jean recognized "family."

After a moment, David said, "He's glad you're going to be part of our family."

Chris glanced at his father as though to ask, *Is that good enough?*

David nodded at him, a cue for the next step.

Looking at David again, Chris moved forward and hugged Jean around the neck.

A charade, she thought. *At David's insistence?* Courtesy was important, but how did Chris really feel?

She hugged him back—an abbreviated hug—and looked into his eyes.

He turned away.

David, who had come down to the foot of the stairs, seemed dissatisfied but tolerant. He told Chris, "You may go."

Chris gave them both a final, opaque look and trudged back up the steps. David stood silently at the bottom of the companionway until his son had gone out and closed the door.

Jean said, "David, if he's unhappy about it, we don't need to—"

"He doesn't necessarily know what's good for him."

Jean swallowed that answer. It wasn't what she'd been hoping for. First, he had not denied Chris's unhappiness. Second, why hadn't David said *he* cared for her and that was the bottom line?

Because it wasn't. He was acquiring a mother for Chris.

Setting that aside to ponder later, she asked, "What did he say?"

David hesitated. "Not everything. I'm sure of that." With obvious reluctance he admitted, "He has an idea his mother is coming back—that I go out on the channel looking for her." Before Jean could feel more than one hard, pounding heartbeat, he said, "I should say, he *had* that idea. I think I dispossessed him of it."

Jean recalled her own parents' death. Morning after morning she had awoken with the feeling that everything was as usual. Then, each day, when she'd realized they were dead, the world had fallen around her. She had wanted to go back to sleep, to wake up from the nightmare.

If somewhere in his subconscious Chris still held the recollection of his mother falling off the ship and never surfacing, his idea made a kind of sense. Hardly knowing she spoke, she whispered, "Poor Chris." And poor David, who had seen his wife's blood and would never lose the memory of it.

David watched her, his thoughts divided between the emotion on her face, the unseen feelings in her heart and his own conversation with Chris—his effort to convince a child who did not even remember his mother or her death that the woman was in fact dead. And all the while trying to preserve something of a six-year-old's innocence.

He told Jean, "Truthfully, I think he was focusing on that to avoid other fears. Being sent away. My no longer loving him or loving you more."

It was the first time he had mentioned loving her at all and now only as a possibility to be denied to his son. Jean said, "You reassured him?"

"Of course." Apparently eager to close the subject, he glanced at the office. "When you're done here, come on up. Some people have arrived, and it's time for introductions."

AS JEAN LOCKED the desk drawers and made sure nothing could be dislodged at sea, she heard the loud hum of the engines warming up. It sent a faint vibration through the ship, the sound of a vessel preparing to move. It excited her, helping to erase the gloom of a morning whose bright buds of hope had been blown away by the winds of reality.

Still, the gravity of her situation immersed her. She was engaged to a man who didn't love her and whose son might or might not accept her as a stepmother. David was marrying her for Chris's sake, and yet Chris wanted his own mother, whose picture still hung in the salon.

As she passed through the salon, Jean noticed the watercolor again. How long did David intend to keep the portrait there? Forever, as permanent tribute to his first wife?

Jean wondered if she could stand it—and if she could stand always being second. But David came with a past.

As she opened the salon door, she found him coming through the diving alcove accompanied by a tall, white-haired man. He said, "There you are. Jean, this is Dr. Grant Geary, our expedition doctor. Dr. Geary was a friend of my father's. Besides being an MD, he's also a qualified veterinarian and a cetacean specialist. Grant, this is my fiancée, Jean Young."

Fiancée. Even hearing him utter the word didn't make it seem real.

For a moment she and Dr. Geary assessed each other. Studying the doctor's face, Jean recognized him from the shark video as the man who had tended David's wound. Now, as he returned her appraisal, she saw something behind his eyes that disconcerted her. Reservation. But the look was well concealed as he held out his hand and said,

"I'm pleased to make your acquaintance, Miss Young. I've already met Baby."

Jean smiled and shook his hand. She could hear Baby outside, whistling from the side of the ship. She said, "It's nice to meet you, Dr. Geary."

They exchanged pleasantries for a few moments more, and Jean began to relax. Then Dr. Geary went below to his cabin, and David invited her outside to meet the other members of the expedition—biologist Ken Lightman and Australian cinematographer Robin Frost. Jake had gone into town for last-minute supplies.

Jean spent the time until departure on the diving platform with Baby and the inflatable Christmas wreath, now patched with duct tape. Part of her worried that it was a mistake to show the dolphin attention at this time. If Baby followed the ship away from Santa Barbara, she might become separated from them and never find her way back. What was more, the unknown southern waters seemed to offer infinitely more peril to the lone dolphin. But surely Baby had the sense to remain behind in a place familiar to her.

At one in the afternoon they cast off and the *Skye* churned slowly out of the harbor. Seeing Chris occupied in the salon with an aircraft carrier and fleet of die-cast metal planes Dr. Geary had given him as an early Christmas gift, Jean went to the wheelhouse to find out if there was anything she could do for David.

The channel was calm, with only the wind disturbing the water. Jean discovered she liked the motion of the ship; the ocean was in her blood. She liked feeling the sun on her skin and the salt spray in her hair as she made her way along the railing toward the bridge.

Nearing the wheelhouse, Jean realized Jake must be inside with David, smoking a cigarette. The starboard window of the cockpit was open, and his voice drifted out with the smoke.

"Your first marriage made more sense to me, and I have to say, that one never made a lot. Marrying a woman you've known two weeks makes *none*."

Jean froze, listening for David's response, but Jake drowned him out. "Oh, Jean's got secrets, all right." He paused. "I know because I know, David. Say the word to her sometime. Watch what happens. What word? *Secrets*. That word."

Jean's heart clenched and unclenched a hundred times. Wondering whether to go into the wheelhouse or try to hear more, she hesitated outside the cabin. She heard the murmur of David's voice beneath the engine but couldn't make out the words.

Jake said, "Okay, okay. I like her, David. You know that. I wish you joy."

Bracing herself, Jean pulled open the door of the wheelhouse and stepped inside.

Jake's back was to her, but David's was not. Eyes dark on hers he said, "Hi, Jean."

Jake shrugged at David. Reaching for his pack of cigarettes, he echoed, "Hi, Jean." Then he slipped out of the wheelhouse, leaving the helm to David.

As the door shut behind him, Jean recalled why she had come. "Chris is playing with airplanes. Do you have something for me to do?"

David looked thoughtful. Watching his profile, Jean wondered if he knew what she had overheard. Did he want to uncover her secrets?

He nodded toward the bow. "I think Baby's up there, playing off the prow. If you go down in the observation chamber, you can see her."

A number of reactions went through her. Worry that Baby was swimming with the ship. Excitement at seeing the inside of the underwater observation chamber, which David had never shown her. And worry over what suspicions Jake might have awakened. She'd sensed David had defended her, but that was what she would have expected of him. It would be a violation of his personal code to let anyone criticize his family or choice of fiancée.

Jean decided to test the waters. "I guess Jake doesn't approve."

David glanced at her. "I wondered if you'd heard that." He turned his eyes to the channel and said, "Don't think about it. You and I have known each other a short time. People will have their say."

Jean thought of Jake. He would say plenty if he knew the truth.

Unexpectedly David put his hand on her back, over her braid. Coming out from in front of the captain's seat, he guided her into his place and set her hands on the ship's wheel. Jean gripped the glossy hardwood of the helm and realized she was steering. Gesturing to the distant islands, David said, "Point the nose under that southernmost mountain. I'm going to see what Chris is up to."

Then he left.

For a moment, Jean felt overwhelmed. There was tremendous power in her hands, and she could feel the other power, the sea, beneath the vessel. Yet the sensation of being at the helm was intoxicating. Other concerns crept away, and after a minute or so she moved and sat upon the leather-covered captain's seat, moving the wheel slightly to keep the bow pointed toward the island mountain David had indicated.

A moment later, the door of the wheelhouse opened again and Jake came in, smelling of cigarettes. She started to move from the seat, and he said, "You're fine," then increased the throttle.

Jean was uneasy, not because she felt Jake might try to ferret out her past, but because he was bound to stumble upon it. Both Jake and David had connections in Baja, and now they were going there. With her. Possibly to Cabo San

Anselmo. She didn't dare ask if the cape was really on the itinerary.

Feeling almost as though Jake might read her thoughts, Jean shifted them to the other part of his conversation with David. Why had Jake said David's first marriage hadn't made sense to him? Jean longed to quiz him, not only about that enigmatic statement but about Erika's accident and the puzzling comment he had made to her earlier about David "doing penance." Jake was a well of information begging to be tapped with questions Jean couldn't bring herself to ask. David would be her husband; if she wanted to know something she should ask him. Except that he wouldn't talk about what she wanted to know.

She was watching the channel through the windshield, but she felt Jake studying her. He lit another cigarette and said, "Sorry about what you heard, Jean, but David's my friend, and I had to say it. Strangers shouldn't marry."

Jean said, "Please consider the possibility that we know each other better than you think."

Jake said, "Please consider the possibility that you don't know David *at all.*"

Jean's palms grew damp on the steering wheel. She told herself it was just Jake, Jake with his way of turning life into gothic intrigue. But there was enough truth in his remark to set her on edge.

And, as though he couldn't keep quiet, he said, "David wouldn't thank me for this, but I've got to say it, Jean. You marry him, you marry his past. And you're sitting on it. *Skye.*"

Because he had said the name, Jean couldn't stop herself. She looked at him and asked, "Did you like her, Jake?"

"Skye?" Jake spread his hands wide, drawing a plume of smoke across the cockpit. "I loved her. I hated her. Everyone did, David most of all. They were screaming one minute and screwing the next. Skye was a bitch and a lush, but she was great. Funniest woman you ever met. Sweetest, too, when she wasn't the meanest. But, baby, Skye made trouble like a baker makes bread, and she made David a lifetime supply. *His* lifetime, not hers. You want to live with that?''

Paralyzed by his speech, Jean hardly saw Jake's eyes drift toward the channel.

He said, ''Watch your course.''

Blinking, stunned, Jean faced the sea. The ship had veered sharply, and she concentrated on regaining her heading as Jake's words spun through her mind. *Bitch? Lush?* Jean couldn't focus on that, only on David and Skye, together. In one breath, she saw them in moments of passionate rage; in the next, making love in every cabin and on every deck of the ship, from engine room to fly bridge, from bow to stern. She saw David buying pearls for Christmas, and she remembered, with horror, that Skye had killed herself. Did Jake know that?

Jean didn't have long to ponder it. The door of the wheelhouse opened, and David came in.

He did not look at her but gazed off the bow, checking her course. Then he stole one of her hands from the helm and said, ''Come on. I want to show you something.''

NOT RELEASING HER HAND, he led her out onto the bow and opened the forwardmost hatch, which Jean knew led down into the underwater observation chamber. Nodding below into the darkness, a darkness shining with faint aquamarine light, he said, ''You first.''

Jean noticed he held her hand until she had crouched on the deck to lower herself down the hatch. The bow, she thought. He's nervous because we're near the bow.

His concern made her heart ache. *David, what did she do, this incomprehensible woman you loved? How did she go over that bow rail? Drunk?*

But there were no answers, could be none until he decided to give them. Which might be never. Watching David's running shoes, inches from her eyes, Jean continued below, into the hull.

Portholes followed the ladder down the ship's nose. Through the layers of glass she saw sunlight rippling in the foam produced by the prow. As she descended the ladder, her eyes caught a sleek, silver shape in the blue and she gasped. Baby, swimming fast and strong in the wake.

David said, "Go on."

At his urging, Jean continued down the ladder, and David followed, shutting the hatch over their heads. The space was small, with barely room for the two of them to stand comfortably. But the chamber curved aft, creating a low-ceilinged nook where the floor was covered by an old mattress. A quilt lay on top, shielding the mattress, and Jean knew in a glance it must be another of Skye's. The colorful, intricate style was like that of the spread on David's bed.

David drew her eyes away from the quilt with the touch of his hands. They were on her waist, and Jean looked at him in surprise.

He said, "Hi." And he kissed her.

CHAPTER ELEVEN

HE HAD KISSED HER on the street that morning, but this was a real kiss, a private kiss, and there was a moment of adjusting mouths, of finding each other again, of remembering.

As the ship hit a wave and the bow bounced, David locked his arm around her, simultaneously holding the ladder. He said, "We'll do better on the floor."

Her heart racing, Jean let him steady her as they slipped down onto the mattress, not sitting but lying, facing each other. Her blood rushed down through her stomach, pooling heat and desire, and she let her legs press against David's as he kissed her again and began unbuttoning her work shirt. Jean did not stop him, but she was shocked. Weren't they supposed to be working? What was happening on deck? Would they be missed?

David's single-mindedness left no room for questions. He made short work of the front closure of her bra, pushing aside the cups to expose her breasts to the cool air and the soft aqua light.

And to his eyes.

Aside from the time they had glimpsed each other through the fog of the steamy shower room, he had never seen her naked. And Jean had never felt so revealed. Years ago, she had joined her body with someone she knew as well as she knew herself. But she felt more now in simply allowing David to look at her. More intimate, more excited, more vulnerable. More right.

As she trembled David kissed her and dragged his lips down her throat to her collarbone and breastbone. He said, "I've wanted to do this for a week."

Here? wondered Jean irrationally. *In this chamber?* Or was he simply talking about taking off her clothes, caressing her? Again came the echo of Skye, a taunting mystery. Had he and Skye lain together on this spot? Had they made love while the foam broke away from the prow?

David touched her, drawing her mind from the thoughts. His hand on her bare side, he let his lips graze her breasts, then one nipple. He tasted the pink skin with his tongue, then closed his mouth over her.

Jean's breath folded inside her, and her fingers caught his hair. His mouth and hands tasted and explored, kissed and stroked. It was not the way he'd touched her the night before—with restraint, as though he had somewhere to be and must leave shortly. No. Now, he kissed and caressed her as though he might continue for hours.

His mouth wandered to hers again, and they kissed with their tongues. Jean's breasts pressed against his shirt, and with wonder she felt his hand between her legs, cupping her over her jeans. She jerked against him, hard, unrestrained.

David murmured something she didn't understand, and she drew closer to him, one of her legs slipping between his. He released the buttons on her jeans. The denim was worn, and the fly parted with one movement of his hand. He said, "Are you all right?"

She nodded, her eyes holding his for one flustered moment. As he'd known she would be, she was a mass of feverish confusion and want. When he slipped his hand under her clothes, into the tangled silken down beneath the cotton scrap of her panties, he found no surprises. Only her, wet and clinging to him, reaching for his pants.

He moved her hand away. "Let's keep things simple." As though anything about it was simple.

He stroked her, and she cried softly, "David."

He felt as though no one had ever said his name before.

But she hadn't surrendered. David felt part of her fighting—herself, not him—as though she didn't picture herself finding sexual fulfillment in his arms in a hollow chamber beneath the sea while others walked overhead. He felt sorry for doing it, but not sorry enough to stop. He wanted to make her come.

It was very easy, the work of quiet minutes.

Jean felt her whole body rushing, burning, floating against him. His name came from her mouth three times, like a spell, and she felt a swift rush of realization, then embarrassment. What had she done?

He wasn't letting her think about it. He was kissing her, touching her hair that had fallen from her disheveled braid, then hugging her against him tightly, as though she were a dear friend he hadn't seen for a very long time.

Her words muffled by the barrier of his body, she said, "No one else has ever done that to me."

Liking the information, that whoever had shared her body had never succeeded in awakening her and that he had, David said, "No one else ever will."

Jean could hear a trace of a smile in his voice but something else, too. A warning? Or a vow? The possessive words filled her like nourishment, and she rested her head against his heart.

After a moment, David moved her onto the mattress, onto her back, then fitted his mouth to hers again, kissing her at leisure.

Jean said, "You're like a dream come true."

Against her cheek and her hair, David murmured, "It's fair to warn you I have total recall of statements like that. Those words may come back to haunt you."

A moment passed before Jean understood the allusion to the long road of marriage. David's comment promised something lasting—the ordinary fights and reconciliations of a lifetime together. But it also reminded her of what Jake had said about him and Skye.

David seemed in no hurry to go, but spent long moments with his lips against her bare skin, his hands caressing her as though he required them to memorize the curves of her form. He cared for her in every way she could imagine before he at last buttoned her jeans, then fitted her bra around her and fastened it.

Dreamlike and wanting to stay in the dream, Jean asked softly, ''Where did you learn all this, *Sabumnim?*''

''Books.''

He met her eyes, and Jean knew it was a lie, but one that for the space of a moment she could believe. With the sea moving around them like an ever-changing cocoon, in the cool depths of the dark chamber with only his body to warm her, she could almost believe it had always been only her for him. That Skye had been unimportant, a trivial mistake.

As David finished buttoning her shirt, he glanced through the glass of one of the deadlights and remarked, ''Baby has company.''

Jean had forgotten about the dolphin. She sat up and saw Baby leap out of the way to allow another dolphin to play in the waves. Realizing David's thoughts beyond his words, she said, ''It doesn't mean she'll be accepted by a school.''

''True.''

Jean wished Baby wasn't following the ship. The last thing she wanted at this beautiful, perfect moment was a disagreement with David, so she changed the subject, asking a question that had crossed her mind earlier in the day. ''When are you going to tell Erika?''

''I already did.'' On the phone that morning. Erika had said, *I knew you were in love with her.* He wasn't, but he hadn't disagreed with his sister. Erika wouldn't understand. Being in love was nothing he wanted, and it wasn't what he felt with Jean.

No. Jean was the ominous approach of a hurricane. When she'd shuddered against him, calling his name, he'd felt things inside him coming unglued. The pieces were breaking apart and mixing up. He couldn't find the dark places anymore, and he had the uneasy feeling they had made a run toward the exit and were lurking near the top.

The thought scared him very much.

JEAN SPENT THE REST of the day in the salon with Chris, playing airplanes. Except for being more subdued, the interaction between them seemed unchanged from any other day, but Jean could not ignore the difference in their relationship. She was going to be Chris's stepmother, and everything they said and did together took on greater significance. But over her head still hung the memory of a long-ago error she had made, a failure less mistake than misfortune. If David ever found out, would he still think her good mother material? Would he find her to be a fit guardian for his son?

Jean wasn't sure.

In any case one thing she could never be was Chris's biological mother. He would always feel the emptiness of missing Skye, whoever she had been.

As she made a P-51 Mustang take off from the deck of the carrier, Jean watched Chris's plane bomb an enemy base made from an encyclopedia volume. The bomb exploded without sound. The engines of his planes were silent.

In a way she never had, Jean felt frustration at his speechlessness. Now she was going to be part of David's family, and the anomalies seemed more glaring, their sting sharper. She began to think of Chris as the boy who would be her son, and she understood more than ever the agony David must face daily in witnessing his child's endless silence. More than ever, she wished Chris's speech restored—and doubted she could in any way effect such a change. Worse, it was a change she now feared, because she sensed it might come with the return of a memory too monstrous for a child to bear.

She wondered how a man could bear it.

LATE THAT AFTERNOON the *Skye* anchored in a cove on one of the southernmost islands, and Robin Frost asked Jean if she'd get in the water with Baby so he could get some footage of them swimming together. Jean agreed, and when Chris asked to join her, David allowed it.

Nor did he raise any objection to Robin's filming Chris with Baby. Taking advantage of David's tolerance, Jean asked to use one of his underwater cameras and took some shots of Chris snorkeling with the dolphin. Then she climbed into the Zodiac, the inflatable motorized pontoon boat, with the others for an excursion to a nearby coral reef, where Robin wanted to film her diving with Baby.

David joined her on the dive, and Jean was acutely conscious of what they had shared earlier in the afternoon. She had never felt so close to anyone, and as they dove together near the reef, she reminded herself that their love of the sea united them, too. There was an easy chemistry between them in the water, a silent communication of spirits, as though they were meant to share the deep.

Robin wanted footage under a variety of conditions that took the whole party—Jean and David, Robin, Dr. Geary and Ken—to more than a hundred feet below the surface. It had been months since Jean had dived at such a depth. She welcomed the world of blue and was spellbound by the slow, graceful movements of large sharks below. Jean had learned in many ocean dives that sharks, while unpredictable, seldom bothered divers. Still, when Baby skirted away, a wave of uneasiness washed over her, and she remembered, as in a trance, the film of David's attack.

David, she thought, meeting his eyes and finding them absorbed with her. He seemed aware of the sharks but uninterested in them—only in her. He was so close Jean felt as though they were children in the same womb, or lovers, naked to each other as she had been naked to him that day.

We *are* lovers now, she thought. He must care.

Then, another truth came to her, subtle and sure. Though she couldn't be certain if Jake's impression of David's and Skye's marital interaction was accurate, she knew this: the David she loved would not relish the kind of constant emotional turmoil Jake had described. David craved tranquillity and clarity of mind. She saw that daily.

And as her eyes met his, Jean knew what she wanted—to bring peace to his soul.

Dr. Geary and the others swam upward, but a powerful allure begged Jean to remain below. She could stay at these depths with David forever, watching his eyes behind his mask. But as she watched, those eyes grew resolute—and regretful. David firmly took her hand and drew her up with him.

Forcing herself to heed the threat of nitrogen narcosis, Jean followed, grateful for his hand in hers. The rapturous high she'd felt gave way to emotional exhaustion, and each time they paused for decompression David stayed close, as though sensing her need for him. He was at her elbow when her regulator went out and her airflow stopped.

David grasped the problem immediately. His gaze locked with hers, and the expression in his eyes calmed her as he passed her his secondary regulator. Frightened, Jean glanced uneasily at his dive computer, doubting he had adequate air, but David thrust the mouthpiece into her hand with a gesture that defied argument. Aware the only alternative was a rapid ascent that would leave her bent and in peril of an embolism, Jean exchanged mouthpieces. David held her, his arm half-around her, as they alternated breaths. Using her buoyancy compensator, he regulated their ascent so they wouldn't have to swim and use precious air.

As they paused for a last decompression stop, Jean

wished she could tell him she loved him. She loved everything about him. His intelligence, his competence, his spirit. In two weeks, he had become the person closest to her, the man she would marry. The dearest gift of the season and of her life.

She *could* tell him she loved him. Freeing her hand from his, Jean faced him in the water and signed the phrase she had learned from him.

I love you.

In response David stared at her for a moment, then drew his hand across his throat.

They were out of air.

JEAN GASPED as they broke the surface. The air at the top was sweet, and the setting sun cast a brilliant glow over the water, momentarily blinding her. Trembling, she pushed her mask up on her forehead, buoyed by her vest.

Beside her, David inflated his vest, and as Jean squinted at him through her dripping lashes he would not meet her eyes. When he looked up it was to wave at the Zodiac, some distance away. Chris was leaning over one pontoon, petting Baby, but Jake returned the wave. Pushing back his mask, David ducked under the water then shook his hair, blinking the salt from his eyes. He still wouldn't look at her, and Jean thought of what had passed between them before they'd swum for the surface.

She had told him she loved him.

Seeing she wasn't going to get a response to that, she said, "Thank you, David."

"You're welcome."

The answer was cool, and Jean realized his mood had nothing to do with her silent underwater confession of love. He was angry about her regulator. Unquestionably and with good reason. He'd criticized her equipment the first day they dived together and had warned her about it since.

Jean told him, "You have every right to be mad."

480 The Third Christmas

Mad didn't touch it, and his maelstrom of emotions wasn't all for her. David's dark eyes met hers with icy brevity, and when Baby swam near them, lifting her head from the water to kiss Jean, he said, "A good thing you weren't alone with your old diving partner, isn't it?"

"I wouldn't have come out here with just Baby." Jean touched the dolphin, stroking her skin in long, soothing motions.

David watched, irrationally wishing she was touching him, instead. He had never before had the impulse to kick an animal. Or to yell at a woman, *And by the way, I don't love you.*

But as she rested her cheek against the curve of Baby's back, David couldn't stop his eyes from tracing the contours of her face, and he thought, *I can't afford to love you.*

DAVID CAME into the galley as she was rummaging in the cupboards. He'd said nothing to her during the ride back to the ship in the Zodiac nor since, but as Jean started turning the pages of a cookbook on the counter he said, "Make spaghetti. Lots."

Jean looked up at him. Her hair, still wet from a shower, tumbled down her back in an indifferent ponytail, and she was wearing a white T-shirt and a pair of faded Levi's that hung loosely from her small hips. She made him think of raw sex, and without wanting to David remembered her in his arms that afternoon. The vision had come and gone all day, pleasant but teasing, like the recollection of her taste and scent and the feel of her skin. Unfortunately, equally strong was the memory of her air stopping at eighty-five feet. It had been a reminder, not that she was heedless but that she was mortal.

David hadn't planned to care, but he did.

Seeing her gaze still upon him, he said, "Don't cook the noodles too long, and you'll be fine."

Jean was glad he'd decided to speak to her. Recognizing

good advice, she put water on the stove to boil, then took a bulk jar of whole-grain noodles from the shelf and unscrewed the lid. She glanced at him. "How much?"

"More." He watched her, his eyes drawn to the curve beneath her small breasts. "More."

Jean held out two huge handfuls. "Enough?"

"One more," said David.

She bowed, eyes flirtatious. "Thank you, *Sabumnim.*"

David felt himself getting hard and made a mental note to speak to her later about calling him that. Someone would ask what it meant and never stop laughing over her addressing him by his title as a master instructor, no matter of what.

But they were alone, and she was making him smile. He answered in Korean—at some length.

Jean stared up at him, her mouth round. "What does that mean?"

"I was just putting you in your place."

But he had looked as though he was promising carnal delights. Eyes flickering like candle flames, Jean answered, "That's something I'd like to hear in English—if you can say it."

Sassy wench, thought David. He could say it. Turning his back to the door, blocking her body from view to anyone who might interrupt them, he drew her close to him and put his hand on her breast, stroking her nipple through her bra. Meeting her eyes, he translated roughly, in a low voice. "You have beautiful hair. I've tasted your breasts and your lips and your tongue. I want to put my mouth between your legs. All parts of you belong to me, and someday I will spill my seed inside you." Watching the flush in her cheeks and knowing it was flamed by desire as much as his frank words, he said, "You did ask," and kissed her mouth lightly, then released her.

Watching him leave the galley and go up to his cabin, Jean decided being put in her place by David was the best thing associated with cooking that had ever happened to her.

The next best thing was that the meal worked, garlic bread and all. She even made brownies from a mix and didn't burn them. Over dinner with Chris and the members of the expedition, David remarked, "You'd hardly know it was amateur hour in the galley tonight." But as the others laughed, his hand clasped hers beneath the table. It didn't hurt her feelings when later that night she heard him tell Jake they would stop in L.A. the next day to hire a cook.

THE FOLLOWING DAY the *Skye* tied up at a large industrial port near Los Angeles. Jean was playing chess with Chris in his stateroom, and when the game was over she went up on deck and found Jake smoking a cigarette and reading a sci-fi novel. No one else was in sight.

Jean asked, "Where is everyone?"

"David's looking for a cook. The other guys went to get lunch."

Jean surveyed her surroundings. The air was laden with smog and factory smoke and tar, and the sky had a yellowish cast. The neighboring ships ranged from a barge to large commercial vessels to luxury yachts. On shore, Jean could see a metropolitan area to the north and industry to the south. Thinking of the letter to Ceci she had never mailed, she asked, "How long will we be here?"

Jake shrugged. "Two hours."

Time enough for an overseas phone call if she wanted. This would be a chance to talk to Cecily in privacy, away from the ship—and the ears of Jake Doherty. Jean thought of other things she would like to do on shore, such as look for a gift for David. There were only five days till Christmas, and what she'd made for him with Chris seemed too little to give a fiancé.

Mentally Jean made a list. Phone call. Christmas gift. Clothes.

If David planned to take her to a party, she was unprepared. She hadn't packed even a skirt for the simple reason that she couldn't go to a party on Cabo San Anselmo. She would be crazy to try.

What she ought to try was telling David the truth.

Deciding that more than anything she wanted to reach Ceci and get her sister's advice, Jean told Jake, "I'd like to call my sister."

Jake said, "I'll watch Chris."

AFTER GOING BELOW to tell Chris what she was doing, Jean tucked her sister's number, a credit card and some cash into a pocket of her jeans and left the ship and the docks. The port had a completely different feel from Santa Barbara, but she welcomed the change. It was a symbol of what she had wanted for years. To be on the move, seeing different places, different people, different waters.

The street outside the marina's chain link fence was alive with activity, but it was the impersonal hubbub of an urban transitional zone. A businessman hurrying to catch a cab. A bicycle courier racing through a light. Dock and factory workers in grease-coated coveralls. Panhandlers. As Jean scanned the sidewalk, then prepared to cross a busy avenue, no one met her eyes. The only signs of the Christmas season were impersonal civic banners hanging high over the boulevard and a billboard inviting drivers to take advantage of holiday bargains at a nearby factory-outlet mall.

Crossing a grassy park shaded by palm trees, Jean saw a sign for a pay phone and rushed toward it to make her call, but when she reached it she found the receiver had been torn out. Dodging cars across another street, she headed for a row of three pay phones on the sidewalk. All were in use.

She hurried farther up the street, two blocks, with a close eye to her surroundings. There was less traffic here and fewer pedestrians. Nearly all were men, and though it was a weekday only a few looked as if they were on their way to or from work—unless they sold drugs or bartered in prostitutes for a living. They all noticed her, and it occurred to Jean that she was in an unfamiliar area and not a safe one. She was about to turn back toward the commercial district when she saw a deserted phone.

Rushing across another street on a yellow light, she dashed down the side street. The phone hutch was attached to the stone wall of a fire-damaged factory building with a realty sign hanging from an upper floor. No phone book, but the phone was intact, and when she lifted the receiver she heard a dial tone.

She got the long-distance operator and charged the call to her home phone, but when the number finally rang in Cecily's apartment an answering machine came on with her sister's voice, speaking in French. Jean bit her lip. She wanted Ceci to know she was engaged, but she couldn't leave her a message to that effect. Ceci would want the details.

The machine beeped, demanding an answer.

She said, "Hi. This is Jean. I'm on my way to Baja. I love you. I'll, um, talk to you when I get back. Merry Christmas." She hung up the phone and turned to go back to the waterfront.

She saw she was in danger.

DAVID FOUND A COOK in twenty minutes.

He asked first at the waterfront diner, wasting more time than he wanted with acquaintances there, and was on his way to check the boards outside the harbor master's office when a meaty hand grabbed his shoulder.

"David Blade! I'll be damned."

Jack "Jolly" Holly, 250 pounds of professional diver and ship's cook. They had dived and fished together in the South Pacific, and David recognized the hand of fate. Five minutes later Holly had signed on, then gone off to throw together his possessions. David jogged back to the ship, thinking of taking Chris and Jean to look at a mine sweeper farther along the waterfront. More than once he'd thought of buying one and converting it to a research vessel. The *Skye* was small and laden with ghosts and memories.

But a pretty ship.

Jake and Chris were sword-fighting on the foredeck with cardboard wrapping-paper tubes, and David smiled as he watched his son land a blow to Jake's knees.

Jake said, "Avast you, matey!" and attempted to take off his head in return.

Chris raised his left arm in a tae kwon do high block and warded off the blow.

Not bad, thought David. He wondered where Jean was, and the words came out of his mouth while he was still standing on the dock. "Where's Jean?"

Jake dropped his sword to his side. "Now, don't get riled at the nanny. I told her I'd watch Chris. She's making a phone call."

"Why didn't you go with her?"

The question sounded like an accusation, and Jake lifted an eyebrow but did not respond.

David tried to quiet the alarm tolling through him. A woman should be able to walk a few blocks alone to a phone booth without coming to harm. But he remembered the night he'd taken her home from the gym. She'd been headed for a lonely bike path, a bad choice. She might make another one, and in this neighborhood there was opportunity. Only yards from the waterfront were streets crawling with junkies, dealers and pimps. Drive-by shootings over drug territory were weekly fare.

He felt panic inside him—less for her safety than at the knowledge that suddenly he cared a little too much, that suddenly she was first and last in his mind, that suddenly a small worry for a woman he'd known a few weeks had become the sort of fear a man felt only for those he cherished. He asked Jake, "How long has she been gone?"

The first mate shrugged. "Ten, fifteen minutes. She's calling her sister."

In Europe. Jean was probably telling her sister-model who didn't come home for Christmas about their engagement.

He never moved toward the gangway. Conscious that Jake was tuned in to his every move, he tried to sound casual. "I think I'll go look for her."

But as he headed up the dock, he realized he was hurrying, mapping in his mind all the nearby phones whose locations he knew. Driven by a force he neither named nor analyzed, he jogged across the thoroughfare toward the park. When he saw the phone with the receiver torn off, he started to run.

THE VERY BEST METHOD of self-defense, Frank always said, *is run.*

It was what she'd taught Chris, but it wouldn't work now. Her only avenue of escape would take her farther from help, and any of the men in front of her could outrun her in two strides. Three were nearly as tall as David, and one was as big. Another, a man with bleached blond hair and a skull dangling from one ear, had a knife and had already detailed how he would use it. Altogether there were four—long-legged young men with feral eyes.

She knew they would hurt her with relish.

Laughing and talking obscenely about her, they moved closer, and Jean watched the knife, mentally processing the comparatively little she recalled about fighting armed assailants. Knowing she should get her back to a wall to protect herself from the blade, Jean focused on the man who held it and saw his eyes quivering in their sockets— a new reason for fear. If they were strung out, they would be harder to take down.

She had no doubt they would do everything they promised. If they could.

She glanced behind her down the side street and saw it ended at another narrow passageway, edged by a tall, windowless building. Was that a street or an alley? Where were the cars? Where were the people?

Jean looked at her opponents again and wondered if she could make a run for it to the main street. As she started to, she saw a car passing and waved at it, yelling at the top of her lungs, "Help! Rape!"

The driver never noticed, like a bad dream. This couldn't be happening to her now, in broad daylight, on a city street.

But it happened every day.

Jean told herself she would not be overcome by fear—that was what the black of her belt symbolized. The thought steadied her, but it did not make her unafraid. As they came toward her, she began yelling at them, using words she hoped would attract passersby. She no longer hoped to scare them. She hoped to distract them and find a path of escape between them.

Remembering the essence of her training, she summoned confidence the only way she knew—by focusing utterly on the task before her.

She ran.

The one with the knife stood in front of her, and another grabbed her arm. She pulled free, but the knife lunged toward her. Blocking instinctively, her arm perilously close to the blade, she grabbed the wrist of her attacker and twisted it as she drove a side kick into his knee. It was weak, and she panicked, abandoning years of advice to keep her kicks low during an assault. She slammed her foot hard into his solar plexus, then up toward his chin. Miraculously she hit his temple, instead.

Someone tackled her, a human shape falling on her like a demolition ball, and she hit the curb with the side of her head. For the space of a few seconds, her eyes closed.

When she opened them with a sick, searing pain, it was to a face of pimples and savage eyes. The pain of his weight was full on her knees, and her nose was filled with his rank, alien scent. Reflexively Jean stabbed at his eyes, but the blow to her head had set the world in slow motion. She was late.

Your timing is off, ma'am.

Someone else grasped her arms, pulled them back, and she was being dragged. As she rolled to free her arms, her head hit the walk. Her right arm was seized again, squeezed hard enough to bruise, bent hard enough to break. It was locked behind her head, and then wrenched. Her shoulder slid from its socket, and she moaned at the unfamiliar pain. She tried to shut out the voices.

"She's not so scary. She's just a bitch. We're going to have fun with you, bitch."

"Sledge ain't gettin' up. Get up, Sledge!"

She remembered kicking that one and wasn't sure he would get up. She wanted to beg them not to move her. She was going to be sick. The viselike grip on her arm was released, sending another slough of pain pouring through her. She felt faint, and the bile rose in her throat again. Someone was ripping at the buttons on her jeans, uttering profanities and spitting on her with each obscene promise. She tried to raise her legs but she knew it was useless. She felt fear, numbed by semiconsciousness.

They were going to kill her.

"No." The word fell from her mouth, and she knew it would become a mantra. "No. No."

CHAPTER TWELVE

WHEN HE SAW THEM David felt only numb shock that his intuition had been correct, that Jean was coming to harm. But as he drew close, horror crawled his throat and squeezed his heart, revulsion he transformed immediately to something more useful—total awareness and focus. He half expected someone to step from that slot between the building with an automatic weapon, but he saw none, and the decision was easy. He ran, his mind clear and centered on his targets and what would take them down.

Number one on top of Jean. Number two behind her.

Number three would run—if no one had a gun.

His body felt swift and solid as a well-tuned machine, but faster and finer. He did not doubt its capabilities for a moment, because he knew that hesitation could cost him his life and Jean's.

He was prepared to kill.

SHE THOUGHT of David and imagined she heard the sound of running feet, of a warrior answering a call to arms. But it was not imagination. A dark, killing cry rang in her ears, the first *ki-hop* of its kind she had ever heard, a deep, ultimately frightening, "*Hi-yah!*" that seemed to come from another land and time. It was accompanied by the flight of a black shadow, a body shooting over her like a missile, and the sound of hard, certain contact.

Someone stepped on her left arm, escaping, and feet

pounded the pavement, running fast, then fading away. Jean forced her eyes open.

She thought she must be dead or dreaming, because he was there, staring up the street after the fleeing thugs. Then he looked at her.

She said, *"Sabumnim."*

He seemed dark and eerie. A shadow in the shadows of the concrete buildings. Vaguely Jean realized she'd been dragged into an alley or niche between two of the structures. Feeling tears in her eyes, of relief and misery, she said, "David?"

He crouched over her, not touching her at all, just looking. Her jeans were unfastened, and he resisted the urge to turn and kick the head of the still body behind him. The restraint he'd already shown would keep things cleaner for everyone. The man was alive and would walk away—eventually.

Closing his mind to his own decision of mercy and his private reason for it, David focused on Jean. "Tell me where you're hurt. I see your shoulder. What else? Can you move?"

Jean started to sit up, but the dislocation of her shoulder sent a primal warning through her system. She said, "I don't want to."

"Is your back or neck hurt?"

"No. Shoulder."

David nodded soberly and reached for her. Jean cried, "Don't!" at the same moment she realized his hands were on her arm and his foot against her side. As he pulled on her arm and the joint realigned itself, she felt as though she'd had the wind knocked out of her.

David gave her a few seconds' rest and watched her breathe shallowly, her face contorted. Then her breaths grew deeper. He hadn't wanted to touch her and would have let her shoulder be if he had met more resistance, but everything about the situation made him nervous, and the street still felt like a place where violence could explode without warning. The squeal of tires and a burst of gunfire. He had to get Jean away to a safer place, preferably the ship.

He said, "Can you walk?"

Jean nodded, eyes half-shut, and began to sit up. She was white, and he put his arm around her.

"Easy. Take it slow."

She nodded and leaned on him as she stood.

David watched her knees fold, then straighten. He picked her up and saw her wince as he jostled her shoulder. With a last glance at the body he'd left behind, he strode toward the main street, his eye marking the spot where he'd launched the flying kick. As he carried Jean toward the traffic, he saw the other figure lying in the gutter, showing faint signs of motion. Jean's work.

David looked down at her.

Her eyes were closed, but they flickered at him for a moment, two flashes of the sea, and she said, "I can walk."

Indomitable spirit, thought David. He hoped she really possessed it, because she would need it. He said, "I know you can."

DR. GEARY STEPPED OUT onto the landing over the galley, and David followed, shutting the door to his cabin all but a crack.

Grant gave him a reproving glance. "You were lucky with that shoulder."

David knew. He thought of Jean in his own bed, going without painkillers because of the lump on her head. "Is she all right?"

"Seems to be, but she needs X rays." Grant's eyes met David's. "And some counseling might be in order. Where's her sister?"

"Europe."

The doctor nodded. After a moment he said, "The police are done?"

"Yes." David could still hear one radio outside, but he knew they'd leave soon. The thugs had escaped, which was just as well. Jean didn't want to press charges, and he hadn't argued. Her spending months tied up in the courts with people she should never have to see again hadn't sounded like justice to him.

Thinking of her, he looked at his door, not even knowing he did. Grant touched his arm and went down the companionway, and David went back into his cabin and shut the door.

Catching sight of him, Jean closed her eyes. She didn't want to see anyone, least of all David. Even less herself. The endless pain in her shoulder was good. It matched what her mind felt.

Everything was still foggy, but clear enough that she could begin to remember details. Clothing. Hair. Teeth. Scent. The feeling of a body lunging against her and taking her down like a bowling pin, just when she'd landed some solid blows. Just when she'd thought she could make a space in which to flee. Instead, she'd been beaten. If not for David, she would have been raped. She might be dead.

And he had found her lying there like a broken doll, a woman who should have known better than to go alone down the side street. A woman with the awareness of a black belt.

David folded his arms across his chest and watched her, wondering why she'd closed her eyes when he walked through the door. What was she thinking? Was she angry he hadn't come sooner? Was she imagining what would have happened if he hadn't come at all?

Again he thought of the moment in the street, the split second in the air after he'd yelled, when he'd seen his target paralyzed by the sound and had known he could kill him— and probably should. And had decided not to.

He lived by the *do,* the way of tae kwon. *Never take life unjustly.* Staring at the dark ink of Jean's eyelashes against her pale cheeks, he knew it would have been justice to kill to save her. The warrior inside him wished he had. But in that moment in the air he'd seen blood and remembered its taste, and he'd seen Skye's face in the petrified eyes watching him, empty eyes waiting for death. And he'd pulled his kick.

Jean's eyes were still closed, and again David wondered why. What had they done to her before he arrived? What had they said? Where had they put their hands? Everything about her said, *Don't touch me. Don't come any closer.*

And all he wanted was to lie down and hold her for a thousand and one days and nights. He wanted to undo the damage he hadn't been able to stop.

Feeling choked him. What he'd told himself about the two of them was a lie. What he felt for her was too frightening to think or utter.

Jean held her eyes tightly shut, wishing he would leave yet feeling him all around her. She leaned back against the pillows, which, like the faded T-shirt she wore, carried the faint scent of David. A sling bound and supported her arm, and ice was packed around her shoulder, her only relief from the steady throbbing that seemed to increase with each breath she took. Her head, like her shoulder, ached with intensity, and so did her heart. She wished David would leave.

He didn't.

He came to the side of the bed and sat down on the edge with the grace of a cat, never jostling her shoulder. Avoiding his eyes, Jean stared dully across the room at her bonsai tree. David had made a nest for it in a top-opening locker in a corner of the cabin. It seemed like a symbol of his faith in her—and of the hope of Christmas that had seemed so bright hours earlier.

David still watched her, but she wouldn't meet his gaze.

At last he reached for her hair and gently pulled the end of her tangled braid over her shoulder, then removed the elastic band. Her eyes dropped lifelessly, emotionlessly, to his hand. Struck by the flatness of her expression, David carefully stroked a lock of hair away from her face and withdrew. He said, "This isn't how I've dreamed of getting you in my bed."

He saw her swallow and thought she was going to cry.

She didn't. When his arms went around her, her eyes were squeezed shut, frozen against everything. The unending ache in her shoulder seemed less, but the reality of what had happened hurt more. And David was holding her, David who was both stranger and lover, David who she'd thought would no longer care for her. His fingers were in her hair, combing free the remnants of her braid, while his other hand rubbed her back in a soothing motion that was as rhythmic as the tide.

She wanted to jerk her head up, to cry at him, *Do you love me?*

Waves of shame washed over her, and she wished he would speak to her.

He didn't. He pulled back, and Jean felt him looking at her face, but she didn't want to look at his.

David backed away and stood up, then went into the bathroom and opened the cabinet where he had seen her hairbrush. It lay on the top shelf, a simple, wooden hairbrush. She had never used it in front of him.

When he glanced back into the cabin she was lying on her side, turned toward the port windows. He went in and climbed onto the bed beside her, at her back. First he checked her ice packs and balanced them over her injury. Then, not touching her scalp, he dragged the brush gently through her hair.

She shivered.

He held a lock and brushed a snarl from the end in small, gentle strokes. "If you want me to go, you should say so."

She was silent, and David realized she was thinking about it. He closed his eyes, glad she couldn't see his face.

Jean lay in agony, fighting down the only words that came to her lips. *I love you.* If she could have, she would have grabbed his hand, held it against her cheek, against her lips. Finally she whispered, "Thanks for staying." But as she spoke, she discovered what she really wanted, even more than his hands in her hair and the weight of his body next to hers.

She wanted to be away from the smoggy, smoky smell of the port.

She wanted to be at sea.

Safe.

David was surprised by her sudden movement, more surprised when she rolled slowly onto her back, knocking two bags of ice into his lap. Moving them, he eased his leg out of the way and let his hand fall to her side. *Look at me,* he thought.

She did. With eyes not her own, eyes that seemed pained to meet his. She asked, "Can we please leave this place?"

He felt relief, huge relief, that there was something he could do. He said, "Yes." And he stood and went up the stairs to the door to the wheelhouse.

A moment later, the engines started.

JEAN FELT SOMETHING soft on her cheek. Delicate. Small. Then on her arm. Her eyes fluttered open, and she saw Chris looking at her. He held a muffin on a plate in one hand and a notepad in the other. In the late-afternoon light that shone through the stained-glass windows of the cabin, Jean squinted at the words Chris had written in his child's printing. "Jolly made you this. It is a banana-bread muffin. I love you."

Conscious of the forward motion of the ship through the sea, Jean sat up, wincing at her shoulder. It had not improved with time. Her voice husky from disuse, she told

Chris, "Thank you, sweetie. I love you, too." She bent over to kiss him, and the pain streaked forward in her head. Chris raised his face for her kiss. Then he started signing at her, something about Hank the Cowdog.

Jean said, "Slow down. I'm not as fast as you." When he complied, she saw he was offering to read to her.

Jean realized the magnitude of the gift, how difficult it would be for him to translate a whole chapter of a book into sign language. She wouldn't be able to follow him, either, certainly not in her present state. She watched him, unsure what to say. Her head felt as though it had been hit with a brick.

She reached for the muffin with little appetite and told Chris, "I'd like that. Unless you'd rather I read to you."

She could tell from his response that the latter was his preference. He scampered to the door of the cabin, slid it open and went out onto the galley landing, then closed the door. Slowly Jean set down the muffin and used her good arm to prop pillows behind her. Who was Jolly?

The new cook?

She bit into the muffin, which was moist and warm from the oven and smelled heavenly. Then she set it on the plate again and turned carefully to switch on the reading lamp over the bed. David's bed. There was a glass-encased bookshelf built into the wall behind the headboard containing titles ranging from Pulitzer Prize winners to bestsellers to Eastern philosophy and world history. Jean saw a well-worn copy of *Don Quixote* in Spanish. As she spotted a tae kwon do manual written in characters she assumed were Korean, a long, sick pain flowed through her head, and she sank against the pillows once more.

Chris came back into the cabin with a book and crawled onto the bed beside her. Jean opened to the place where he'd left the bookmark and forced herself to read. The chapter was particularly amusing, and soon she was trying not to laugh over the cowdog's adventures, because laughter hurt her body. She did not hear footsteps on the companionway.

Dr. Geary said, "And I was going to offer you something for pain."

Jean said, "I'll take it."

"I thought so." He came inside and looked sternly at Chris. "You told us you were going to read to *her,* young man."

Chris smiled sheepishly and shrugged, then snuggled closer to Jean, against her injured shoulder.

Jean said, "Whoa, Chris. Move over to the other side."

But Dr. Geary shooed him out of the room so he could examine her shoulder and shine a flashlight in her eyes. As he was finishing up, the door to the wheelhouse opened, and David entered the cabin. Grant handed him a small pill bottle and said, "One every four to six hours as needed." Then he turned and nodded to Jean with a kindly smile. "No more laughing."

When he had gone, David glanced down the companionway, slid shut the door behind him and said, "If you were laughing over Hank, you're out of luck. Jolly's put Chris to work in the galley."

Jean said, "Oh," but she wasn't thinking of Chris. She was looking at David, who seemed so solid and strong and familiar—and very kind. It was easier to be near him now than it had been earlier. Everything seemed easier since she had awakened to Christian's small face watching her, waiting for her attention. Since she had felt the motion of the ship and realized they must be far from the port city where she had been assaulted. Remembering what David had said, she asked, "Jolly who makes great muffins?"

"Yes." David was conscious of the beat of his heart, faster and harder than usual. He knew it was because she was meeting his eyes. Not as she once had, but even the way they skirted away now was an improvement over what he'd seen when he'd brought her back to the ship. Conscious of her hold on his heart—and his blindness in not seeing it earlier—he climbed onto the bed beside her and kissed her temple very lightly. He said, "How do you like my bed?"

Looking down at the covers over her lap, she answered, "I like it best with you in it."

David felt a tightening in his chest, yearning and reluctance exerting their separate strengths. This was it. Jean was here, in his bed; she couldn't climb in and out of her own berth with an injured shoulder. He knew she didn't want to. She wanted him.

Jean felt the long silence. The sound of the engines seemed eternal, like the pulse of time, counting how long it could take a man to find a way to tell a woman he didn't want to sleep with her.

David leaned back against the headboard beside her and examined the bottle of pills in his hand. Narcotics. They seemed both a symbol and an easy excuse. He took off the cap and handed her one. He said, "I want you to be conscious and healed."

He didn't say, *when we make love.* Jean heard the omission even more than she heard his words. Inside, all along her throat, she felt as though she was strangling. She remembered lying on her back in the street, strange hands tearing at her jeans, a strange person breathing on her.

Her jeans were gone now. When he'd brought her back, David had taken them off, along with her sweatshirt and everything else she'd been wearing. Then he'd dressed her in a T-shirt of his and a pair of clean underwear from her locker. Jean was glad. She never again wanted to see the clothes in which she'd been dragged on the pavement, the clothes another man had tried to tear from her body.

David climbed off the bed and went into the bathroom. Jean heard him fill a water glass, and in a moment he brought it out to her. She swallowed the pill, then gulped down the water, wishing it could ease the pain in her heart. But only David could.

Staring out the starboard window, she saw nothing but ocean with the sun setting upon it. She asked, "Where are we?"

David met her eyes for a moment, then said, "Let me get the chart, and I'll show you." He went into the wheelhouse, returning with a couple of charts, then sat down on the bed beside her and began explaining how to read them. After pinpointing the ship's bearing, still off the California coast in U.S. waters, he showed her the port where they would stop that night.

Her voice was little more than a whisper. "Can't we anchor?"

David sensed the fear and anguish behind the question. It was all he could do to control his own features, to grip his own heart. He said, "You need X rays. This is a different kind of port, a different kind of town." He spoke as steadily as he could and tried to smile. "Ritzier than Santa Barbara."

She was quivering like an animal, and David wished they dared forego the X rays. He said, "I'm sorry."

Anyone could see that he was. Jean wondered if he knew he had grabbed her hand and was hurting it. He seemed to realize it and released her.

He looked down at the chart as though it was a foreign object. After a moment he said, "I'll show you our itinerary." He did, starting with the chart on top, then switching to the one beneath, which showed the Baja coast. Jean listened almost indifferently until he pointed to a big cape on the Mexican shoreline. He was saying, "Cabo San Anselmo on Christmas Eve. Then Scammon's Bay the next day."

Jean's stomach plunged. Until David had said it aloud, even the possibility had seemed unreal. But what had happened during the afternoon was a reminder that nightmares, like dreams, could come true.

David studied her face, noted her pallor. A crash course in navigation wasn't the kind of distraction she needed. Setting the charts on the far corner of the bed, he knelt over her so that his legs straddled her body. Then he kissed her mouth and, when he felt her response, slipped his tongue inside.

She made a soft sound in her throat, involuntary and needy.

He said, "It's an hour till we're in port. Would you like me to take your mind off your shoulder?"

"Yes." The word was faint, altered by the kiss they'd just shared.

Lips still near hers, David said, "Thank you." Trailing kisses along her jaw and her neck, he drew the covers away from her body.

CHAPTER THIRTEEN

SHE TOSSED in hot, shivering confusion, surrendering to a rapture she had only imagined. What he had said the evening before was the only hint she'd ever had that David would want to know her this way, to taste her and venerate her so intimately. She had to draw the knuckles of her hand against her mouth to silence her lips.

Most of the time, their hands were clasped, but David had felt hers stray to his hair more than once as he let his tongue roam inside her, tasting her. He could feel the smooth skin of her slim, taut legs around him. Those legs were shaking, and she was shuddering. He heard her muffled, almost tearful gasp, and a sob that was his name.

There was a heat high in his own throat, emotion riding a river of rushing blood and breath. He continued to tease her and caress her till her quaking ceased, and then longer, because he didn't want to stop. And then his mouth rested on the inside of her thigh, and he couldn't speak.

But she was pulling at him, calling him, like a voice from the sunlight dragging him up from a very deep dive, saving him from a fatal high, from rapture of the depths. He wanted to tear off his clothes and become one with her.

And it felt good to want it so badly.

He sat up and moved over her body to her left side, then lay down beside her and buried his face in the cascade of her hair. *Someday,* he thought. *Someday, Jean.*

She said, "Can I do that to you?"

David almost inhaled her hair. For the second time that

day, he was glad she couldn't see his face. He said, "Sure." Then he sat up, not looking at her. "Not now, though. I need to get back to work."

But for a moment he remained immobile on the edge of the bed, feeling like an indebted property owner who has just received the final extension on his taxes. His hour of reckoning was near. David groped behind him for Jean's hand and felt it slide into his.

And when he turned to kiss her it was he who could not meet her eyes.

HE TOOK HER to an exclusive facility where he knew there would be no questions, and when Jean had received a clean bill of health they drove back to the ship in the rental car he'd had delivered to the marina. No cabs. No strangers. Only the two of them, much closer than before. He held her hand while he drove.

When they reached the ship, Baby was there, chattering under the dock lights. David saw she had drawn the attention of people on the decks of yachts nearby—and entertained them by pulling a string of large plastic candy canes off the side of a nearby cabin cruiser. The owner had retrieved the decoration and was trying to hang it back up.

Jean stooped by the edge of the dock to pet the dolphin and lower her face to Baby's for a kiss, and the cocktail-sipping spectators across the way oohed and aahed over Baby's friendliness to her.

David barely noticed the reactions of the audience. He saw only the effect of Baby's closeness on Jean. He found himself saying, "If you feel well enough, we could go out on the diving platform." The stern was out of view of the other boats. It lay in shadow. Private.

Jean heard David's suggestion and felt her heart stir. He must be worried about her to propose they spend time with Baby. Straightening up, she managed a smile. "Thanks."

He put his arm around her and guided her toward the

ship. As he helped her aboard and led her past the lights of the salon to the darkness of the aft deck, he tried to catch her eye, but she wouldn't look at him.

Thinking of her attack, he felt the same constriction in his chest he had felt periodically all afternoon as he imagined them touching her. They'd never gotten her clothes off and she hadn't been raped, but other than that he wasn't sure what had happened.

As he debated asking her, Jake stepped out of the diving alcove, and a lighter flared, illuminating his face. David nodded to him. Jake returned the nod and edged around the cabin toward the bow, giving them privacy.

David lifted Jean down to the diving platform by her waist and saw Baby waiting for them there. He said, "Let me find a toy for her," and scouted the deck in the darkness until he found the inflatable wreath, pathetically deflated. He blew it up, then joined Jean on the diving platform. She was sitting down.

He tossed the ring to Baby, hoping to keep her occupied, and asked Jean, "Did they touch you?"

"No." She watched Baby swim the ring back to them. David leaned forward to retrieve it and hurled it farther this time. Jean said, "You're playing with her."

In other words, David thought, *let's talk about something else.* He didn't answer her. She couldn't know how inadequate he felt. There was not a single woman on his ship with whom she could share her feelings. He would do anything to ease her trauma, even lie beside her in his bed that night. Without touching her. He'd already made that decision. And though the solstice was still two days off, he knew this would be the longest night of the year.

When Baby came to the platform, he petted her, feeling her heart. She was a sweet animal. He had never thought anything else. Not facing Jean, he said, "I spent some time with a lone beluga whale many years ago, when I was fishing. I had a Japanese trawler, a sailboat. She used to come feed near my nets.''

Jean sat silent in the darkness, listening as though the water might tell David's secrets. It was hard to believe he was telling her one himself.

''Then, some fishermen killed her. I…sort of…came upon it.'' Baby rolled for a caress on her belly. David gave it, then reached for the ring and threw it as far as it would fly. She took off like a missile.

Jean didn't say anything. But she finally understood the thing about him that had puzzled her most—his trouble with Baby. His revelation threw her off base. She was unready when he said, ''I want you to tell me everything that happened today. Every word, every touch, every ugly threat.''

She did. And when she cried against him he felt outrage for her but also relief that she wouldn't hold it inside. That she wasn't like him. For a moment he wanted to call her his master instructor. Instead, because it seemed years too late for him to learn the lesson, he carried her inside through the wheelhouse to his cabin and his bed.

HE COULDN'T WORK without sleep, and lying beside Jean's dozing body was a recipe for insomnia. The only relief would be inside her, but she was in no condition to bear his weight or lie on top of him. And their first time together should be very, very good.

Right now David wasn't sure he could be even mediocre. Sleepless and horny as hell, he lay staring at the ceiling and weighing the odds. Bad. How could the life force, the *him* inside him, be simultaneously so urgent and demanding, yet fickle? It was the worst of both worlds.

He heard the echo of a woman's laughter in his mind. Skye's. He could see her with ease. He could imagine what she would say. But he didn't believe she was saying it now.

He didn't believe in ghosts, except those that lived in the human psyche. He had a roomful, and they were all her.

Jean made a quiet sleeping sound, not of pain, but when she rolled toward him David saw the flicker of discomfort on her face, and her eyes opened. Shut. Opened and stared at him. She didn't say, *Why are you awake?* but he felt it from her.

He glanced at the glowing red dials on the alarm clock and asked, ''Want another pill?''

He heard Skye saying, *Good idea, David. Keep her drugged as long as you can. Then she won't find out.*

Jean was shaking her head against the pillow.

Thinking of Skye taunting him—and wondering why she still could—he moved closer to Jean. Why did he war with a woman who no longer existed except as a memory?

Because the havoc she'd left was everywhere. In Chris, in Erika, in him. In those shapes and colors in his mind, in that horrible sensation surrounding his whole body. He could feel it now. He wanted a shower.

Jean watched him in the glow from the dock lights that shone through the window. Didn't he ever sleep? A number of possibilities, reasons he wasn't sleeping, occurred to her. The most likely seemed desire, and if that was David's problem she'd like to ease it. Didn't he know that?

Yes. She'd offered that afternoon—plainly and more than once. He hadn't been able to meet her eyes, and Jean thought she knew why.

Since Skye's death David had never had another woman in his bed. She was nearly certain of that. And now her own presence must be keeping him awake. Was that why he wouldn't share himself with her? Because she wasn't Skye?

Or because, like Jake, he believed she had secrets?

Jean felt a chill pass over her.

David saw. His hand went at once to her cheek.

She said, ''I'm fine.''

He reflected that she hadn't bathed since that scene in the street. He still caught the scent of the place on her. Without asking her preference he got out of bed and went into the shower room.

Jean watched his tall shape, clad in only a pair of dark sweatpants that hugged the muscles in his legs, pass out of her field of vision. The water went on. Tub water.

A moment later, he came back into the cabin. Returning to the bed, he pulled the covers from her, exposing her small, long-legged body clad only in another of his T-shirts and a pair of pale pink panties. He said, "Say something if I hurt your shoulder." And he picked her up.

THE SHOWER ROOM was lit by sconces, two of them, flickering high on the wall over the big sunken tub. David set her down and dipped a toe in the water. Hot, but not, he hoped, too hot for her.

They were inches apart. With the precise perception of a martial artist, David knew exactly how close they stood, how little he would need to move to touch her. He knew when she was going to touch him and where.

On his scar.

A tremor passed through him as her fingers found his chest, and when Jean dropped her eyes she saw and felt he was aroused, stemmed hard against her body. She wanted his sweatpants off. She wanted him to love her.

Eyeing the tub, still filling, she said, "Are you getting in?"

Eyes on her face, David reached for the hand on his chest and guided it downward. "Yes, ma'am."

THEIR BODIES were entwined, slick with soap, their tongues in each other's mouths. David felt her hand sliding over the length of him again and again, bringing him higher than he had ever thought he would go. At first his fingers had played inside her, too, but now he could only draw her closer, so she was sliding along his leg. She was slippery, but not from the soap.

He said again, "Jean." It was all he could say anymore, and he said it a lot. Didn't her shoulder hurt? They'd taken off her good sling and replaced it with one made from the T-shirt she'd been wearing. Now it was wet.

Everything was wet. Clean hair and bodies. Mouths. Everything.

Jean watched his face, his half-closed eyes. Giving to him was the deepest pleasure she'd ever known. He'd entrusted himself to her at last, as she had long ago to him. And now, as she touched him, he was incoherent, his head back, his mouth relaxed, then moving with reaction to the feel of her hand. She sank harder against the muscles of his thigh, hardly knowing what she did, only that he was guiding her, holding her, dragging her nearer to him. She could feel his longing for her, and she could see it in his face, now so altered by emotions and passion. Not lust, but a need of the heart. And maybe something more.

She said, "Make love to me."

David's mind was foggy as the room, floating on scent and sensation. Her words changed none of that. They were what he wanted to hear.

He reached for Jean, slick and wet, and lifted her to the edge of the tub, then lowered her back to the floor. Wanting her to feel what he felt, a hunger so intense he could hardly stand it, he caressed her—first with his hands and then with his mouth until she cried. Then he rose up in the tub, his eyes on hers, coming closer. Their bodies touched, more intimate than ever before, poised for the greatest intimacy of all. David's voice shook, rough, as he said, "Put your legs around me, Jean."

She did, never knowing that her head was already tossing, not knowing her eyes were flickering open and shut and she was making a small animal sound of want, the same sound over and over again.

He said, "I love you," and he drove himself inside her.

IT WASN'T A NIGHTMARE, but it was intense and complicated. And sweet.

Afterward, empty and sated, he lay against her on the wet floor and the towels, knowing he must be hurting her and yet needing to stay a minute longer. On top of her. Inside her.

She said, "David," and he made himself move, slipping away from her and then joining her on the cold floor. He neither spoke nor looked at her, only closed his eyes and placed a hand on her breast, on the body that belonged to him.

She told him, "David, that was perfect."

Thank God, he thought. If he'd done anything right, she was responsible. She gave him a power purer than desire and stronger than death.

He was in love with her.

He couldn't speak, so he moved closer to her and rested his face in the curve beside her breast. *Jean.* He touched her skin with his mouth, feeling her heat, knowing her scent. His mouth against her skin, he hugged her close, like a drowning man clinging to a life raft.

Jean felt the emotion in him as she had ever since they'd begun making love. When they were joined it had escalated, and she'd met a David she hadn't known before. Vividly she remembered her own panic as he filled her, then his drawing her into his arms and back into the tub, holding her against his heart and kissing her long and deep as he let her know what it was to have all of him. She had pictures of him in her mind, pictures she would treasure of his eyes on hers, his mouth drinking her wet skin, of water beading in the hair on his chest and on his scar, of his head back against the edge of the tub and his eyes closed as he brought her down on him. Of how he looked before he kissed her and when he came.

She belonged to him.

She loved him madly.

And she had seen his darkness. A communion of minds, perhaps, spurred by the union of bodies, but now she knew with a certainty beyond intuition where his pain must lie. Only the details remained unknown.

Feeling the air on her damp body, she shivered, and David stood up to get more towels from an overhead locker.

Her shoulder aching, Jean sat up. He toweled her hair and body, then untied her wet sling. Working quickly and carefully, he secured her dry sling, wrapped fluffy towels around her, and dried her hair with her hair dryer.

Last, he blew out the candles in the sconces and led her back into the cabin.

THE ROOM SEEMED cold as a tomb, which surprised David. It had always been his cabin, never Skye's, and he had always liked it. Now, he noticed the quilt on the bed. And without seeing them, he was aware of the scars she had left on his windowsill. Four letters.

His eyes flickered to the corners of the room. A faint light from outside flickered on the Christmas ornaments on the bonsai. The tree of life and renewal, a promise of Christmas and the cyclical return of the solstice, of longer days and shorter nights.

Jean was beside him, clutching the arm that must be aching now. Thinking of her, of the seeming impossibility of meshing past and present, he drew out his desk chair and said, "Can you sit here for a minute?"

She nodded with a small movement and sat down. David brought her a pill for pain and a glass of water, then efficiently stripped the bed and changed the sheets and pillowcases, thinking that they, too, must carry the scent of the street, of what had hurt her. Thinking also that he could get the quilt out of his sight.

Jean watched him, contemplating his silence. Not even

love made him talkative, but what he had said and done
was perfect. Even the soreness between her legs was welcome, an ancient earthy symbol that he had bound her to
him, that she was his. She had believed lovemaking could
be so perfect, and David had proved it.

Briefly it occurred to her that they had made love with
nothing between them, that he had come inside her, that
they'd been reckless. She had no regrets. In her mind he
was already her husband. He was hers forever.

Seeing he had finished with the bed, Jean stood up. David helped her into his bed and covered her with the sheet
and blanket. He kissed her, and Jean remembered the feel
of him inside her. She reached for him, but he was gone,
gathering up the laundry and taking it down into the office
where the washer and dryer were.

With effort Jean sat up, looked around the cabin, then
fell back against the pillow. The quilt was gone. He had
taken it, the quilt made by Skye, the wife who had killed
herself.

David, she thought, *how can you ever forget?*

Remembering the way he had made love to her, the gentle intensity, the unstoppable overflow, she wondered if a
man could live a healthy life and raise a family without
ever talking about the things that had hurt him most. She
wondered if David would ever talk or if he could.

And she thought of the irony that his son, too, was silent.

She was drowsy when at last he returned and slid shut
the door. Jean's eyes wavered upon him as he came to the
berth and threw a thick, plaid wool blanket over the bed
and over her.

He got into bed with her and lay his body alongside hers,
then kissed her. No words, just the intimacy of touch, of
skin against skin. Glad for his heat to chase away her dark
thoughts, Jean rested her head on his shoulder for long
minutes, feeling his skin and the solid length of his muscles. He stirred only once, turning and resting his hand on

the inside of her thigh, as though to make sure she was still there and couldn't leave.

Moments later he slept.

DAVID LIKED MORNINGS. He liked the alarm on his watch, he liked swimming before the sun rose, he liked meditating and working tae kwon do forms on the deck of his ship before anyone else was awake. Jean in his bed was a perfect addition to mornings.

Her hair spilled over the pillows, and the sheets were half-off her, exposing her breasts and shoulders and arms—and the sling that was a reminder of violence. As David debated touching her, the alarm on his watch beeped, and her eyes opened, reminding him of a waking kitten. Asleep one moment, alert the next.

David didn't bother apologizing for the alarm. Seeing the sea green of her eyes made him unsorry for waking her, and he asked the only thing that seemed essential. "How's your shoulder?"

"Stiff. Okay."

David was glad she wasn't in agony, because of what he wanted to do. As he reached for her and felt her respond, moving closer, seeking him, he thought of responsibility and what they'd risked the previous night. Now he would take more care. And someday later, he very much hoped, she would be the mother of his children.

As her fingers slid down his stomach, she said, "You can always wake me up, David. Even in the middle of the night."

That meant more to him than she could know. Thinking of the progress of her hand, he said, "I will." A moment later he choked out her name and pulled her close, all the other words lost against her skin. But when he was inside her, what she had said came back to him. And it occurred to him that that was what she had done to him. She had woken him in the middle of an endless night—and from a horrible dream.

He sank deeper inside her.

OVER THE NEXT THREE DAYS the *Skye* followed a leisurely, zigzagging course to Baja. Whales appeared every day, and David slowed the ship to follow them, changed course to see them better.

Jean assisted the scientists. She took copious notes on the activity of the cetaceans, as well as that of other marine life in the vicinity. Ken Lightman put her to work sketching slide samples of seawater and recording related information for him. Robin made her his favorite photographic subject, next to Baby. And Dr. Geary asked her to research past observations from texts and journals in David's collection.

Yet it felt more like Christmas than any season of her memory. Playing the calendar game in the morning with Chris. Making construction-paper ornaments together in the afternoon. Singing carols to him at night.

And lying in the dark of David's cabin with the olive tree a silent witness to their passion. Hearing him say again and again that he loved her.

It was a love without censure or criticism, and Jean could almost believe it wouldn't be altered if at some point he learned about what had happened when she'd worked for Michael and Jennifer Avery in Cabo San Anselmo. She could almost believe that in his eyes she could do no wrong, that if he ever heard the story he would see her side and take her part. After all, he'd even accepted Baby now. He seemed resigned to the dolphin's attachment to his ship and to his son, and early Christmas Eve morning Jean found him alone in the water with Baby, playing with her.

In the predawn light, Jean climbed down onto the diving platform in time to see Baby kiss his cheek and hear David say, "We can't, Baby. Jean would never forgive us. Her fiancé and her best friend. And you're a dolphin, don't you know that?'' As Jean watched Baby attempt to hug him with her flippers, David glanced toward the ship and saw her. He told Baby, ''See? Caught.''

Baby maneuvered around his body, four hundred pounds of possessive female, impeding his progress back to the ship.

Jean laughed, wishing she had a camera.

Finally David climbed onto the diving platform, dripping, and Jean grabbed a towel to throw over his bare shoulders. He kissed her mouth, glanced briefly at the sky and asked, ''Want to go ashore this morning? I have to pick up mail.''

Baby cried at him from the water, and he leaned forward to touch her beak.

Jean stared across the water at the shoreline, the coast of Baja California. Condos lined the beach, reminding her of Cabo San Anselmo. She shook her head.

David thought of the last time he had gone ashore—two days earlier with Chris, to one of the towns south of the border where junk was beautiful and treasures could be found if one knew where to look. He had asked Jean to come with them then, and she had declined. It had bothered him then, and it bothered him now. He said, ''You can't stay on the water forever.''

Jean swallowed an attack of conscience. He thought she didn't want to go ashore because of what had happened in L.A. when the problem was her being in Baja. And the fact that they would anchor at Cabo San Anselmo that night.

She looked at his eyes, sable in the morning light. The red dawn turned his skin to rosewood. She said, ''I'm all right, David. Really.''

He let it go, mainly because he didn't have time for anything else. The sky was red, and storm bulletins the previous night had played out the sailor's verse. Sensing the sea brewing, he said, ''If you're not going, watch Chris, will you? I won't be long.''

He went inside to dress, and Jean went below to the galley to suggest to Chris that there might be a cowdog named Hank behind the twenty-fourth door of the advent calendar. There wasn't.

There was a wreath.

IT WAS STORMING when David returned with the mail. Conditions were so bad that he, Jake and Ken were all needed to manage the Zodiac as the hoist lifted it back onto the canopy beside the dinghy. They weighed anchor immediately afterward, and everyone but David promptly became seasick.

For the first couple of hours Jean could do nothing but care for Chris and deal with her own nausea, but then her symptoms subsided. Seeing Chris asleep in his stateroom, she went up through David's cabin to the wheelhouse.

He was alone, the only one able to tolerate the onslaught of twenty-foot waves, and he smiled when he saw Jean.

She said, "You look lonely."

"You look better."

Jean smiled weakly. They'd met an hour earlier at the railing.

David nodded to the navigator's seat and a small stack of letters tucked into a well in the cockpit. "Read me Erika's letter. It's to both of us."

Jean held the back of the captain's seat for balance as she made her way to the navigator's station. Climbing up on the stool, she reached for the stack of mail and leafed through until she found Erika's letter, addressed to Miss Jean Young and Mr. David Blade. She opened the envelope and withdrew a single sheet. The loose, even writing was like Erika, relaxed and approachable. Her greeting went straight to Jean's heart.

David said, "I'm waiting." With a glance at the sky, he said, "Better start before the lightning comes."

"Lightning?"

"Read."

Jean eyed the dark horizon and saw a distant flash, faint in the gray. She turned to the page in her hand. "'Dear Brother and Sister-To-Be, I have very good news for you. I have sensation in my legs.'" Jean looked at David.

He was watching the sea, but when she stopped he said, "Keep reading. She's right. It's good news. Great news."

Jean lifted the sheet again. "'Hard to believe, yes? And the fault of my Swiss miracle doctor. He's put me in AN-GER therapy.' That's in caps, David."

"I'm sure."

The bland reply struck Jean, but she forced herself to keep reading. "'It's incredible. We throw things and say every horrible thing we ever wanted to say about anyone. I strongly recommend it, *David*.' That's underlined."

This time he said nothing. Looking up, Jean watched waves come over the bow and saw the first slivers of electricity in the sky. A low roll of thunder mingled with the sounds of the sea and the wind and the engines.

Returning to the letter, she resumed reading Erika's words. "'I was never willing to express my real feelings about the accident before, but I can now.'"

Abruptly the letter was taken from her hands.

Jean said, "David," in protest as he held the page against the steering wheel and read it, glancing intermittently toward the sea.

Jean thought, *He's worried about what she's going to say about that accident. Why?*

David flipped the page over, scanned the other side and handed it back to her without apology.

Cool, Jean said, "Do you want me to read it to you anymore?"

"No."

He seemed irritated, and Jean recalled what Erika had said about anger therapy. David had plenty to be angry about, but his sister's letter? Jean turned it over and read silently.

> ...I was never willing to express my real feelings about the accident before, but I can now. For one thing, I no longer call it an accident. The only thing accidental was that you weren't in the driver's seat, David.
>
> Enough already, I know. In thirty minutes, I get to give an earful to my therapy group, so I'll save some for them.
>
> I mostly wanted you to know about my legs and that I like the Swiss Marvel, and I wanted to tell Jean how happy I am you're going to be my sister, dear. Crazy me, when I feel my legs, I wonder if we might dive together someday.
>
> Squeeze Chris for me, but don't tell him anything about me that might get his hopes up. I love you all, and I want you to know that my heart is with you on Christmas. We're all together in spirit.
>
> Tidings of comfort and joy,
> E.

Jean could hardly contain her feelings. Erika's news was wonderful, confirmation that the problem with her legs was at least partially psychological and might be overcome. The thought of diving with David's sister someday thrilled her, and she held the image in her mind, as hope for Erika.

But everything Erika had said about the accident was puzzling, an invitation for questions. David *hadn't* been driving.

Jean looked up in time to see a flash of lightning illuminate the cockpit. She asked, "Who was driving the car?"

"Erika." A clap of thunder followed his words.

Jean had to raise her voice over the sound of the storm. "Why did she say it wasn't an accident?"

His reply was louder than it needed to be. "Probably so you'd ask me that question."

She'd never have a better chance. "Was it an accident?"

David didn't answer at once. His eyes traced a lightning bolt in the sky, and at last he said, "No."

The reply was drowned out in the thunder, but Jean understood it. She said, "Please tell me what happened."

David seemed not to hear her, but Jean was sure he had. A bright flash exploded the sky near the ship, a huge crack of thunder following. He peered uneasily out the edge of the windshield, as though awaiting the next bolt. Then he looked at the Global Positioning System.

Jean realized he wasn't going to say a word.

Maddened, she stuffed Erika's letter into the well with the others and climbed off the navigator's stool. Grabbing the back of the captain's seat for balance as she prepared to go below, she said, "No wonder Chris can't talk, with you for a role model."

As she spoke, the ship hit a big well, and a blinding light, accompanied by an earsplitting boom, seemed to shake the world. Jean saw sizzling blue.

David, voice tight, said, "Call Jake on the intercom."

Shaking, holding on to anything she could find, Jean reached for the intercom and punched a button. "Jake to the wheelhouse." She asked David, "Are we going to sink?"

"No. That hit the lightning protection." As Jean started to slip past him to the cabin, he grabbed her wrist, his eyes never leaving the sea. He said, "First rule of sparring, Jean. Never hit below the belt. That's for street fighting with the people who want to hurt you."

Feeling him bruising her arm, she said, "*You're* hurting me."

He released her, and she swayed against the side of the wheelhouse.

Grabbing the edge of the cockpit, she added, ''And it hurts when you don't talk.''

David took his eyes from the sea and met hers. ''Skye hit her. All right? She was leaving a party at her parents' house, she was angry at me, and she pulled out of the driveway and saw my car. Erika was driving. If you read the rest of that letter, you can figure out the rest. Now don't ask me about my wife again. *Ever.*''

Jean took a step back.

He was still gazing out at the sea and the storm. He said under his breath, ''I won't malign her.''

The door from the cabin opened, and Jake came up. He looked at Jean, then at David. ''Any sign of Baby?''

Jean's mouth fell open, her thoughts changing direction, and she watched David shake his head, his mouth a tight line. He glanced once at Jean and said, ''Sorry.''

She knew he was.

Baby was gone.

CHAPTER FOURTEEN

THEY ANCHORED in a cove on Cabo San Anselmo that night, and it seemed to Jean like a good place for gloom. The ingredients were readily available.

One, Jake and the other members of the expedition were going ashore that night to a party on the cape where she was notorious.

Two, Baby was still gone, and Chris was heartbroken about her disappearance.

And three, the conversation with David in the wheelhouse felt like a mistake. He had broken his silence, but at whose expense? Jean felt as though she had degraded their relationship by prying such an ugly truth from him. He hadn't told her everything about Erika's accident, but she could assemble the pieces. Jake's story about David's old car that Skye had hated and totaled. David's doing "penance." Jake's description of Skye as "a lush and a bitch." Probably alcohol was one of the factors David had omitted from his account. Another would be Erika's statement that the only accident was that David hadn't been driving.

The question that remained unanswered was what could have made Skye so angry.

Obviously David returned the feeling. His remark that he wouldn't malign his wife seemed to indicate that he couldn't talk about her without doing so, which was both telling and curious. Jean wondered how much of that was the result of Skye's suicide, how much Erika's accident, how much other things.

The puzzle came and went from her mind. More urgent was what the evening might bring down on her own head. Although David, as far as she knew, would stay home with her and Chris, Jake's going ashore to the party seemed a one-step plan for disaster. Jean could picture it easily, a casual comment to the wrong person. *No, David stayed on his ship tonight with his fiancée, Jean Young.*

Every time she thought of it, she wanted to moan aloud. Yet she felt helpless, as though she was in the grip of events spiraling out of her control.

And Chris's reaction to Baby's disappearance had the same flavor.

That night, after Jolly's four-course Christmas Eve dinner, Jean waited on the steps of the aft companionway with David while Chris changed into his pajamas for bed. In the salon, the others were drinking rum-and-eggnog, warming up for the party at nine. Behind her on the steps, David was taking out her braid. His impatience to be alone with her made the threat of exposure seem even more dire, and Jean was glad when Chris emerged from his stateroom.

But he did not look like a boy waiting for the sound of sleigh bells.

David nudged Jean to her feet and stood up. He told Chris, "Better set out one of Jolly's cinnamon rolls for Santa Claus."

Chris hardly looked at him but squeezed past them both and up the companionway to the salon. Jean closed her eyes, feeling culpable. David had tried to keep Chris from loving Baby. Only she had swayed him.

As though he knew what she was feeling, David told her, "He'll get over it. And so will you."

Jean wanted to sink into the hold of the ship. Now David thought her moodiness was the result of Baby's absence.

She had to tell him the truth. Tonight, before the others came home. As she watched him follow Chris across the salon, she wished she'd found the courage to tell him sooner.

IN THE GALLEY Chris climbed onto a stool to take down a plate and a glass for Santa Claus, then set out a cinnamon roll and a napkin. Watching him fill the glass with milk, David asked, "Going to write a note for him?"

Feeling superfluous, Jean said, "I'll get the paper."

Minutes later she sat at the galley table beside David as Chris wrote a note to Santa Claus, but her mind was elsewhere, on the evening ahead. It was going to be very hard to tell David the truth and hard for him to hear it. He would be angry, but at some point that anger would fade, wouldn't it?

Maybe she should wait until after Christmas.

But after Christmas might be too late.

David's voice, stressed, called her away from her musings. "Chris, Santa Claus is not going to bring Baby back. That's not part of his job."

Chris signed something at him, and Jean followed the words. *He knows where Baby is. He'll find her. You wouldn't go back to look for her today. You wouldn't even find my mother.*

Jean tried to draw an even breath.

David's face went still. Evenly, quietly, he told Chris, "Please go to your room."

Chris's face collapsed in tears, and he scooted out of the booth and ran up the companionway. The sound of his door sliding shut with a bang rang through the ship like a gunshot.

Jean looked down at the note he had written. "Dear Santa Claus, Please bring Baby back."

David slid out of the booth. "I'm going to say goodnight to him."

Jean sat behind at the galley table, thinking of what Chris had said and of what she had read in the *South Coast Sun,* that David had dived beneath the ship looking for Skye's body. A chill passed over her. What had he told Chris? What could he tell him?

David was gone so long that at last Jean went up to his cabin, intent on taking a shower. After the stormy day, her hair and skin were caked with salt spray. But she had shed only her sweatshirt when David came in, closing the door. Catching a glimpse of his face, an expressionless mask, Jean asked, "Shall I go say good-night to him?"

"He's asleep." David stepped toward her, ran his eyes over her body and asked, "Taking a shower?"

"Yes."

"Good." He drew off his shirt and threw it indifferently in the corner. "So am I. Saves water." He smiled at her—almost—and Jean saw he was exhausted.

Her courage evaporated.

HE MADE LOVE TO HER against the tile wall of the shower, her legs wrapped around him as he moved inside her. After the turmoil of the day, Jean wondered how they could still want each other. Yet the pleasure filled her, overwhelming her, while she clutched his shoulders, feeling the ripple of muscle in his arms and back.

He said, "I love you." The words came out again and again, more than he'd ever said them before, and Jean held him tightly, needing him and feeling at the same time that their lovemaking was a travesty, that she was unworthy of what he was giving her.

David sensed it without knowing what he was sensing, only a sadness in her. Baby? Chris? He didn't analyze it. He made her forget it. Under the water of the shower, he spoke to her softly. The intimacy of words was magic, and soon he felt her clinging more tightly, heard her crying for him low in her throat, an animal with her mate.

Then the hot shivers raked through her, shattering around her, shuddering over him. David drove harder inside her and hardly knew he was saying her name over and over while he came. It was a long time before he let her slide to the floor, rinsed the water over her many more times and turned off the tap.

When he looked at her she was crying. He said, "Are you hurt?"

She shook her head. "I just love you."

"Good." He handed her a towel. "Wait here."

JEAN STARED at the dress on the bed. Waltz-length skirt, draping tiers of gauzy black cotton and a scooped neck embroidered with every color in the rainbow. Birds and flowers in exquisite detail, the work of weeks or months. From the blanket hem dangled six inches of fringe like uncombed hair, woven with trade beads and scraps of silver—silver like the ornate coin belt that must have cost the earth. David had also thought to find her some beaded rope sandals, beautiful and perfect. Everything reflected and would enhance her style, which seemed to Jean some kind of miracle—and testament to how well he knew her.

But the gift seemed ominous. She asked David, "Are we going somewhere?"

"Carlos's party. Grant and Jolly volunteered to stay with Chris so you and I could have a date." Watching a tremor pass over her, David thought of the industrial port in L.A. and the man who had straddled her, ripped at her jeans, promised her pain a woman would never forget. Blinking the image from his mind, he said, "Chris and I found the dress together."

She said, "It's beautiful." And she made herself meet his eyes. "Thank you." She had many excuses to plead, from a headache to the truth. But David was counting on having her beside him, and letting him down would be cowardice.

By going she could remind herself she was innocent. By going she could show David her innocence. And only by going could she convince him there had never been reason for her to tell him anything.

But she knew in her heart he would never agree with the last.

For a wrap Jean wore the gift from the London shop, which Ceci had said she could open early. When David saw her, he said, "And I thought I'd have to keep you warm."

As he touched the fine wool of the long, woven, hooded shawl, Jean stared at him, mesmerized. She'd never been anywhere with a man in a tuxedo, and she couldn't imagine another looking so perfect in one. Tall, broad-shouldered, sinewy. This was her companion, her lover, the man she would marry.

The man she might lose.

There were five in their party—David and Jean, Jake, Robin and Ken—but they took both of the *Skye*'s auxiliary craft, the Zodiac and the smaller glass-bottomed dinghy, across the cove to the party. Jean rode in the dinghy with Jake while the others went in the Zodiac with David, something she knew David had arranged as a matter of courtesy to the expedition members.

In his tuxedo, the holly berries on his battery-powered bow tie blinking in the night, Jake gave her an abbreviated rundown on Carlos, who owned a fishery in Le Paz. As they motored along the shore under a swelling moon past two other craft glowing with Christmas lights, he told Jean, "This is a big party. We'll see most of the people who own property down here and more from up north. You might run into someone you know from Santa Barbara."

As he spoke Jean understood how foolish she'd been to come. When she had fled Cabo San Anselmo it had been with the conviction that she would never want to return— and the certainty she never could. Now she was going back, plunging into a social situation where she was bound to see people with whom she had bitter, unresolved differences. Worse, she realized belatedly that if she'd leveled with David, given him some warning, he might have protected her. Now he could only be angry.

And this was Christmas Eve, a night for peace and joy.

When Jake steered the dinghy up to the dock, the Zodiac, with its more powerful motor, was already there. David took their bowline and helped Jean from the small craft onto the weathered dock, touching both her hands as he steadied her.

Just that contact in the night quickened her pulse, and Jean knew from his eyes that David felt the same. He said, "Ready, ma'am?"

She would never be ready, but she looked toward the lights of the sprawling hacienda on the hill and accepted the arm he offered her. As he guided her up the dock, Jean peered at a building she realized must be a three-car garage. Colored lights etched a nativity scene on each of the doors. The star, the shepherd, the family, the wise men. Symbols of hope and promise of the morning. Christmas Day.

But the emotional anticipation she should have felt was missing. There was only fear. And a sense that she, by her deceit, had broken something beautiful and fragile. It was only a matter of time till David discovered the damage.

THE SMELLS OF THE CAPE were the same, but Carlos's place added its own. From the moment the black-skirted maid took her wrap at the door, Jean inhaled the fiesta of aromas brewing in the kitchen. Fajitas, flan, mole, cinnamon cookies, hot chocolate, and almond torte. Creamy corn soup and flounder rolls, everything a feast for the senses.

Music from the ballroom drifted out to the palatial red-tile foyer, bringing with it the sound of tinkling glasses and many voices talking at once. As David introduced her to Carlos, a short, wiry man with dancing eyes and a surplus of charm, Jean felt short of breath, faint. What would happen when she walked into the next room? Who would be there? Would anyone recognize her? It was all she could do to concentrate on the introduction and keep her eyes on their host as he spoke in perfect, barely accented English, praising her beauty and congratulating David.

As Carlos turned to the others, greeting Jake with familiarity and Robin and Ken with attentiveness, Jean's gaze drifted to the church-size nativity set at the end of the hall, lit with lights and surrounded by flowers. Its beauty reminded her of David's love. And of her own unworthiness.

She deserved coal in her stocking.

David's touch drew her attention back to Carlos, who was urging them toward the ballroom, saying, ''I'm so pleased you're all here, my guests. David, you can take care of your *novia,* yes? My wife is showing the upper level to friends, but when she comes down I'll bring her to see you.''

Jake, Ken and Robin went ahead, looking for the punch bowls and tables laden with food, and Jean found herself alone with David, gazing upon a majestic room of high stucco arches and ornate chandeliers, all decked with holiday color. She searched the faces in the crowd, but recognized no one. It gave her no ease. Heat was rising over her in waves, and she could not escape the feeling that her minutes were numbered.

David's hand slipped from hers and touched her back near her waist. ''Are you all right?''

''Yes.'' Jean made herself smile at him. She would not use his concern to her own advantage, to escape. She owed him this night, and she wanted him to have it. She only hoped it wouldn't end in disgrace.

She saw no one she knew, except a few vaguely familiar faces who seemed not to place her at all. David brought her food and drink, introduced her to a few close acquaintances and danced with her on the starlit patio outside, occasionally trading her into other hands. Ken, Robin, Jake and, once, Carlos, who asked her many questions about herself and how she'd met David. He seemed to know David very well, and by the end of the dance Jean sensed his approval of her. When he handed her back to David, he called her a treasure.

David did not relinquish her again, and Jean felt herself relaxing as the evening wore on and she spent it at his side and in his arms. Though he never voiced it, she sensed his pride in her. No one had ever made her feel so cherished.

When they had been at the party for nearly two hours, he drew her off to the edge of the patio and said, "I think I'm wearing you out, which I'd rather do at home." He met her eyes significantly. "Ready to go?"

Jean nodded, giving silent thanks that they were escaping now, that nothing had happened to mar the evening, that tonight he would hear the truth from her own lips, not distortions from someone else's. She said, "I need to find the ladies' room first."

David said, "I'll get your wrap."

HE WAS WAYLAID by a brunette in a black-and-white dress that reminded him of the clothes Skye had worn so well. On this woman, whose carriage seemed stridently athletic, the style was more forced, and it was the sense of forced fashion that David remembered about her. He didn't know her name.

"Jennifer Avery," she said. "I'm sorry. It has been a while. Two years perhaps."

David started at the name, then said, "Of course. I remember you." He knew she must be aware of her husband's proposal still on his desk, and he wasn't sure he was glad she'd chosen to speak to him. He found himself glancing down at the empty champagne flute in his hand as though it was a burden he was impatient to lay aside. He searched for something to say to Jennifer and recalled where they had met and the substance of their conversation two years earlier, the horrifying story she had told, the story Erika had said must be incomplete.

He said, "Let's see… You and I met at the gallery opening on the wharf. You'd had trouble with your nanny."

"Yes," said Jennifer. "And how surprised I was to hear just now that you're going to marry her!"

Jean was descending the stairs, her hand tight on the wrought-iron railing. She had spotted Jennifer Avery at once and felt her stomach take a kamikaze dive. Now she saw David's startled movement, the stem of the champagne flute break off in his hand, the remaining drops of wine spill onto the tile floor. He stepped back, staring at the spots on the floor, then at Jennifer Avery.

Knowing what must have been said, Jean felt her insides shatter. She should have spared him that moment.

She should have spared herself.

DAVID PULLED HER WRAP around her silently and nudged her toward the door. They had already bade farewell to their host, David with a smile that Jean could hardly believe he had summoned and that fooled her not at all.

As they moved outside under the moon, Jean said, "The others…"

"They'll take the Zodiac." He glanced both ways as they walked onto the flagstone. They were alone but too close to the house to speak. Touching Jean as little as possible, he led her down the stone steps to the water.

Jean said, "I'd like to know what Jennifer Avery said to you."

They stepped onto the dock. David didn't answer until they'd reached the dinghy and he'd handed her inside. Then he climbed in after her and crouched over the outboard. Before pulling the starter, he took a breath and said, "It's been two years since she told me the story, but it stayed in my mind. Two children left alone in a condominium while the nanny went AWOL with her boyfriend. The children set fire to the condo and barely escaped with their lives, one of them with burns.'' He pulled the starter. Once. Twice. It caught.

Jean was kneeling in the bow, untying the line. As she shoved the dinghy away from the dock, she looked into his eyes.

David said what had been building inside him for twenty minutes, ever since Jennifer Avery uttered those words and that champagne flute came apart in his hands. ''You lied to me.''

''No.'' She shook her head, eyes wide and clear.

David turned the throttle and steered the boat away from the dock out into the cove. He headed the dinghy not for the ship but for a stretch of beach farther south from Carlos's hacienda, deserted and out of reach of the ears on other boats in the cove.

On the forward seat, far from him, Jean asked, ''Where are you going?''

''The beach.'' He silently cursed what the sand would do to the outboard, but it couldn't be helped.

At the shore he helped her out, then turned away.

Jean said, ''You should have my side of the story.''

''First you're going to have mine.'' He spun on her tensely, his tuxedo incongruous with their surroundings, the empty, moonlit beach. ''Say what you will, say you never told me a lie, and I'll tell you there are lies of commission and omission. Yours was the latter. Whatever happened down here, and I'm not sure I care what it was, you lied to me a dozen times about it. You lied when you told me about your mother. You lied when I hired you to care for my son.''

''I did *not*.''

''You lied when I asked you to read Michael Avery's proposal. You lied every time I asked you to watch Chris. It was a *lie,* Jean. A living lie. Day in and day out. God, and to think I was worried you didn't want to come to this party because somebody had tried to rape you!''

Jean was glad of the dark so she didn't have to see his face. But she could feel the anger snapping from him—and the betrayal. She could think of nothing to say in her own defense. Except, ''I'm sorry.''

''So am I,'' he said tautly. ''So am I.''

His words plunged through her like a rock, and the sound of the waves on the shore seemed mournful, as though the tide was playing ''Taps'' over the remains of David's respect for her. Jean said, ''You should try to understand.''

He had turned partially away from her, but she had his full attention now. ''Forgive me for not understanding that you neglected to tell me you'd been a nanny before and that two of your charges almost died from your negligence.''

''They did not!''

''Don't shout at me.''

''Then listen to me.'' Her hair waved around her, curling from the dampness of the sea air. She felt wild, out of control. She couldn't lose David's love over this. It would be the final insult.

He said coldly, ''I'll listen, but go light on the details about your lover. This is where it happened, isn't it, Jean? Was it your boyfriend? Or your professor? Or both? How many other lies have you told me?''

For a moment Jean couldn't speak. When she could she said, ''I don't deserve this. I've never lied to you. I withheld something, and that's my right. I wanted a job, and I knew you wouldn't give me one if I told you this story.''

''Then you *lied!*'' He was shouting now—because she hadn't answered his question. ''That's what it's called, Jean. A lie. You lied because you wanted a job from me! And when I took you into my bed—''

''That's irrelevant, and you know it.'' He was advancing on her, and she stepped back. ''I planned to tell you.''

"When? Tonight?" David swore at her. "Every time you shared your body with me, you lied."

"Stop saying that. If my not telling you this was a lie, then you lie to me a hundred times a day!"

"Explain what you mean."

"Do you tell me everything?"

The question made him furious. "Some things are none of your business."

"Wrong. I'm going to be your wife."

And then they both fell silent in the moonlight, hearing only the water.

David said, "Perhaps."

Jean expelled a breath. "You—"

"Dream come true," he supplied. "Remember? Now, tell your story, if you have the nerve."

"You don't deserve to hear it." Hugging herself, Jean turned toward the water. "Just take me home."

Her words inflamed him. Not deserve to hear it? Who did she think she was talking to? David grabbed her arm and wheeled her around. The emotions building inside him had obliterated all thoughts except one, the question that he'd already asked—that she'd never answered. That he knew she shouldn't have to answer. The question that he couldn't ask again. He shoved her down on the sand, mindless of her dress, hating the feel of manhandling a woman's body. It reminded him of Skye, of their screaming, shaking fights. And her constant, unending deceit.

Jean hit the wet sand hard and stared up at him, gasping.

Seeing her eyes begin to tear, David snapped, "Pull yourself together and start talking. I've got more to cry about than you'll ever know."

Jean didn't doubt it. She told him, "Never touch me that way again."

He said, *"Talk. Now."*

Jean felt the breath steaming like fire through her nostrils, but she knew that if she didn't tell him they would never sort it out. She said, "It was my day off."

"Start before," David said sharply. "How you got the job—you, who said you were no good with children, who said your mother put you down."

"That was why. I wanted to prove to her I could do something useful." Jean swallowed, watching the tiny waves sweep into shore, then crumble to nothingness. "I could talk about this all night, but the bottom line was that she didn't like how I spent my time, except for school. Tae kwon do, surfing, diving—all worthless. All self-gratification, according to her.

"The Averys were friends of my mother's, and they mentioned the job to her, thinking of Ceci, but Ceci was already modeling, getting better assignments all the time. I said I wanted to do it." Jean didn't add her mother's doubts and fateful predictions. They didn't matter. But something else did, something David wouldn't want to hear. She took a long breath and continued.

"Billy Moss was going, too. He had a job at the condos as a sailing instructor, surfing coach, et cetera."

David stepped away from her in the darkness, kicking off the shoes he wished he'd removed earlier, before they'd gotten out of the boat. "Who is Billy Moss?"

"He was my boyfriend. We were high school sweethearts and best friends." Jean looked at David, trying to gauge his reaction. His back was turned. "We dated for three years. Two years of high school and one of college."

David thought of this boy's hand on her breast. He thought of him making love to her, never satisfying. Or had Jean lied about that?

Behind him she said, "David, it was never like what I have with you. The first time—I knew he wasn't the one. It was...rather traumatic." She drew another shaky breath. "That's another reason I came down here. To be alone. He followed. That's why he got the job, to be near me."

David didn't look at her. He moved yards away and sat down on the dry sand above the tide line.

Jean said, "It was strictly platonic by then—on my side, anyhow. We surfed together. On my day off we always went up the coast to San Marcos Island, where the waves are big."

David knew the place. He hadn't known Jean could handle swell of that size. And he didn't care.

"That day—it was about a month after I started the job—we went surfing as usual, and late in the afternoon Billy did a face plant on an easy ride, one of those you think is going to be a piece of cake. I saw him not get up, just lie in the water, and when I went over he wasn't moving. His neck was broken."

David looked at her, and Jean suspected he thought she was lying, but she went on because she didn't know what else to do. "I pulled him out of the water, using everything I knew about lifesaving, and I sat there on the beach holding his head all night."

"All night?" said David. "Wasn't anyone else out?"

"It was cloudy, and the swell was bad. We had talked of going farther up the coast. We'd heard Gila Point was good, but it was too far, because I was supposed to be at the Averys' at seven." She was surprised how calm she sounded now, how calm she felt. "At dawn, some other surfers showed up. People we knew. They went for help, and it took hours. Someone knew someone with a chopper. Finally they came and took him to San Diego."

"And?" said David.

"At the hospital, they drilled holes in his head and put him in traction, if that's what you call it. He had this halo thing around his head. Eventually he walked away."

If it was a lie, it was an ambitious one. David said, "And you?"

"I drove his car back to the condos, and the Averys' was still smoking. They had gone out the night before—'just over to the clubhouse.'" Jean heard the bitterness in her own voice, the mocking of her accuser, Jennifer Avery, who should have been accused herself of criminal negligence. "The boys started a campfire in the TV room." She felt her old ambivalence toward the children, both hellions; toward the parents she felt outrage.

She remembered that David was waiting for her to speak. "The younger boy, Baker, was hurt in the fire. The Averys were threatening lawsuits." She closed her eyes. "I was afraid—being in a foreign country, not knowing the laws. While they were occupied, I took Billy's car and drove home."

David sat still, his reactions mixed. It wasn't what he'd expected to hear. Part of him didn't believe it, was afraid to believe it, afraid it was a lie. He had heard so many from Skye that for a time he'd believed everyone told them habitually.

Jean was still talking. "My parents were shocked to see me, and when they heard the story my mother didn't believe me. She called the hospital in San Diego—not to check on Billy but to see if he was there at all. Even when she found he was, she insisted that I shouldn't have gone up the coast if there was any chance I couldn't get back on time. Maybe she was right." Jean swallowed. "We never had a chance to work things out. A few weeks later she and my father were killed on the interstate, just two miles from home."

David knew how that unresolved argument must have felt—probably still felt. For Jean's sake he wished her mother had retracted her words.

He wished he could believe her himself, but the fact that she had concealed the incident ate at him. He no longer trusted her, and he wasn't sure he ever would again.

He stood up and brushed off his pants, grabbed his socks and shoes, and said, "Let's go home."

CHAPTER FIFTEEN

JEAN WATCHED HIM remove his jacket and place it on a hanger over the door of his open locker. As he pulled off his bow tie, she said, ''I didn't know those things really tied.''

Skye had taught him how. He wanted to tell her that, a cruel tidbit about his first marriage. She wanted details. He'd give them.

On a wave of self-disgust David slid open the door to his cabin and went out, up into the wheelhouse, before he could say something he'd regret.

Left behind, Jean was unsure what to do. It was late, time for bed, but he hadn't invited her to his, and the last thing she wanted to do was creep up to him and ask him where she should sleep. She went to her own cabin and retrieved a paper shopping bag from the locker. Christian's Christmas gifts were inside, and she made her way down through the office and aft to his stateroom, where his stocking hung, to leave them for him.

David and I should be doing this together, she thought. But there were good reasons why they weren't. His lack of conviction about her story hurt—more, even, than her mother's distrust had at the time.

Tiptoeing into Chris's room, Jean took a moment to reposition the covers he'd kicked off in the night, then turned to set the wrapped packages under and inside his stocking. With thoughts of St. Nicholas, she tucked the hacky sack in one of his small shoes, a pack of stickers in the other.

A shadow hid the glow from a night-light in the hall. It was David, still wearing his white tuxedo shirt and black pants. He had a drink in his hand, and he sipped from the glass as he looked at the gifts she'd tucked into Chris's shoes. He said, "Did you know St. Nicholas was credited with bringing the dead back to life?"

Jean shook her head. She reached for the hacky sack to put it in Chris's stocking instead. She hadn't forgotten about St. Nicholas's Day, but she'd thought the baggage of *that* day wouldn't matter on Christmas morning. Of course she was wrong. It would always matter.

David said, "Don't bother. He'll like it that way." The glass hovered near his lips as he said, "I was just sharing trivia. My mother liked saints, and she used to tell me stories about St. Nicholas. In Greece they say he controls the tempests and the winds. There are churches and shrines all over the coasts dedicated to him, and the icons show him with a dripping beard and brine on his clothes from pulling drowning people out of the sea."

Jean closed her eyes. Erika was right. David did get black at Christmas.

"In other countries they said he could reassemble dismembered bodies."

Jean's heart stilled. She thought of the props on the *Skye,* the blood in the water. On St. Nicholas's Day. She looked at him and said softly, "David?"

But he was looking at his son. "He went to sleep telling me Santa Claus is going to bring Baby back. To you." David swallowed another draft of tequila. He'd poured it into a glass this time—so he would stop. "Your present, not his."

Jean said, "I wouldn't ask that of Santa Claus."

"Good," said David flatly. "I can paint sleigh tracks and hoofprints on the foredeck, but that's the bottom of my bag of tricks."

Jean wondered if he really went to such lengths. She heard no humor in his voice, or warmth.

Chris tossed in his bed, and David watched him dispassionately, as though he were someone else's son. Mirthlessly, bitterly, he said, "Here we go. Time for a little night music."

Chris began to scream. David set down his glass, stepped inside and shut the door. As he moved to the bed to pick up his son, Jean glanced toward the hall. Thinking of the expedition members in the nearby staterooms, she asked, "Should I go out and explain to the others?"

"I already told them." Then, not wanting to see her there in his son's room doing mother things and still less wanting her to witness his family's shame again, he said, "But if you're done you can go."

Jean said, "You're not being fair to me."

Instead of replying, he lifted Chris in his arms and opened the door for her. "Good night."

Jean went out, to her own cabin.

THAT NIGHT the dream was the worst it had ever been but only because it was the most vivid. The details never changed. It always started at the same place, her last words, her strange backward topple over the railing. Then everything else, just as it had been the first time, never getting better. As always David awoke with the feeling that his hair and skin were caked with her blood and worse. He got up to take a shower.

Under the spray, he scrubbed himself with a wood-handled brush, feeling like Lady Macbeth trying to cleanse her hand of the blood of her murder victim. For perfumes of Arabia, substitute white bar soap. Had Jean ever noticed how much of the stuff he went through?

In the midst of his furious scrubbing, she came in and stood on the wet floor looking at him, her legs strong and fine beneath the hem of one of his T-shirts.

David set the scrub brush on the shower caddy and slammed off the water.

Jean handed him a towel and asked, "Why do you do that?"

"Do what?" He dried his face first and shook his hair on her.

"Take showers at three in the morning."

"Because I can't sleep." Feeling his own lies now, he stepped past her to his cabin. Damn her body, she made him hard. He would have banged the door shut behind him if he hadn't wanted her so badly.

Jean saw the invitation and followed him. "Showers help?"

"You help," he said tersely.

Hoping that if she bent, he would, Jean said, "I'm here, David."

He turned so she could see what she did to him. "Then get in bed."

It was better with her arms around him, better still with everything off her. As he felt the heat of her skin, the soft places on her body, relaxation went through him in small shudders. Like a house settling in the ground, he settled against her inch by inch, feeling her hand stroking his hair. He buried his face in hers, wishing he didn't want her. Wishing he didn't love her.

Jean whispered, "Please forgive me, David."

He wondered if she meant, *Please believe me.* And he thought of her boyfriend. He wanted to ask, *Only once?* But he knew it shouldn't matter if it'd been a hundred times—and a hundred men. It was because of Skye that it did. And because he loved Jean so much he could hardly stand it.

He moved against her, anticipating the heat of her around him, hating the thought of the synthetic barrier between them. He longed to forgo it, as he had the first time, but now it seemed more important than ever. He didn't know her as well as he'd thought.

He kissed her, postponing the moment, and as he did it all came to the surface. The same images as the dream, in vivid color. He shut his eyes.

Jean's arms went tight around him almost as though she knew everything inside him, but David knew she couldn't.

He moved her arms away, got out of bed and reached for a pair of sweatpants hanging over a chair. Without a word, he left the room.

HE WAS PULLING on his pants when she opened her eyes the next morning. Without greeting her he said, "There are some whales in a lagoon out there. It's foggy, but Ken was already out and saw them. We're all going now, so watch Chris, will you?"

Jean said, "Merry Christmas?"

David walked to the bed, touched her hair and went up to the wheelhouse.

Thinking of Chris, Jean climbed out of bed, hurried into the crew's quarters and put on an old pair of sweatpants and a sweatshirt. Then she went down through the office and up into the galley. As usual Jolly's domain was ship-shape, except for the note and empty plate and milk glass on the table. Jean paused and read the note again. Beneath Chris's request for Santa to bring back Baby was a reply in David's writing, somewhat disguised:

Dear Chris,
Sorry about Baby. She's celebrating Christmas up north, and I couldn't budge her. But thanks for the cinnamon roll. Ho, ho, ho! People call me jolly, too. Hope you won't mind cleaning off those tracks we left on the deck. Dasher and Dancer just can't seem to get a clean landing on the water.
    You're a good boy.

                                                    Love,
                                                    Santa

In a rush, Jean recalled what had happened before they went to Carlos's party—Chris's *You wouldn't even find my mother.* Poor David. Christmas Eve had been the worst kind of day for him: the storms, Baby's disappearance, Chris's accusation, discovery of her own deceit. And deceit it was, one way or the other. Alone in her berth before she slept, Jean had faced that.

Yet after such a miserable Christmas Eve, David had found the kindness to write a Santa Claus note to his son. And, apparently, leave reindeer and sleigh tracks on the foredeck.

Noticing the last closed door on the advent calendar and thinking that David had left her with a child waking up to Christmas morning, Jean hurried back to Christian's stateroom. But his door was still shut. Sleeping. That wouldn't last long, so Jean took advantage of the time to shower and dress.

As she did she tried to tell herself it was a new day, but her heart wasn't in the thought. David had not kissed her since the night before, when their lovemaking had abruptly ended. Probably he still doubted the story she had told him about working for the Averys.

Everything had turned upside down.

After dressing, Jean hurried back out to the salon. It was fully light now, and Chris's door was still shut. She sat down to wait for him and saw a package with her name on it under the tree. It was from David, she knew. Wondering what it was, she thought again with misgiving of her own presents for him. And when she turned back to look toward Chris's stateroom, Skye's eyes seemed to mock her from the painting over the stairwell.

Before Chris awakened, the Zodiac returned, and Jean went up on deck into the fog-banked, misty morning to greet the men. Jake was saying, "She must have taken him out somewhere. I'll go look for them. Don't sweat it, David.''

David was gazing toward the diving platform as though something displeased him, and when at last he glanced up and saw Jean on the deck, his eyes were a portrait in shock. He said, ''Where's the dinghy?''

Jean looked toward the diving platform blankly. No dinghy.

David clambered out of the boat, took the aft deck in three strides, then ran into the diving alcove, leaving the door swinging behind him. Jean heard his feet on the companionways, the sliding of a door inside, then his voice shouting through the ship. ''Chris!''

The name slammed her in the chest.

A moment later David was back on deck, facing her. ''Is he here?''

Jean couldn't answer. She shook her head.

David went to the aft railing and stared out of the cove toward the grayed-over obscurity of the open sea. Jean followed, while behind them Jake said, ''I'm on the radio, David.''

Never taking his eyes from the water, David said to Jean, ''You know where he's gone, don't you?''

She didn't answer, couldn't.

''He's looking for Baby.''

THERE WAS NOTHING for her to do but pace the deck and listen to the crackle of the radio. David had taken Grant, Jake and Robin and made her stay behind. He wasn't kind about it, either, just direct, wasting no time on recriminations. They would come later.

It was worse than anything Jean could have imagined, had ever imagined. And it had happened on her watch. A six-year-old boy gone to sea in a seven-foot boat.

Behind her, she heard Jolly talking on the radio. A moment later he stepped out of the wheelhouse and joined her at the rail. He was unshaven, still in his red, long-sleeved undershirt and a pair of olive fatigues held up with dirty, rainbow-striped suspenders. He said, "Nothing yet. You see anything, Jean?"

She shook her head, wishing there was more she could do. Her eyes lingered on the shore, and it occurred to her that if she were a frightened child that was where she'd go. And by now, Chris must be frightened.

She thought of the surfboards in the alcove and her shoulder, still compromised. But the shore was close. She could be there in ten minutes.

She looked up at Jolly. "If I paddled over to the beach on one of the surfboards, would you watch to make sure I don't drown?"

Jolly stepped back uneasily, as though she'd asked a sticky question. "I don't know if David would like that."

All that could matter to David right now was getting his son back. Jean said, "The shore's close. I think that's where Chris might go."

"On the ocean is where he'll get hurt," said Jolly. "If he's on the beach, he'll be fine."

"Not if he's cold and wet." Hypothermia. It was a wet morning, and Chris was a slight child.

Jolly sighed and turned back toward the wheelhouse. "Ah, go look. Yeah, I'll watch you. Just don't get hurt, or David'll have my hide. He probably will, anyhow."

Jean hurried below to put on her wet suit.

JAKE SAID, "I can't believe Chris started that motor."

David wished he hadn't taught him how. Staring off the bow of the Zodiac and into the fog bank, he said, "Keep close to the shore. The tide will sweep him toward those rocks on the point."

Jake pulled a cigarette from the pocket of his slicker, tucked it in a corner of his mouth, then groped for a lighter and lit it, all with the same hand. His other was on the tiller. Drawing on the cigarette, he said, through half-closed lips, "At least the gas was down."

David had refilled it last thing before he turned in. He answered, "No such luck. He's got a full tank."

Robin trained binoculars along the shore, then in the other direction, out into the fog. David wanted to snatch the field glasses from his hands and throw them on the floor of the boat. Visibility was fifty yards, max.

Jake said, "The chopper's coming from north of San Marcos. I'd give it twenty minutes yet. And Carlos took both his boats out."

Twenty minutes. Chris had already been gone forty-five at least, maybe longer. David thought of his son in the dinghy, a boat too small for the open sea. Why had he gone?

But he knew the answer.

Jean.

Baby.

And Skye, the mother he, David, had never tried to find. *She was dead, Chris. I saw her.*

What if she wasn't? Why did you let her sink?

That conversation had been a nightmare.

I couldn't hold her, Chris.

Jake suddenly pointed at the rocky point where the spray leapt twenty feet in the air. "There he is, David. And there's your girl." He gunned the outboard.

WHEN SHE SAW the dinghy near the rocks, Jean began to run. The boat was going to break apart, and then Chris's small body would be tossed in the foam and smacked hard against the point. He was going to die.

There was no chance of wading or swimming into the swell to the boat. The water would be ten feet deep out there, and as the waves hit the rocks they sprang up in foam to triple that. The only approach was over the black, craggy rocks.

They cut her feet as she climbed them, and her wet suit ripped on a ragged edge. What was worse, her shoulder could support almost no weight. She was reduced to one arm, a hand that could be used only for balance, and her legs. Those legs were her strength, and she stretched them long over the steep side of the point, determined to make faster time.

Hang on, Chris. Hang on, baby. Then, desperately, she thought, *Don't die!*

But there was no way she could get him. As she climbed she imagined hanging from the edge of a steep face and letting Chris grab her foot. But one-armed pull-ups were not her specialty.

When she crested the top, she couldn't see the dinghy, but she saw the Zodiac, farther out, headed toward the point. Where was Chris? She scrambled over the rocks until she could peer down to the waves, just in time to see the dinghy wash up on top of a low boulder, the terribly small boy inside. As the waves receded, the boat came to rest, perched on the black rocks.

Jean yelled, "Get out, Chris! Climb!" At the same time, she began climbing down toward him. She saw the next set of waves coming in as he put his leg over the gunwale and stepped out of the boat. "Hurry, Chris! Climb!"

He made for the higher rocks, moving from her view.

Jean saw the waves come in and thought how wet were the rocks down which she was climbing. The tide smashed against the point with a sound like thunder, and the spray showered her. All Jean could think was that Chris was farther below. The waves must have swallowed him. Crushed him.

Drowned him.

The dinghy, still in her view, washed off the boulder and fell down between the rocks on a wave of foam, swamped by the tide. Jean kept moving, sliding down one long ledge after another, feeling a numb certainty that all she would find at the bottom was a small body crushed in the rocks, broken.

Or nothing.

Her feet slipped on the wet surface, and her toes grappled for each fissure in the rocks as she climbed downward. The waves had gone out, and soon they would be back in. As they came she peered down again.

There was Chris, his face crumpled in fear, wet with tears, drenched with water. He clung to the crags below her, his feet on a narrow ledge. Jean knew he must have held on when the last waves came. Now his eyes were on hers. She couldn't get to him before the next breakers came in. She could only make the ledge above him.

She said, "Hold on, honey. You're doing fine. Don't try to go anywhere yet. Here's another wave." It hit, washing over him and drenching her. Jean looked down, drawing a breath when she saw him still there. The next step was too high for him.

She slid down beside him, cutting her palms on the crags and her feet on the knife-blade ledge, the ledge that had saved Christian's life. Knowing that the weakness of her shoulder left her only one option, she braced a foot on the rocks farther down and her knee on the ledge. "Climb up me, Chris. Now."

He did, pulling her hair as he scrambled up on her back, then onto the higher ledge. Jean straightened up just as the next wave hit, knocking away her balance, the onslaught of water suffocating her. She grabbed for rock, anything, as the water threatened to wash her away. Then it was gone, and she fell, a hard drop to the boulder where the dinghy had washed up.

Jean knew the waves were returning and scrambled to her feet on the slick surface; she made it back to the ledge, climbing up to the knife-edge as the water came back. This time she had a firm purchase when the tide came and slammed against her. Feeling her body pressed against the rocks by the force, she thought, *How did little Chris stand it?*

But he had, and he was waiting for her on the rock above. She climbed up to him.

DAVID LIFTED HIS SON down from the rocks and clasped him against his chest, held him tight in his arms. Chris was sniffling and making a humming noise in his throat, and Jean watched him bury his face in his father's neck.

David looked at her once and said, "Thank you." Then, his son against his shoulder, he turned and started across the gray of the beach to where the Zodiac waited on the calm side of the point. Jean was left to climb down the last short pitch by herself, and by the time she reached the Zodiac Chris was bundled inside, his drenched body nestled in the folds of Jake's slicker.

David said, "Jake, see that he gets warm at the ship. I'm getting the dinghy."

Jean said, "You can't. It's down between those rocks."

"I saw where it is." David was scooping spare lines, a bail bucket and a life preserver from the Zodiac.

Jake glanced at David and indicated Jean. "Is she coming with us?"

Jean backed away from the water.

David said, "No."

Robin started to get out of the pontoon boat. "You'll need another hand."

"No, thank you." David didn't want the dinghy as badly as he wanted the privacy in which to tear Jean of Arc limb from limb.

The cinematographer sat down and Jake said, "Give us a shove, Jean."

She did, and then they were gone, leaving her and David alone on the beach without a boat.

David did not even look toward the point. He threw the lines, bail bucket and life vest into the sand and took a desperate step toward Jean, not sure if he was going to shake her like a rag doll or hold her so tight he would drain the life from her.

She saw the wildness in his eyes and remembered the way he had turned away after he'd taken Chris down from the rocks. She said, "I watched his door, David. I took a shower, that's all. I never heard the outboard."

"I'm not blaming you!" David wondered where the yell had come from. She had saved Chris's life—at the risk of her own. For long minutes he had watched the two of them on those rocks fighting for their lives, and him with no way to assist. He had learned the meaning of impotence.

Again.

He screamed at Jean, "Don't ever do that again! I'm *done!*" He spread his hands to each side of his body in a swift cutting motion. "No walking bike paths alone at night, no bad diving equipment, no phone calls in crack districts! You want to live like that, you don't live with me!"

Jean didn't ask if she should have left Chris on the rocks. She drew a hand to her face to push a wet lock of hair out of her eyes. Her hand was bleeding.

David saw it, but all he wanted was to keep yelling. He grabbed her shoulders and shook her until her teeth rattled. She looked unafraid, just accepting, a warrior of the way choosing passivity, and her calm drove him wild. Again he saw Chris's small head and shoulders barely clearing the gunwale of the dinghy as it washed up on the point. Again he saw his son climbing out, to certain death David had thought.

Again he felt the grinding in the props of the ship, and he shook Jean again, as though if he shook her hard enough it would somehow help. He saw her hand come up, trembling from what he was doing to her. Yet she touched his face. "Tell me."

"No!"

His body shook against his control, and Jean watched, wanting to hold him.

His hands jerked away from her, pushing her back, and he wheeled, then turned back and yelled at her. "I saw her, Jean!" A pause lingered like a rest in a requiem mass. He whispered hoarsely, "In pieces."

And then there was silence on the beach but for the waves. Jean felt the muscles in her face straining oddly as though they didn't know what expression to form.

"I saw her come at me...." He was barely articulate, and Jean watched him clutch his body like a man whose heart was being ripped out. His hair whipped in the breeze, and tears blurred from his eyes.

She moved toward him cautiously, feeling as though she was approaching a wounded animal. A large, dangerous animal. A weeping moan rose out of him, a long sob from fathomless depths, from the black well she'd known was inside him, and he sank down on the sand and lay face-down, shaking. Jean sat beside him and put her hand on his back, against the salty yellow slicker he wore.

"Her blood was everywhere, and there was... Oh, God. You couldn't see from the surface, but once you were down there..." The cry came again, broken, from his throat. "I tried to go to the screws, and the sea was rough. The water...those colors... It was my wife. It was my *wife!*"

Jean clutched him, feeling his scream expand through his body, hearing it terrify the empty beach. She held her cheek against the back of his hair, clumsily, desperately.

"This *thing* came at me, jarred loose from the screws by the swell, it must have been. It looked like a big dark shape falling through the water, and I knew it must be her, so I grabbed her, and my hands sank into her hair—and I saw her *eyes.*" The anguished, choking cries fell on each other.

Jean combed his hair with her fingers, holding his head, hardly breathing. His voice was so strangled she could barely understand him, but the words were coming out.

"And then, I dropped her—shaking—and I tried to get her again, but she just sank away from me, and I couldn't get her again. The snorkel came out of my mouth, and I swallowed her blood, Jean. Her blood…" He let his face fall to the sand, unable to go on. "In my mouth."

Jean lay against his shaking body and held him, stroking his hair, her heart crooning his name softly with every beat while he cried. Gradually he moved and lay his head against her breasts, against the neoprene of her wet suit, and Jean held him and caressed him, knowing what it was to be a mother and a woman in the comforting of a grown, grieving man. A man who had swallowed death and let it eat away inside him.

His tears were hot and wet against her and as soundless as Christian's. She stroked his cheek and his hair, and without knowing she spoke, she whispered, "I love you."

David pressed tighter against her, fighting the rest, the other things rising in him. It hurt, and he cried, afraid he would never stop. "She said goodbye. 'Goodbye, David.' Like that was all the thought she gave it. 'I'm blasted, and I think I'll tweak my husband by doing a back flip over the bow rail and never coming back.' Chris was right there. Three yards aft."

His voice broke again, and Jean held him hard, hearing his strangled sob. "My son."

My son who cannot talk.

"The bitch. I wanted her to die. I used to look her in the eye and think, *Die. Do me a favor and die.*"

Jean drew a shallow breath, put both her hands on his head, in the strands of his hair. She brushed the hot tears from his face.

David tried to stop the escaping words. He didn't want to say them, didn't want to feel them. He wanted to stop.

He wanted peace. He sat up, jerking away from Jean. "I can't say these things."

He sat with his head between his knees, like a man fighting illness, and Jean said, "You can say anything."

"She was my *wife.*"

Jean understood him better than she ever had, understood that honor could devour him. She suggested, "Pretend she's a stranger."

David shook his head, making a sound that was a mockery of laughter. "It's so bad, Jean." And the words spilled out. "She was an alcoholic. And drugs. Everything. She took *everything.*" Jean knew he was crying again, or still, but she didn't try to move closer to him. "And sex. Completely faithless. She thought fidelity was something stereos had. God!" He yelled the word at the sky. "I wanted a divorce so badly.

"And I wanted Chris. I wanted the bad thing, to take a baby from his mother. But if I didn't stop her, she'd go driving with him when she couldn't focus four feet in front of her. Once she said, 'Who are you?' to me, two minutes before she tried to take him out the door." David looked up at the sky, at the receding fog, the growing brightness heating his face. A cloud-covered sun shining on his shame.

He lay back in the sand, his arm over his face. "I thought I could do it. Divorce her, get Chris. Then she told me what she'd done with the Blade Institute accounts. It amounted to tax fraud in my name, big time. Even when she was sober she was Machiavellian."

And then his features tensed again, and he turned from her, averting his face because he was crying. "That's not true, either. I loved her. She used to... She really loved me. And she had so much brain she didn't know what to do with it. Never even made it through college for sleeping with professors and fixing grades on her computer till she got thrown out."

The two European universities took on new meaning. And so did his asking if she had slept with Michael Avery.

He was shaking his head against his arm. "And then Erika. You want the good part, Jean?" He turned and looked at her. "After she does this senseless thing—gets mad I took her car keys, has the chauffeur hot-wire her car, pulls out of the driveway and tries to take me out, but it's Erika. After all that, when she's lucid enough to know what she did, she wants to make sure none of us thinks she feels guilty. So she sleeps with my sister's fiancé! Comprehend it! I don't." He stood up, pulling off his slicker. "I'm going in the water."

As he stripped off the rest of his clothes, Jean peeled off her wet suit. The Mexican sun was shining through the faint misty remnants of the fog, a light water vapor in the air. It did nothing to warm away the chill in her bones. Goose bumps crept over her skin, and she was glad for the little protection of her purple swimsuit. She'd only taken off her wet suit so David could feel her skin, if he wanted or needed it.

As he walked naked to the shore, she followed, wading into the low breakers a few steps behind him, grateful that a curve in the coastline put them out of sight of the ship and the other boats in the cove.

David waited for her, and then they dove into the sea together and swam out until the water rose to his shoulders and Jean no longer touched bottom. She treaded water and ducked her head back in the salt and watched him do the same, a dozen times, rubbing his skin and his face. And she understood what he had been doing in the shower the night before.

She accepted that he might do it again, for the rest of his life.

At last he moved close to her in the water, reaching for her body, pulling her against him, settling her legs around him. He said, "Jean," and held her close in a tight bear hug while the salt sea washed around them on Christmas morning, trying to make him clean.

CHAPTER SIXTEEN

THEY DID NOT RECOVER the dinghy. Jake picked them up in the Zodiac, and when they were back on the ship it was only to weigh anchor and set out for Scammon's Bay.

Chris, subdued, stayed with his father in the wheelhouse until David could open presents with him. Jean left them alone and went down into the underwater observation chamber seeking solitude. For hours her stomach had been in knots, not only over what had happened on the beach, but over what had brought them there. Whatever the outcome, Chris had left the ship while he was under her care. David might be able to forgive that, but she couldn't. Not yet. And she doubted either of them would ever forget.

Down in the nose of the ship, she lay on the shark quilt Skye had made and thought of David, everything he had said, words that made the obituary in the *South Coast Sun* a lie. But the answer was easy. Discretion could be bought.

And then she realized it wouldn't have to be. The Haverford family owned the *Sun* and every paper on the south coast, lock, stock and barrel.

She was dense not to see it earlier. That and a few other things.

Her mind returned to the horror David had described, and suddenly the chamber with its motion and its blue light and the waves frothing past seemed suffocating and frightening. She stood up, banging her head on the overhead, and started climbing the ladder as fast as she could, wanting to get out, wanting to be near David.

DAVID OPENED Chris's package and lifted the lid on the box, gazing down at what lay inside. His son's face, in plaster-of-paris relief, painted with bright colors and decorated with feathers and buttons—child things. Jean must have helped him make it.

As he turned to say something to his son, who sat beside him on the stateroom's single berth, David heard a gasp from the hallway and looked up and saw her. Jean's eyes were wide, her hand over her mouth, as she stared at the mask. She said, "Oh, God," and moved out of his sight. He heard her stumble up the companionway, almost as though she were running.

David smiled at Chris, wearing his new tae kwon do uniform, and said, "It's beautiful. I love it. Let me find out what's wrong with Jean. Stay here, okay?" He set the box in Chris's lap and went out of the room, following Jean's course across the empty salon and down into the galley.

He found her in the dark by the sink, making a low moaning sound like a woman in torment. She was clutching the sink and crying, but he sensed the tears were mostly within. He said, "Jean?"

She jumped at the sound of his voice and turned to face him, hardly knowing what she was saying. "I'm sorry, David. I don't know why everything I've tried to do is turning out this way, but it is." Unable to do anything but ridicule her own appalling thoughtlessness, she exclaimed, "What to give the fiancé whose wife was run over by his own ship? plaster-of-paris body parts of his family!"

It took David a moment to follow her. When he did, he realized she must mean the mask. It was a moment when the only safety from tears was mirth, and what she had said struck him as very funny. She was upset, so he tried not to laugh, but without success.

Looking helpless, as though he were coming apart before her eyes, Jean said disconnectedly, "I didn't mean it, David. I love you. I'm just stupid. *Stupid.*"

David shook his head at her, and grabbed her before she could go anywhere. Feeling her shaking in his grasp, he said, "It's beautiful, baby. And I love it that you and Chris made it for me together. I never thought of it for a minute as body parts." Pulling her against him and stroking her hair and her back, he said softly, "Is it too much to hope there's one of you?"

THERE WAS—and also a photo of her and Chris peering around the sides of a hastily built sand castle. Beautiful smiles, Jean's like the one she'd given him that night when she opened her gifts, a new regulator and a silver brush and comb embellished with blue and green tourmaline. The last two he had won for her through lengthy and pleasurable bartering with an enterprising border trader, and after she had opened them he had brushed her hair for a long time.

Now while Jean slept beside him, David stared in the moonlight at the photograph of her and Chris, now on the night table. He thought of all it represented. His silent son, offspring of the marriage from hell. And Jean, who shook him, who never stopped shaking him. She had ridden him hard that night, so hard, as though she loved him more now that she'd seen the worst.

Which David wasn't sure she had.

He felt a numbing awareness of all he had dragged her through, what they had dragged each other through in the past days. With shame, he saw himself shoving her in the sand on Carlos's beach. This morning he had grabbed her and shaken her. He'd never touched Skye that way, ever, nor any other woman. It was beyond apology, and it made him sick.

It also made him wonder if they should be together, because something about it reminded him of Skye. The intensity. And it wasn't Jean, it was him. It was what he had felt in L.A., what he had felt in front of Jennifer Avery, what he had felt when he saw Jean on the rocky promontory with Chris.

He could also hear Erika saying, *Cold feet, David. You're getting cold feet. That's all. Just go on.*

But his feet weren't cold. They were ice.

He looked at Jean and rolled toward her to touch her and wake her in the night, as she'd told him he could, as he often did. And as she moved sleepily against him, reaching her arms around him, he knew he would go on. But only because he couldn't make himself stop.

TAE KWON DO KEPT HIM sane, and he realized neither he nor Jean had practiced for nearly a week. The next morning, before the sun rose on Scammon's Bay, he awakened her and said, "Tae kwon. Let's take the Zodiac over to the beach and get in a workout before the others wake up."

Jean sat up slowly, more slowly than he had expected she would.

He said, "We'll go easy with your shoulder. I know you have some healing to do."

Jean didn't answer but climbed out of bed and went to her cabin.

She was slow dressing, and at last David went to look for her. He found her standing beside her open locker all in white, her black belt in her hand. Her eyes were closed. She couldn't have seen him, but she startled him by saying, "I don't know if I can do this."

David understood. He'd felt something of the same thing when he'd dressed minutes earlier, but he'd moved past it. She needed to do likewise.

He stepped toward her, took the belt from her hands and wrapped it around her waist. Once. Twice. She did not meet his eyes then, or as he knotted it.

Looking at her bowed head, he said, "Ma'am, tae kwon do is a journey toward loss of self. You've lost some. So have I. Now let's get out on that beach and do what we do.''

THERE WERE WHALES in the water, all distant but in such numbers that Jean felt as though she was traveling in a world that was theirs and not hers. David used the outboard but kept it low. Nonetheless, the nearest whales dove, disappearing from sight as the first crescent glow of the sun appeared on the horizon.

Jean watched them in reverent silence until the Zodiac reached the beach.

There, her feet feeling the cool of the sand, she knelt opposite David to meditate, realizing that since the last time they had practiced together they had become lovers. Yet here nothing had changed. There was a timelessness to the ritual—and a peace. In it she knew she still possessed the strength and courage to fight.

They practiced for an hour, until David said he needed to get back to the ship and to work. But as he helped Jean into the boat at the shore, her eye caught a commotion in the water about two hundred yards out. She paused, staring, and David followed her gaze.

He said, ''Get the paddles. It's a hell of a way to move a boat like this, but it's best. The outboard scares the whales.''

As he shoved the boat hard from the shore and climbed on, she did as he asked, found the paddles and gave him one.

They both dug into the water, moving in the direction of the turbulence, and David said, ''I hope you're a good observer, because you're all I've got.''

At the moment she thought her powers of observation were failing her. She squinted at the sea for long minutes before she discerned whales rolling in the water with great agitation, raising waves from the sea. Her pulse picked up as she realized what was happening before her eyes.

The whales were mating. There were three of them, a female and two males, David said. At first it looked as though the males were taking turns, and then it appeared as though one male was helping the other with the female, attempting to hold the pair in position in the water. It was a scene of incredible confusion.

David rowed as close as was safe, given the excitement of the huge creatures. The wake from the whales' aquatic lovemaking rocked the boat. He took two notebooks from inside an ammo can on the floor of the Zodiac and handed one to Jean, along with a pen.

"I don't want to write. I want to watch," she confessed, enchanted. She had never seen any mammal mating in the wild and in her college years studying whales had never dreamed she would observe them in their most intimate act. Now she was mesmerized, heartstrings pulled tight as she witnessed the noisy, clumsy, yet endearingly erotic endeavors of the gigantic cetaceans.

"You can watch now and write later," David said.

They gazed at the whales in awe, stirred by their awkward dance of love. Observing the whales' bodies struggling for union, David said, "It looks frustrating."

Thinking how easy it was with David, Jean turned to him, but he was staring at the leviathans, and she followed his eyes. Watching the female press her flippers to the sides of the male's body, Jean said, "David, she's hugging him. Oh, David, I love them."

David let his notebook fall to the floor of the boat. Pulling her back against his chest, between his legs, he hugged her tightly. Together they rocked over the water, voyeurs to the primal act of passion of the largest creatures on earth as the sun lifted slowly over the land.

ON NEW YEAR'S DAY on the way home from Scammon's Bay, they spotted the orcas. Jean was on the foredeck with

Chris, Dr. Geary and Robin Frost when Robin saw them and leapt up for his camera, saying, "Killer whales."

Jean felt a flicker of uneasiness, remembering that they were near the spot off the Baja coast where Baby had vanished. Of course Baby was nowhere in sight now, but the tall, black fins broad off the port bow belonged to nomadic orcas. As David identified them over the hailer, Jean lifted her binoculars for a closer look, watching the sleek black-and-white bodies rise and fall in the water. They were her favorite cetaceans, although mortal enemies of others. Ruthless killers, highly intelligent. Jean admired what she'd read of their hunting strategies, but she was glad Baby was nowhere near the ship.

The orcas were swimming toward the *Skye* and abreast of it, but slowly, and watching through the field glasses Jean saw why. They were at the edges of a torn drift net that seemed to extend some distance just beneath the surface of the water. Drowned seabirds and a few other unrecognizable animals floated in the net. Jean flicked past something that moved and went back for a better look. A trapped shark.

She turned to Chris, beside her on the aft cushions, and offered him the binoculars. "Want to see?"

He shook his head. He was playing with plastic horses, making mesas and buttes of the white cushions.

The *Skye* drew closer to the whales, to within a few hundred yards, and slowed to stay clear of the net. Jean continued her observations of the environmental disaster, the untended net, until she found the dorsal-finned animal struggling at its edge. The fin was not triangular but curved, and marked with a black scar.

Jean set the binoculars on her chair and jumped up, rushing to the wheelhouse and throwing open the door. "David, Baby's in that net."

Jake shook loose a cigarette from his pack and glanced toward the net.

David said, "I'm sorry."

Jean stared at him incredulously. "She's alive. Let's get her out."

David said, "Take the wheel, Jake." He moved toward her.

Jean stepped back. "Don't. I don't want to be comforted. I want to get Baby out of that net. We can take the Zodiac. David, the orcas will get her if she doesn't drown." Looking out the windshield, she saw the ship would soon be abreast of the net, but the killer whales were already closing in on the struggling dolphin. Jean could imagine Baby's frightened cries. The thought made her wild. "Think of Chris. Think of me. Dammit, David, stop the ship!"

He didn't touch her, but Jean sensed he would grab her if she moved a muscle. Eyes focused and calm, he said, "I care about you infinitely more than that animal, and I'm not going to let you drown in that net with her—or swim into a killer whales' banquet."

Jean said, "We could take the Zodiac, confuse them, chase them off. We could get her out, David, please. I'll take my tank. You can come with me. The orcas wouldn't hurt a human. You know they never have, ever."

David shook his head. "I've never interfered in the natural order that way, protecting one animal from others. I won't do it."

"David, this isn't just any animal, it's *Baby*. And that net isn't part of the natural order!"

"My ship is in danger from that net, Jean. We don't know how big it is, and those things can drown people. Jean, she's *under* the net. You can't get her out. You can't. Believe me." He looked honestly regretful, heartbroken for her. "All we can do is leave so we don't have to watch."

Turning from him, Jean pushed out the port door of the wheelhouse, going to the railing. The ship still hadn't reached the net, and the orcas hadn't given up. Jean thought of how faithfully Baby had swum with her on dives. There were times she'd been so lonely that the dolphin was her only friend. Because of her, Baby had come to Baja. And now she had to cruise past her and leave her to die? She would never forgive herself.

She spun around to go back in the wheelhouse and landed in David's arms. She looked up into his eyes, pleading. "David, even if she's going to die I want to see her once more. Please. Please stop the ship. Take me in the Zodiac. David, I love her. Even if she's dying, I want to be there. Even if I can't do anything." Laying her head against his throat, she breathed, "Please."

"Okay."

Jean looked up at his face, then back at the net.

"I'll let Jake go farther, and we'll stop. You can help me with the Zodiac."

It would take forever to launch the boat. Jean gazed back across the water at the net and saw an orca rise from beneath it. The others were tearing at the net. Her stomach lurched.

David said, "You couldn't have made it."

Jean did not turn from the sight. She moved from David's arms and faced it, the blood, the devourment. Baby, dying the death of a wild thing. A wild thing caught in a trap of man and left helpless against her natural enemies. Jean's heart felt sick, full and empty, as though she were dying, too. And she remembered the beluga David had known and seen butchered by fishermen.

They were even now.

"Jean! David!" It was Robin Frost on the foredeck, holding his camera in one hand and pointing to starboard with the other.

Four dolphins had joined the *Skye,* catching the wake off the prow.

The photographer said, "It's Baby! She's right here!"

Robin would know. He'd spent a week filming her. The dolphin who'd died in the drift net wasn't Baby! Jean took one look at David and hurried forward to the bow rail, over the sea-sprayed deck.

She was moving fast. Too fast. Watching, David felt a strange presentiment creep over his heart, darker and more certain than anything he had ever felt. He yelled, "Jean!" Then, without waiting for a response, he slammed through the door of the wheelhouse and went for the kill switch.

Skidding on the wet surface of the deck, Jean barely heard his shout. She had gained a momentum the water beneath her feet only increased. Stumbling on the forward hatch, her feet threatening to hydroplane out from under her, she slid across the water-washed bow and crashed against the bow rail. Clutching it as she wavered over the water, Jean stared down at the silver bodies of the dolphins, barely seeing them for fear she would fall.

A child's cry rang through the wind to her ears.

"Mommy, don't!"

Jean realized the engines had stilled. One by one the dolphins looked out of the water as though wondering why the ride had stopped. Baby lifted her head and whistled at Jean, but instead of responding, Jean spun around.

"Daddy, help! Help Mommy. Help, Daddy! Help!" Chris stood in front of the forward cushions, a distant, stunned expression in his eyes. Then, he began to scream.

David had emerged from the wheelhouse, and now he crouched by his son, watching but not touching him. Once, his eyes darted to Jean.

Robin and Dr. Geary peeled away toward the aft deck, Grant saying, "Don't forget I'm here if you need anything, David."

Slowly Jean started across the deck toward David and his son. Chris's screams had turned to sobs, and as David took the boy in his arms Jean knelt beside them.

"Daddy," cried Chris, "where's Mommy? I want Mommy!"

Jean had never felt so helpless, nor such a strange mixture of agony and joy, because she fully understood what had just happened. Chris's memory had opened, probably because of seeing a woman fly against the bow rail. And now he was suffering. What he must be remembering would be every bit as painful as David's experience.

David said, "Christian, Mommy is dead."

"No!"

Jean realized the child was really hearing it for the first time, the horrifying words that would bring down the world. Because now he remembered.

Tormented, she stood. David's eyes followed her and he nodded, as though he wanted her to leave. Before Jean could feel the hurt, Chris's face, squished against his dad's shoulder, turned toward her. His brown eyes solemn, he reached out one hand, looking dazed.

Jean knelt down, and David gave his son into her arms. But Jean felt his reluctance. It quivered through her like an arrow hitting a target.

It scared her.

JEAN LAY in the underwater observation chamber watching Baby trade places with the other dolphins as they played in the wake off the prow. Baby had found a group, and now, seeing what had happened to the lone animal in the drift net, Jean was glad.

Her nerves were raw. David and Grant were still with Chris, as she had been for nearly an hour, sitting in David's desk chair like a bug on the wall while David and Chris talked about what had happened that day.

Yes, we were fighting. No, I didn't tell her to jump off the ship. It was something she decided to do. She wasn't in her right mind, Chris. She was drunk and on drugs. We've talked about what that means.

But didn't she know she would die?

Jean had been glad when at last Grant knocked on the door of the cabin and David suggested she find something to do. They were the first words he'd spoken to her after he'd brought her to the cabin with them, and since then an eerie sense of disquiet had sunk into her bones. A dread she couldn't pinpoint.

Overhead, the hatch opened, and a square beam of sunlight shone down on her, blotted out as David came down the ladder. Jean watched his long legs in faded blue jeans until he sat beside her on the quilt.

There were shadows under his eyes, and his expression was unlike she had ever seen it. He looked at her once, then eyed Baby through the portholes. But he said nothing about the dolphin. Instead, he told Jean, "We're anchoring in a few minutes. I'd like you to come ashore with me."

Jean studied his profile. "With Chris?"

David shook his head, then stood and started up the ladder again, never touching her.

Jean felt a numb foreboding in her heart, too inconceivable to credit. She didn't credit it. She reminded herself that David's moods were mercurial, that the restoration of his son's power of speech signified a major change in his life, and that Chris's grief must now absorb him totally.

And she told herself that if not for her and the unforgivable thing she had done by accidentally falling against the bow rail, Christian would still be silent.

THEY MOTORED to shore alone in the Zodiac, Jean bringing her wallet and her address book. David was still quiet, his eyes resting on her only occasionally, and the anxiety she had felt earlier returned. As she spotted the dock where he planned to tie up she blurted out the words. "David, is something wrong?"

He looked at her, eyes steady, his lips parted as though he wanted to speak and didn't know what to say. He nodded.

Jean knew. She said, "Will you please stop the boat?"

He tossed his head toward the dock. "We're almost there."

No! Her heart and her head screamed the word, not once but many times. She could hardly think or hear. There was nothing but the blood rushing in her ears. Feeling dizzy, she watched the fishermen on the dock draw near, was aware of David easing back on the throttle and steering carefully around their lines.

Minutes later they were on shore, and he held her hand as they walked up the rocky beach, heading north as the sun came down in the sky.

David was aware of her shaking beside him. He told himself she was going to be all right, they both were. More all right than if they went on this way. Together.

Even before they reached the dock he had seen she knew what was happening. She wouldn't look at him now, and he knew she was gathering herself. He tried to do the same, but it was impossible. He might spend a year finding himself again, maybe the rest of his life, but it wouldn't happen with her. He couldn't afford it. Emotionally he was in the red, had been ever since Skye, and Jean was too expensive.

She'd proved it again today.

Her voice shook him from his thoughts. "I don't want to hear you say the words. I already know what you want. But I want to know why."

David saw a big boulder being licked by the low waves near the shore. He led her toward it because it looked like a good place to talk. As they walked he thought about what she had asked. The answers were ready, because they'd been building in him longer than he'd known. He needed only to arrange them in cohesive order.

He thought of telling her the things that were right and decided it was only hypocrisy to mention what they both already knew. He wanted to keep it simple, yet it wasn't. Struggling, he said, "I don't need to tell you how grateful I am for what happened today with Chris. But I doubt I need to tell you, either, what it was like for me seeing you swaying over the bow rail.''

To her credit, the look she gave him was not of contempt. It was disbelieving. *You're breaking our engagement over that?*

David said, ''You didn't do anything wrong, Jean. You just did what was natural. You never even ran. I watched. It was just an accident, just something no one could prevent.'' He drew in a breath, pausing as they reached the boulder he had picked out. ''A lot of things happen no one can prevent. Others can be stopped. But I can't keep you in a cage, Jean. You're an independent woman capable of calling your own shots.''

Jean stared up at him, dumbfounded. It took her less than a second to conclude he was sparing her feelings. Nobody broke an engagement—a deep love affair—for such a reason. Not even David. She said, ''There's more.'' She could guess what. That she hadn't told him about the Averys. That she had let Chris slip away in a seven-foot dinghy on Christmas morning.

That in bed they were so crazy for each other it was hard to tell love from lust.

That Skye Haverford Blade had killed herself and her husband had come upon her freshly mutilated remains in the sea.

David tried to answer her. ''I...'' He fell silent, letting the waves talk, instead. He closed his eyes, shook his head. ''I can't do it. That's all, Jean. I can't.''

Jean knew he was certain. David would not take such a step unless he was. And he would never change his mind. She felt as though she had suddenly run into a wall she hadn't known was there. And there was no way through.

A frightening combination of anger and fear and desperation mounted inside her, a reaction to pain that seemed beyond her, beyond anything she had experienced before. Seeing him standing in front of her, looking like what he was, a man of the sea whose eyes had seen much, she wanted to grab him, shake him, kick him, punch him. Hold him. Scream.

But David would think of her again as he saw her now. In the coming hours and days she might regret showing restraint in this moment, but someday—much, much later—she would be glad.

So she said only what she must. "May I leave now? The ship, I mean."

David nodded, thankful she had suggested it and he hadn't had to. "I can get a car and a driver to take you home. Or to San Diego, if you like." He watched a light sea breeze lift the tendrils of hair that had loosened from her braid. The same strands that always came out. He wanted to tell her that her hair was pretty, that he had always thought so, even before he knew her. Instead, he looked into her eyes, and asked, "Would you like to talk more, or shall we go?"

"Go," said Jean, starting back toward the dock and the road into town. She wanted it to be over.

As they made their way around a private oceanside enclave and out to the road, David said, "I have money for you. I never paid you."

Jean gave him a baleful stare, and he closed his mouth. He knew he could never pay her enough, and she knew it, too. But he said, "I'd like you to take it."

Jean surveyed the flowers in the bed along the path. The sunset was turning them to a crimson sheet. Red sky at night, sailor's delight. She knew the sky was red, but she did not look toward the ocean. It was part of him at the moment. It seemed to belong more to him than to her.

She considered what he had said about paying her, and said, "I'll accept pay for my work up until the night of December eighteenth."

David didn't have to ask what night that was. It was the date he had taken Erika to rehab. The night he had given

Jean his pledge. Now he was breaking it. He drew a crumpled envelope from his pocket and put it in her hand without looking at her.

Jean opened her wallet and stuffed it inside. It was cash, imminently practical. Combined with the money in her checking account, it would take her to Ceci, straight from San Diego. She told David, "Thank you."

There was more to settle. "I'll have someone bring your things to your house." He glanced at the cotton sweater and jeans and denim jacket she wore, which reminded him of the student he had hired weeks earlier. She was a different woman now, and he felt dismally the responsibility of changing her. But marrying her to pay that debt would be no favor to either of them.

He said, "You have enough money to...take care of yourself. If you like, I'll pay plane fare back to Santa Barbara."

They had reached a road, but before David could steer them both toward the next village of condos, where he could find a driver he knew, Jean paused and said, "Please don't insult me again."

He hardly knew what he had said, and he blinked at her.

"The plane fare," said Jean. "You don't have to pay to get rid of me. I'll go."

David winced internally. If she hadn't liked the plane fare, she was really going to hate the next one. So did he. Everything about it. But he made himself say it, because they were standing still and because soon they would be among others and never be alone again.

"There's a chance you could be pregnant."

Jean refrained from asking if this was a biology lesson. She could think of nothing to say on the subject that wasn't ugly, that wouldn't tarnish the preciousness of what they had shared. She remained silent.

He said, as though the words were hard to get out,

"You'll tell me."

She nodded.

THE DRIVER DAVID FOUND was American, a longtime security man for people he knew well. It was a person he could trust.

When the luxury car pulled up to the drive where they waited together, David opened a back door for Jean.

She moved toward the car, then turned and looked at him, her eyes brimming, glossy wet where they hadn't been a moment earlier. She was beautiful and good and didn't deserve what he was doing to her or what he had done.

He bowed to her and reached for her hands.

She gave them with her bow, and a moment of peace passed between them in the touch.

He said, *"Kamsa hamnida."* Thank you.

Jean echoed his words and did not rise from the bow until he did.

David suspected those two displays of courtesy might be the hardest things she had ever done. And the kindest.

As he watched the car pull away, lifting dust in its wake, he put the last memory of her in his mind, and turned back to his ship.

CHAPTER SEVENTEEN

The fourth Christmas

IT DIDN'T FEEL like winter—or like Christmas Eve, although the decorations were out in force. Santa Clauses, Christmas trees and *karavakis,* tiny boats decorated with lights and ornaments, stood in all the shop windows. But on the shores of the Aegean Sea, the real anticipation was reserved for the bigger holiday the following week, New Year's Eve. That was the night for caroling and exchanging gifts, for games of chance and kisses at midnight.

Today was only the twenty-fourth, but the seventy-degree weather felt like summer. Minutes earlier, Giorgio had rolled down the corrugated metal door of his shop and closed up for lunch, and now everyone was home sleeping.

Except her.

As was her routine, weather permitting, Jean raised the sails on Jean-Claude's wooden sloop, *Time-Stealer,* and unwound the line from the dock. Ceci's friend was generous with everything. His house, his boat, his diving equipment. *You go away and spend a year in my little house in Greece, Jean, and you will forget David.* David, said the French way.

Now Jean sent Jean-Claude rent for the house. What Giorgio paid her at his shop was little, but she had money saved from her parents' estate and she used it. She couldn't stand the thought of returning to Santa Barbara, and here she was closer to Cecily. But Ceci had gone to Chamonix for Christmas, and Jean had decided to stay by the sea. This year it seemed easiest to be alone.

Months earlier, after she had left Ceci in Paris and settled into Jean-Claude's vacation home, a package had arrived from Santa Barbara, a huge, well-protected box with the return name Blade. It was from Erika, a watercolor of Jean and Baby swimming underwater. Jean had cried when she saw it, cried more when she read Erika's brief note, written on a card just like the one David had sent with the orchids so long ago.

Jean—
I never paid you, and I hope you will accept this. You might want to know David has been working on a book about Baby.

I want you to know I can walk and that I'm very sorry about you and my brother.

E.

Jean put the painting on Jean-Claude's white mantel and tried to remember the days when it was only her and Baby in the harbor. But she could never remember only that, because the harbor was connected with David. Now, Erika's painting still sat on the mantel, but the little *karavaki* Giorgio and his wife had given her was beside it, a reminder of a new season, a new year, a new life.

She'd already spent a year without David.

Now, pushing the tiller so the boom jibed over her head, Jean let Jean-Claude's sailboat take her away from the dock and the marketplace on the Greek waterfront, the oceanside so different from others she had known. Here, the water was turquoise and so clear she could see the bottom. The people were dark and pleasant, and she liked learning their customs. She also liked Jean-Claude's sailboat, with its salt-sprayed icon of St. Nicholas, protector of seamen, mounted in the bow. The icon always made her think of David— and of Skye—but the *Time-Stealer* did exactly as the name implied. It stole the days.

She only wished something could take away the long winter nights.

Studying the sea, the Greek and American naval ships, she thought of an officer on one of the ships who had cooked her a delicious Thanksgiving dinner at Jean-Claude's house weeks before. She hadn't felt able to see him again. The same thing had happened months earlier, with Orion, the sponge diver.

Time had changed nothing. She still loved David.

Her mind flashed unwillingly through thoughts she had tried to obliterate from her consciousness. His face, so many expressions. The sensation of him holding her. His arms around her, her face against his naked chest, her lips on him, touching the scar where the shark had bitten him. His hands on her. His mouth on her. His body pressing down on her and into her.

The pain had not dulled. She could still hear his voice, talking low to her. *I love you.*

He had. Deeply. She knew she would be lucky ever to be loved so much again. But what had happened to that love? Had David just shut it off?

Or had she just imagined it, imagined that a two-week-long engagement really meant something, that a shipboard romance was true love?

Weary of questions she knew she could never answer, she studied the other ships at anchor. A huge yacht. Fishing boats. A barge. And a black-and-white minesweeper flying a Jolly Roger.

Her breath caught at the sight of the pirate flag. The ship

was anchored farther south, straight out from the cobblestone street where Jean-Claude's white house perched on a hill. The vessel wasn't the *Skye;* it was much too large, completely wrong. But she brought the sailboat about, wanting to take a closer look. He might have bought a new ship.

If it was David, his presence in the Aegean would have nothing to do with her. But part of her was quaking, and her mind began spinning daydreams, the same as always. *Take me away, my pirate captain, my warrior, my love. Come, David, and take me away.*

The breeze flowed through her hair and she felt the sun on her face and saw the beautiful colors of the jellyfish in the water, and for a moment she could believe in Christmas again.

But the dream was short-lived. The name on the stern was a single Oriental character, and the national flag flying from the stern was not the Stars and Stripes. It was blue and green and white, probably from one of the smaller countries in the Far East.

She wasn't sure what she felt, but she turned the sailboat again, and lay back under the low winter sun, waiting for the thief with the sail to steal her afternoon.

AT TWO O'CLOCK the metal doors of the shops rolled up, and Jean met Giorgio in front of the table of candles. Candles were a big item during the holidays. Candles, nuts and small boats.

Giorgio said, "You've been out in that sailboat, haven't you? You're a crazy woman. Do you notice it's winter? You should sleep at lunch and stay out of the sun. Your legs are sunburned."

Jean looked down at the skin showing beneath the hem of the colorful Lapland-style dress Ceci had bought her in

Paris, fresh off the runway, a dress that had cost too much to sail or work in but that Jean had been wearing since November for whatever she wanted. Ceci had promised her another like it for Christmas, and Jean had already guessed which box it was in.

She told Giorgio, "I use sunscreen."

"You've got sun in the brain. I'm going to watch you make change."

Jean laughed as she stepped behind the tables to the counter. It was the fact that Giorgio could speak English that had drawn her to his shop in the waterfront market-place. His wife was from Canada, so Jean was particularly glad for their friendship in a country where the native language was difficult. And the job in his shop, little as it paid, was a godsend. It was another time-stealer.

She resumed the work she had been doing before lunch, stocking nuts in bulk bins, until a shadow cut out a tall block of afternoon sunlight from the concrete walkway outside.

Giorgio said, "May I help you, sir?"

"Yes, please. I know your shop assistant. May I speak to her?"

Jean froze, knowing the voice, remembering the ship in the Aegean, the minesweeper with the Jolly Roger. Disbelieving, she looked up and saw him, a bearded silhouette against the masts of the boats rocking at the dock behind him. She'd forgotten he was so tall.

Giorgio was regarding him suspiciously.

Jean stepped toward the candle table, uncertain of her legs. "I do know him, Giorgio."

Giorgio eyed her doubtfully. Then, suddenly, he smiled, as though it had just dawned on him what David was to her. As though the appearance of the tall, handsome American explained something that had puzzled him forever. He told Jean, "You want time off? You can have the afternoon off. Just stay out of the sun."

Jean stared at David. He was wearing a long-sleeved shirt with wide, bold stripes, black and red, that made her think of pirates. He looked as he did in her memories, and she wondered why he was there, what he wanted.

If he was her dream come true.

David made a slight motion of his head, a *Please come*.

She said, "Thanks, Giorgio," and squeezed between the bulk bins and the candles.

David watched as she stepped onto the boardwalk. In the black Scandinavian-style dress with its accents of red and blue she looked like a painting, more vivid than reality. Her hair was held back with a red crocheted ribbon in a ponytail so loose it seemed to be slipping out, and David could tell she'd been on the water that day. It was on her skin and her hair. She looked only a little different than before, a year different. It made him uneasy, aware of the chasm he'd put between them. She was beautiful, more beautiful than he remembered, and he was surprised she had chosen to speak with him at all.

But she had always been polite.

She looked up at him expectantly, and he saw that her eyes were the color of the sea they stood beside. The Aegean.

He finally remembered how to talk. "Will you walk on the beach with me?"

She smiled a little. "Sure, David."

Hearing her say his name changed the rhythm of his breath. He said nothing more, just indicated the path at the edge of the waterfront, past the shops and the docks and the shrine to St. Nicholas, the path that led down to the sea.

The beach was rock, and Jean couldn't help saying,

"This really isn't a walking kind of beach. It's a sitting kind of beach." She felt proud of herself for saying something so impersonal, casual and light. She felt none of those things. Her heart was racing.

David glanced behind them toward the marketplace with its Santa Clauses and lights, holiday decorations from the West. He eyed the wooden fishing boats offshore, and the white houses set back on the dry, rocky hill. They were alone. Jean stood before him with a stillness he remembered and admired.

Pained by his own stupidity, by things that couldn't be undone, he asked, "May I hold your hands?"

Jean looked down at his. She nodded and watched him reach for her, hold her fingers and her palms. She thought of his hands touching her, gently and roughly both. She remembered everything, not least what he had done in the end.

David felt the wind of the Aegean blowing over him, mild as the afternoon, and it affected him, made him do the only thing he could. He dropped her hands and fell to his knees on the rocks before her. And bowing his head, he made himself speak, formal words that fell from his mouth unrehearsed, in lieu of others he had planned. "I don't have the right to touch you or to stand holding your hands. When I broke our engagement a year ago, I showed you dishonor—my own. Now I ask your forgiveness, though I don't deserve it."

Jean stared at him, the muscular man at her feet, bowing to her. And she knew that act as no sign of abasement but as the ultimate show of respect. For her.

She couldn't deny his plea, and she whispered with as much honesty as she'd ever felt, "David, I hope you didn't come to Greece to ask me that." He straightened his shoulders but did not move, and she said softly, appreciatively, "You're forgiven, sir."

She sat down on a low rock beside him, and he sat back on his heels looking at her, studying her, possibly wanting her. She wasn't sure. There was respect in his eyes, and as she watched him, her eyes caressing the bones of his face, she realized that whatever happened from this point onward, she was healed. Being apart from him could not feel good, but he had shown her in the most powerful way that she still owned his respect.

And she remembered that respect was love in plain clothes.

She found herself saying, "David, I'm not going to get down on my knees to say this, but I've had time for thinking here, especially about the Averys. After you asked me to marry you, I should have told you." Before he could comment, she said, "As for what happened with Chris on Christmas morning, well, I don't know how I could have stopped it."

"Neither do I, since you and I were both in bed when he left," said David.

Jean blinked at him.

"When we left that morning, Ken, Robin and Grant all noticed the dinghy missing and made up their own explanations in their heads. I didn't know that until you were off the ship. Then each of them told me." And what they'd told him, obliquely, was that he'd done a stupid thing. Chris had been more direct; he had cried. David told Jean, "In any case, that had nothing to do with why…" He drew a quiet breath. "Why I did what I did." After a moment he said, "I denied Avery's grant. I'm sorry for the things I said to you that night." He moved and sat on a rock nearby and looked out at the ships.

He was silent for a long time, and at last, because he

wasn't saying what she wanted to hear, Jean made herself be sociable. "Did you buy a new ship?"

He glanced at her. "Yes. It's a 130-foot minesweeper. It's called *Him*."

Jean smiled. "That's a funny name for a her." But she knew that *him* was the Korean word for the internal life force. She admitted, "I saw her when I was sailing today. What's that flag you're flying? Is it Korean?"

David stared at her for a moment, puzzled. Then, comprehending, he said, "Jean, that's the Blade Institute flag." For a moment he enjoyed the color flooding her cheeks. Then he said, "Actually I hoped you'd come out and see it tonight. The ship, that is. I still have your bonsai tree."

It sounded like it was something he'd been meaning to return. A wave of misery washed over her. She didn't want to be friends or kiss him casually on the deck of his ship or under the mistletoe or make love to him before he cruised away. She wanted him to take her along, forever.

He said, "Or we could go dancing. Isn't this a big night for parties here?"

It was. The twenty-fourth was Reveyon, the night of revelry, and there were dances everywhere. But it was also Christmas Eve, and Jean asked, "Where's Chris?"

David nodded toward an island, a landmass across the water to the east. "He's with Erika. He's made some little friends, and they want him to go caroling with them tonight. They go from house to house and play drums and ring metal triangles—"

Jean grinned. "And people give them money."

"Yes. He likes that idea."

Jean thought of Chris singing carols. Chris, whom she had wanted to be her son. She wouldn't know his voice if she heard it. She asked David, "How is he?"

"Great. He barks a lot."

Jean smiled, bent to rearrange a damp stone near her feet. "Playing Hank?"

He nodded. "I'm the cowboy, and Choong-Moo is Drover the deputy."

"Choong-Moo?"

"Ship's cat. A very fat kitten. You're not allergic, are you?"

Jean shook her head, wondering why he'd asked. *Please,* she thought.

David's eyes held hers in the sunlight, and Jean watched the emotion flicker over them. At last he said softly, "Jean, you've given me your forgiveness, but I know nothing can make up for what I've done."

Jean felt her throat swelling. She said, "It's okay." She realized she did want to hold him and be held by him, even if he was leaving. Not touching was too hard.

David said, "I was scared, Jean. Scared of what I felt. Do you understand?" When she looked into his eyes but didn't answer, he said, "This year I've tried to put things back as they were before I met you. But everything is too different." He thought of the long months, the nights when he sat in the dark with only her bonsai for company, listening to the indifferent water sloshing the sides of his ship. He'd ached for her body, and for a long time had convinced himself it was only that. He hadn't known his sadness was visible, tangible to those around him.

He said to Jean, "I think I told you once about a place I go to in Ventura to practice tae kwon do. The master is a very old Korean. He's taught me a great deal, and a few months ago he told me a story. An allegory. It was about a man who had a valuable vase he was always afraid would be broken. He kept it for years and years, never enjoying it as completely as he might have if he hadn't feared for it so. One day it did break, and he realized then that it had been broken all along, that its destructability was inherent and that he should have let himself love it and not worried about its safety.''

Jean was watching his face and he told her, ''Jean, you're the vase I've been afraid to have for fear you'd break. And now—I want to love you.'' He tried to read the expression in her eyes, and he saw she was near tears. Emotion threatening to close his own throat, he whispered, ''May I?''

She was huddling on the rock, biting her lip, and David wasn't sure if she was thinking of refusal or if she was simply vulnerable. She had given him her heart once, and he had stepped on it as he walked away.

Rising, he reached for her hands, and after a moment that seemed too long she gave them. He pulled her to her feet, then led her to a large flat rock on the ground nearby. When they both stood upon it, he said, *''Anj-oh.''*

Sit, thought Jean. Responding, she kicked off her shoes, knelt on the rock across from him and sat back on her heels. David knelt in front of her, his knees touching hers.

Closing her eyes, she listened to the sea and the creaking of the nearby docks and the silent chant of time. She felt him take her hands.

His voice was low, carried on the wind. ''Ma'am, you are precious to me, like the life you gave back to me. Your goodness is more than I deserve, your beauty more than I ever wanted. I love you more than I have ever loved a soul on earth. Please look at me and tell me now if you will make me the happiest of men by becoming my wife.''

Jean opened her eyes. David was there, eyes on her, the only man she had ever wanted. She said, ''Yes, sir. I will.''

He took her hand and slid a band around her finger, a band of gold for a pirate's maiden. As her hair blew around her in the breeze by the sea, she seemed like one to David. His maiden.

Jean looked down. A black pearl was set alongside a ring made by the curved body of a dolphin.

David said, "The wedding ring is the mate, another dolphin. They look after the pearl together."

Jean smiled down at the ring, then up at him. "It's a beautiful pearl."

"I found it."

Jean's eyes teared. "I love you, David."

He reached for her and drew her down beside him on the rock, then put his mouth near hers, wanting her as he had for so long. Now she was really his, and he was hers. His heart felt as though it would explode with the knowledge. He said, "Merry Christmas, Jean," and he told her again how much he loved her.

And he kissed her while they lay by the sea.